D0494953

3 8014 08328 9790

THE
WINDS
OF
FOLLY

By Seth Hunter and available from Headline Review

The Time of Terror
The Tide of War
The Price of Glory
The Winds of Folly

SETH HUNTER

THE
WINDS
OF
FOLLY

headline
review

Copyright © 2011 Seth Hunter

The right of Seth Hunter to be identified as the Author of the Work
has been asserted by him in accordance with the
Copyright, Designs and Patents Act 1988.

First published in 2011 by HEADLINE REVIEW
An imprint of HEADLINE PUBLISHING GROUP

1

Apart from any use permitted under UK copyright law, this publication
may only be reproduced, stored, or transmitted, in any form, or by
any means, with prior permission in writing of the publishers or,
in the case of reprographic production, in accordance with the terms
of licences issued by the Copyright Licensing Agency.

All characters – apart from the obvious historical figures – in this
publication are fictitious and any resemblance to real persons,
living or dead, is purely coincidental.

Cataloguing in Publication Data is available from the British Library

ISBN 978 0 7553 7899 9 (Hardback)
ISBN 978 0 7553 7900 2 (Trade paperback)

Typeset in Sabon by Avon DataSet Ltd,
Bidford-on-Avon, Warwickshire

Printed in the UK by CPI Mackays, Chatham, ME5 8TD

Headline's policy is to use papers that are natural, renewable and
recyclable products and made from wood grown in sustainable forests.
The logging and manufacturing processes are expected to conform
to the environmental regulations of the country of origin.

HEADLINE PUBLISHING GROUP
An Hachette UK Company
338 Euston Road
London NW1 3BH

www.headline.co.uk
www.hachette.co.uk

For Pat

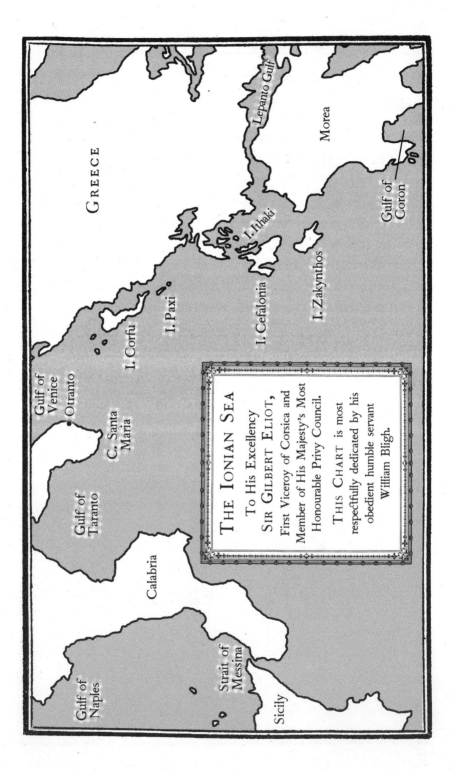

THE IONIAN SEA

To His Excellency
SIR GILBERT ELIOT,
First Viceroy of Corsica and
Member of His Majesty's Most
Honourable Privy Council.

THIS CHART is most
respectfully dedicated by his
obedient humble servant
William Bligh.

GREECE

Lepanto Gulf

Morea

Gulf of
Coron

I. Ithaki

I. Paxi

I. Cefalonia

I. Zakynthos

I. Corfu

Gulf of
Venice

Otranto

C. Santa
Maria

Gulf of
Taranto

Calabria

Strait of
Messina

Gulf of
Naples

Sicily

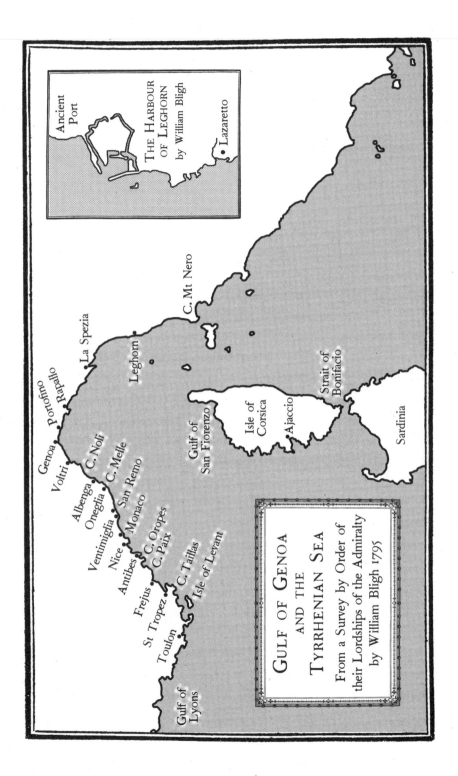

THE HARBOUR OF LEGHORN
by William Bligh

Ancient Port

•Lazaretto

C. Mt Nero

La Spezia
Leghorn

Portofino
Rapallo

Genoa
Voltri
C. Noli
C. Melle
Albenga
Oneglia
San Remo
Ventimiglia
Nice Monaco
Antibes C. Oropes
C. Paix
Frejus
St Tropez C. Taillas
Toulon Isle of Levant

Gulf of
Lyons

Gulf of
San Fiorenzo

Isle of
Corsica
Ajaccio

Strait of
Bonifacio

Sardinia

GULF OF GENOA
AND THE
TYRRHENIAN SEA

From a Survey by Order of
their Lordships of the Admiralty
by William Bligh 1795

I am but mad north-north-west: when the wind is southerly I know a hawk from a handsaw.

Hamlet, II. 2. 405.

The Devil's Carnival

—•◦•—

May, 1796

The man known to his associates as Cristolfi, and to the rest of Venice as the Devil, passed unnoticed through the crowds on the Piazza San Marco. He wore a mask, of course, for it was *Carnevale* and most people were watching the fireworks, but such anonymity was rare in one whose status made him the most feared individual in the Republic. Indeed, so great was his notoriety, it was said that his mere presence on the fringes of a crowd was enough to disperse the most dangerous of rabble-rousers before they could make a proper nuisance of themselves.

But this was not always convenient for an agent of the Inquisitors, and so it was gratifying for him to hear the occasional murmurings of dissent from those who may have thought the pyrotechnics a sufficient distraction from their sedition and would have quaked in their elegant footwear had they comprehended that *Il Diavolo* was anywhere in the vicinity.

'I find it quite remarkable,' proclaimed one whose beaked

domino disguised his features but whose stout frame and lofty tone betrayed him as a prominent member of the Senate, 'that with a French army at our borders and the Treasury unwilling to expend a single ducat on our defences, the government finds it entirely within reason to waste a small fortune on fireworks. But then who am I to question the wisdom of our masters? *Ooooh!*' he exclaimed mockingly, a second or so later than the crowd, as another starburst splintered the velvet sky and a shower of red and golden rain descended upon the black waters of the lagoon.

'It keeps the people happy,' his companion demurred, 'and I dare say the money would be wasted whatever it was expended upon.'

Il Diavolo smiled beneath his mask and made a mental note of these indiscretions, though his own private views were not dissimilar. Venice, the Most Serene Republic, mistress of the seas, the greatest maritime power in the history of the world – until the English stole her trade and the Turks her empire – was reduced to a mere hulk, floating on a tide of nostalgia, while a French army, inspired by the rhetoric of Revolution and the prospect of plunder, swept across northern Italy.

Cristolfi marvelled that the Republic continued to indulge her infinite capacity for pleasure in the face of a threat to her very existence, but then as the Doge had remarked to him not half an hour since: 'Without pleasure, my dear, what reason *is* there for our existence?'

Even so, to spend six months at Carnival and the other six preparing for it might be regarded as excessive by less indulgent rulers, Cristolfi reflected as he moved through the thinning ranks on the edge of the crowd. Nor did it make his job any easier to permit people to hide behind a mask for half the year: a cover for all manner of villainy and subversion.

He viewed the current crop from behind his own disguise: the plain white *volto*, the ghostly *bauta* and the effeminate *gatto* cat mask with its meowing admirers, the black velvet *moretta* – a popular choice with women these days – and of course the entire cast of the *Commedia dell'Arte*: Pulcinella, Pantalone, Scaramuccia and poor Arlecchino with his expression of astonished idiocy. Every subtle contrivance of the *mascherari*'s art to intrigue and beguile the observer and afford the wearer a degree of anonymity, a measure of freedom from the constraints of conventional society. Or, as *Il Diavolo* expressed it more frankly to his subordinates, to bring out the beast in man and the harlot in woman.

He himself wore the mask of *Pedrolino*, the simpleton whose good and trusting nature makes him the target of tricksters and wrongdoers: the naive buffoon, unaware of what is happening around him. A small, private irony.

He moved on – into the warren of back streets behind the Doge's Palace, through a long, dark tunnel and over a bridge on to the *fondamenta*, the paved walkway along the canal: in this case more mud than paving, with pools of stagnant water that obliged Cristolfi to tread carefully in parts, feeling his way like a blind man with his stick. A gap opened on to the black void of the Basin, with a distant glimmer of the lights on the Isola San Giorgio. Into the dark canyons again, permeated now by the smell of the sea, or rather that particular smell of Venice – a distillation of seaweed, mud and effluvia, mingled with damp hessian and rotting wood, and the tantalising scent of spices: the smell of trade. Another canal, a backwater, its quietude disturbed only by the tap-tap of the Devil's cane on the *fondamenta*, the soft slap of water against stone and the clink of the boats at their moorings. And then the sudden startling screech of a rocket and the surroundings flaring into violent light, the buildings revealing their own mask-like façades, with the black eyeholes of countless windows arched in astonished wonder.

He met no one in the streets, but once, crossing another bridge, he saw a gondola come gliding out of the shadows like a sleek black swan and there was a clink of glass or jewellery and a seductive chuckle from within the silk-shrouded cabin before it slid away into the night.

On he walked into a deeper, denser labyrinth until, as happened in Venice, he moved abruptly from darkness into light. Light and laughter, loud conversation and music. His instinctive reaction was to draw back into the shadows, from which vantage he viewed the fantastic spectacle of the Rio della Pietà filled with boats of every size and description, from the slender gondolas to fat barges, all ablaze with flambeaux and packed with spectators, heads craned to watch the fireworks – though not a few, Cristolfi noted, were gazing with equal rapture at the immodestly dressed young women leaning from the balconies of the Convent of San Paolo di Mare, itself so brilliantly illuminated it appeared to float on its own reflection in the waters of the canal.

Il Diavolo observed this prospect with quiet satisfaction. He had made careful preparations for this evening and for once he desired an audience – awe if not appreciation, horror if not applause. The nuns of San Paolo di Mare and their eager young pupils had become notorious, even in libertarian Venice, for their indulgence in the pleasures of the flesh, though the extent and precise nature of their depravity was a mystery, even to the Devil. He had sent his infiltrators, of course, under suitable disguise, but they brought back mixed report: some so lurid he suspected a degree of exaggeration to earn his approbation, others painting a picture of such pious adherence to the vows of the Order his men could only have been bribed by those they had been sent to watch. And one dedicated subordinate had exhibited the marks of a cane upon his posterior, though it could not be ascertained for certain whether they had been inflicted with sexual intent or out of a normal Christian zeal for chastisement.

Il Diavolo did not care either way. His current preoccupation with the inner workings of the Convent of San Paolo di Mare had nothing to do with rumours of sexual or spiritual excess, but with more recent report that the good sisters, and one in particular, had been dabbling in affairs that were the exclusive domain of the ruling Council of Ten. And must, of necessity, be discouraged.

From his eyrie across the water he scanned the crowded balconies opposite. The nuns had made a special effort for the occasion. They were adorned in their finest apparel – not a single black tunic or veil between them – and their guest-list almost certainly included some of the most esteemed names in the Golden Book. This, too, was entirely to Cristolfi's satisfaction. He was of the enlightened opinion that for justice to be done, it must be *seen* to be done, even if the means of applying it might be deemed excessive by more squeamish authorities.

His keen eye spotted a movement on one of the upper balconies. Two figures had emerged from the room within. Both were masked, but Cristolfi knew exactly who they were. The woman was Sister Caterina, the Deputy Prioress of the convent, formerly the actress Caterina Caresini and a famous beauty. Which was presumably why she had chosen an elegant Colombine, masking only the upper part of her lovely face. And the man, who wore a plain white *volto* with black tricorn and cloak, was the English Ambassador, Sir Richard Worsley.

Fireworks were clearly not the chief reason for the Ambassador's presence here tonight, for the couple had missed most of the display. One final extravagant bombardment and it was over. There was cheering and applause – but not a lot, not enough to justify the expense, in Cristolfi's view. Then balconies began to clear and boats to disperse as their varied occupants sought other, less innocent diversions.

Not yet, the Devil silently instructed them, not yet. There was one more spectacle for them to watch: one that would, he hoped, make what had preceded it appear tawdry by comparison. He scanned the crowded canal with unusual concern. Everything depended upon timing and this was an element not entirely within his control. Then he saw it – a simple, black gondola, with no especial mark of distinction, weaving its expert way through the ruck of boats on the canal. Only its direction and a certain purposeful manner gave it away, for it was heading against the flow of traffic and towards the steps of the convent. Cristolfi's eyes rose to the upper balcony. She had seen it, too. Her head bent towards that of her companion as if to murmur some endearment or instruction. Then the Devil stepped into the light and raised his cane.

'Here he is.' Caterina Caresini gazed down from the balcony as the gondola emerged from the chaos of dispersing craft and glided swiftly towards the convent steps. She turned to her companion. 'Perhaps we should go down to greet him?'

Her guest gave her his arm and together they re-entered the building and descended the stairs.

It would not have been immediately apparent to a visitor such as the English Ambassador that this was a convent. The corridors echoed to the sound of girlish laughter, the rustle of silks and satins, the soft patter of dancing pumps and the louder clack of platform shoes – worn in flagrant defiance of the sumptuary laws – on parquet and marble floors.

'I take it yours is not a silent Order,' the Ambassador murmured smoothly as he viewed this excess of feminine zeal through his quizzing glass.

'We have a special dispensation from His Holiness,' Caterina replied with a composure that equalled his own. 'For Carnival only. The rest of the time we are quiet as mice and are glimpsed fleetingly, through a grille.'

It was the Ambassador's first visit to the convent and she trusted it lived up to his heretic expectations so far as the Church of Rome was concerned, though in truth Rome had very little to do with the conduct of religion in the Most Serene Republic. Rome had washed its hands of them years ago, though it was not averse to taking a share of the revenues from its Venetian benefices, no matter how scandalously they were earned.

In fact the Convent of San Paolo di Mare was by no means the worst of its kind, not in Caterina's view, not by Venetian standards. It ran a small private casino for invited guests, and gentlemen were hospitably entertained in the parlour, but it was not a bordello in the true sense of the word. More a finishing school for young ladies of good family, though Caterina conceded the distinction could appear trifling at times. But as far as she was aware, neither the nuns nor their pupils took money for their favours. Gifts, of course, were a different matter. Caterina had accepted gifts herself: she was wearing not a few of them at present. And you could not blame an enterprising young woman of good family for accepting what she might quite justifiably consider her due. Most of the girls here had been sent to the convent against their will, their fathers wishing to avoid paying the penalty of a dowry when they were married, and they were disposed to resent it and to try to make up for it by whatever means were available to them.

Caterina's own route to San Paolo had been less straight-forward. At the height of her career as an actress she had become embroiled in a scandal of such monumental proportions – even for Venice – that the convent had been presented as the only alternative to exile or prison. A substantial fee had been required, of course, and certain favours granted to the Prioress which were a little distasteful at times but nothing Caterina could not deal with. Since when she had risen rapidly through the convent hierarchy until it was for all practical purposes hers to command. A secure base from which to launch her political career.

Caterina had devoted much of her youth to the amorous intrigues which occupied any lady of leisure in Venice during these final years of the century. There were times, indeed, when she had imagined everyone of a certain class and disposition to be engaged in his or her own private version of *Les Liaisons Dangereuses*, which had been popular reading at the time of her arrival in the city twelve years before in 1784. But she had grown tired of such diversions. Indeed, she came to hold them, and all who practised them, in contempt. As she had entered her thirties, she had become involved in a much more interesting and far more dangerous game.

Caterina was not Venetian by birth. She was a native of Verona, whose citizens considered themselves far more passionate, far more idealistic than their aloof overlords in Venice. For the true Venetian considered it the grossest form of bad taste to care about *anything*, especially politics. But Caterina did care. She loved Venice, as deeply and more openly than any born Venetian. And she was much distressed by its present predicament.

The thousand-year-old Republic had been as shocked as any king, queen or emperor by the excesses of the French Revolution. But she had refused all invitations to join the coalition of powers aligned against the regicides in Paris. Austria, Prussia, Spain and Great Britain, with most of the principalities of Germany and Italy, might be united for once, but the powers that ruled the *Serenissima* maintained a policy of strict neutrality. Thus did they hope to preserve what remained of their empire – one could not say their integrity – from the conflagration that engulfed Europe.

The actress-turned-nun thought they were mistaken.

Of course, the prevailing view was that this was of no concern to either actress or nun, or indeed any female of the species. But Caterina begged to differ. No, she did not beg – Caterina never begged – she set her mind upon a course of action and she pursued it with ruthless tenacity. Subtly, of course, until the moment came to strike, and even then her victims were sometimes left wondering how the knife had appeared in their ribs and who had wielded it. She was circumspect: she knew her weaknesses as well as her strengths, but what she had, she used. If the winged lion, the traditional symbol of Venice, had forgotten how to roar, the lioness must show her claws.

She crossed the long reception hall and stepped through the open portal on to the broad terrace above the canal. The recently arrived gondola bobbed at the foot of the steps, the silken curtains drawn across the front of the cabin, shielding its occupant from inquisitive eyes. He had waited for them to come down to greet him, Caterina noted with approval, pleased that he rated himself so highly. But at her appearance with the English Ambassador the curtains parted and he stepped nimbly ashore. Giovanni Galeazzo Dandolo, Admiral of the Fleet, youngest of the Council of Ten, the man who would be Doge if Caterina had her way.

She greeted him with a smile and advanced to meet him, still with her arm on the Ambassador's. She had no eyes for any other, though she was vaguely aware that others were there. The gondolier, of course, and a servant or bodyguard who had stepped ashore after his master. The musicians who had been assembled here, providing an accompaniment to the fireworks, and were now packing away their instruments. A few spectators, still loitering at the water's edge, pushing and shoving at each other with loud voices and laughter. Caterina felt a slight unease but no sense of threat, none at all. She was still smiling, up to the moment of the attack, and even then she did not recognise it as such. She thought one of the spectators had staggered into Dandolo's path, or been shoved in that direction by one of his companions in their horseplay. She frowned and was about to utter a rebuke when she saw the glint of steel and uttered a cry of warning instead. Too late; they were all around him, lunging with their stilettos, and she heard a scream like a rabbit taken by a fox. She thought later that it was like the scene in *Julius Caesar*, which she had performed once in Verona, and perhaps it was intended as such, for theatre played an important part in the politics of the Republic. Later she remembered the masks, too, though she was not taking any particular note of them at the time. The assassins moved in on him as swiftly and mysteriously as ghosts and then, like ghosts, they vanished, melting into the crowd and the shadows. And then there was just the gondolier and the servant and the musicians. And Dandolo, lying there on the steps, in his blood.

He was still alive when she reached him but he had been stabbed many times. In the chest, in the neck, in his beautiful face. She tore off his mask, shouting for a surgeon. There was blood everywhere. She tried to stop the flow with her hands but there was too much. His eyes were open, gazing up at her, but there was no recognition in them. Then more blood came gushing from his mouth and she knew he was gone.

She felt hands pulling at her, trying to lift her to her feet. Voices urging her to come inside the convent. She resisted. It occurred to her to say a prayer for Dandolo's soul, but the dominant emotion in her breast was one of rage. But then something made her look up and across the water, and her eyes found the exact spot where he was standing, as if she had known he would be there. And she saw the mask of Pedrolino, the simpleton, in the lamplight.

She stood and pointed like some demented creature from the Greek chorus, pointed and screamed, the blood of her lover on her hands and arms, on her face, on her chalk-white mask.

'*Assassino!*'

And she cursed him, a curse that was also a prayer – that the Avenging Angel would come out of the sea and destroy him: the man who had destroyed her dream.

'*Assassino!*'

The word echoed back to her from the walls of the surrounding buildings, like laughter.

Part One
The Tramontana

———◆◆◆———

Chapter One

The Captain of the Unicorn

———◦•◦•◦———

Captain Nathaniel Peake of His Britannic Majesty's Navy was not normally given to the sin of Avarice. Lust had been a problem at times and Gluttony was not unknown to him, but Avarice, he would have thought, stood low on his list of moral propensities; so he was a little surprised to find he had been lounging against the stern rail of the frigate *Unicorn* for a not inconsiderable time gazing with some complacency at the four vessels sailing in her wake whilst calculating how much wealth they represented and how much of it would accrue to him personally.

Three of the vessels were blockade runners, caught sneaking along the Ligurian coast with munitions and supplies for the French Army currently fighting the Austrians in the mountains. The fourth was a French privateer of eight guns, the *Bonne Aventure*, which the *Unicorn* had taken off Cap Ferrat, and which was by far the most valuable of her prizes, not least because of the small velvet bag containing ten pieces of jewellery which had been discovered in the safe in her Captain's cabin and which now belonged to Nathan. Or more accurately, to His Britannic Majesty. Nathan, however, was entitled to two-eighths of their value, this being the share assigned to him in their wisdom by their Lordships of the Admiralty as an incitement to initiative, and he was more than content with this arrangement. If a fraction of the profit found its way into King George's purse, which was doubtful, Nathan wished him joy of it: the unhappy monarch had thirteen children to support and the tradesmen to pay, not to speak of the doctors who were treating him for his current mental disorder.

The Captain's gaze shifted from the little flotilla to the mountainous coastline a mile or so off his larboard bow. He had been cruising up and down it from Cap d'Antibes to Genoa for half a year now and could have drawn a detailed chart from memory with the depths of every cove and inlet, the projection of every headland, and the strength and position of every fort and battery. Liguria. An enchanted province of mountain and forest, olive and citrus groves, vineyards, deep valleys and mountain streams, remote monasteries and ancient hill towns. In the light of the afternoon sun it looked entirely at peace: a mossy haze veiling the mountains, the sea lapping gently at its rocky shores, a mild northerly breeze bringing the fragrant smell of pines from the lower slopes. But it was a fragile, illusory peace, for although the Republic of Genoa maintained an official policy of neutrality, the French had insinuated their garrisons into every port, and a squadron of English frigates patrolled the coast, seizing any vessel suspected of trading with the enemy.

And in the distant mountains, a young Corsican General called Napoleon Bonaparte led the French Army to victory after victory against the demoralised troops of the Austrian Emperor, Britain's last remaining ally of note in a war that had divided Europe for the past seven years and spread across the seas to the Americas and the Caribbean. A war that would, if it continued to go badly, bring Britain to her knees.

Nathan was aware that Italy was regarded as a sideshow, Bonaparte's sortie across the Alps a mere diversion to the main battle on the Rhine. But the General's spectacular success had brought matters to a head. If the Austrians lost their Italian provinces it was odds on that they would throw in the towel before the enemy advanced to the gates of Vienna, and it seemed unlikely that Britain would fight on alone, expending more blood and treasure in a futile bid to restore the Bourbons to the throne of France.

Nathan had not met an Englishman yet who thought the Bourbons worth a fart, much less worth dying for. As for the wider motives that Edmund Burke and his friends propagated in press and Parliament – that one must fight the spread of Revolution and its evil progeny, Terror – well, Nathan had witnessed the Terror in Paris during the dark days of Robespierre, and he would have been the first to agree that it must be opposed, but the Terror was over, the Revolution had lost its sting. Robespierre had been overthrown, the guillotine dismantled and put into store – even if Billy Pitt still used it to scare people into paying their taxes. France had new rulers now and they were too busy feathering their own nests to burden themselves with principles or ideals, much less export them to London.

Nathan had read Bonaparte's proclamation to his troops before he crossed the Alps and it smacked more of piracy than idealism.

'*Soldiers! You are hungry and naked; the government owes you much but can give you nothing. The patience and courage which you have displayed among these mountains are admirable, but they bring you no glory – not a glimmer falls upon you. I will lead you into the most fertile plains on Earth. Rich provinces, opulent towns, all shall be at your disposal;*

there you will find honour, glory, and riches. Soldiers of Italy!
Will you be lacking in courage or endurance?'

That was the stuff to give the troops. No wonder they loved
him. You could only have so much Liberty, Equality and
Fraternity; you could never have too much Loot. And that was
what they fought for, those boys up in the mountains: like
every army that had marched into Italy since the Renaissance.

Nathan's eyes moved to his own plunder, keeping station at
the rear, and experienced a slight twinge of conscience. But
only slight: not enough to take the edge off his appetite for
more. He began to scale the hills of Avarice again, pushing his
moneybags before him. Two barques and a snow – worth at
least £30,000 with their cargoes, he would have thought – and
it was almost certain the *Bonne Aventure* would be bought into
the service: the fleet was short of lean, fast sloops that could go
close inshore. Say another £10,000 to make it an easy sum.
That would bring in £5,000 for Commodore Nelson, his flag
officer, who was always going on about how poor he was as
the son of a Norfolk clergyman; £5,000 to be shared between
the *Unicorn*'s three lieutenants, her sailing master and surgeon;
£5,000 for the principal warrant officers, the Captain of
Marines – *and the flag officer's secretary, God damn it!* Though
why this gentleman should be included in a division of the
spoils provoked the first symptoms in the *Unicorn*'s Captain of
that condition to which the wealthy are often prone when
obliged to share their fortune with the undeserving poor.

Another £5,000 for the midshipmen, the warrant officers'
mates and the Marine sergeant; £10,000 for the crew – that
was near enough £50 per man – almost five times the annual
pay for a great many of them.

And £10,000 for the Captain.

£10,000!

And that was without the jewellery – the gewgaws, as he

believed they were known in thieves' cant, which was uncomfortably appropriate in the circumstances. Nathan reviewed
the individual gems in his mind's eye. A blue sapphire set in
garnets, a pair of emerald earrings, a ruby set in filigree, and
six diamonds mounted in silver. He had no idea what they
were worth but he reckoned it could easily add another few
thousand to the tally. He might even buy one of the diamonds
himself as a gift for his future bride.

Nathan's thoughts veered in a more romantic direction,
though one that was not without its own pitfalls and problems.

Sara Peake. The name did not seem very real, somehow; it
did not seem to fit. Sara Marie Peake. No better. Perhaps
because she had previously been Sara Marie de la Tour
d'Auvergne, Countess of Turenne. That had a ring to it, all
right. Even her maiden name – Sara Seton – had a ring to it.
But Sara Peake? Unlikely.

They had not actually spoken of marriage, but there was an
'understanding' between them. At least he thought there was.
Or there had been when he had put her aboard the Gibraltar
packet two months ago. Perhaps, on the long voyage to
England, she had thought better of it. If he could win a knight-
hood it might improve matters a little. Lady Sara Peake. Yes.
He liked the sound of that. It was not quite up to the level of
Sara de la Tour d'Auvergne, but it was a definite improvement.
Captain Sir Nathaniel Peake did not sound too bad, either.

He turned back from the rail and assumed an air of gravitas
in keeping with his position as Captain of a thirty-two-gun
frigate: the lord of all he surveyed. Six months in the Mediterranean sunshine had so darkened his complexion he had grown
quite saturnine, especially when he frowned as he did now,
drawing himself up to his full height, which was a little over
six feet, clapping his hands behind his back and casting an
eagle eye over his domain.

Not that anyone took a blind bit of notice, of course, much less quaked in their boots, but this, too, might be taken as cause for satisfaction, in that every man aboard knew his place and function, no one had been flogged for as long as he could remember, and the smooth running of the ship was something her Captain could more or less take for granted.

It had not always been the case. Nathan had taken command of the *Unicorn* in the aftermath of mutiny and murder, when a score or so of her people had risen up against their officers and made off in the ship's cutter, taking their previous Captain as hostage. His body had later been washed up on the shores of Louisiana with its throat cut, and the mutineers had taken to a life of piracy on the Spanish Main while the *Unicorn* had endured hurricane and near-shipwreck in a futile pursuit.

Nathan had come aboard in the Havana to find both ship and crew in a sorry state. The first lieutenant was a martinet and a moron, the junior officers morose and uneasy, the people whipped into a dogged and surly subservience. But after a shaky start, he had presided over a dramatic improvement. The *Unicorn* had fought and won two encounters with larger frigates, and though both her opponents had run upon the rocks and foundered, depriving him of a considerable fortune in the way of prize money, the victories had done much to bond officers and crew into a fighting unit. By a strange series of events, Nathan had secured the freedom of a number of African slaves in Louisiana and many of them had volunteered for service on the *Unicorn* where they had proved ideal recruits, particularly in the working of the guns. The fact that they could not under any circumstance be described as loyal subjects of King George was of no account. Not that many of the crew were.

Once, going through the ship's books with the purser, Nathan had been startled to discover that ninety-six of the hands, almost half the total, were listed as foreign-born, including twelve Frenchmen. He hoped the latter were Royalists, but he did not count on it. The hands comprised Scandinavians, Latvians and Lithuanians, Italians, Americans, the Africans – and a pair of Lascars who had been found drifting in an open boat off the west coast of Ireland and had yet to satisfactorily explain their presence there. And then there were the Irish, of course – the Catholic Irish – who made up almost a third of the remainder and were at best reluctant subjects of King George, at worst out-and-out rebels, at least in their Papist hearts.

As for the native English, most of them were the scourings of the jailhouse or the waterfront, forcibly brought in by the press, or fleeing from a worse fate than the King's Navy.

Nathan had decided he was more pleased than not by this multiplicity of nationalities and races, as if their very variety gave them some common cause, like Crusaders. Though God only knew what it was. The restoration of the Bourbons to the throne of France hardly counted as a crusade. The prize money probably helped.

The officers, of course, were a different matter, and here Nathan had more cause for satisfaction. Death had removed the main impediments to his contentment, the first lieutenant having been struck by a musket ball in the Caribbean, and the sailing master, a notorious Jeremiah, having lived up to his own expectations and succumbed to a perforated ulcer on the voyage home. Their replacements, Mr Duncan and Mr Perry, were their superiors in every way. They could be relied upon to manage the crew and to sail the ship in whatever direction was required without troubling their Captain for an opinion on either subject. And should he feel compelled to offer one, or even to issue an order, he could always turn for advice to his particular friend, Lieutenant Tully, presently commanding the

Bonne Aventure. The third lieutenant, Mr Holroyd, was an exemplary officer in every way – if you discounted the loss of an ear, sliced off by a cutlass in the Caribbean – and the midshipmen and other young gentlemen were coming along nicely.

In fact, Nathan had very little to do most of the time besides sink into long bouts of the introspection to which he was prone, though he did his best to divert himself with music and prose, even the occasional line of verse. He practised upon the flute, wrote long letters home and shorter despatches to his seniors, swam around the ship to keep himself fit, and played chess with whoever of his officers could be relied upon to give him a respectable game and not let him win too easily – which usually came down to the surgeon McLeish and the youngest but most assured of the midshipmen, Mr Lamb.

He shifted his position slightly so he had a better view of the waist where a number of the hands had appeared with buckets and swabs. He wondered what new occupation the first lieutenant had found to divert them, for the swabbing of the decks always occurred in the forenoon watch, and from Nathan's present vantage they still looked as spotless as even Lieutenant Duncan might desire. But it soon became apparent that this was a different kind of ritual. The buckets contained a quantity of fat derived from the boiled meats which coagulated in the galley coppers – commonly known as 'slush' – and the hands were applying it to the wheels of the gun trucks to make them slide more easily and make less of a fiendish scream when they were about it.

Nathan could only approve such zeal, though he wondered idly what kind of bargain had been struck with the ship's cook, for the slush was one of the perks of this satrap and he usually had some deal going with the purser to sell it off as tallow or even for human consumption as 'dripping'. But then he noted that the operation was being conducted under the supervision of George Banjo, who was the acknowledged leader of the African contingent among the ship's company, and whose impressive powers of persuasion were reinforced by his gigantic bulk. Banjo – Nathan had no idea if this was his real name – had lately been rated gunner's mate, for his love of the 18-pounders that constituted the *Unicorn*'s main armament was only matched by his skill in handling them, and he had since embarked on a series of measures designed to improve their already creditable performance. Clearly the ship's cook had been compelled to cooperate in this ambition.

Nathan had lately been informed by Tully that Banjo's leadership of the Africans had now been extended to include the entire lower deck, and that even the boatswain's mates, the official policing agency of those realms, stood in awe of him. As there was no reason to doubt his loyalty to Nathan personally and his manner was generally benevolent, Nathan had no serious argument with this, though he did wonder sometimes if his own position was more nominal than actual and whether the real powers aboard the ship more properly belonged to the triumvirate of gunner's mate, first lieutenant and sailing master.

None of which diminished Nathan's current sense of complacency for he had much to be grateful for, quite apart from the promise of £10,000 in prize money – £12,000, possibly, with the gewgaws thrown in. Though he was approaching his twenty-eighth birthday, he remained in excellent health, he was in possession of a good head of hair and most of his teeth – and the sounding of the ship's bell alerted him to the fact that it was nearly time for his dinner.

There was nothing more certain to improve Nathan's opinion of the world and his position in it than the imminent prospect of a meal, for he possessed a prodigious appetite, and today he had been invited to dine in the wardroom with his officers. They had done some brisk business with the fishing fleet off Savona and picked up a large blue-fin tuna which one hoped would not prove too much of a challenge for the ship's cook. Nathan would have had it cut into steaks, griddled, and served up with a pease pudding, but he had not thus far been summoned to the galley for his opinion on the matter. Notwithstanding, he would contribute six bottles of his best white wine, which had been brought down from the Alps packed in ice and straw and were now residing in the darkest, deepest part of the orlop deck.

But there was still over an hour to go; he must think of something else to ease his torment. The cry from the foremast lookout supplied a welcome distraction.

'Sail ho! Two points on the starboard bow.'

Nathan crossed to the starboard rail and peered forward, but could see nothing from so low a vantage – and nor did he expect to, not if the masthead men were as alert as they should have been.

'Mr Holroyd, I am going aloft,' Nathan informed the officer of the watch, in case he should notice his Captain's absence from the quarterdeck and wonder if he had jumped overboard out of a sense of his own inconsequence.

He made his way forward and climbed rapidly up into the rigging, his Dollond glass tucked firmly under his arm. He made a point of going aloft whenever he had an excuse to do so – in part to reassure himself and the crew that he was as capable as any of swinging like an ape 120 feet above the deck – but he knew he was a mere sloth among the accomplished simians who normally resided here, while the midshipmen, he had no doubt, would be watching his progress from the deck with amused tolerance.

He paused for breath at the crosstrees and the nearest lookout considerately swung down to him and knuckled his forehead, before using the same arm to point in the direction he had so recently communicated to the deck, as if his Captain needed special guidance in the points of the compass. Hanson, Nathan recalled – a Dane, taken off a Bristol slaver in the Caribbean.

From his present vantage Nathan spotted the sail almost immediately, even without the Dane's thoughtful assistance, hull down and on the larboard tack. She must be an outwardbounder from Genoa or one of the ports to the east: a merchantman most likely, for though there were several French privateers lurking thereabouts, on such a day as this they could scarcely have evaded the British blockade – and for the same reason she was almost certainly a neutral, unless she was part of the blockade herself, sent westward on some mission for the Commodore.

Nathan hooked one arm through the topgallant shrouds and lifted the glass to his eye. With its assistance the individual sails became more distinct and he could see at once that she was no man-o'-war. But even as he began to lose interest, he saw that she was changing course, and now heading directly towards the *Unicorn*, or as directly as the wind would allow. This was strange, for even a neutral would be wary of encounter with a British man-o'-war, eager for trained seamen to supplement her crew. He rested his eye for a moment and when next he looked he saw the small puffball of smoke blossom from her bow and heard the distant report of the signal gun carried across the still waters towards him. Closing the telescope with a brisk snap, he tucked it down the front of his coat and slid down to the deck by the backstay as nimbly, he flattered himself, as any young gentleman, or ape.

'Hands to the braces, Mr Holroyd,' he called out, and to the quartermaster at the helm, 'Bring her two points to leeward. Ah, here you are, Mr Perry . . .' catching sight of the sailing master who had emerged from below and was already frowning up at the sails as if they had been perfectly all right as they were and no one but he had any business to be fooling around with them in his absence. 'There is a packet to leeward with a signal for us and I have altered course to converge with her. Doubtless it is from the Commodore desiring us to engage the enemy with more vigour.'

He meant this as a witticism, for their Commander was prodigal in his employment of signals and eager to convey his own zeal for action at every opportunity. But despite his apparent composure, Nathan could barely control his impatience to know the precise nature of this instruction, for it must surely portend some new move by the enemy. He was obliged to endure a wait of almost an hour, however, before the vessels were close enough for a boat to be lowered and the despatch conveyed to him.

It was, indeed, from the Commodore, and apparently written in some haste for it abjured the usual eloquence:

To Capt Nathaniel Peake Esq., Unicorn

From Captain, *off Genoa, June 24th 1796*

Sir,

Being advised of the rapid advance of French forces upon Leghorn I am proceeding thereto with Captain *and* Meleager *to render such assistance as may be required. You are therefore requested and required to follow as speedily as you may with* Unicorn *and what other forces you may have under your command.*

Your obliged
Horatio Nelson

Short as it was, Nathan pondered the missive with a frown. Leghorn – or Livorno as it was known to its inhabitants – was a major centre for merchants engaged in the Levant trade and possessed a sizeable community of British expatriates. It was the most important provider of supplies for the British fleet east of Gibraltar. Moreover, the British Consul, Mr Udny, acted not only as prize agent to the fleet, but as a procurer of female companions for the officers, a service which many of these gentlemen had come to rely upon, even the Commodore himself. Its loss would be a serious blow – which was presumably why Nelson had decided to raise the blockade of Genoa and go there himself in the *Captain*.

Catching the enquiring eye of his first lieutenant, Nathan passed him the despatch without comment. Leghorn was not much more than thirty leagues to the south-east. Even with this wind, the *Unicorn* might be there before tomorrow sunset, but the prizes would take a while longer. There was nothing for it but they must follow on at their own pace, though he thought he could, without risk of censure, leave *Bonne Aventure* to guard them from recapture.

'Signal Mr Tully to come aboard, if you would,' he instructed Holroyd. Then, turning to the sailing master: 'I am afraid I must trouble you to set a new course, Mr Perry – for Leghorn, and with all the sail we can carry.'

Chapter Two

The Vipers' Nest

———◆◆◆———

The French had beaten them to it. Nathan stood on the quarterdeck of the *Unicorn* gazing out in dismay at the huge pall of smoke spreading over Leghorn. His first impression was that the entire port was ablaze, the populace fleeing in everything that could be made to float. But as the frigate crept closer he saw that the fires were confined to the northern outskirts, the lurid glow produced by the rays of the rising sun filtered through a pall of smoke and morning mist. This was far from reassuring, however. Nor was the steady report of gunfire that came rolling across the water from the surrounding hills and the sight of hundreds, if not thousands, of refugees crowded upon the mole and the adjoining quayside, mostly on foot but some mounted or in carriages, all laden with baggage, even furniture, intent on boarding the vessels crammed into the harbour and its approaches. But there was no sign of the *Captain* or the *Meleager* among them – or, indeed, of any other ship-of-war. If Leghorn was to be defended from the sea, it was going to be down to the *Unicorn*.

It had taken them the best part of two days to reach the

port, with the wind remaining fickle. He could barely feel a whisper now on his cheek, and the sails flapped inelegantly against the masts. He shifted his gaze to the outer suburbs, though his view was considerably impeded by the dense pall of smoke. Through it he could make out the glow of burning buildings and the stabbing flash of what he took to be artillery on the hillside, where the French must be lodged. But it was impossible to discern their strength or disposition.

'We had best take in sail, Mr Baker,' he instructed the sailing master, 'and stand off the mole. Well off, mind.' For he had no desire to be drawn into that impossible crush of shipping. He turned to the first lieutenant. 'And Mr Duncan, let us clear the ship for action.' This with the suggestion of a sigh, for he had no idea what action might be contemplated.

He ran up the ratlines a little and focused his glass on the end of the mole. His initial impression of chaos and confusion was clearly mistaken, at least in this area, for the refugees appeared to be in good order as they waited to board the transports. He moved the glass further down the mole and to his great surprise saw a number of figures in the distinctive red coats and black shakoes of regular British infantry or Marines – though it was possible, he supposed, that they were soldiers of the Grand Duke of Tuscany. So far as he could make out at this distance, they appeared to be marshalling the crowd.

He rejoined his officers on the quarterdeck but before he could discuss what he had seen and seek their opinion, he was alerted to the approach of a ship's cutter which had emerged from the ruck of vessels in the harbour and was clearly heading towards the *Unicorn*. He brought the glass to his eye once more and picked out the blue ensign of Admiral Jervis flying at the masthead – and in the stern-sheets, looking very much at ease, the portly figure of Captain Thomas Fremantle of His Britannic Majesty's frigate *Inconstant*.

*

'Well, I must say you took your time getting here,' Fremantle observed cheerfully, the moment he stepped aboard. 'I don't suppose you passed Nelson on the way, did you? I sent to him all of five days ago to tell him what was afoot.'

Nathan conveyed the gist of the Commodore's message to him, adding that he had thought he would already be here.

'Well, as you can see, he ain't,' Fremantle assured him, not without satisfaction. 'And if he don't get a crack on, it will all be over, which won't please him a bit.'

Nathan proposed they continue their discussion in the Captain's day cabin, for Fremantle was notoriously indiscreet and though he claimed to be Nelson's great friend, he not infrequently revealed intense feelings of rivalry, even envy towards his senior officer.

'I cannot say I am too put out,' he continued loudly as Nathan led him below, 'for doubtless he would require us to take on the whole French Army – with or without the Grand Duke's blessing.'

The Grand Duke of Tuscany had steadfastly refused to join the coalition against Revolutionary France, but he had permitted the British fleet to use Leghorn as a port of convenience and this – in Fremantle's view – was what had provoked the French attack.

'Bonaparte informed His Nibs that he was nurturing a nest of vipers – meaning us – and that he was determined to smoke us out,' he announced unconcernedly as he took a glass of Madeira in Nathan's day cabin. 'Your very good health, sir.'

'So Bonaparte is leading the invasion personally?'

'I don't say that,' Fremantle replied cautiously, 'for I've no information on the subject. Why? Do you wish to become acquainted?'

They were, in fact, already acquainted. Though this was not

something Nathan would reveal lightly, certainly not to a tittle-tattle like Thomas Fremantle. He had met Bonaparte in Paris little more than a year ago when the current hero of the French Army was an unemployed artillery officer down on his luck and desperate for a job. He had cut a pathetic figure with his sallow complexion and long greasy hair, his features pinched and scowling, invariably wearing a threadbare greatcoat and a battered bicorn hat. In fact, apart from the hat, he looked more like a street urchin than an army officer: one of those barefoot Savoyards who used to act as messenger boys to the Convention. He even spoke like them, with a thick foreign accent, for he had been born in Corsica. His associates called him Captain Cannon – though not to his face; he had a terrible temper.

'Well, he has a reputation for winning battles,' Nathan replied shortly, for to universal astonishment, not least among the French, Bonaparte had won a series of victories over the armies of the Austrian Emperor and the King of Savoy, and advanced right across the north of Italy to the borders of Venice.

'Oh, I doubt there will be anything approaching a battle, not here,' Fremantle assured him. 'The Tuscans ain't got the bottle for it. And to be fair to them they ain't got the men neither.'

'So who is doing the fighting?'

'Oh, that is just the French vanguard announcing their presence. I think they're trying to hit *Inconstant* for I've took her close inshore on a spring cable. But the range is too long for 'em. Most of the rounds are falling on the town,' he added complacently.

'Hence the fires?'

'No, no, the fires were lit by Spannochi – he's the Governor here – to cover the evacuation. Stop the French from spying on us from the hills. He has told them they cannot enter the city until he has instructions from the Grand Duke. But I expect

Bonaparte will put him right about that – if and when he gets here with the rest of the army.'

Nathan nodded as if this all made perfect sense. In a mad world he supposed it did. 'So – what are we going to do?'

Fremantle was a couple of years ahead of Nathan in the Navy List which made him the senior officer present – at least until Nelson arrived.

'Well, we can hardly oppose them – even if the Tuscans were prepared to help us out, which they ain't. So I talked it over with old Udny and we decided to evacuate everyone that don't want to stay and take 'em to Corsica.'

'Old Udny' being the British Consul, prize agent and pimp. A silver-haired gentleman with a mild manner who collected harpsichords.

'Everyone?' Nathan queried.

Fremantle shrugged as if this was a minor inconvenience. 'Every foreigner, that is, who don't fancy being here when the French arrive. We've took off most of the British already – them that's from Leghorn, that is – but they keep coming in from all over. You would think Tuscany was a British colony, the number that's living here. Some fair-looking dollies among them, too, I don't mind telling you.'

Fremantle was known to have an eye for the dollies. By all accounts he was Udny's best customer.

'And we are taking them all to Corsica?'

'Unless you have a better idea. I don't see we've much choice in the matter. Not the way Bonaparte's been talking. Nest of vipers, you see. Burn 'em out. Scourge 'em from the temple. Anyone who trades with the British tarred with the same brush. Hollanders, Armenians, Persians, Jews – though I hear tell the Israelites may have decided to stay, Bonaparte not being what you might call Christian.'

'And have we got room for them all?'

'In Corsica?' Fremantle frowned as he tried to recollect who else lived there.

'I meant in the way of transport.'

'Well, I've commandeered every sail that was in the port. Don't see what more I can do. Might be a bit cramped for some of them. I've given up my own cabin as a matter of fact, to an English family from Florence. Four daughters.'

Nathan thought of querying this but on second thoughts he let it pass. 'And how long do you think it will take to get them all off?'

'Way things are going – most of the day. Sent my Marines ashore to control them – and to hold the harbour as long as possible.'

'And what would you like me to do?'

Fremantle considered. 'I think you had best stay out here. Guard the transports. Once word gets out of what is happening we shall have every corsair between Nice and Genoa heading our way. Form a convoy,' he added brightly. This expression appeared to give him considerable satisfaction, for he nodded to himself several times, as if it were a salve for all life's problems. 'You might let me have a few of your Marines, though, if you can spare them.' He finished the Madeira and picked up his hat. 'Now I had better get back to *Inconstant*. I've taken her as close inshore as I dared – did I say?'

'You did.'

'Cover the coast road, d'you see? Might persuade the Frogs to stay up in the hills for a while.'

This proved to be wishful thinking. When they returned to the quarterdeck it was to find most of the officers training their glasses on the hillside where a long column of troops could be seen advancing towards the port.

'French cavalry,' Duncan reported confidently, handing his

glass to Fremantle who observed them for a moment before declaring that he must be off.

'If I cannot delay them we had better save what we can,' he called back to Nathan as he made for the quarter-ladder, 'and the rest must take their chances with Bonaparte.'

Nathan sent Whiteley and his Marines after him in the *Unicorn*'s two cutters – a pitifully small force to throw against the French Army of Italy, he reflected as he watched them go. But he had his own problems to consider. There were already up to a dozen transports standing out from the harbour and he had very little notion of what to do with them. For most of his fourteen years in the service the country had been at peace and he had never been called upon to perform the duties of a convoy escort, an omission that had previously appeared more a cause for congratulation than not.

'It is usual to appoint a Commodore,' Duncan instructed him when Nathan sought his advice.

'A Commodore,' Nathan repeated doubtfully, thinking of Nelson and the considerable authority attached to this office.

'From among the merchant Captains,' Duncan explained, 'with the duty of maintaining the agreed order of sailing.'

'I see. Keeping the buggers in line.'

'That is about the measure of it, sir.'

Nathan hesitated but Mr Duncan, being some ten years older than him, had seen service in the American War and then with the Russians during the peace. His experience was invaluable and in truth, he did not appear to resent sharing it. 'And are there any particular principles one should acknowledge in agreeing this order of sailing?' Nathan enquired.

'It is customary to order them in several parallel lines,' Duncan offered, 'with the largest and better armed on the outside, the most vulnerable in the middle.'

Common sense really, thought Nathan, though he suspected it worked rather better in principle than it did in practice. But he was impressed with the notion of a Commodore, now he was aware of its limitations when applied to the merchant service. It only remained for him to appoint this unfortunate.

He surveyed the vessels currently standing off the mole. A mixed bunch. The largest and most shipshape appeared to be a barque of some 1,000 tons with a broad white stripe down her side pierced with ten black gunports. This did not mean she was endowed with as many guns, of course, but it was a promising sign and he sent young Mr Lamb over in the gig to request her Captain to come aboard.

This individual turned out to be a Scot by the name of McNabb, a cagey-looking brute of about fifty or so with the sanguine features and red and rheumy eyes of a man much exposed to the weather or the bottle, possibly both. His ship was the *Selkirk Castle* out of Leith, under permanent lease to the Levant Company. Which was not quite the East India Company but of a similar pedigree. Nathan took him down to his cabin, gave him what Fremantle had left of the Madeira, and put the proposal to him. Rather to his surprise, for he had been anticipating an argument, it was accepted with a terse nod, as if it were of no great consequence.

'You have done this before,' Nathan guessed.

McNabb confirmed with another nod that this was indeed the case. He put Nathan in mind of those Highland cattle he had seen in landscape portraits, standing in a loch under a lowering sky. Not that he was particularly hairy or be-horned; just something in his manner suggested the comparison.

'Well, I am very much obliged to you,' Nathan assured him with what he hoped would be an endearing grin, 'for I confess I have no experience at all.'

McNabb did not look in the least surprised.

However, he concurred with Duncan's proposed order of sailing and suggested that Nathan post an officer in a cutter or similar vessel to convey these instructions to each of the transports as they left the mole.

'And may I ask how many guns do you carry?' Nathan put to him as he prepared to depart.

'Sixteen,' he replied shortly. 'Six-pounders.'

It was more than Nathan had anticipated, and though the calibre would serve to deter only a half-hearted pirate, it was a great deal better than nothing.

'And you have sufficient crew to fire a broadside?'

This moved the Captain to eloquence. 'She is a Levanter, sir, not a Leith collier.'

Nathan accepted the rebuke with good grace but he did wonder about sending Holroyd over to take a look at the guns, even to stay on as gunnery officer. But it would not do at all. Not with Tully and four of the midshipmen already away in the *Bonne Aventure* and the other prizes. And many of his best seamen with them. In fact, he wondered if he might press a few prime hands from the transports but he was unsure of the ethics of pilfering seamen from ships under one's protection. Perhaps Duncan would know. He decided against consulting McNabb.

He escorted the new Commodore over the side and sent Mr Lamb after him in the gig to perform the duty they had agreed upon.

'So you may play the sheepdog for once, Mr Lamb, but remember that a bark is more instructive than a bleat.'

Mr Lamb rewarded this poor attempt at humour with a glazed grin. He was sensitive where his voice was concerned, for though he normally had it under control it rose, when excited, to a piping treble. It would not be pleasant to spend the best part of the day in an open boat in this heat but it would teach him how to order a convoy, which was more than Nathan had ever learned.

Once he had gone Nathan returned his attention to the shore. The cavalry appeared to have advanced no further than the outer suburbs. Certainly there appeared to be no serious attempt to attack the harbour – and the artillery had stopped firing from the hills, possibly for fear of hitting their own men. Nathan guessed they were happy enough to let the vipers flee the nest, rather than be put to the trouble of slaughtering them out of hand, or accommodating them elsewhere, for there were a good many women and children among them, and despite rumours to the contrary he did not suppose that French dragoons had any more relish for that line of work than British soldiers. But perhaps they did not like the look of *Inconstant*'s guns covering the road down to the harbour. If Fremantle had her on a spring cable she could cover most of the waterfront with a lethal arc.

Nathan would have liked to moor the *Unicorn* in a similar fashion but he needed more room for manoeuvre. If there was a concerted attack by several privateers at once he might have to cut his cables. So, not wishing to lose his anchors, he had the frigate heave to with her foretopsails braced against the main, about half a mile north of the convoy with her guns run out on both sides. He now had some thirty sail gathered under his command, moored in four lines, with about half that number still waiting to load up at the mole – a considerable responsibility for just one ship-of-war, and he scanned the seas to the north and west with some concern. Happily there was no sign of the expected raiders, but nor was there any sign of *Captain* and *Meleager* – or *Bonne Aventure* for that matter, with her own small convoy.

A little before noon the lookouts in the foretop alerted him to the approach of two sails to the north-east, close into the coast. Nathan climbed up the ratlines to have a look for himself, but his hopes were swiftly dashed. The sails were too small for Nelson and it was the wrong direction for Tully. He focused his glass on the leading vessel and then his lips moved in a silent oath, for she was long and lean with the look of a predator about her – and as she came closer and the smoke cleared a little he saw the tricolour flapping at her stern.

Worse, there were four more of them, emerging from the haze behind her.

'Beat to quarters, Mr Duncan,' he instructed the first lieutenant, 'and signal the convoy to prepare for battle.'

He wondered if he could alert Fremantle to the danger but *Inconstant* was still lost behind the press of vessels inside the harbour. He would know soon enough, however, when he heard the sound of the guns.

Chapter Three

Corsairs

———•◆•———

They came out of the smoke-thickened haze to the north, five of them: spectral at first, slowly taking shape and substance. Corsairs out of La Spezia, Nathan guessed, or one of their other bases on the Ligurian coast. Legalised pirates, the wolves of the sea.

Not that he cared what they were, legally or morally, or where they came from. His chief concern was how to stop them.

He studied them through his glass as they came closer. Two brigs of sixteen guns or more and two small sloops about the size of *Bonne Aventure*. The fifth was lagging somewhat, and still too distant to tell what guns she carried, but she was schooner-rigged which would give her a considerable advantage sailing into the wind. Individually, or even combined, they were no match for a thirty-two-gun frigate, but they were unlikely to make their attack from the same quarter and *Unicorn* could not be everywhere at once. The schooner could run right past the convoy and attack from the south, and if Nathan took *Unicorn* after her it would take a long time to beat back and engage with the others.

He wished now that he had sent young Lamb off in the gig to alert Fremantle to the danger, for if *Inconstant* could work out of the harbour she could run down on them with the wind on her quarter. But it would be no easy task to bring her safely through that mass of shipping and it would mean leaving the harbour undefended. Besides, Fremantle had asked him to guard the convoy, and if he looked into his heart Nathan suspected he would find a deep reluctance to admit he could not do so unaided.

'Mr Perry, I believe we must tack to the north-east,' he informed the sailing master, 'and lay her as close to the fort as you are able.'

The sailing master glanced towards the Fortezza Vecchia, the ancient fortress on the northern tip of the harbour, and then up to his sails, pursing his lips thoughtfully. Nathan knew what he was thinking. It would mean sailing perilously close to the wind, and if they were taken aback there would be hell to pay in such a crowded anchorage. But being Perry he made no verbal expression of dissent. Instead it was hands to the braces and the topmen swarming aloft to spread more canvas the instant the yards came around. But the frigate could not be so easily cozened. She was barely making steerage way and the wind, such as it was, was pushing them far too close to the harbour entrance. They would have to wear ship and come up on the starboard tack, and Nathan was not at all sure if he had sufficient sea room for the manoeuvre – already he was alarmingly close to the transports waiting off the mole.

'We will have to use the boats,' he declared, trying to sound more positive than he felt and avoiding Perry's eye for he knew the master would have anticipated this problem long before he had.

They used the crews from the starboard guns, but it took a

good few minutes to haul the boats up from the stern and as many more to man them. Then there was the time-consuming business of rigging the cables through the hawsers with Duncan red-faced and roaring and Perry chewing upon his lower lip and Nathan wishing, not for the first time, that he had kept his mouth shut. But eventually they had the frigate in tow and the effect was felt immediately. Her head came round and she began to move across the crowded anchorage with some purpose. Nathan looked to the privateers. They were still holding to their course, close enough now for him to see the guns run out and the studding sails spread out like wings, aloft and alow: more geese than wolves but no less threatening.

There was the sharp report of a cannon and he jerked his head round to see the puff of black smoke from the fort. A warning shot, no more, but it was enough to make the corsairs bear off a little. Their course was now sou'-sou'-west, which was more or less where he wanted them, but he could not count on their holding to it for long.

A thin, piping voice at his ear and he looked around to behold a small, fat midshipman, his face shining with eagerness. 'Mr Holroyd's compliments, sir, and he thinks he can reach them with the foremost guns.'

Nathan looked back at the privateers. But the range was extreme and the recoil would inevitably have an effect on the tow.

'Thank you, Mr Anson,' he replied, 'but I believe we must wait until we can give them a better show.'

The midshipman's face fell and for a moment Nathan thought he was going to argue the toss. He frowned as fiercely as the circumstance required and discipline prevailed; the boy ran back to instruct the lieutenant to hold his fire.

They were at the edge of the northern road now, and the corsairs about a mile further out to sea, still bending to westward. Nathan guessed they would continue on this course until they drew level with the convoy and then make their move. But he did not wish to make his own move too soon, for if he shot too far ahead of them he would have a hell of a job beating back against the wind.

'I think we may get the hands back from the boats,' he informed the first lieutenant; and to the sailing master: 'Stand by to brace the yards round, Mr Perry, and let us go straight at 'em.' He glanced aloft. 'And break out the battle pennant, Mr Duncan, why don't you? It is time we gave it an airing.'

Which was all very well and might have won a round of applause on the stage and even three hearty cheers from the more receptive audiences, but he was in a private agony of frustration until the last man was back aboard and they could finally wear ship.

Round she came, ponderously at first, but then as she took the wind on her quarter he felt her bite into the sluggish sea and a few spittles of spray came flying back from her bow. Hardly a charge, but at least they were moving in the right direction. Looking up, he saw the battle pennant doing its best to stream from the masthead, less of a spear pointing at the heart of the enemy than a long, quavering finger. He laughed aloud, more from nervousness and a sense of his own absurdity than exultation, but he saw Duncan and the other officers on the quarterdeck grinning back at him, and even some of the hands, too, and if they thought he laughed at the prospect of battle or imminent death then who was he to contradict them?

They were now on a parallel course to the five privateers and a little behind the third in line, and every minute that passed pushed the enemy further out to sea. If they did not turn soon they would sail right across the front of the convoy, shepherded by the frigate at their heels.

But they were not sheep. They would not come on such a hunt only to sail away unsated and the prey in sight. They would lose too much face with their men – and each other.

Further, further he hounded them out to sea. Then, at the very last moment, just when he was beginning to think they had missed their chance, they made their turn. First the two large brigs, then the smaller vessels. On a course that would bring them across the frigate's bows and into the heart of the convoy.

Still he let the *Unicorn* run on. He could sense the tension on the quarterdeck. Perry staring up at his sails, Duncan fixedly out to sea. No one would look directly at him. The first brig was just off his starboard bow at a distance of about five hundred yards. He had no need of the glass now to see her guns. They were only 6-pounders, he told himself, and they would be firing at extreme range. But the distance seemed to grow less, the black muzzles larger the longer he looked at them until, with a suddenness that made him flinch, a rippling line of fire and smoke erupted from stem to stern. His mind even registered that they were firing chain shot before he heard the peculiar whining, whirring sound of their approach, like angry, darting hornets – if two iron balls joined by a murderous length of chain could be thought to resemble anything as insignificant as a mere insect. They would do more than sting if they hit you, he reflected grimly – he had seen a man cut in two by them – but their real target was the rigging. They could cause mayhem aloft and leave a ship dead in the water. But they had fired too soon. Most of the rounds fell harmlessly into the sea – all but one, probably from the last gun to fire, that struck the bower anchor with a tortured screech of metal upon metal. And then another scream that was entirely human as the shattered fragments went spinning off into the crew of the starboard bow chaser, the only gun to have fired back.

Then, only then, did Nathan give the order to port the helm and they came heavily round to larboard and fired their own rippling broadside – thirteen 18-pounders and the four 6-pounders on the quarterdeck – the successive reports rolling down the gundeck towards him so that to his deafened ears it sounded like one long roar as if the air itself had been torn asunder by a giant hand.

He ran up the mizzen shrouds a little and when the smoke of the guns cleared, he saw the brig, still running on to the south-east, apparently unharmed. But then as he stared – astonished and appalled that every single round had apparently missed its target – the brig's foremast came toppling slowly down, like a giant tree in a forest, bringing spars and rigging with it, forestays, jibs and all, crashing down across the forecastle and into the sea, pulling her round by the head.

She was well within range of the big 18-pounders, and every shot of the second and third broadsides hammered home, bringing down mainmast and mizzen and tearing huge bites from her gunwale, for she was not built to withstand 18-pound round shot, and they left her a dismasted hulk, drifting away to the south.

Nathan backed the mizzen to let the second brig draw level. But she had no stomach for this kind of fight and he did not blame her. She fell off the wind and began to wear away to the south-west with the two smaller brigs behind her. But not the schooner. As he had predicted, she was making a dart for the south, right across the front of the convoy.

For a moment Nathan was tempted to follow and trust the other three had seen enough to deter them from taking any further part in the proceedings, but it was too great a risk. If they saw the frigate chasing off to the south they would resume their attack on the convoy, and the *Unicorn* would never beat back in time to prevent it. He could only hope that the transports could fight the schooner off by themselves. Already several of them were firing at her as she crossed their bows, though their shot was dropping well short. He saw Perry looking towards him with a trace of anxiety, for if the *Unicorn* stuck to her present course she would plough straight into the convoy.

He nodded. 'Wear ship, then, Mr Perry.'

Young Anson came aft with a damage report. Three men injured from the chain shot that had come aboard, only one seriously, but that was Mr Clyde, the gunner, with a head wound. Nathan sent to the surgeon to see how he did, but the news was not good. McLeish had stitched up the wound but the gunner was unconscious and it was too early to say what his prospects were. The gun, Anson reported cheerfully, was undamaged.

So they harried the enemy to the south-west for a good mile or so, concentrating their fire on the biggest of the three brigs, which was also the slowest, and reducing her to such an extent she came up into the wind and struck her colours. Nathan was unimpressed. He had no men to spare for another prize crew and if he left her as she was he had no doubt she would make good her escape, or even resume the attack, for she did not seem at all damaged aloft. He sent word to Mr Holroyd to load with chain and fire every gun into her rigging as they went past, quieting what little conscience he had in the matter by telling himself it would do no further injury to her crew – unless they got in the way of a falling block – and they were little better than pirates anyway.

They left the brig in a tangle of torn rigging and continued their pursuit of the two smaller craft, but Nathan was concerned not to stray too far from the convoy, and after one final discharge from the bow chasers he gave the order to wear ship once more.

Rather to his alarm, in his enthusiasm for the chase he had allowed the *Unicorn* to drop a good deal further to the south than he would have wished. They would have to sail very close to the wind to resume their station, and if anything it had shifted a little to the west, making the job far more difficult. Sure enough, as they braced the yards round on a course that would bring them back to the edge of the mole, the sails began to feather alarmingly and even to flap back against the masts.

'We will have to take her off the wind a point,' the sailing master informed him glumly, 'and come about on the other tack.'

'Very well, Mr Perry, make it so.'

His dismay was increased when he heard the continuing sound of gunfire and he saw smoke drifting southward from the far side of the convoy. The schooner had done exactly what he had predicted and closed in on them from the south, for with her fore-and-aft rig she could sail a lot closer to the wind than *Unicorn* or any other square-rigged vessel.

Nathan consoled himself with the thought that the firing was unlikely to be coming from the schooner itself, for no privateer would wish to damage a potential prize. Sure enough, as *Unicorn* came up on the larboard tack, he saw her break away to the south with one of the transports hard on her stern. The crafty fox had snatched her from right under his nose.

For a moment Nathan wondered if he should let her go – one transport out of forty was not such a disaster, and he had no wish to be lured downwind while the two remaining predators resumed their attack. But only for a moment. He was damned if he would let them have even one of his charges. The schooner's one advantage was sailing into the wind. With the wind behind her she was no match for the *Unicorn*, especially with a cumbersome transport to slow her down.

So they fell off from the wind again and ran with her,

clapping on every sail they could carry, studding sails and all, and within minutes the transport hove to and they saw a boat drop away from her stern, presumably with the prize crew aboard. The schooner paused just long enough to pick them up and then continued her run to the south.

This time Nathan let her go.

They clawed their way back to the convoy, the transport lumbering in their wake, and though they made a cursed slow job of it, there proved to be no compelling need for haste. The privateers had had enough. The two that remained unscathed were hull down on the western horizon and their crippled consorts limping after.

There were cheers from the crew and though Duncan checked them with his usual firmness, they were all looking mighty pleased with themselves. And from the looks they gave him, Nathan could see they were not overly discontented with their Captain. He only wished he could feel the same way about himself.

'I am going below, Mr Duncan,' he told the first lieutenant, 'to see how Dr McLeish is doing with the wounded.'

Chapter Four

The Courtesans

———•◦•———

The gunner was dead. He had died without regaining consciousness, the doctor said. Nathan looked down at the body. Clyde had been a big man, even for a gunner, but he seemed to have shrunken somewhat in death. He did not look at peace. Nathan remembered when they were in the Devil's Jigsaw, off the coast of Louisiana, after the hurricane, when *Unicorn* was grounded on a mud bank and they had been obliged to haul her off with the help of George Banjo and his fellow slaves. But Nathan had left Clyde aboard to fire one of the bow chasers in the hope of dislodging the keel from the mud. He remembered when the ship slid off and he had dived into the water and swum out to her. He remembered standing there, dripping water on the deck and shouting up to the gunner in the bows, 'Well done, Mr Clyde! I swear it was your gun that did the trick.' And Clyde grinning back at him and scratching behind his ear and saying, 'Aye, sir, I reckon it may've helped a bit.' And for the first time since Nathan had come aboard the *Unicorn* in the Havana he had felt he had something other than a crew of malcontents under his command. He saw himself so clearly, dripping water on that deck, and grinning away, happy as he would ever be, he thought now, and Clyde grinning back at him. It was scarce eighteen months ago. He seemed so much older now, and the gunner was dead.

He went back up on deck and his officers saw the black look on his face and left him alone at the rail. It was not just the death of Clyde – Christ knows he had lost enough good men since he had come aboard – but it was a mood that invariably took him after an action, whether they had won or lost. He felt drained and depressed. Diminished, too, in a way he could not easily explain, even to himself. As if he had failed to live up to some exalted expectation of himself.

It seemed to him now that the 'victory' the crew was celebrating with such evident satisfaction had been a very shabby affair. How could you call it a victory? They had simply beaten off a couple of privateers – merchantmen converted to ships-of-war by the addition of a few piddling guns and issued with a licence to plunder. Where was the glory in that?

He gazed out over the sea to where his vanquished enemies were making their escape. Not so much wolves now as whipped curs, tails between their legs. So how many more men had he killed and maimed today? A dozen? A score? More?

And for what?

When this war began Nathan had not really questioned what he was fighting for. It was just another war against the French, the old enemy. They were always fighting each other, the English and the French – it was what they did. He'd lost count of the times they had fought each other over the last couple of hundred years, or the times during the peace when he had raised a glass with his fellow officers and drunk to 'the next war and promotion for us all'. Promotion and prize money. That was what you fought for. Later, when he was in

Paris and witnessed the Terror at first hand, he had discovered a worthier cause. But then . . . the Terror ended. The French calmed down a little. Became, if not less excitable, at least less fanatical, less eager to cut off people's heads. They still called themselves Revolutionists, still refused to restore the monarchy – which was the official, government-authorised reason for fighting them – but Nathan could not find it in his heart to condemn them for that. He supposed that since the start of the war he had moved to the Left, as the French would say. Perhaps it was sharing a prison with Thomas Paine. He had been subverted by his ideas on monarchy and revolution. Though frankly, the more you saw of Tom Paine, in Nathan's view, the less likely you were to believe a word he said, or wrote. But without being too radical, it seemed to Nathan that the men who now ran France were not much worse than the men who ran Britain. Perhaps not so fastidious. Not so polite. But then you could hardly expect them to be when the crowned heads of Europe were baying for their blood.

And that was another thing. Who were these men in whose cause so many others fought and died? The Hapsburg Emperor, the Kings of Spain and Prussia, the King of Sardinia and Piedmont-Savoy, the King of the Two Sicilies . . . and their own King George. Nathan had a fondness for King George, what he knew of him. He seemed like a decent enough fellow. Farmer George, people called him. Of course, he was stark, raving mad, by most accounts. Forever trying to mount the Queen's ladies and making lewd conversation – if that was a sign of madness. Half the court would be in Bedlam if it was. But it didn't stop at that, apparently. The latest story was that he had jumped out of his coach in St James's Park and started talking to a tree. When his attendants tried to get him back in the coach he assured them that it was the King of Prussia. Perhaps he was trying to make a point. Perhaps it was a form of political satire. Talking to the King of Prussia was like talking to a tree.

Still, it was not an entirely satisfactory image if you were fighting for the cause of Monarchy against Republicanism. And now the crowned heads were all sending their envoys to Paris in the hopes of making peace. The only ones left in it were mad King George and the Hapsburg Emperor. They said even Billy Pitt wanted to make an end to it, that he was only fighting on in the hopes of making an honourable peace, whatever that was. It probably meant swapping a couple of sugar islands in the Caribbean. We get to keep Saint-Domingue, the French can have Guadeloupe.

Not a great cause to die for. Or kill for. What would God make of it all? Nathan raised his eyes to the masthead, as if he might find Him there, keeping a tally on some eternal abacus. How many was it now? Two hundred men had died in his fight with the *Virginie* off Cuba, another two or three hundred when he lured the *Brutus* on to the rocks off Cap Martin. And all those women and children at Quibéron. He may not have killed them himself, but he had been in command at the time; it was his fault. 'You are nothing more than a band of assassins,' his mother had said once, speaking of the Navy as a whole. Admittedly she was biased in her opinion, for the British naval blockade had played the devil with her family fortune. But he suspected that God, that old man at the masthead, was more of his mother's way of thinking than not.

Not that he believed in God any more. Not the God of the Church of England at any rate, and not the God of any Church he had ever heard of. Yet he could not shake off the need to believe in *something*. Some order in the universe. Nathan was an astronomer by inclination. And he would have been by practice, perhaps, if it had not been for the war.

He still occupied much of his leisure time with a study of the night sky. Lying flat on his back in the maintop, wrapped in his boat cloak with his telescope resting in a kind of cat's cradle he had made so he was not overly troubled by the movement of the ship. Some of his most peaceful moments had been spent like that, gently rocking to the movement of the waves, his ears filled with the creak of rope and tackle, observing the wonders of the universe. There was order there, surely. But was there anybody *ordering* it? He would have liked to think so. A kind of Divine Clockmaker, not unlike Mr Harrison who had invented the first marine chronometer. A Divine Tinkerer with a pair of glasses perched on the end of His nose and a small screwdriver in His hand, trying to make everything work. Trying to put things right. It was a pleasant thought. But Nathan did not really believe it.

His thoughts turned to more practical considerations. The mole was almost clear of evacuees, with just three or four transports waiting to take off their remaining charges. He could see *Inconstant* clearly on the far side of the harbour now, still covering the approaches with her guns. But the French were still lying low. There was no sign of them at all in the town, and the guns on the hillside remained silent. The flag of the Grand Duchy still flew from the Fortezza Nuova in the centre of town.

He began to think more cheerily about dinner. They had scarcely resumed their station on the convoy's flank, however, when his attention was drawn to the approach of *Inconstant*'s cutter. Nathan half-thought it might be Fremantle again, come to congratulate him on his defence of the convoy, though it would scarcely be in character. But it was not Fremantle. It was something altogether more alarming.

*

'They are *what*?' Nathan addressed the impudent-looking midshipman who commanded the cutter and now stood, hat in hand, on the *Unicorn*'s quarterdeck.

'I think that was the word the Captain used, sir. He says they are under the protection of Mr Udny, sir.'

'They fucking would be,' said Nathan. He looked down once more into the cutter, scarcely believing the evidence of his own eyes. One of its occupants looked up and waved at him. He vaguely thought he recognised her, but from where?

'Courtesans?' he repeated in bemusement.

'I think it means whores, sir,' the midshipman confided in a low voice, smirking.

'I know what it means, sir,' Nathan rebuked him sternly. 'But what the devil does he mean by sending them to *me*?'

'He says to tell you he is desolate, sir, but—'

'Desolate, is he?'

'But he has no room for them aboard *Inconstant*, owing to having given up his own cabin . . .'

'To a family from Florence with four daughters. Yes, I know all about that. But why could he not have them stowed aboard one of the transports?'

'Well, as to that, sir, he said to tell you that . . . that . . .' The midshipman quailed at the look in Nathan's eye but continued gamely: 'He says that they have formed so strong an . . . an *attachment* to certain officers of the fleet, sir, that, that they are entitled to be treated as officers' wives, sir.'

The bare-faced effrontery of this temporarily deprived Nathan of the power of speech. Not that he had any principled objection to the comparison, but that it should come from Fremantle was, he thought, a bit rich.

The midshipman pursued his advantage. 'And he said to tell you that one of them is Signora Correglia, sir.'

Nathan stared at him. The woman who had waved at him.

No wonder she looked familiar. He had dined with her aboard the flagship. Adelaide Correglia was Nelson's dolly. It was common knowledge that he paid the rent on her apartment in Leghorn and she was frequently to be found in residence aboard the flagship.

Nathan closed his eyes for a moment. Then he sent for the purser.

'They are *what*?' McIvor echoed Nathan's own initial reaction when informed of the situation. Nathan told him. The purser stared over the side.

'How many of them are there?' he enquired finally.

'I assume, McIvor, you can count as well as I,' Nathan rebuked him coldly. His normal good humour was beginning to fray a little at the edges. 'Probably better, given your occupation.'

'Seven of them?' McIvor's tone expressed his rising astonishment and indignation. 'But where on earth are we going to put them all?' Nathan kept his counsel. 'And if I am to draw upon stores to feed them, how am I to account for it in the ledger?'

'You may enter them as whatever you goddamn like,' Nathan replied shortly, doubting it a proper subject for the Captain of a King's ship upon his own quarterdeck. But he could not leave it at that. Nor did he want McIvor making unsuitable entries in the ship's books. If they were read by the wrong persons there would be hell to pay. The press might get hold of it. Questions might be asked in Parliament. 'Enter them as supercargo,' he suggested more reasonably. 'And you may stow them in my cabin until more appropriate accommodation can be arranged for them.'

'But they are whores,' Mr McIvor hissed, in the low but scandalised tones of a Scotsman, a citizen of Edinburgh, provoked beyond his normal reserve.

'Courtesans,' Nathan corrected him mildly, though the distinction, as it had been explained to him, was a fine one.

'But why do they want to leave Leghorn?' McIvor demanded forcefully.

This question had occurred to Nathan. While it might be considered unpatriotic to confess it publicly, he would have thought there was little to choose between a French Captain of Hussars and an officer in His Britannic Majesty's Navy. If you were a whore, that is. Or even a courtesan.

'I am told they have formed certain "attachments" to some of our officers,' Nathan informed him in a low voice.

But McIvor was still looking mutinous. 'Now lookee here, McIvor.' Nathan tried a different tack. 'This is a delicate matter. Several of these young persons are under the protection of very senior officers on the Navy List. I have entrusted you with their care because I can count on your discretion and your . . . your diplomacy.' And also, though he did not say it, because he was the only ship's officer of any seniority whose dignity could be compromised in this way. 'I trust you to steer a fine course between Scylla and Charybdis,' he concluded vaguely. 'And now if you will excuse me, I have rather more urgent matters to attend to.'

He clapped his eye to the glass and pretended to be observing the French positions above the town. But despite the rigidity of his stance and the gravity of the military situation, his mind remained very much preoccupied with the problem of his new charges. He watched covertly as they came aboard – were helped aboard, in fact, by an outrageous number of the ship's company, far more than was needed to bring seven fit and healthy young women up a quarter-ladder. But they were a comely crew; there was no getting away from it. A vision in satin and lace. He closed his glass with a sigh. He supposed he must be civil. After all, she was the

Commodore's particular friend and they had dined at the same table.

'Signora Correglia,' he enthused, making an elegant bow. 'Welcome aboard. Delighted to be of service.'

She smiled and gave him her hand, but her eye, he noted, was cold. He had, after all, kept her bobbing about in a small boat for the best part of half an hour.

'I am so sorry to have kept you waiting,' he babbled, 'but as you can imagine, there were certain arrangements to be made. We were not prepared for such . . . that is, for female company.' He was blushing himself now, for the female company was making the most of the effect it was having on its exclusively male audience. 'However, I have made my own cabin available and I trust you will be comfortable there until . . . until other arrangements can be made for you. My steward will show you below.'

But Signora Correglia apparently had no desire to be shown below. She and her companions distributed themselves about the quarterdeck like visiting royalty, supervising the disposal of their baggage and conversing animatedly with each other in the local dialect.

'This is intolerable,' Nathan informed the midshipman from *Inconstant*. 'You would think they are embarked upon a pleasure cruise.'

He was further incensed by the amount of baggage they had brought with them. Not only a remarkable number of personal items but a great deal of household furnishings including some Turkish rugs, an extraordinary number of velvet drapes and cushions, several songbirds in elaborate cages and a parrot. And a large unwieldy crate which he was informed by the midshipman contained Signora Correglia's virginal.

He made another attempt to engage the woman in debate. 'This is a ship-of-war, Signora,' he insisted. 'We might be called upon to fight an action at any time. I beg you to take your party below.'

She rewarded him with another of her dazzling smiles before turning back to her companions. Nathan recalled that on their previous encounters she appeared to have very little command of the English language. He tried again in French, even in what little he knew of Genovese, and finally managed to convey his desire that the ladies should remove themselves from the quarterdeck so he could get on with fighting a war.

They were led below by his steward, Gilbert Gabriel, who showed every appearance of complacency at this new responsibility. After a few minutes he was back.

'They are asking if I can move out the guns, sir,' he reported with as straight a face as he could muster, 'to make more room for their duds.'

Nathan did not dignify this request with a reply.

'And what about your cot, sir? Shall I have that moved out, or will you be joining them later?'

Nathan rewarded him with an icy glare but Gabriel had been his father's servant before him and had known him when he was in skirts. The man was impervious to anything short of a kick up the arse, which was not to be undertaken lightly. He had been a highwayman in his youth and retained the murderous demeanour that had proved so useful in his former occupation. He was widely known – with that flair for irony not uncommon on the lower deck of a British ship-of-war – as the Angel Gabriel.

'You may leave the cot where it is,' Nathan informed him. 'They will be moving out before nightfall.'

Nathan was already regretting his hasty instruction to have them quartered, even temporarily, in his own cabin. He hoped rumour would not spread about the fleet that he had turned it into a bawdy house and set himself up as the Madam.

But as he had informed the purser, there were more urgent matters to consider. He returned his attention to the harbour. The *Inconstant* was standing out to sea, bringing the last of the transports with her, and as they cleared the harbour entrance a squadron of French cavalry galloped on to the mole.

'Putting on a show for us,' Nathan murmured to the first lieutenant, for he thought he was right in assuming that the French wanted only to be rid of the vipers and parasites, as they described them in their press, who were draining the lifeblood of Italy. But the cavalry were clearly intent on putting on more than a show. It soon became clear that their target was the battery on the edge of the mole, and the Grand Duke's soldiers had no intention of contesting it with them.

The guns must already have been loaded and ready, for within a very short space of time they were firing on the departing transport and its escort. Firing wild, fortunately, for being cavalry they were no great shakes as artillerymen. But they had plenty of targets to practise upon and the approaches to Leghorn suddenly became a very uncomfortable place to be. Nathan spent the next hour or so shepherding his charges further out to sea under a barrage of gunfire.

And there were more problems on the horizon, for the surviving privateers had been joined by several newcomers and there were more sails reported to the north-west. Though they kept their distance for the moment, Nathan had little doubt they would resume their attack at the first opportunity.

Help, however, was at hand. The sails to the north-west turned out to be *Captain* and *Meleager*, bringing *Bonne Aventure* and the *Unicorn*'s three prizes with them. Nathan now had high hopes not only of defending the convoy but of transferring his other charges to the more commodious quarters of the flagship. But they were soon dashed. A succession of signals informed him that Nelson intended to remain off

Leghorn with *Captain* and *Bonne Aventure* while the three frigates escorted the convoy to San Fiorenzo.

Nathan began to give some thought to his personal predicament. With the wind remaining fickle, they could hardly hope to reach Corsica much before tomorrow sunset. Which raised the question of where he was to spend the night.

He sent for the purser.

'Well, Mr McIvor, have you solved the problem?' he quizzed him with false bonhomie.

'The problem, sir?'

'Of the . . . of where to put our passengers.'

'But you said to put them in your cabin, sir.'

'I did, sir. For the time being. But I seem to remember expressing the wish that you find them alternative accommodation as soon as possible.' He was not sure if this was true and McIvor, judging from his expression, was certain it was not.

'Well, as to that, sir, I am not sure there *is* any alternative accommodation.'

'Don't be ridiculous, McIvor.'

'Not lest we turn out the officers, sir, and give them the gunroom. Unless you wish them to berth with the hands.'

'What about the orlop deck?'

'You would berth them in the orlop, sir?'

McIvor might very well query it, for the orlop deck was below the waterline, a notoriously dank, airless pit where the ship's stores were kept – and the livestock – and any prisoners when they had them. And of course being closer to the bilges it smelled worse than the rest of the ship – and was a great place for rats.

'It is not for long,' Nathan persisted, closing his ears to his conscience. 'Just one night. And I am sure you can make it comfortable for them. Hang a few lanterns.'

'And I suppose I am to give them hammocks to sleep in.'

'Well, what else are they to sleep in? Damn it, man, this is a ship-of-war, not a bordello.'

And who has made it so? McIvor did not say this to his Captain's face but his expression conveyed this sentiment at least as eloquently, and he probably muttered it to himself as he left the quarterdeck, shaking his head.

Only to return a little later to report, not without satisfaction, that 'the ladies' had spurned his offer of alternative accommodation and were intent on staying where they were for the duration of the voyage.

'But have you not explained that it is the Captain's quarters,' Nathan demanded indignantly, 'and that . . .' He sought for a convincing reason to maintain it for his exclusive use. 'And that the safety of the ship depends upon my having instant access to it at all times?'

'I did my best, sir,' the purser replied, 'but there is only one of them that speaks more than a smattering of English and what she does speak, she speaks with a certain *authority*, if you take my meaning, sir.'

And to Nathan's astonishment he solemnly laid a finger against his right eye and pulled down the lid. Just as he was about to berate him for insolence, Nathan realised the significance of the gesture. It was widely known that the Commodore had lost the sight of his right eye at the Siege of Calvi. The lady in question must therefore be 'Nelson's dolly' – Signora Correglia.

Nathan considered the problem at his leisure. He could, of course, order the Marines to clear the cabin for him, but this was fraught with complications. Injuries might occur and even if they did not, the damage to his character would be considerable. It was the kind of story that could spread. Captain Peake's heroic action in the Tyrrhenian Sea – against seven unarmed courtesans.

Nathan's youth made him overly conscious of his dignity, and such an incident could make him a laughing stock throughout the fleet. Already he was aware that the officers and crew awaited his next move with interest. Of course, it would be easy enough to take over one of the officers' cabins for the remainder of the voyage, but he felt this would not enhance his reputation as a fighting Captain. He had yet to win the ship's approval for his skills as a seaman, or a disciplinarian – too soft on the cat, was the general opinion – but he did have some standing as a strategist. Surely he could devise a strategy for this particular occasion.

It had still evaded him by six bells in the afternoon watch, the time when he usually had his dinner – in his cabin. He was saved from going hungry, or the embarrassment of eating on the quarterdeck, by an invitation from the first lieutenant to dine with the rest of the officers in the gunroom.

He accepted with alacrity, but the atmosphere would have been more cheerful, he felt, without his presence. No one felt at liberty to raise the subject uppermost in their minds and an uncomfortable silence fell upon the company, which was broken, with an air of desperation, by the first lieutenant.

'Caught any rats of late, Mr Lamb?' he enquired of the youngest officer present who, as such, was frequently the butt of his humour. Mr Lamb's exploits as a ratcatcher could always be relied upon as entertainment, for though young, he was not shy of putting himself forward.

He replied at length. He had caught six of the creatures during the last twenty-four hours, with a new method he had perfected, and they were now hanging in a cage – two cages, in fact – in the midshipmen's berth where they were in the process of being fattened with ship's biscuit. Midshipmen, being composed for the most part of growing boys, were invariably hungry and none too fussy about what they ate. Rats, fed on ship's biscuit, were much prized as a supplement to the ship's diet.

Prompted with further questions, Mr Lamb was prevailed upon to describe his patent methods of entrapment and where, in his opinion, the most prominent 'rat-runs' were situated. In this he revealed an impressive knowledge of both rodent behaviour and the more obscure regions of the *Unicorn*, but Nathan had stopped listening. He was recalling a similar conversation some months earlier when he had described his own custom as a midshipman of cooking them spatch-cocked – split open and skewered – with a bread sauce. Somehow this story had reached the ears of the Commodore, who had asked Nathan to repeat it for the amusement of the assembled company when next he dined on the flagship.

It happened to be one of those occasions when Signora Correglia was presiding as hostess, and as he told the story Nathan had noted the brief look of disgust on her lovely features. He concluded that she was not as ignorant of the English language as she would have it supposed – and that she had a natural aversion to rats.

The recollection of this gave him the germ of an idea. When dinner was concluded he took Mr Lamb aside for a quiet word.

'These rats of yours,' he began. 'What would you take for them?'

The midshipman gazed at him in some surprise. 'Take for them, sir?' he repeated foolishly.

'Yes, take for them, sir. Clear enough, ain't it?' He thought of one possible reason for misunderstanding. 'In coin.'

The midshipman still appeared bemused. 'You want to buy them from me, sir?'

'Yes, Mr Lamb, I want to buy them from you.' The boy was an idiot. 'Would six shillings suffice?'

A small pause. 'Each, sir?'

Clearly not that much of an idiot.

'For all six,' replied Nathan severely.

'I think ten would be a fairer price, sir. With the cages.'

'I don't want the cages, sir, I just want the rats.' But this was becoming undignified. Nathan sighed. 'Very well, Mr Lamb, ten it is. With the cages.' He counted the coin into the midshipman's grasping hands and in a short while he reappeared upon the quarterdeck and held the cages up for his Captain's inspection. Six gibbering rats glared furiously out upon him.

'You want me to kill 'em for you, sir?' enquired Lamb obligingly. 'Or would you like to do it yourself?'

'I'll tell you what I want you to do, Mr Lamb.' Nathan lowered his voice significantly. 'When I give the word, I want you to lower yourself over the lee rail and distribute them through the gunport of my cabin. Taking care that you are not observed in the process, do you understand me?'

'Oh yes, sir,' replied Mr Lamb, his features creasing into a delighted grin.

Nathan summoned the Marine sergeant and informed him that the moment the young ladies emerged, he was to post two sentries at the door of the Captain's cabin, with fixed bayonets. Then he gave the signal to the waiting midshipman.

Mr Lamb vanished over the rail. Nathan paced the quarter-deck. He was aware that a significant number of the ship's company had been alerted to the stratagem and were awaiting the outcome with a covert but lively interest. Mr Lamb reappeared with the two empty cages. Together they awaited the crescendo of screams that would herald the stampede of seven scantily clad females to the upper deck.

There were screams, certainly. Then a series of loud crashes and bangs and a strange squealing noise. But not the expected stampede. Nathan met the midshipman's puzzled eye.

'Thank you, Mr Lamb, that will be all,' said Nathan.

Time passed. The Marines were stood down. The convoy proceeded at its leisurely pace towards Cap Corse. The corsairs kept at a safe distance to windward. Nathan brooded on the quarterdeck.

At the end of the second dog-watch, he was approached by the Angel Gabriel.

'Signora Correglia's compliments,' he stated formally, 'and she requests the pleasure of the Captain's company at his earliest convenience.'

Stemming an angry retort, Nathan descended to his cabin. He was resolved to take a firm approach. The ship's discipline might well depend upon it.

He found the Signora presiding over her court. He bowed warily. She had been brought up in the slums of Genoa, he had once been told, and for all the elegance she had since acquired, she retained the robust and expressive nature of her class.

'Ah, *Capitano*,' she greeted him, 'we prepare the little dish for you – to thank for you that you give to us your little room.'

She stepped aside and Nathan saw the object simmering in the small silver chafing dish in which Gabriel normally prepared his nightly supper of toasted cheese.

'I think you like,' the harlot crooned as her companions collapsed in hysterical laughter. 'Spatch-a-Cock the Rat – with the bread sows. You take it away now, please, and if you like we make you another.'

Chapter Five

Night Attack

———•◆•———

Nathan spent the night on deck, wrapped in his boat cloak. He was comforted by the thought that he would have been obliged to do so anyway, given the constant threat of attack. There were now up to a dozen privateers stalking the convoy, hoping for the opportunity to slip between the escorts in the darkness – *Inconstant* and *Meleager* to windward, *Unicorn* bringing up the rear, with the lumbering transports spread out across a mile or so of ocean. But it was never that dark at this time of the year, especially on such a clear, cloudless night. The sky was full of stars, the moon shining a rippling path to the west, and scarcely a breath of wind to fill the sails. They cast the log at regular intervals but their speed never attained more than two knots and one fathom. A sluggish but steady progress towards Cap Corse.

Nathan sat in a canvas chair at the stern, hunched into the collar of his cloak, for even midsummer nights in the Mediterranean could be cool with the wind in the north. He was aware of a certain obstinacy in his manner, a dogged determination to suffer for his own perceived inadequacies. The first lieutenant had graciously offered to give up his own cabin. The doctor, McLeish, less graciously offered him a cot in the sickbay. Nathan had declined them both. He did not see why others should be inconvenienced, he said, by his own exaggerated sense of honour – though honour was not what he privately called it. And because the Captain stayed on deck all night, so did most of his officers. Including the first lieutenant. Nathan appreciated the contrariness of this but decided there was nothing he could do about it. It was the way of the service.

As the night wore on, his self-contempt ebbed a little and he began to feel a strange kind of content. Or perhaps there was nothing strange in it, for it was as beautiful a night as he could remember, and if you could forget the continuing vexations of courtesans, corsairs and the French, all seemed right with the world. The sails flapping lazily against the masts, the ropes creaking a little in the blocks. The ship riding easy on the gentle swell.

And of course the stars. Nathan was tempted to climb into the tops and take his glass to them, but he felt too lethargic to make the effort – and despite the ingenuity of his cat's cradle it was always a trial to hold the glass steady on a particular object in the night sky. Far more pleasant to just sit back and take in the whole panoply with the naked eye, especially as the master of *Inconstant* had the duty of navigating the convoy safely to San Fiorenzo. He had rarely seen such stars, so bright and so apparently close to hand, as if the topmasts were moving delicately through them, the *Unicorn* a starship gliding through the Milky Way.

He wondered what Sara was doing now and whether she was gazing at the same celestial panoply. Perhaps she had reached England by now and had been reunited with her son Alex in Sussex.

England. It was such a strange concept for him now, after

so long an absence. But when he thought about it, it was always the same little patch of it, the England of his childhood – and Alexander's childhood now – an area of the south coast from the market town of Lewes to the village of Wilmington on his father's estate, bounded on one side by the rolling hillocks of the South Downs and on the other by the sea. It was strange to think of Sara there, in the place he had grown up. Walking along the same woodland paths, climbing the Long Man, gazing out over the rolling Downland to the sea. He wished he was there with her, to be her guide. To show her the places he had roamed as a child, the ancient woodlands that were a riot of primrose and bluebells in spring, foxgloves and sweet violet in summer, a shadowland of foxes and badgers and half-wild pigs and the mythic creatures of Faerie that had been as real to Nathan's immature mind and the country folk that helped groom it as anything in *The Book of British Mammals*. And the chalk Downs that hosted a myriad of wild flowers and insects and butterflies as well as the hundreds of thousands of sheep that gave it a more material worth to Nathan's father and his fellow landowners. The gentle, shaded rivers where he had fished, filled with their basking trout and bream, perch and dace; ponds full of frogs and newts and other creatures of that slimy netherworld between earth and water; and of course, the sea. The headlands and havens, the rock pools and shingle beaches, the smugglers' haunt of Cuckmere and the chalk-white cliffs of the Seven Sisters. This was the paradise land of Nathan's childhood and early youth before he went to sea, where he still spent the best part of his leave, when he had it, where he still went in his mind, whenever he had the inclination or the leisure.

But it was a land under threat. Not from the French – the old enemy over the water, who would be dealt with one way or another – but from a young woman called Frances Wyndham, whom his father wished to marry. Which would mean divorcing his wife, Nathan's mother.

This was the only cloud that disturbed Nathan's content. Not Bonaparte in the mountains, not the Directory in Paris, not the ghost of Robespierre or the irritation of sharing a portion of his prize money with the flag officer's secretary. Sometimes it was no more than a distant blot on the horizon, at other times it loomed large as a thundercloud. But whatever its proportion or distance, it was always there. He had warned Sara about it, before he had sent her off to join them, but she had scarcely turned a hair. He supposed it was nothing after all she had endured in France at the time of the Terror.

Nathan's father and mother had lived apart for many years, for the whole of his life almost, though only in the formal sense since his adolescence. Nathan's father, Sir Michael Peake, was a retired naval officer and landowner who now devoted his life to hunting, fishing and the improvement and maintenance of the breed of Southdown sheep. Nathan's mother, Lady Catherine – Kitty to her friends – was an American, born and bred in New York, who harboured views and aspirations not at all compatible with life in the English countryside. It was difficult to imagine what had ever attracted them in the first place. 'We were young and foolish,' his mother had assured Nathan on more than one occasion, always with the same affected sigh, 'and he was a handsome devil in those days.'

And she was an heiress and a beauty. It was enough for most people.

But now she lived in London where she pursued a certain notoriety as the friend and patron of dissidents and dissenters and Republicans. Men such as Charles James Fox, the leader of what was described without apparent irony as His Majesty's Loyal Opposition, the radical brewer Samuel Whitbread, and the out-and-out Revolutionists Thomas Hardy and Francis

Place, whilst her closest female friend was Mary Imlay, née Wollstonecraft, author of *A Vindication of the Rights of Women*. Mrs Imlay was undoubtedly a woman of genius but she was prone to alternate periods of melancholy and passion which made her, in Nathan's view, a most unsuitable companion for his mother, who tended to excitability when encouraged.

On Nathan's last visit to London, upon discovering Mr Imlay's attachment to an actress from a strolling theatre company, Mrs Imlay had thrown herself into the Thames from Putney Bridge, obliging Nathan to jump in after her in his uniform coat, and then challenge Imlay to a duel in Lincoln's Inn Field which had caused him no little embarrassment with the gentlemen of the Holborn Watch and their Lordships of the Admiralty.

Nathan loved his mother but he could understand why it might be impossible to live with her for any length of time. Divorce, however, was unthinkable. At least so far as Nathan was concerned. It obliged the parties concerned to utter the most ill-natured slanders, whilst exposing their private lives to the voyeuristic gaze of press and public. Reputations were ruined, friends and family were compromised, servants were called upon to give evidence of the grossest indecencies. All of which conjured up the picture of an England very different from the pastoral idyll of Nathan's fond imagining: an England very like one of Hogarth's more critical depictions – debauched, decadent, seedy and corrupt. An England of fat and frowsty lechers robustly indulging their vices in an atmosphere of shameless abandon.

Not that this did not have its attractions, of course, but it was not a *worthy* image; it was not an image of England to carry into battle; it was not an England to die for.

His thoughts turned to what they would do when they

reached Corsica. The British had seized the island from the French two years ago and installed a Viceroy in Bastia – Sir Gilbert Elliot. Presumably Sir Gilbert would have a say in what happened next, but his options were limited. With Admiral Jervis and the best part of the fleet occupied in the blockade of Toulon, Nelson's squadron was the only naval force available to him. One ship of the line and a handful of frigates to patrol the west coast of Italy from Genoa to Naples, protect British trade from the hordes of French privateers and Barbary pirates swarming the Med, and do what they could to support the Austrians on land.

There was no escaping it: the war was going very badly for the British – and the allies as a whole. Bonaparte was making fools of the Austrians and the bulk of the British Army was in the West Indies, dying of yellow fever and malaria. Every military expedition in Europe had ended in disaster. In fact, the capture of Corsica was the only victory of any note since the war had started – and that was largely due to the Navy. Nathan doubted if Elliot had more than 5,000 British troops on the whole of the island. And if they lost Corsica they would be left without a single base east of Gibraltar.

Would Bonaparte make it his next target? He had been born there, Nathan recalled – in Ajaccio – shortly after the island was ceded to the French, a quarter of a century ago. Bonaparte would have to cross seventy miles of ocean to get there, but for a man who had crossed the Alps with an army of starving peasants, nothing was impossible; Nelson's little squadron could not be everywhere at once.

Suddenly, Nathan became aware that he could no longer see the stars. It was as if his Divine Clockmaker had leaned down from His superior height and blown them out, like so many candles. Puzzled, Nathan looked to the officer of the watch, Mr Holroyd, to see if he had observed the same strange phenomenon or whether it was gifted to him alone. Then the true culprit became apparent.

Fog. It had risen unseen from the still waters and within minutes it had masked not only the stars but everything else that mattered to a ship at sea: *Inconstant* and *Meleager*, the convoy itself and, of course, the wolf pack at its tail. Nathan could barely see beyond the *Unicorn*'s bowsprit.

There was no immediate threat. *Unicorn* had been stationed well to the rear of the convoy, and provided none of the lumbering transports stopped dead in the water, there was little risk of a collision. It was the privateers that gave him more cause for concern. He stood up and made his way to the stern rail. Ghostly shapes formed and dispersed in the haze but he could not tell if they were real or imagined. A gun went off over to starboard, roughly in the direction he had last seen *Inconstant*. Fremantle firing a warning – but of what? That there was fog? They all knew that, save those fortunate enough to have a cabin that was not occupied by whores. Again. Nathan saw the flash this time but was no more enlightened. He gazed into the impenetrable gloom beyond the *Unicorn*'s stern. He did not seriously think the corsairs would attempt something in this, but still, it was wise to be ready for any eventuality. Reluctantly he gave the order to beat to quarters.

The drum roll sounded strangely muffled in the liquid air but it had the desired effect. In a trice the upper deck was transformed into a scene of apparent Bedlam as the sleeping watch emerged from below and above 200 men ran or were chivvied to their allotted stations. Nathan observed this exercise with an expression of aloof detachment, his hands firmly clasped behind his back, very much as the supervisor of Bedlam itself must observe, he thought, as the lunatics went about their own unfathomable exercises. No matter how often he had seen it happen – in action or in practice – it always gave him a feeling of immense wonder that such Chaos could resolve itself into Order, and without any visible effort on his part. There was a time when he had been intimately involved in the operation, a junior officer barking his orders, herding his division into their correct pens – although even then they had known their place and function far better than he. But now . . . Provided he just stood there and did not say anything to disrupt it, it would all happen as if according to some divine plan. Gunports thrown open, tompions removed from the mouths of the guns, the lead aprons from the touch holes. Quoins thrust under the breeches to depress the barrels. The guns themselves, already primed and loaded, run out with a fiendish squeal of protest from the truck wheels – despite all the cook's slush that had been lavished upon them, Nathan noted with a perverse satisfaction. Spare shot and cartridge brought up from below. Powder horns and wads, lanterns, handspikes, sponges and worms neatly laid out beside them, like a surgeon's instruments in the cockpit. Matches and match tubs between every two guns in case the flints failed. Nothing missed. Everything in its place, even at night and in a fog. Wonderful. And the same impressive discipline would be transforming the lower deck . . .

By God, he thought, the whores!

He had completely forgotten them – but now he came to think of it, there had been certain sounds from below that might have alerted him to their presence: sounds not unlike the squealing of the gun trucks but less mechanical, more persistent. More *determined*. He was about to call for Gilbert Gabriel when that worthy appeared before him with a more lugubrious expression than was normal even for his countenance. What, he demanded, was he to do with the persons that was below decks, for they refused to be moved and was getting in the way of the guns.

Nathan looked about him and encountered the wary eye of Mr Lamb who hastily looked away. But no, tempting as it was, the midshipman was too junior for such a task. He raised his voice for Mr Holroyd and begged him, if he could be spared from his present duties, to present his compliments to Signora Correglia and inform her that he was obliged to clear the ship for action and that for their own safety she and her companions must retire to the orlop deck.

'And take a pair of Marines with you to enforce their compliance should they become obdurate,' he added callously, for in the circumstances he was prepared to brook no dissent.

He was considerably relieved, however, if not a little surprised, when Holroyd reported that his instructions had been carried out to the letter and his charges consigned to the orlop deck, the which – being below the waterline – could be considered the safest place in the ship: unless she was unexpectedly to founder, of course, in which case it was as bad a place to be as anywhere upon the planet.

This minor crisis being averted for the moment, Nathan turned his mind to more compelling matters, for the fog pressed in ever more closely and a palpable air of tension fell upon the ship.

'Strict silence, Mr Duncan,' he enjoined the first lieutenant sternly, for a certain amount of muttering had come to his ears. 'We must hear what we cannot see.'

And so, after a necessary interlude of abuse, strict silence it was, only the creaking of ropes and timbers and the steady slap of water upon the hull defying Nathan's command as the *Unicorn* crept on through the murk with every eye straining to discover substance and form in such an ethereal world.

Nathan, who was of an inventive disposition, had often considered the possibilities of deploying some kind of beacon or guiding light that would assist in navigating a vessel through such conditions, or give some warning of the presence of other ships, be they friend or foe. Unhappily, he had yet to discover a means of suspending it in the air, or directing it with sufficient force to pierce the miasma that surrounded them. But now he considered the possibility of towing it at their stern. It might not succeed in entirely dispelling the gloom but it would surely serve to betray any movement in the vicinity. A simple tar barrel might suffice, or a vat of tallow. He wondered if Mr Clyde, who shared his talent for invention, might be disposed to rig up such a device, or provide an alternative form of illumination, but then he recalled that Mr Clyde was dead and he had yet to appoint a replacement. George Banjo was the obvious choice but it would mean appointing him over the head of the gunner's mate, Dodds, a reliable enough individual but somewhat lacking in imagination.

Nathan was still considering these issues when the darkness was disturbed by a series of bright orange flashes a little off their starboard bow. For a fraction of a second he thought that someone had forestalled him in providing the very illumination he desired, but then he realised it was gunfire. More to the point, it was directed at *him* – and with startling accuracy, given the violent mayhem that suddenly exploded all around him. Splintered timber, a shriek of tortured metal, a loud thud as of a giant hand knocking upon the hull, and the scream of a man whose arm, Nathan saw, had been taken off at the elbow; he was standing beside his gun with the stump leaking on to the deck like some macabre pump, spurting blood.

Nathan's reaction to this assault was more indignant than alarmed. The damage he saw at once was superficial – though the man with the severed arm might conceivably entertain another view – and it was clear, even in the immediate aftermath of the attack, that their assailant carried no great weight of broadside. Nathan was more concerned with how she had managed to locate them in such a fog while remaining invisible from his own decks – apart, of course, from that brief eruption of flame. The only rational explanation was that the frigate's position had been betrayed by the lights she carried at her stern and masthead, or even the red glow from the slow matches that burned beside each gun as a precaution against the failure of the flintlocks. He ordered them instantly dowsed but they endured another broadside before this could be accomplished, and this time Nathan brought their own guns to bear, more as an angry retort than in hopes of hitting anything.

'Shall we close with them, sir?' Duncan prompted him when the last gun had fired.

But Nathan was thinking hard. The corsairs had been shadowing the convoy all day long. They knew the *Unicorn* was bringing up the rear. Why fire at her, and bring attention to themselves – unless it was to lure her out of position. The frigate was stationed slightly to windward of the convoy and their attacker was at least another quarter-mile or so off their starboard beam. It was far more likely that an attack would come from the opposite quarter. He crossed to the larboard rail and glared into the fog. Nothing. Nothing he could see, at any rate. If he got it wrong it would look as if he was running away, putting distance between himself and his attacker. Certainly it must have crossed Duncan's mind – he could tell by the look on his face when Nathan gave the order to veer to larboard.

Minutes passed. They were now sailing diagonally across the stern of the convoy – if it was where Nathan imagined it to be. God help him if it wasn't, he thought. In another minute he would have to give the order to beat back against the wind and hope to God the wolves were not yet among the sheep.

They almost ploughed straight into her. At the very last second someone up forward let out a shout and Nathan bawled at the quartermaster to port his helm an instant before he saw the ghostly shape of her sails in the fog. More shouts – in French – from the gloom ahead. He saw the white faces peering out at him across the rail, the scurrying figures. A glimpse of the open gunports, the black muzzles of the guns run out. A flash of flame from a musket or swivel gun. And then the *Unicorn*'s bowsprit slowly came round and they emptied their entire larboard broadside into her at point-blank range.

Nathan backed the mizzen and they lay off her at a distance of twenty or thirty yards. She was a brig of no more than three or four hundred tons, and even in the murk they could see the havoc they had wrought. The 18-pound shot had torn through her thin timbers, carrying away whole lengths of rail and leaving gaping holes in her hull, and as for her crew – the shouts of alarm as they saw the frigate bearing down on them had turned into screams of agony and frantic pleas for mercy. She was still flying her colours but Nathan forbore to fire into her again. Instead he brought the *Unicorn* alongside and sent Holroyd off with a boarding party.

'Put the survivors into the boats,' he told him, 'and then fire her.'

Holroyd looked at him in bemusement. Crippled though she was, she might still fetch a few thousand in a prize court once the damage was repaired: a good 100 guineas might find its way into Holroyd's pocket and a lot more for the Captain. But Nathan had other uses for her.

He stood off her at a distance of about a cable's length and watched her burn. Here was his beacon, his guiding light in the fog. And there was his quarry – two of them trying to creep past her stern. He gave them each a broadside before they veered to leeward and vanished into the gloom, but he had seen the 18-pound shot tear through the rigging of one and make a shambles of the stern of the other as she turned away, and he suspected they would have no stomach to resume the attack. Still, he kept the *Unicorn* hove to off the burning vessel until she sank beneath the waves, and then followed slowly in the wake of the convoy for the rest of the long, grim night with the men standing to at the guns and the lookouts straining their eyes in the fog. It was only when it dispersed a little before dawn, and there was no sign of a single sail – no convoy, escorts or enemy – in the several miles of ocean thus revealed to him, that Nathan finally gave the order to stand down.

He lowered himself into the canvas chair Gilbert Gabriel had provided for him on the quarterdeck and closed his eyes. He was desperately tired but he had the satisfaction of knowing that he had made the right decision for once – and every man in the crew must know it, from Duncan down.

Nathan's moods tended to the extreme. He was either plunged into a pit of self-loathing or floating upon a cloud of self-esteem that he would have considered excessive in the heroes of Antiquity. In this latter mood he would bask in the imagined approval of all his acquaintance, even going so far as to dwell fondly upon the terms they might employ in praise of his sagacity, valour, generosity, or whatever other quality he had displayed. '*How in God's name did he know they were there?*' he imagined Duncan exclaiming in wondrous tones to Holroyd, and Holroyd shaking his head in mute reverence at such godlike perception. Alas, he had learned that such periods were invariably followed by a sharp reminder of his human failings. The ship had been put back to her normal state: the guns secured, the bulkheads restored and the hammocks returned to the lower decks before he once again remembered his passengers. His consideration for their welfare was somewhat secondary to the realisation that while they were confined in the orlop deck there was nothing to stop him moving back into his cabin. He could inform the Signora that the constant threat of attack made it imperative for them to remain in a place of safety.

He passed the word for Gilbert Gabriel and had begun to state this intention – and of partaking of his breakfast there – when something in the fellow's manner alerted him.

'What?' he said.

'They've already moved back in,' reported Gabriel, with grim satisfaction, 'and asked me to bring them coffee and warm rolls as soon as the galley fires is lit.'

Chapter Six

The Seraglio

—◦◆◦—

A little after sunset they sighted the long promontory of Cap Corse far to the west. But then, as so often happened in the Mediterranean in high summer, the sparse wind dropped to a whisper and they barely advanced any closer throughout the whole of that long, sweltering day. By noon the timbers were too hot to touch and the tar was bubbling up from the deck seams. Nathan cast off his uniform jacket and dozed in his chair in a sennit hat like an old curate, but he missed his cabin now, more than he had at night: his cabin and his cot. He would have given much to absent himself below decks and snatch an hour or so of proper sleep with the stern windows thrown open to what little breeze remained. But it was not to be. Signora Correglia and her company remained in possession of his quarters, keeping the Angel Gabriel cheerfully busy fetching fresh-squeezed lemon juice with water and wet towels to lay on their fevered brows. He made none of his usual complaint – Nathan gathered from a chance-overheard conversation that the women had shed most of their outer garments and he could only imagine the scene that must greet the eager steward on each foray into the shadowed sanctuary at the stern.

For those on deck, or for the off-duty watch in the foetid stews below, there were no such luxuries, not even for Nathan – no lemons, no cool towels; Gabriel was far too busy with his other charges. But the first lieutenant had canvas awnings swung up from the yards to provide some shade for his blistering paintwork and had half the crew hauling buckets of water from the sea to dampen down the decks, and though it was not his principal intent – paintwork and timber being high on Mr Duncan's list of priorities – these measures afforded some little relief to the human components of the *Unicorn*. And the awnings gave Nathan one of his rare inspirations.

He sent for the sailmaker and asked him if he had any spare pieces of canvas with which to make a tent.

'Make a tent, sir?' The sailmaker was an ancient of forty or so who rarely saw the light of day, being content to conduct his business in the gloomy confines of the sail-locker, leaving others to admire the result of his labours when his precious canvas billowed out from the yards in all its glory.

'A tent, Mr Sweeney,' Nathan repeated. 'An awning with sides. I have made a rough sketch for your instruction.'

The sailmaker scrutinised this object with a bewildered frown, scratching his bald pate.

'Is there a difficulty?' Nathan enquired coldly – and for the benefit of the first lieutenant whose expression bespoke a measure of concern: 'Are the materials available without detriment to the smooth running of the ship?'

The sailmaker reluctantly conceded that he supposed he might find something lying around.

'Very well, Mr Sweeney. Make it so. And as near to the stern-rail as you are able. My coxswain will assist you with any fixtures you may require.'

And so, to the bemusement of the ship's company and the tight-lipped disapproval of Mr Duncan, a canvas structure somewhat resembling the pavilion of a medieval knight at a tournament gradually rose to prominence at the stern end of the frigate, with the blue ensign hanging somewhat flaccidly above its peaked extremity. Nathan availed himself of the Turkish carpets and cushions brought aboard by their passengers and a table was improvised from timbers and empty casks covered with a damask cloth. Well content with this arrangement, Nathan retired there for the best part of the afternoon, reclining upon the cushions in a silken robe which he had thrown over his shirt and breeches, and reading *Tom Jones* by Mr Henry Fielding, which he had borrowed from Fremantle's extensive library.

He rarely smoked, but in the circumstances he allowed himself this luxury, filling his long, curved pipe with a special ingredient of tobacco and herbs provided by the ship's surgeon, McLeish, which he was assured would induce a mood of calm composure. Nathan had initially taken this as a criticism of the more volatile aspect of his nature, but he had given the mixture a trial and conceded its merits. It induced feelings of serene equanimity, a benign acceptance of the many things he could not change but which had so often tested his patience in the past. When he enquired of its content, the surgeon merely winked and laid a finger upon his nose, but more persistent probing elicited the information that it contained a portion of the species *Cannabis sativa*, closely related to the hemp used in the manufacture of ship's cable. McLeish advised against overuse, explaining that it could induce a level of complacency not advisable in the Captain of a ship-of-war, but at moments such as this, floating upon a flat calm under a cloudless sky with no obvious threats upon the horizon, Nathan felt that it could be resorted to with an easy conscience.

He had drawn back the flaps at the rear of his domain to allow a little air to flow and provide a view over the ocean to the distant Isle of Capraia, which grew more attractive a prospect as the hours slipped gently by. He imagined a life of seclusion and contemplation among the goats and herbs of the island pastures, far from the cares of command and conflict, dwelling upon the mysteries of the earth and the heavens in the manner of one of the Ancient Greek philosophers. In such a mood he concluded that he was far too inclined to worry about matters over which he had little or no control. Matters such as the wind and the tide – though admittedly the latter was not an issue in the Mediterranean. The war. And more particularly, the behaviour of other people. His mother, for instance, could often drive him to distraction with her whims and wiles, and yet she was really a very good-natured woman, very affectionate. He missed her a great deal. He must show her how much he appreciated her the next time he was home.

And then there was Sara.

They had met in Paris during the Terror, when Nathan was occupied on confidential business for His Majesty's Government. They had fallen in love. At least, Nathan knew he had been in love and he was reasonably sure that Sara felt the same. But after only a brief courtship they had been thrown apart by the political upheavals of the time. Nathan had thought she was dead, a victim of the guillotine. In fact she had fled Paris and sought refuge in the Vendée where she had fought with the Catholic rebels. And then, after their bloody defeat, fled south to her birthplace on the shores of the Mediterranean.

Nathan had found her in the *manoir* that had once been her family home and brought her back to the *Unicorn*. But they had not made love during their brief reunion on the frigate. Nathan had experienced a certain delicacy of feeling about it and indeed, there had been little opportunity before Sara's departure for England. Even so, it was regrettable. He wondered if they would ever rekindle the passion they had felt for each other in Paris. And he wondered at his own feelings, whether they were as strong now, knowing she was alive, as they had been when he had thought she was dead.

These reflections were brought to an abrupt end by the return of the Angel Gabriel, who staggered through the tent flap, burdened with Nathan's flute, his music-stand and a leather folder containing his music. He also brought a request from Signora Correglia. She wished to speak with him in private.

'Send her up,' Nathan instructed him as he removed the flute from its case.

Gabriel considered him coldly. 'Then you will be wanting your uniform coat,' he proposed.

'No, no. It is quite all right. She may take me as I am,' Nathan instructed him cheerfully.

Gabriel's jaw moved fractionally. Their relationship was a long and enduring one but it was not without its trials. When Nathan was a child – and Gabriel his father's steward – they had frequently failed to see eye to eye in the matter of Nathan's dress and deportment. Nathan could recall times when he had been seized by the collar and given a salutary thwacking before having his head thrust under the kitchen pump and his recalcitrant limbs forced into the preferred attire. It was clear from Gabriel's expression that he had not put this recourse entirely out of mind, but the subsequent alteration in their status making this a hanging offence, he gave a perfunctory nod and departed upon his errand. To be succeeded, in due course, by La Correglia.

'Signora,' Nathan greeted her with feigned enthusiasm, laying aside his flute and making a bow.

'*Capitano*,' she responded graciously. Her eyes settled upon the Turkish carpet and Nathan perceived a glint of recognition. 'You make yourself *comodo*, I see.'

'I do indeed. And you are as comfortable in my cabin?'

'It is of this I wish to speak with you.'

Nathan indicated that she should be seated and they took up their stations at opposite ends of the table like wary negotiators at a peace conference. 'If it is about the guns . . .' he began. Even in his present state of lassitude, Nathan was not prepared to compromise over the guns. He would have defended his guns to the death. But it was not about the guns. The Signora, it appeared, was concerned about what would happen when they reached their destination.

'Ah.' Nathan had been somewhat concerned about this himself. 'Well, I assume you would wish to find suitable accommodation for yourselves in San Fiorenzo,' he replied smoothly enough and with a creditable effort to hide his unease on this score.

'Where?'

'Where? Well . . .'

'You think the women of San Fiorenzo make the welcome for us? Ha! You think the English wives leave the room for us? Ha! Seven lady without the 'usband?'

'I am sure something can be arranged,' Nathan persisted. 'You will not be left destitute, I do assure you.'

This elicited another *Ha!* Even louder and more scornful than those that had preceded it.

'And what we do there?'

'What do you do there?'

'*Sí*. In San Fiorenzo, what we do?'

Nathan, if he had thought about it at all, had imagined they would do much the same as they had done in Leghorn, with whatever adjustment to their standards and fees as might be required. However, it would probably not be diplomatic to state as much.

'Well, what would you *like* to do?' He caught the Signora's eye. 'I mean, I am sure you will find sufficient to amuse your . . . I appreciate there is no opera house but . . .' He then recalled that the opera house in Leghorn was where the initial introductions were made between officers of His Majesty's Navy and ladies of the Signora's persuasion, and felt himself beginning to blush. 'And though I am not myself familiar with the port, I am assured the people there are friendly and hospitable . . .'

The Signora gazed at him in unfeigned astonishment. 'They are Corsi,' she pointed out.

'Indeed. But the Corsicans are now subjects of King George . . .'

'The men they cut your throat, the women they rob a blind beggar. And the 'ores they fuck a dog for a *denaro*.'

'I see.' Nathan was briefly taken aback by this insight. He considered several responses but rejected them as inappropriate. 'But I was informed that you were most anxious to be transported there.'

She shook her dark curls in vigorous denial. 'Only we wish to leave Livorno. So the French they do not cut off our 'eads.'

Nathan felt obliged to point out that the French, though continuing intolerable in many regards, had become less sanguine of late, at least in the matter of decapitation.

'That is not what I 'ave 'eard,' the Signora muttered darkly. 'The *Commodoro* 'e say the French they round up the 'ores and cut off their 'eads.'

'Did he? Did he, indeed?' Nelson, he was aware, nursed a passionate loathing of all things Gallic. He got it from his mother, it was said. But it was by no means unusual among a certain class of English gentleman.

'Is not true?'

'Well, it is true that in the time of Robespierre and the Terror a number of women of a certain – status – suffered a certain—'

'They cut off their 'eads.'

'Unfortunately.'

'They cut off the 'ead of Marie Antoinette.'

'Yes, but—'

'And all the other 'ores.'

'Well, actually Marie Antoinette . . .' Nathan gave up. Why was he defending the French, for pity's sake? Because he had a hint of French blood in his veins? 'Well, certainly you will be safer in San Fiorenzo,' he agreed.

But she was shaking her head more firmly than ever.

'But where else would you go?' he enquired helplessly.

'We go to Genova,' she said firmly.

'Genoa? But . . . Genoa is closed to the British Navy.'

'But not to us.'

'No, but . . .' Nathan recalled that the Signora's mother lived in Genoa and that the Commodore used often to set her down there. There were rumours that he used her as a spy. For a moment Nathan was tempted, but it was impossible. 'I cannot take you to Genoa,' he said.

'Why not you take us to Genova?'

'Because I have my orders to take you to San Fiorenzo.'

'Who give you these orders?'

'Well, Commodore Nelson for one, and—'

'I speak with the *Commodoro*,' she declared with satisfaction.

'I am afraid the *Commodoro* – the Commodore – has remained at Leghorn. That is to say, *off* Leghorn. In the flagship.'

'Then we stay 'ere. With you.'

Nathan returned her look of stubborn obstinacy with one of

despair. 'Signora, this is a ship-of-war. We may be required to go into battle at any time and—'

'So we go into the battle with you.'

'No, really, that is not—'

'My friends, they do anything for the *Capitano*.' Her voice and expression softened. She smiled seductively at him. Nathan felt himself blushing. 'They say the *Capitano* 'e save them from the French, 'e give up 'is little cabin for them, 'e give up 'is little bed for them. 'Ow do they show 'im 'ow much they love the *Capitano*?'

'I assure you, that is quite unnecessary.'

'Perhaps they ply for 'im.'

'I beg your pardon?'

'They ply upon the 'arp for 'im.'

'The what?'

'The 'arp. They ply the 'arp. They ply for 'im, they sing for 'im.' She smiled fondly.

Nathan considered her carefully. 'They want to sing for me?'

'And ply the 'arp.'

'You mean, all together?'

The Signora lowered her eyes demurely. 'As the *Capitano* 'e like it.'

'No, no, I mean . . . That is not what I . . . No. One at a time is perfectly in . . .' He began again. 'When you say the 'arp – the *harp* – I presume you mean the virginal, that you brought out of Leghorn?'

'The 'arp, the virginal, *sí*.'

Nathan thought about it. A succession of young women tripping into his tent might be taken amiss by the other officers. And it would encourage some merriment among the crew at his expense, which might be very bad for discipline. Certainly Mr Duncan would consider it so. But a succession of young ladies tripping into his tent with a harp – or even a virginal – that was surely a different matter. It might give Nathan a mild reputation for eccentricity but this in itself was no bad thing. Fremantle would be beside himself with envy.

'There is a Handel Larghetto for flute and harpsichord which is a particular favourite of mine,' he mused, 'but which I have not had the opportunity of playing in tandem, as it were.'

Strangely, and a little to Nathan's chagrin, the appearance of a tent at the tail end of the *Unicorn* and the succession of personable females who were to be observed entering and leaving it did not cause the stir he had anticipated. He detected a degree of awkwardness, or embarrassment, among his fellow officers, but as if by tacit agreement no reference was made to the evening ritual – which began at the commencement of the first watch of the night and ended about an hour later. Naturally he would not have expected a direct reference to the visits themselves – that would have bordered on vulgarity – but he had imagined there might be some comments about the music. Something along the lines of, 'Was that Bach's Sonata in C major I heard last night – or something else?' Possibly delivered with the trace of an ironic smile. But there was nothing of the sort. Even the Angel Gabriel appeared indifferent to the arrangement, providing such refreshments as were required without question or quarrel.

As for the wider world, it either failed entirely to notice the proceedings or turned its back upon them. Even when anchored in the commodious bay of San Fiorenzo, each vessel close enough to its neighbour to permit conversation, there was no immediate indication that the diversions of the *Unicorn*'s Captain had attracted the slightest interest, let alone censure, beyond the decks of his own ship.

Admittedly, there were other distractions. As Signora Correglia had predicted, there was a great rush to claim the available accommodation ashore, but once lodgings had been secured, the new tenants showed no inclination to remain there. Having staked their claim they returned with alacrity to their shipboard quarters. There were probably several reasons for this. One was the cool sea breeze, for the wind continued to blow mildly from the north and made shipboard life vastly preferable to the suffocating squalor of San Fiorenzo. Another was the company of their fellow Englishmen – and women. And then there was the entertainment.

Captain Fremantle had somehow acquired a seven-piece orchestra, which was to be seen and heard playing upon the forecastle of *Inconstant* most evenings, while the officers and their guests danced the night away in the waist, as gaily as at any Assembly Rooms in England. It was not unusual to see upward of a hundred couples engaged upon this exertion beneath the starry sky, with a multitude of coloured lanterns suspended from the frigate's yards.

Nathan felt that Fremantle had once again stolen his thunder. His performances upon the flute, even with the pleasurable accompaniment available to him, appeared paltry in comparison. It was not until the fourth day of their stay in the port that the first signs of interest became apparent.

It was a Thursday – washday aboard ship – and the *Unicorn* was transformed into something more closely resembling a prison hulk in the Medway than a crack frigate. Great tubs of soapy water steamed upon the decks, each surrounded by a companionable crew of washermen, scrubbing and sloshing and wringing, while clothes lines were rigged fore and aft to accommodate the several hundred pair of duck trousers, shirts, handkerchiefs and smalls that constituted the normal slops of the crew of a sixth-rate. But this mundane picture of domestic content was considerably altered by the appearance of items not normally associated with a ship-of-war, not at least in the service of His Britannic Majesty.

Given the nature of the convoy, articles of female apparel were to be observed on many of the vessels in the anchorage – washday being a universally observed phenomenon – but they were largely functional in their purpose and appearance, and those undergarments that were exposed to public view did not deviate substantially from the male variety.

They were nothing to the articles displayed aboard the *Unicorn*. Items of silk and satin and of the flimsiest lace that illustrated the true purpose of their manufacture. Items that would, as the Angel Gabriel put it, stir a eunuch to lust.

It certainly stirred something. On the two frigates and several of the larger transports, a number of officers could be observed training their telescopes on the objects in question before roving the *Unicorn*'s decks in search of their former occupants. In the next hour or so, several ships' boats arrived at the *Unicorn*'s larboard quarter upon one frivolous pretext after another, and towards the end of the forenoon watch Nathan was alerted by the cry of '*Inconstant*!' to the arrival of Captain Fremantle himself.

'Well, I'll be damned,' he murmured as he gazed about Nathan's new quarters. His speculative eye took in the Oriental carpets, the embroidered cushions, the Benares brass tray with its selection of refreshment, the gilded virginal in the corner . . . 'The Grand Turk ain't in it.'

'Hardly up to his standards, Thomas. But unlike the Grand Turk we do serve hard liquor, unless you would prefer sherbet.'

'Be damned to your sherbet. I will take a glass of Madeira with you, to assure myself you have not turned Musselman.' He settled his stout frame among the cushions, resting his hands across his abdomen and viewing Nathan through narrowed eyes. 'You know what they are calling you – the ship, that is? The *Seraglio*. What do you think of that? It means Harem, you know. The place the Musselmans keep their concubines.'

'Thank you, Thomas, I know the meaning of the word.'

'The *Seraglio*. Captain Nathaniel Peake of the frigate *Seraglio*.' He rolled about a little on his cushions.

Nathan shrugged. 'I am glad it amuses you, but I think I prefer the *Unicorn*. Who are "they", by the by?'

'Too many for you to fight, Nat, so don't come the boyo with me. Besides, it seems damned appropriate, if you ask me, from where I am sitting.'

'Whereas you consider the *Inconstant* is not?'

'As to that, I have had my share of banter on that account. I take no heed of it. The ship was named long before I took charge of her. Though I have always thought it a damned silly name for a ship-of-war, now you mention it. Thank you kindly.' He took the proffered glass and looked about him again. 'So this is where you entertain the charmers.'

'I beg your pardon, this is where I *live*. This is where I sleep and eat and command my ship. Since you saw fit to impose "the charmers" upon me and deprive me of my proper quarters.'

'I did not instruct you to surrender your cabin to them.'

'And where else was I to put them?'

'I would have thought the orlop deck would do, my dear, or even the chainlocker. They are only whores.'

Nathan choked back an angry retort. For all his familiarity, Fremantle and he were not the closest of friends. Nathan entertained strong doubts about him and not only for his attitude to women. 'You did not call them that when you sent them to me,' he pointed out. 'At least not according to the arsewipe of a snottie you sent with them. You said they were the wives of serving officers, as near as damn it.'

'Never in life, sir, never in life. You must have misheard the brat. Or he mistook my instruction.'

'"They had formed so strong an attachment to certain officers that they deserved the same consideration as officers' wives."' Nathan mimicked the piping tones of the midshipman. 'That's what he said you said.'

'Nonsense. I said nothing of the kind.'

'And that is why I made my cabin available to them.'

'Well, I am sorry for that, but you appear to have made the best of it. I wondered that you did not attend any of our evening revelries. Now I know.' He dropped his voice for fear of being heard by the Marine sentry at the flap. 'So what's the score?'

'I beg your pardon?'

'How many have you had so far? I am told it is a different one every night.'

'You must not listen to tittle-tattle, Thomas. It is invariably ill-informed. My commerce has been more with Bach than Eros.'

'The Devil, you say!'

'No, Bach, and some Handel. You must not suppose that we are all of your inclination when it comes to that sort of thing.'

Fremantle frowned. 'What do you mean?'

'Thomas. The whole fleet knows of your reputation for lechery. It was you who told me who to go to in Leghorn if I ever fancied a dolly.'

Fremantle had paled a little under his tan. He looked quickly round to check that they were private. 'For God's sake, Peake, do not be saying that.'

'Why not? Thomas, we all know you are led by the prick, you have boasted of it oft enough. I am sorry if I have offended you,' he added, for Fremantle had turned from wan to scarlet and Nathan began to think he had gone too far. 'But I had no idea you were sensitive on the issue.'

'No, but – I have been a very rake in my time, I'll not deny it – but I have changed, Nat. I have put it all behind me.' His voice was hoarse, his skin sweating. He leaned forward and dropped his voice even lower. 'I have found love.'

'Bugger me,' said Nathan. 'Where?'

'Aboard *Inconstant*. Now there's a thing I never thought of.' His eyes became dreamy. ' 'Twas on *Inconstant* I became constant. There is a verse in that somewhere, Nat.'

'Thomas, what are you talking about?'

'I am telling you. I have cast aside the tawdry trappings of licentiousness. I have sown my wild oats and walk in fields of barley.'

'Who with?'

'Miss Elizabeth Wynne.' He pronounced it as if it were a saint. 'Betsey. One of the Misses Wynne that we brought out of Leghorn. They are on the *Achilles* now, but we still contrive to see as much of each other as is possible in the circumstance.'

He gave a look around his present surroundings as if another possibility had just occurred to him.

'I see.'

'I don't think you do, Nat, not when you say it in that tone of voice. There has been nothing like that. Not the least impropriety. She has her father and mother with her, for heaven's sake, and her three sisters. Where was I to do it?'

'There is always the orlop deck. Where you would have me put my whores, as you are pleased to call them.'

'I will treat that with the contempt it deserves. You are speaking of the future Mrs Fremantle.'

'You never mean to marry her?'

'I do indeed, sir. I do indeed. For all that she's a Papist.'

'A Papist? Is she Irish then?'

'Don't be a fool, man. Irish, indeed. I may be 'sotted but one must draw the line somewhere. Her mother is Venetian. 'Tis where she gets her looks from, I suppose, for the old man is an ugly bugger. English, though, and a thorough gentleman. Turned Papist when he married which I'll not do, even for Betsey Wynne, for it would mean leaving the service. But I would burn for her, Nat, I'd burn in Hell for her. And she says I will – if I stay in the Church of England.'

'A beauty, is she?'

'Well, I would not say that. Not a beauty,' he replied thoughtfully. 'It was not her looks that captivated me. Not but that she is not handsome.'

'Handsome?' Nathan frowned. It was not a word he would have used of Sara, or anyone he might consider marrying, he hoped, though he supposed it might come to it if you were pushed. Fremantle was not being pushed, however.

'But that is by the by. She has a wonderful heart, Nat, a wonderful heart. And such eyes.'

'You have always been one for the eyes. And the heart.'

'Now that is low, sir, very low.'

'You have fallen for an honest woman then, at last.'

'Honest as the day, Nat. And innocent as the dawn. You never saw such innocence, Nat. Eighteen years of age. And the light of love in her eyes.'

'She returns your affection, then?'

'The way she looks on me, Nat. The trusting, gentle . . . *adoration* in her eyes. You would have to see it to believe it. It makes me humble, Nat. I say, you're a bit stingy with the wine, you know, my glass has been empty these past five minutes or more. Much more of this and I will think you have turned Musselman. Thankee. Your very good health.'

'To Miss Elizabeth Wynne. And your future happiness.'

'Thank you, Nat. I can see you don't believe me, of course. But you always were a cynical sod. You never saw the romantic in me. Don't you ever think of marriage? What happened to that wench you brought out of France? Came swimming out to the ship with you? That was romantic. It was the talk of the squadron for a day or two. Did you pack her off again, or is she stowed aboard with your other charmers?'

'She is in England I hope, by now. With my father.'

'With your father? Damn me. Is that wise?'

'What do you mean by that?'

'Nothing. Not a thing. Only that . . .' But whatever it was, he thought better of it. 'So you have a mind to marriage too, then?'

'We have not spoken of marriage.'

'But you think on it.'

'I suppose.'

'Well, you cannot afford to wait too long. How old are you now?'

'Twenty-eight next month.'

'There you are then. You do not want to end up an old bachelor.'

'Thomas, not ten minutes ago you were calling me the Grand Turk.'

'Yes, well, there are women and women, you know. Find yourself an honest one and marry her, that is my advice to you.'

'Thank you, Thomas, I shall bear it in mind.'

'We all need someone to come home to, you know. And to think on when we are away. Look at Ulysses.'

'I beg your pardon?'

'Do you know your classics?'

'As well as you do, I expect.'

'Well, you are half-American, and one has no idea what

they taught you at school. *If* you went to school.'

'I was raised in Sussex, Thomas, and was taught at Charterhouse till I went to sea.'

'No need to go all hoity-toity on me. Charterhouse, was it? So you know who Ulysses was?'

'Yes, they did teach the *Odyssey* at Charterhouse, along with a few other things of no particular import, but what has Ulysses to do with it?'

'I am about to tell you, if you will let me. He had his adventures, enough to fill a book, but he had an honest woman waiting for him at home, that is the point I am making. Penelope.' He frowned. 'I think that was her name. Not the most romantic, I agree, but it might sound different in the Greek. Anyway, she was waiting for him. And he was hot to get back to her, for all it took him twenty years or so. That was what made it such a good story. Without that it would just be so much beating against the wind, fucking about with trollops and harpies and the like, do you see? There would have been no point to it. It gives the story a meaning.'

'So you think marriage gives your life meaning?'

'It does, sir, it does. A wife and a family and a fine estate on the south coast of England with a view of the sea. Same as your father has. Well, not that he has a wife, of course, given the situation with your mother, but we all know what she is like, and he still has the view. But that is what we are fighting for, Nat,' he added quickly, lest he had given offence. 'That is what gives it point and meaning, do you see? Not that I wouldn't say no to a leg-over from time to time, same as Ulysses when it came his way, but it ain't the be all and end all.' He belched and reached out an arm. 'Now you must excuse me for I had best be getting back to *Inconstant*. 'Tis all go, you know, we have another dance this evening. Do you want to come, or will you be playing Bach again on your flute?'

Nathan saw him over the side and retired thoughtfully to his quarters. Fremantle talked rubbish, of course, most of the time, but he had touched a raw nerve with his mention of marriage. Marriage, in Nathan's mind, was an essential ingredient of that English pastoral idyll he venerated, and yet . . .

Was venerated the word? Or was it just an idle fancy, a romantic illusion? Not even that. More a kind of . . . whim. A response to the shambles his parents had made of it. In reality, he could no more think of Sara living quietly in Sussex than he could his mother. Not after the life she had led. She was the daughter of an Italian countess and a Scottish soldier in the French Army. Her father's family name was Seton and he had been laird of some impoverished tract of the Highlands before his attachment to the Young Pretender obliged him to follow that most hopeless of lost causes into exile. But he had some claim to nobility and Sara had her mother's looks, so at the age of seventeen she was married to Henri de la Tour d'Auvergne, Count of Turenne, one of the noblest families in France. It would have been counted a brilliant match had he not been a libertine and a profligate almost twenty years her senior. Then came the Revolution. The count had fled to the Royalist court in Germany and died there – of a fever of the blood – leaving Sara and her young son alone in Paris where Nathan had met her.

After the report of her death on the guillotine, Nathan had returned to England with her son, Alex, only to learn that she had escaped execution and joined the Royalist insurgents in the Vendée.

It was what had happened to her there over the next twelve months or so that gave Nathan cause for his present disquiet. It was strongly rumoured that she had become the lover of François de Charette, one of the most charismatic of the rebel leaders. That she had fought by his side until she was taken captive and Charette was shot by a Revolutionary firing squad. Then Sara had been exposed to whatever torments were devised for female rebels in that most brutal of civil wars.

Some preparation for a life in Sussex. But perhaps after such experiences she was ready for it.

And when Nathan came home from the wars he could join her there. They could move in with his father and his mistress. Or wife as she might be by then. Help his father raise sheep. Or Nathan could build a house of his own with a view of the sea. Sara would have lots of children and Nathan would become a Justice of the Peace, maybe even stand for Parliament. Invest in government stock at 2 per cent, ride to hounds and drive to church every Sunday in a carriage.

And walk back through the graveyard, past the family tomb where he himself would be buried. Feel the coffin lid pressing down upon him, hear the earth rattling upon the lid . . .

He shook his head at his own perversity. What was he fighting for, if not for a continuation of the life his father had led, and *his* father before that? For most of Nathan's fellow officers it represented the very height of achievement. And as for death . . . All must die one day, either in their own homes, among family and friends, or sewn up in a canvas bag and tossed into the sea.

But it was the journey you lived for, not the ending of it, for all Fremantle's talk of Ulysses. Did you remember Ulysses for his life back in Ithaca? Was there a sequel, chronicling the life that awaited him upon his return? And if there was, would any bother to read it?

No. It was the journey. Long may it continue.

If only he did not miss Sara so much.

'I will wait for you,' she had said, when she had left for England. 'But come soon.'

He had not thought too much of that at the time. But he did now. There was a contradiction there, sure. *Come soon, for if you do not . . .*

The thought of her with another man was torture to him. But it was strangely, disturbingly stimulating, like an addiction to some dangerous drug. It had started in Paris when Imlay – Mary Wollstonecraft's lover – had told him that Sara was in the custom of posing naked for the students at Regnault's art school in the Rue St Honoré. Nathan doubted it was true, but it was an image he could not dismiss from his mind. It haunted him, tantalised him, drove him to distraction. Then he learned that she had become the lover of Charette – and that she was known to the rebel leader's men as *La Renarde* – the vixen.

These were the thoughts Nathan must carry with him every day of their separation, and every night.

He recalled the words of a song that was popular with some of the men on the lower decks. Not a sea shanty as such, for it had the wrong rhythm for capstan or cable. They sang it in their leisure moments, accompanied by the fiddle or the Jew's harp, and one of the men had told Nathan, rather shamefacedly, that it was a skipping song, popular among the street urchins of Liverpool.

> *Johnny Todd he took a notion*
> *For to cross the ocean wide*
> *And he left his true love behind him*
> *Walking by the Liverpool tide.*

The story continued much as one might have predicted, with the fair maiden meeting up with another sailor, marrying him and having his child. But it was the last verse that stayed in Nathan's memory. It had snagged on some barbed point of his brain and stuck there, playing monotonously over and over and over again.

> *Now all you young men who go a-sailing*
> *For to fight the foreign foe,*
> *Don't you leave your love like Johnny,*
> *Marry her before you go.*

He could have married her. They could have been married by the Commodore, on the flagship, before she left for England. But he had let the opportunity pass. And might live to regret it.

He was disturbed in these sombre reflections by the stamp of the Marine sentry upon the deck and a discreet cough, both of which served to alert him to the presence of a visitor, there being no door to rap upon.

It was Mr Duncan. He removed his hat and stood just inside the flap of the tent as if to advance further might compromise him. Nathan was aware that he had been a disappointment to the first lieutenant of late and wished to make amends. 'Mr Duncan,' he greeted him with a smile. 'All well, I trust?'

'Very well, thank you, sir. *Meleager* is signalling that the flagship is in sight. And the Commodore aboard.'

And the look in his eye said, That will cut your capers, my lad.

'Thank you, Mr Duncan. I will be on deck directly.'

When the first lieutenant had gone, Nathan took one final look around his temporary quarters. Then he put on his coat and stepped out on to the quarterdeck. The flagship was in plain view now and she was not unaccompanied. In her wake came a frigate which Nathan recognised as the *Blanche* and in the further distance a couple of armed brigs, one of which, he thought, might be the *Bonne Aventure*. A puff of smoke issued from the *Captain*'s bow and the first gun of the salute echoed around the steep flanks of the harbour.

'Be so good as to send for my coxswain and my steward,' he instructed Mr Lamb. And when the former had reported: 'Strike the tent, Young, if you would, and have the furnishings packaged up and ready for transport.'

The coxswain hesitated a moment. 'And shall I have them stowed in the orlop deck, sir?'

'No. You are to have them loaded into the launch. And have my barge ready.' Then, turning to Gabriel who was hovering in the background and had overheard this exchange with interest, he said: 'My compliments to Signora Correglia, and I would be obliged for the privilege of an interview – in my cabin.'

And so it was done. More easily than Nathan had imagined, though he could tell the Signora was not entirely convinced.

'Without delay?' she repeated, looking doubtfully about her at her scattered belongings.

'That was the signal from the Commodore,' Nathan insisted firmly.

'And with all my company?'

'I imagine the Commodore will be most anxious to be assured that you and all of your friends are in good health and spirits, and have suffered no alarm or discomfort.'

A condescending smile. 'I will assure the *Commodoro* you have make the most excellent of host.'

Nathan bowed low. 'It has been my pleasure,' he assured her.

He watched from the starboard rail as the barge left for the flagship, followed by the overloaded launch. The ladies waved tearfully. Nathan returned a dignified salute. He sighed. Gabriel gave him a sly look.

'Open the stern windows,' Nathan instructed him. 'Let us

get some damned air into the place, for it smells like a tart's boudoir down there. And take that smirk off your face. We are back to normal, I hope.'

But like the Signora he had his doubts. He awaited the Commodore's response with private trepidation. It was not long in coming.

'Signal from the flagship,' Duncan reported before the barge was halfway back to the frigate. 'Captain of *Unicorn* to report to the Commodore. Without delay.'

Chapter Seven

Council of War

———•◦•———

'Well, sir, I am surprised you have the nerve to show your face here.' The Commodore sat rigid at his desk, a malign presence in the half-light, his good eye glaring.

Nathan returned a look of polite surprise. 'I understood I was to report to the flagship *without delay*, sir.'

'Aye, and had I been in your shoes, I'd have sought my coffin sooner.'

'I hope I know my duty, sir.'

'Your duty, sir, your *duty*? Is it your duty to send a parcel of whores to your commanding officer? Aye, and all their damned chattels, parrots and all.'

'Whores, sir?' Nathan permitted his surprise to grow less polite. 'I cannot think who—'

'Do you have the face to deny it, sir? And a note of your respects, God damn it, to add insult to the injury.' He waved the offending item in the face that had been so brazenly presented before him.

For all his feigned astonishment, Nathan had anticipated a

measure of resentment. He had detected it in the air the moment he stepped aboard the flagship. Nothing obvious, nothing one might take exception to. He had been piped aboard with all the respect due to his rank, the Marine guard drawn up in the waist, Captain Miller there to take his salute with the first lieutenant, Edward Berry, and James Noble, the officer of the watch, both of whom he knew well. They and all the other officers he encountered were entirely correct in their bearing, polite in their address, but – perhaps a little *too* correct, polite to the point of coolness. Certainly a mite less affable than Nathan had come to expect on his not-infrequent visits to the old *Agamemnon* when she had been Nelson's flagship in the Bay of Genoa. Perhaps one might detect a hint of censure on those tanned, graven faces. If one were looking for it. A note of rebuke in the cold instruction: *'The Commodore will see you in his cabin, sir.'*

So the cabin was still his to command then. He was not o'errun. Nathan made a covert inspection but could detect no sign of the Signora or her delightful companions, not so much as a pair of smalls hanging from the line.

'I am very sorry, sir, but I find myself at a loss. Whores, do you say?'

'And what else would you have me call them?'

'If you are referring to Signora Corriglia, sir, I believed her to be a lady of excellent character and a particular friend of yours, sir.'

Nelson observed him for a moment without speaking. The Commodore's gaze was disconcerting at the best of times. There was no obvious damage to the eye that had been injured at Calvi save a slight milkiness, an absence of lustre, but this gave an added intensity to the other, so that Nathan had the impression of being an object fixed in its sight. Like an insect under the cold scrutiny of a magnifying lens.

'I was not referring to Signora Correglia,' the Commodore said at last. 'I was referring to the other bitches you had the damned effrontery to send to me. What of them, sir – eh? What of them?'

'I was under the impression that they were her maids, sir.'

Nelson struggled visibly with his emotions. Then, unexpectedly, the corners of his mouth twitched and to Nathan's astonishment he exploded in undisguised mirth.

'Her maids, do you say? Oh dear. Oh dear me.' He wiped his eyes with a delicate knuckle, his narrow chest palpitating a little. He raised his voice. 'Tom Allen there! Do you hear that? He says he thought they were her maids.'

A gargoyle face was thrust through a companionway on the Commodore's starboard quarter which, from previous visits, Nathan knew led to the pantry where his body servant invariably lurked. 'Well, an' what did he think *she* was, the Queen of Sheba?'

Thomas Allen, like most of the Commodore's personal servants, was from Norfolk and generally held to take liberties. Fremantle said he and the Commodore went at it like a pair of Cromer fishwives at times.

'Never you mind that, sir, and you may fetch us some of that Madeira you've been drinking, I can smell it on your breath from here. Or better still, fetch us the sack we had from the Doge before he kicked us out of Genoa, and those sugared almonds you are so fond of. You'll take a glass with me, sir?' This to Nathan.

'Willingly, sir.' Nathan suppressed a relieved sigh.

'Maids, indeed, but 'twas you who served *them*, from what I hear. Do you hear that, Allen? I said 'twas he who served *them*. Ha, ha!'

An indistinct retort issued from the pantry.

The Commodore, well pleased with his wit, came from

behind the desk and waved Nathan to a chair. 'Be at ease, Captain, I'll not make you take them back with you. You must have had your fill of the virginal by now. Sit down, man, sit down.'

Nathan wondered that the information had come so swiftly to his ear, but he supposed it was a facility that came with rank. 'I trust you have accommodated them without too much inconvenience,' he ventured, chancing his luck.

'I believe some of my officers have been put to considerable inconvenience,' Nelson advised him, 'for they have been obliged to vacate their cabins. But enough of this nonsense, we have more serious matters to attend to. The Viceroy is coming up from Bastia and we are to have a council of war aboard the flagship. He was particularly anxious that you should be present.'

This time Nathan's surprise was genuine. 'The Viceroy?' he repeated foolishly.

'Indeed. I admit I was not aware that you and His Excellency were intimates, so to speak.' Nathan was once more subjected to the cold stare.

'As far as I am aware, sir, we are not,' Nathan assured him honestly.

Sir Gilbert Elliot had been appointed Viceroy of the island upon its accession to the British Crown two years before, but Nathan knew little more about him than that he was a Scot and from a line of established if not ancient nobility.

'Then clearly your reputation precedes you,' Nelson observed. 'We can only hope that the reports were more favourable than not. And yet one can but wonder at his interest,' he added thoughtfully. Given his own reputation, Nelson often appeared to be overly concerned with the good opinion of his superiors, especially those who could boast a title to their name, and it was evident that he considered their regard to be of finite value: what was given to others must, of necessity, diminish the portion due to himself.

Tom Allen re-emerged from the pantry with two glasses upon a tray and the desired sweetmeats which he delivered with some speech that passed Nathan by. He had been a Norfolk ploughman before entering the service and the clay still stuck to his vowels, though the Commodore seemed to have no difficulty in understanding him.

'When I want my steward I will call for him,' he rebuked him sharply. 'And in the meantime I will make do with what poor service is available to me. Now be off with you and leave us in peace. Your very good health, sir,' he addressed himself to Nathan. 'And I hope it has not been diminished by your recent exertions.' Having delivered of this double broadside he drank with evident enjoyment, Nathan more austerely. 'Now, I expect you will furnish me with a written report of your activities by and by – I mean those that are the more inclined to the worship of Mars than Venus – but in the meantime a verbal report will suffice, for I am assured that you have secured a number of fat prizes on your most recent cruise.'

Few things were more likely to earn the Commodore's approbation than the procurement of a few fat prizes, for as flag officer he was due one-eighth of their value if, as appeared likely, they were condemned as contraband. So for the next few minutes Nathan regaled his Commander with a precise description of each article and its contents and the circumstances by which he had arrived by them.

'Excellent,' Nelson enthused, when he had concluded. 'A fine haul from one cruise. And the jewellery is a particular bonus, upon my word.' Nathan had noted how his eyes had lit up at mention of the hoard that had been discovered in the Captain's cabin of *Bonne Aventure*, for he was, like all of them, a pirate in his soul. 'Though we must, of course, be diligent in our pursuit of the legal owner.'

Nathan agreed that must, indeed, be a priority.

'Well, I am assured the *Bonne Aventure* will be taken into the service,' Nelson continued, 'for we have need of good sloops that may enter into shallow waters. But you comprehend there is no prize court in Corsica. It is one of the issues of which the Viceroy must be made aware, though if I have my way . . .'

But the Commodore's way remained unstated for the time being, for there came a scratching upon the door which heralded the entry of a young midshipman with the news that *Inconstant*'s barge was approaching.

Fremantle was the first of several Captains to arrive at the flagship. For the next half-hour there was a constant coming and going of barges as Cockburn of *Meleager*, Sawyer of *Blanche* and the two Commanders of the brig sloops *Sardine* and *Petrel* were separately piped aboard. And finally came the Viceroy himself, conveyed from shore in the Commodore's own barge and greeted with all the ceremony the flagship could muster: all hands dressing ship and a company of the 69th Foot drawn up in the waist as the band played 'Rule Britannia'.

'Which should inform the French we do not mean to be trifled with,' Fremantle murmured irreverently in Nathan's ear as they waited their turn to be presented.

The King's personal representative was a tall, burly Scot, though with rather more of the Edinburgh courtroom about him than the Highlands. He removed his hat on reaching the deck to reveal a great dome of a forehead and a mane of greying hair blowing back in the breeze: a lion's head with a long patrician nose and a wide, slightly twisted mouth which reinforced a certain haughtiness of expression.

'A nobleman by birth, a lawyer by profession and a politician by instinct,' Fremantle offered when petitioned for knowledge of the subject. 'Entered Parliament as a Whig – one of your Lowland Whigs – but soon cosied up to the Tories when it appeared to be of advantage to him.' Fremantle was well-read and prided himself on his knowledge of national affairs. 'Generally thought to be a close confidant of Pitt's. A member of the Privy Council till they sent him to Corsica.' And then with a look towards the rugged mountains above the port: 'I am not sure he would regard it as a promotion, but then he is from Edinburgh so I suppose he is no stranger to savagery.'

They sat at the Commodore's long, gleaming table with the light of the sun, low now in the evening sky, spilling over the stern windows. Motes of dust circled in the still air with the inevitable flies and other insects that had found it profitable to make the journey out from the shore. Above their heads they could hear the sounds of the hands going about their duties, while their betters applied themselves to the more cerebral task of winning the war; or at least not losing it as spectacularly as they appeared to be. The Viceroy sat at the head of the table, his aide-de-camp, Major Logan, on one side and the Commodore on the other, with the Flag Captain and the other officers assembled in no particular order of seniority or rank. And at the far end, the Commodore's secretary, John Castang, taking notes. There was no formal agenda but Nathan gathered that the main topic was to be what they were doing here and where they were to go next.

The Viceroy began with a summary of the current situation. The loss of Leghorn was a serious blow to the fleet. The port had provided shelter, dockyards, supplies and – of considerable import to these gentlemen – a prize court. These facilities now became available to the French, and the port would furnish them with an ideal base for their own aggressive activities, which might very likely include the invasion of Corsica.

A restless shuffling about the table, a grim rearrangement of expressions. There were some predictable slanders upon the French Army of Italy: 'a rabble of half-starved levies with the clothes falling off their backs and not a decent pair of boots between them' and the view was expressed that 'whether they had boots or not they could not walk on water'.

Sir Gilbert was brisk in his rebuttal. In a few short months, he reminded them, this rabble had, under Bonaparte's inspired leadership, crossed the Alps, swept across Piedmont and Savoy and advanced into the heart of Lombardy, driving the Austrians and their Italian allies before them. One strongpoint after another had fallen to them and now they were laying siege to Mantua, within striking distance of the Austrian border.

'And lest you assume this is of no concern to the Navy, gentlemen, I must remind you that it will be very difficult to operate at sea without secure bases on land, especially in the Mediterranean.'

The Republic of Genoa, though maintaining an official policy of neutrality, had submitted to the imposition of French garrisons and batteries all along the Ligurian coast, which in consequence had become a haven for enemy ships-of-war. Now Tuscany and the Papal States had succumbed without firing a single shot, closing their ports to British shipping and turning the entire Italian peninsula between Genoa and Naples into hostile territory. The Pope had paid the French a vast indemnity to stay out of the Romagna but he had permitted them to occupy the port of Ancona on the Adriatic as a base for their corsairs, from where they could blockade the Austrians in Trieste and attack allied shipping throughout the region.

News of the Papal submission brought further expressions of anger and revulsion. The Navy maintained a healthy

Protestant disrespect for the Church of Rome but this, they agreed, achieved new levels of infamy. Had they no memory of the priests that had been massacred by the French, the Flag Captain demanded heatedly, and the nuns that had been violated? Ralph Willett Miller was an American who had stayed loyal to King George during the Independence War and was known to be as ardent in his opinions as he was in his faith.

'I believe the priesthood did suffer somewhat disproportionately during the Terror,' Elliot acknowledged mildly, 'but the French have observed a more tolerant policy towards the Church of late. And there has been no report of violations in Italy so far as I am aware. Bonaparte appears to have behaved remarkably well on that score, at least as far as the nuns are concerned.'

His gaze strayed to Nathan who noted the hint of a smile in his eye and something else that he could not identify, something conspiratorial perhaps, as if they shared a secret or a private joke. He wondered again why the Viceroy had expressed a particular interest in his presence at the meeting. Could he have been informed of Nathan's association with Bonaparte in Paris? It seemed unlikely and yet, if he had been a member of the Privy Council, a confidant of the King's Chief Minister, it could conceivably have come to his ear. If so, Nathan could only hope he would keep it to himself.

He was aware that Nelson was talking, and almost as heatedly as his Flag Captain. He proposed placing the papal ports under blockade and sending a fleet of small boats up the Tiber, armed with carronades and loaded with Marines, to expose the Pope to some 'sharp language'.

The Viceroy raised a calming hand. 'We must not let our feelings get the better of us,' he warned. 'I am persuaded His Holiness had little choice in the matter, with the French Army at his borders and no significant forces of his own, from the material point of view, to resist them. However, it poses an additional difficulty for us, particularly the use of Ancona as a French naval base. But I will return to that directly. In the meantime, perhaps the Commodore will enlighten us about the current situation in Leghorn, for as we all must know, he has lately come from there.'

Nelson reported that within two or three days of his arrival, *Captain* had been joined by the frigates *Lively* and *La Minerve*, with the brig sloops *Sardine*, *L'Eclair* and *Vanneau*, and the *Fox* and *Rose* cutters, all of which maintained a strict blockade of the port. No ships of any nationality had been permitted to enter or leave.

'I believe that faced with the ruin of their trade, the inhabitants will rise up and turn the French out,' he concluded, 'particularly if they are encouraged to do so.'

'And what of the situation within the port?' the Viceroy enquired.

Nelson prided himself on his intelligence reports. He had kept a string of agents in Genoa and it appeared that he had swiftly established a similar network in Leghorn, using the local fishermen as couriers. 'I have let it be known that they may continue their trade under British licence,' he confirmed, 'and every morning up to twenty or thirty tartans have been gathering under the stern of *Captain* to secure leave to proceed. They also bring messages and information from the town.'

By such means he had learned that the French had moved some three or four thousand troops into the port; that all Tuscan troops had been placed under French command, and that General Bonaparte had established his headquarters in the British Consul's house.

'Old Udny's,' established Fremantle unnecessarily, with a bark of laughter. 'Do you think he knows?'

Nelson subdued him with a glance. 'I believe we all know Mr Udny to have been the British Consul,' he interposed coldly. 'And I do not believe it is cause for amusement.'

Fremantle blushed scarlet and stammered an apology. 'Only but you know what I mean. To have Udny and his . . . well, replaced by . . .' He looked around the table but there was no support to be had from his fellows, and if they knew what he meant they were not to be betrayed into revealing it in front of the Viceroy. 'I am surprised he did not seek accommodation in one of the forts,' he attempted lamely. 'Bonaparte, I mean.'

'I believe it may be a symbolic gesture,' the Viceroy proposed smoothly. 'The British are in retreat, the French in the ascendant. And to prove it the tricolour is flying above the British Consul's house. Though I believe Mr Udny himself, with his goods and chattels, is in safe hands.' He caught Nathan's eye again and Nathan, too, felt a blush suffusing his features, though it was surely not possible that the Viceroy knew of the reason for his embarrassment.

Nelson resumed his report. As a further demonstration of the new order, Governor Spannochio had been arrested and sent off to Florence with a demand that he should be punished by the Grand Duke for holding up the French advance. All British and allied property had been confiscated, and Bonaparte had ordered that anyone caught hiding it, or communicating with the British squadron off the coast, was to be shot. This had no noticeable effect on Nelson's flow of information, however, and the previous morning his fishermen had brought him the news that Bonaparte had left the port, taking most of his cavalry with him.

'Left?' Elliot repeated sharply. 'Left for where?'

'For Mantua. He had information that the Austrians were marching to its relief. He has left Leghorn under the command of General Belgrand with the Seventy-fifth Demi-brigade, a company of artillery and a squadron of Hussars. Two thousand troops in all. If Your Excellency can furnish me with the same number of British troops, I will undertake to drive the French from the port before the week is out.'

The Viceroy looked alarmed. 'I admire your zeal in this matter, Commodore, and I do not wish to appear shy, but . . .' He glanced to Major Logan, who stroked his chin thoughtfully in the military manner but offered no further guidance on the subject. 'But our situation here in Corsica is not favourable to an offensive campaign on the mainland. We have fewer than five thousand regular British troops at our disposal and it is a large island to defend. The loss of Leghorn, while serious, is not a disaster. The loss of Corsica would be. It would leave us without a single base east of Gibraltar.'

'So we are to sit here doing nothing?'

There was a small frisson of discomfort around the table. Nelson might be overly impressed by title, but it was nothing to his opinion of his own worth, and he could be scathing in his rebuke, even of a superior, if he felt the war was not being pursued with sufficient vigour.

'By no means. We will maintain the blockade of Leghorn and do what we can to take the war to the enemy,' replied Elliot coolly. 'Additionally, though I do not mean to interfere in purely naval matters, I believe there is a strong case for sending a small squadron into the Adriatic.'

Nelson was clearly taken aback. 'For what purpose?' He recalled his manners. 'If I may . . .'

'To maintain a link with the Austrians through Trieste, to counter the menace of the French corsairs in Ancona and more particularly, to advertise our continuing presence in the region to the Venetians.'

There was a silence around the table. The circling insects appeared to have multiplied. Something dropped with a loud clatter upon the deck above and there was the sound of a half-broken voice raised in brief but violent abuse.

'The Venetians?' Nelson repeated after a moment, but in a tone of wonderment, as if they had but lately landed from Venus.

'Admittedly the Republic of Venice has been in decline for many years,' continued the Viceroy, 'but her navy is still considerable. Almost as considerable as the fleet that is presently available to Sir John Jervis. It is imperative the Venetians do not enter into alliance with the French – and I believe a British naval presence in the Adriatic will remind them we are still very much in the game.'

'How large a presence did you have in mind?' Nelson enquired faintly.

'I leave that entirely to your discretion. It need not be a large force. But as a measure of our intent, I do assure you it will carry far more weight than the weight of guns it carries. I would have thought it was a plan after your own heart,' he added sweetly, 'and in the meantime I will give orders to have the required troops ready to embark at Bastia the moment it is propitious to do so. And now, if we may, let us turn to other matters. I believe there is an urgent need to establish a prize court here in Corsica . . .'

'I doubt I have seen Nelson more taken aback,' Fremantle affirmed complacently as he and Nathan stood apart from the other officers on the quarterdeck, waiting for their barges to fetch them back to their ships. 'If the old boy had asked him to send a squadron to China I do not think he could have been more amazed.'

'And yet it is only the Adriatic,' Nathan pointed out reasonably. 'No more than a few days' sailing, would you not say, with a fair wind?'

Fremantle gave him a sharp look. 'You are contemplating it, are you?'

'Not at all,' Nathan replied deceitfully. 'I only mean that it is not so very far.'

Fremantle sniffed. 'I suppose he thinks of it as a backwater,' he said. 'And yet the Viceroy is right about Venice. Thirteen ships of the line, you know, and as many more on the stocks in the Arsenale. And now Bonaparte is on the borders of the Veneto.'

'What is the Veneto?' Nathan queried him. 'Or should I say where? It is not a term I am familiar with.'

'It is the mainland territory of Venice. What the Venetians call the *Terraferma*, Venice itself being entirely surrounded by water, as I am sure you must know from your time at Charterhouse.'

'I did know that, but I thank you for bringing it to my attention.'

'Indeed, it would be unfortunate to go charging off there without knowing.'

'What makes you think it will be me?'

'I saw how the Viceroy looked at you. He has singled you out, my lad – you are to be favoured. You are the golden boy. I cannot think why.'

'What nonsense.'

'You will see. He is down there now with the Commodore, banging his fist upon the table and saying, "I must have Peake. I will not be denied."'

'Fremantle, you talk the most imbecilic rubbish at times.'

'I might almost envy you, but I have Betsey to think on. She would not wish me to go to Venice. It is full of whores, you know. I suppose that is why they are sending you there.'

'They are not sending me anywhere. And if they are, it is not because of that. I have still not made up my mind to forgive you, you know, for obliging me to take them aboard. It has caused me a great deal of embarrassment. I might have to call you out.'

Fremantle graced him with a small bow. 'I am your servant, sir, whenever you feel disposed. But I could hardly keep them on *Inconstant*, you know, with Betsey aboard. Signora Correglia and I were once attached, did you know?'

'Why does that not surprise me?' Nathan remarked. 'I think because you told me of it, several times. You passed her on to Nelson, you said.'

'Did I? Good God. I trust you would not betray a confidence, Peake,' he warned Nathan sternly.

'Was it a confidence? I had thought it was general knowledge. Oh, do not glare so, it don't frighten me, you know. Now that you are a reformed character I will speak only of your virtues, if I can recall them. Here is your barge.'

'Well, good luck in Venice. It is called the Most Serene Republic, you know. Or the *Serenissima* in the Venetian tongue. The Most Serene Republic of Saint Mark. Saint Mark being their patron saint. And the Doge is addressed as Your Excellency.'

'I shall try to remember that, should I ever have the opportunity of addressing him. But you are quite wrong, you know: there is no prospect of my being sent to Venice. I am the most junior Captain in the squadron.'

But Fremantle was already gone with an indifferent wave, and now here was Tom Allen with some instruction in his own alien tongue.

'I beg your pardon?' Nathan queried him, frowning in concentration.

''Is 'Onour wants to see 'ee in 'is cabin, zor,' Nathan interpreted on the second rendering. 'If you is still 'ere.'

*

They were still seated at the table, but the lanterns had been lit and they had their heads together over a chart. An open bottle of wine and two glasses stood conveniently to hand. The atmosphere seemed convivial. Indeed, the Viceroy was laughing when Nathan entered the room.

'Ah, Peake, I am glad you have not left us,' Nelson greeted him. 'The Viceroy has expressed the desire that we should send you into the Adriatic and I am very willing to oblige him – if you are.'

Nathan had been quite serious in his protestations to Fremantle and this was a considerable surprise to him, but he managed to murmur some suitable reply and the Commodore instructed him to fetch up a chair so that he might join them at the chart. 'And you will take a glass of claret with us, I trust.'

The chart was one of William Heather's showing a part of the Mediterranean from the Tyrrhenian Sea around the long dog-leg of Italy into the Adriatic: from the Ionian Islands in the south to the Lagoon of Venice in the north.

'Here is Corfu,' Nelson indicated one of the larger and more northerly of the Ionians, just off the mainland of Albania, 'which is where the main Venetian fleet has its base, strategically placed as you see, to cover the approaches to the Adriatic and permit sorties into the Mediterranean, though we are told this has happened but rarely in recent times. His Excellency assures me we have a very good Consul at Corfu who sends us excellent report.'

'Spiridion Foresti,' the Viceroy contributed, 'a native of Zante, which is one of the other islands in the group. He has proved one of our most reliable informants over the years.'

'You will take *Unicorn*, of course,' the Commodore resumed, 'with *Bonne Aventure* as your consort. I am afraid I can spare no other, though I am in wholehearted concurrence with the Viceroy on the importance of this mission.'

This did appear to be the case, despite his earlier reticence. It was as if he had adopted the plan as his own.

'You will make a thorough assessment of the strength and condition of the Venetian fleet,' he instructed Nathan, 'and take what soundings of the principal harbours and lagoons as you are able. I am assured that His Majesty's Government takes a long-term interest in the islands, which are ideally situated as a base for both the eastern Mediterranean and the Levant.' This with another glance towards the Viceroy who confirmed it with a nod. 'You will, of course, take whatever steps may be necessary to curb the activities of the corsairs at Ancona.' He indicated the port in question, about halfway up the map, on the eastern coast of Italy. 'Making our disapproval of the facility afforded by His Holiness apparent in whatever way appears appropriate.'

'Within reason,' Elliot interposed hastily. 'I would not like it to be thought that Captain Peake felt he had carte blanche to attempt a landing in the port.' His laugh was a little nervous.

'I think you may rest easily on that score, Your Excellency. With the limited forces at his command I do not believe Captain Peake will contemplate an invasion of the Holy See.'

They shared a good-natured chuckle at this, rather more vigorous on the Commodore's part than upon the Viceroy's, but Nathan was surprised to observe the degree of amity between the two men. Nelson was all charm and affability, while the Viceroy appeared almost deferential in his regard; certainly he seemed more than happy to let the Commodore take the lead in his instruction. Nathan assumed it was the diplomat in him, smoothing the waters after obliging Neptune to bow to his will, but it soon became apparent that it stemmed from a sincere admiration. More than that, as their discussions progressed it became clear that the Viceroy desired the younger man's approval – a rare achievement in one who, for all his merit, was still relatively junior in rank and not much more than halfway up the Captains' List. Still, it said much for Nelson's estimation of his own merits that he accepted the role with such confidence.

'You will also pay your respects to the Imperial Governor in Trieste,' the Commodore continued, moving his finger up the Adriatic to the Austrian port on the Istrian coast opposite Venice. 'It is imperative that the Austrians are made aware of our presence in the region and that we are making every effort in their support. You will find that the *Unicorn* is by far the most powerful ship-of-war in the Adriatic, apart from the Venetians', of course. The Austrians have just a couple of xebecs, of no more than fourteen guns apiece, and a few small gunboats. Nothing to pose a problem for a French national ship or even a well-armed privateer. A demonstration of our own strength would, of course, be appreciated. If you were to sail into Trieste with a string of French prizes at your stern it would greatly improve our standing with the Imperial court.'

Nathan did his best to maintain a neutral expression, as if the capture of half-a-dozen enemy corsairs might be accomplished every day before breakfast.

'And then there is Venice,' Nelson concluded, turning to the Viceroy again.

'Ah yes.' The Viceroy passed a hand over his forehead and frowned a little. 'The *Serenissima* has, as you are no doubt aware, been in decline for many years.'

Nathan nodded gravely, privately reflecting that until his conversation with Fremantle, he would have assumed the Viceroy was talking about a woman, an elderly duchess perhaps. But Elliot had embarked upon a history lesson and he did his best to pay attention.

'There was a time, during one of the many wars with the Turk, when the Arsenale turned out a new warship, fully equipped, every day. She was the greatest naval power the world had ever known, greater than Carthage, Greece or Rome in all their glory. But those days are long gone. The *Serenissima* has become synonymous with decline, decadence and corruption. However, she still maintains a great naval tradition and her fleet, as we discussed earlier, is still one of the most powerful in the Mediterranean.' He paused and took a sip of wine, gathering his thoughts. 'This has not escaped the attention of His Majesty's Government, even before Bonaparte crossed the Alps. It was appreciated that if the Venetian fleet fell into the hands of the French, their combined forces would far outnumber our own fleet in the Mediterranean.'

It would not be difficult, Nathan reflected privately. Sir John Jervis had no more than a dozen ships of the line to bottle up an equal number of the French in Toulon.

'Various approaches were made to the Doge and his advisers, both by ourselves and the Austrians,' the Viceroy continued. 'They were unsuccessful. The Venetians remain wedded to a policy of neutrality. However, less formal overtures were made to the Venetian Admiral of the Fleet, Giovanni Dandolo. Dandolo has lately become a member of the Council of Ten – which is to say, the ruling council of Venice. His family has filled the office of Doge in the past, and he is known to favour an alliance with the Austrians and ourselves. Having seen what has happened to Genoa and Tuscany, of course, he will know that a declared state of neutrality will not save them from Bonaparte if he should choose to invade. This may strengthen the Admiral's case. But if the French *do* invade – and Venice falls – Dandolo is prepared to assemble the fleet in the Ionian Islands which he will then place under the protection of King George.

'I tell you frankly that this is a policy we have much encouraged. The fate of the Ionian Islands – and the Venetian fleet – is more important for us than the fate of Venice itself. However, Dandolo requires certain assurances – securities, one might say. To be precise, one half of a million pounds in gold.'

There was a small silence in the cabin, broken at length by the Commodore.

'He does not sell himself short,' he remarked.

'He has suggested that he will need the funds to provide better facilities for the fleet in Corfu and to place it upon a war footing. And from our point of view, of course, it is a very fair price indeed. I believe the cost of building and equipping a single ship of the line is at least fifty thousand pounds. And the islands themselves will be a considerable asset to His Majesty's Government. A Gibraltar in the eastern Mediterranean.'

He looked to Nathan who nodded his comprehension, though he was wondering quite how much this mercenary Admiral was going to cost him personally. It seemed to him that his journey into the Adriatic had far more to do with supporting Dandolo than with any concerns with privateers or the Austrians.

'May I ask what contact we have with Dandolo?' he ventured.

'The British Minister to Venice, Sir Richard Worsley, has, for obvious reasons, been obliged to maintain contact through an intermediary. However, all seems to be going according to plan, though it has been difficult to discover precisely what is happening in Venice of late.'

Previous experience had given Nathan a nose for prevarication, particularly in the political animal. Nelson sensed it, too, judging from the sharp look he gave the Viceroy from under his brow.

'I should say that *I* have not heard,' Elliot added hastily. 'It is quite possible that Sir Richard has communicated directly with London by way of Germany. However, as you know, communications have been much disrupted by Bonaparte's activities in the north and by the activities of French cruisers at sea. This is one of our reasons for sending Captain Peake into the Adriatic. We need to re-establish our contacts in Venice and assure them that we have agreed to their terms. The amount requested has been made available, in guineas, and will be despatched to Corfu, through the agency of the Levant Company, as soon as the fleet – and the islands – have been delivered safely into our hands.'

Nathan regarded him warily. There was something that needed to be clarified here – and in the presence of the Commodore, who was his direct superior in the chain of command. 'You wish me to deliver this information personally?'

The Viceroy glanced uneasily at Nelson before he spoke. 'We must leave that to your discretion, I believe, and the circumstances in which you find yourself. However, your previous experience as, how shall I put it, a . . . a confidential agent for His Majesty's Government, does make you an ideal candidate for such a mission. And the Commodore concurs with me in this.'

This time Nelson gave a nod. 'Any questions?' he enquired of Nathan. His tone and the look that accompanied it may have been ironic. Nathan resisted the temptation to say it all sounded perfectly straightforward.

'I assume I am to have written orders?'

'Of course. I will instruct my secretary to prepare them as soon as this interview is ended.'

'And when am I to leave?'

'As soon as you are able,' replied the Commodore briskly. 'You may provision at Naples, where you will call on your journey to the south. His Excellency has despatches for the British Envoy there and I will give you a short note to carry to him. Now as to your complement. *Bonne Aventure* is presently under the command of one of your officers, I believe, with a prize crew?' Nathan nodded, though his head was swimming with other considerations. 'I have it in mind to give the command to one of my own officers, Lieutenant Compton. I take it you would have no objection? I assure you I cannot recommend him more highly.'

Nathan bowed his compliance as, indeed, he was obliged to, for it was the flag officer's prerogative to appoint officers to a command, but he had mixed feelings about the appointment. He knew Henry Compton to be a good officer, but Tully would not be happy to relinquish his temporary command of the sloop. On the other hand, it would be good to have him back aboard the *Unicorn*. But Nathan was already working out what might be wrung as a concession. 'I am afraid Lieutenant Compton will find the *Bonne Aventure* desperately under-crewed,' he put in quickly. 'And if I am to take any more prizes . . .'

'I will see what we can do,' Nelson assured him, but with ill grace – Captains were always complaining they were short-crewed. 'Of course, the transports in the harbour may provide us with additional hands.' Nathan's qualms about stealing prime seamen from the convoy were clearly not shared by his commanding officer. 'And I can let you have one of my junior officers as acting lieutenant for he is, I believe, more than ready for a promotion.' Nathan bowed his thanks, though maintaining private reservations so far as the additional officer was concerned, for despite the assurance, he knew Nelson would have no qualms about giving him some elderly snottie or master's mate who was making life hell for his young gentlemen and the crew. 'Then I think that concludes our interview,' Nelson smiled and gave Nathan his hand, 'and it only remains for me to wish you joy of your commission.'

'There is one other thing,' the Viceroy announced as Nathan prepared to take his leave. He appeared a trifle embarrassed. 'You will find that Venice is a city very much addicted to *intrigue*, both of a political and a . . . a *sexual* nature, and sometimes the two are . . . well, you take my point.'

Nathan's expression did not alter but he wondered what on earth the Viceroy was trying to tell him. He looked to the Commodore for assistance but Nelson appeared intent on his study of the map.

'When in Rome,' the Viceroy persisted gamely.

'Or Venice,' put in the Commodore without looking up from his map.

'Or Venice,' the Viceroy conceded, 'it is not *always* advisable to do as . . . as the Romans.' The smile turned into a frown as he realised the Commodore's intervention had not improved his adage. 'Or the Venetians. And as a serving officer of King George you will, of course, at all times preserve your, your . . .'

The word he was probably looking for was integrity. Possibly it stuck in his throat.

At last Nelson lifted his head. '*Virgo intacta*,' he supplied with a thin smile.

Chapter Eight

The Tramontana

'If I were to give you an instruction, but issued a warning to keep your virginity intact, what particular conclusion would you draw?' Nathan enquired of his friend Mr Tully in the privacy of his cabin on the *Unicorn*.

'I would conclude that you were sending me into a situation where I was in imminent danger of losing it,' Tully replied after a moment's reflection. 'Assuming the object was still in my possession.'

Nathan nodded thoughtfully, having come to a similar conclusion. Over the several years of their association he had come to value Tully's opinion as much as he did his friendship, though a superficial knowledge of their backgrounds might consider it an unlikely alliance, for while Nathan was the offspring of a British Admiral and an American heiress, Tully was the product of an illicit liaison between a Guernsey smuggler and the daughter of the local seigneur. Having been raised as a gentleman by his maternal grandfather, he had forsaken the advantages of this situation to follow in his father's calling. An unfortunate encounter with a Revenue cutter had obliged him to abandon this for a career in the King's Navy, if only as an alternative to transportation. He had risen rapidly from able seaman to master's mate, however, and had recently passed his examination for lieutenant, his nautical abilities being matched only by his ease in conversing with men of all rank and situation. Though Nathan was aware of the iniquity of having favourites, Tully was the only officer with whom he felt able to converse as an equal – and on matters that were not solely concerned with the running of the ship.

Even so, there were certain aspects of the current mission which could not be confided even to Tully. Nathan had told him only what he had revealed to Mr Duncan and the other officers: that they were to proceed to the Adriatic with a view to halting the activities of the privateers operating out of Ancona, and that they were to call in at Naples on the way. He was considering now what else he might tell him without betraying any confidences when a knock upon the cabin door signalled the arrival of Dr McLeish, who had been invited to join them when his duties allowed.

The doctor entered with a rush for there was a heavy sea running and the *Unicorn*'s steep ascent had canted the deck sharply towards the stern; he was scarcely halfway across the cabin, however, when the frigate began to slide down the other side, and he was obliged to take several small steps backwards to maintain his balance before making a dash for the relative security of a chair. Such was the comic effect of this, and the expression of surprise on his normally unruffled features, the two officers burst into spontaneous applause and invited him to do it again, for it was as good as Astley's Circus, Nathan assured him.

'I am happy to be a source of amusement,' the doctor declared, 'but when you have recovered your composure a little, you might oblige me by explaining why we are reeling about like a drunken whore in Grangemouth, for I have known the ship steadier in a hurricane.'

This was almost certainly untrue but they did their best to enlighten him.

'It is because, like most of our ships, she is built for the long Atlantic rollers,' submitted Nathan graciously, filling his glass, 'and has difficulty with these shorter Mediterranean affairs.'

'Like a thoroughbred,' completed Tully, 'that finds the fences stacked so high and so close she cannot quite get into her stride.' He demonstrated this by a kind of plunging motion with his hand. 'But there is no necessity for alarm, Doctor. I doubt we shall founder.'

The doctor regarded him with disfavour. 'I have survived greater blows than this without a fit of the vapours,' he assured him coldly. 'I am only surprised to find it blowing so hard in the Mediterranean in midsummer.'

'It is the Tramontana,' Nathan declared with a great air of wisdom, having been informed by Mr Perry before he came below. 'From the Latin *trans montanus* meaning from across the mountains, which are, in this instance, the Alps. It often blows in the Mediterranean at this time of the year, but not often so hard, I believe.'

'I am obliged to you, sir.' The doctor bowed ironically. 'And I thank you for the translation. The Latin, is it? What a wonder is a classical education. I would find it very useful in my own profession, no doubt, for I have observed a great many potions and remedies to be inscribed in the tongue of Pliny – and some doctors even utilise it, I believe, to describe the condition of their patients.'

Nathan received this with a smile, for even at his most amiable the doctor's own tongue tended to the acerbic. 'I am sorry it is distressing for you,' he remarked, 'but it should carry us speedily to Naples, touching wood . . .' he touched the table with proper circumspection, 'though being of a northerly disposition it is not generally to be relied upon.'

'And does it change direction in the Adriatic so it may, with the same good grace, waft us the other way?'

'I regret it is not so obliging,' Nathan admitted, 'for then it would not be the Tramontana. However, there is another wind which we call the Sirocco which blows from Africa and which will, if we are in luck, "waft" us as far up the Adriatic as we wish to go, even to Venice.'

He made a grab for the wine as the frigate plunged into the next trough. He felt that the wind had strengthened somewhat since he had left the quarterdeck, but Mr Duncan had the watch and was at least as capable as his Captain of taking in canvas if he considered it necessary for the safety of the ship.

'Ah, so we *are* to go to Venice!' exclaimed McLeish in a manner that suggested rumours of this destination had been bandied freely about the ship. 'I am very glad of that, for I have long wished to visit the *Serenissima*. To look upon the Doge's Palace and the Grand Canal and other such wonders of the world. This is excellent claret – is it your own?'

This was a pertinent remark, for Nathan had appropriated a considerable quantity of wine from the previous Captain after his throat was cut, but the supply had long been exhausted.

'It is part of a batch I purchased in Genoa,' Nathan replied, 'but I did not say we *were* to go to Venice, I said the wind would take us there *if we allowed it to*. However, I agree it would be more interesting than some of the places we have been obliged to visit of late.' Nathan had made subtle enquiries among his officers, but as far as he could ascertain, none of them had visited what he must learn to call the *Serenissima*, nor sailed the Adriatic – not even Mr Perry, who had travelled more widely than most. 'I dare say you have read a great deal about the place,' he added carelessly, for McLeish was a devoted reader of travel books and periodicals, and his reference betrayed a more than superficial knowledge.

'Well, I would not say I have made a particular study,' the doctor confessed, 'but I am acquainted somewhat with its history and architecture – and other of its attractions.'

'I have heard that it has degenerated somewhat in recent years,' Nathan remarked in the same casual tone, 'in terms of its moral standards.'

'The journals that I have read do not, alas, provide an insight into the facilities provided by your average Venetian brothel, if that is what you mean,' replied McLeish, who had dealt with too many cases of the clap and the implausible reasons for it to have the wool pulled over his eyes. 'But I have heard that the city does offer all manner of diversions to those of a licentious nature and has, for that reason, become a popular destination upon the Grand Tour.'

'They must be interesting diversions indeed for people to travel so far in the hope of experiencing them,' Nathan persisted. 'If, that is, you mean people from our own shores.'

'Englishmen primarily. Germans, too, I believe, of a certain inclination. I can probably find you a more detailed description, if this is of particular interest to you.'

'Not at all, I merely . . . Well . . .' Nathan shot a glance at Tully, who was observing him with a curious regard. 'It is just that I was advised by His Excellency the Viceroy that if we *were* to visit the city I should be wary of letting the young gentlemen ashore, lest they become corrupted.'

'I fear it is too late for that, in most cases,' McLeish countered with a harsh laugh. 'However, if His Excellency told you this, I am sure it would be wise to follow his advice. I personally would let your "young gentlemen" have the run of the place, for I believe corporal punishment is one of the delights widely on offer, not only in the bawdy houses, but even in the convents and monasteries. Indeed, I cannot think of a more salutary lesson for the little scrotes than to have them thrashed to within an inch of their lives by a hefty nun and make them pay for the privilege.' He neatly caught the decanter as it slid across the table and topped up his glass with what was left of the claret. 'But I perceive that I have embarrassed you, or stimulated your own fantasies to an extent that might require bleeding.'

'Not at all,' Nathan assured him, heaving himself upright. 'Indeed, I wish we could continue the discussion but I fear I must temporarily abandon you to attend to my duties.' For that last lurch had persuaded him that Mr Duncan was taking a greater risk with the spars than he was prepared to tolerate. 'But pray take your ease until I return and I will send Gabriel in with another bottle.'

He emerged upon the quarterdeck to find a monstrous sea marshalling its forces at their stern and a heavy rain sweeping the decks. He looked instantly aloft to see the topmen taking in sail, for it had, as Mr Duncan kindly informed him, come on to blow a bit.

There were further signs that the first lieutenant had taken every precaution – and possibly more than was necessary – to meet this condition. The topgallant masts had been struck down upon the deck, anchors and boats secured and, rather more surprisingly, the guns aligned fore and aft and lashed across the ports, a measure which usually presaged a very serious blow indeed. Nathan lurched over to the weather rail and screwed up his face as he peered into the rain. It swept the sea like grapeshot, reducing visibility to not much more than a mile, but he could see the *Bonne Aventure* at their stern and though she was making heavy weather of it he could not find fault with the trim of her sails or the amount of canvas Lieutenant Compton had allowed to remain aloft. He personally found the rain quite exhilarating after the sweltering heat of

San Fiorenzo, but it was as wet and cold as it had no business to be in the Mediterranean in midsummer. He had known better days in the Bay of Biscay in November.

Mr Perry came stomping aft, having finished instructing the topmen, water streaming from his hat and a look as near to satisfaction as his leery features would ever present to the world. They were now running under topsails and staysails alone and there was an immediate improvement in the *Unicorn*'s gait. She still resembled Tully's thoroughbred with the jumps stacked against her, but she was taking them more in her stride. The wind had shifted a little to nor'-nor'-east and was now about two points off their stern, which was near their best point of sailing.

'Perhaps you would oblige me by casting the log, Mr Duncan,' Nathan requested, for he was curious to see what progress they were making. Then he might return to his cabin with an easy conscience, he thought, and see if he could prevail upon the Angel Gabriel to indulge him with one of his famous Welsh rabbits to go with the claret.

The log ship disappeared into the white race of water without a splash and they watched the line move swiftly astern.

'Turn!' yelled Mr Lamb as the ribbon crossed the rail and Mr Anson promptly turned the 28-second timer and held it up to his eye until the last grain of sand ran by. 'Stop!'

Mr Lamb nipped the line between finger and thumb, measured the distance from the last knot and raised his voice to convey the result to his waiting superiors.

'Nine knots and three fathoms, sir.'

'Very good, Mr Lamb,' Nathan responded formally. 'Thank you, Mr Duncan, for obliging me. We may see Vesuvius be— before we die.'

He had been about to say before noon tomorrow, and being

of a superstitious nature even his later estimate seemed to be an outrageous temptation to fate. Sure enough, the words were scarcely out of his mouth when a cry from the foretop alerted them to the presence of a sail a point or two off their starboard bow. Nathan could see nothing from the deck and felt no great desire to go aloft. A sail in these waters was unlikely to indicate anything more intriguing than a merchantman, he told himself, most likely a neutral turned away from Leghorn by Nelson's blockade. But the first lieutenant had already sent Mr Lamb swarming up the ratlines to make a more substantial report.

Nathan watched the young midshipman as he swung into the maintop and then, after a moment's observation, proceeded up into the crosstrees where he hung, a hundred feet or so above the deck, with the glass glued to his eye. The mast swayed through an arc of some 30 or 40 degrees, and the rain and the wind lashed and clawed at him with malign intent, but he maintained this position for several minutes, scanning the heaving seas to windward, before sliding shut the glass and availing himself of the backstay to return to the deck. He had taken the precaution of securing his hat to his head with a Barcelona neckerchief, his face was flushed with wind and wet with rain, and he looked, Nathan thought, like a tearful child with the toothache. He had passed thirteen on his last birthday but his voice had not yet broken.

'Please, sir, she is a ship-of-war. A corvette, I believe.'

'A corvette?' Nathan's tone was doubtful.

'A large corvette, sir, almost as big as a frigate. She is in and out of the waves, sir, and I cannot see if she is flying any colours.'

Nathan nodded thoughtfully. The corvette was an exclusively French class of vessel, something between a sloop and a frigate. Fremantle had captured one of them – the *Unité* – off Algiers earlier this year. Twenty 9-pounders on her main gun deck;

four 6-pounders on her quarterdeck. She had been renamed the *Surprise* and classed as a frigate in the British Navy, but it could not be her, for she had been sent off to the Caribbean some months since. He supposed *Sardine* was a possibility for she, too, had been a French corvette until her capture off Tunis. They had left her at her mooring in San Fiorenzo with the rest of the squadron, but there was a slim chance she had been sent after them with a message and missed them in the rain. However, the likelihood was that she was French.

'Could you tell how far off she is?'

'About half a league, sir.'

That would be the very limit of visibility in this weather, even from the maintopmast. Nathan subjected the young midshipman to a speculative regard. He looked very sure of himself but then he often did and frequently without cause. He had adopted a new policy in chess of clearing the board with reckless abandon in the hope that he could force a draw, or make Nathan so irritated by the tactic he would make a fatal mistake and lose the game.

'Very well, thank you, Mr Lamb.' He looked to Perry who knew what he was going to ask.

'We might chance the fore course, sir,' he conceded doubtfully, 'with a reef or two. But if it comes on any harder . . .'

'Very well, Mr Perry, let us live dangerously for once.'

Mr Perry's smile was as painful to behold as it almost certainly was for him to contrive. The moment they loosed the sail it had an immediate effect, though Nathan was not at all sure it was the one he had desired. The *Unicorn* heeled several degrees further to leeward and the following sea gave her a strange corkscrew motion as she pitched and rolled through the troughs. But now he had to look to his cannon for they were no use where they were, tethered cow fashion across the ports. It would be a devil of a job to unship them, though, and then rig them again with the sea that was running. And he'd look a damn fool if she turned out to be the *Sardine*, or a neutral merchantman. Dear God, he thought, there was no helping it – he had to make sure the midshipman was right in his estimate.

'I am going aloft, Mr Duncan,' he told the first lieutenant.

He tucked his glass under his arm and began the laborious ascent. There was a time he could have run up the rigging without the slightest concern, even in a sea like this, but he was out of practice. He would dearly have liked to go through the lubbers' hole but he could not be shamed before the whole crew. He began to climb outwards along the futtock shrouds, hanging almost upside down as the mast went through its terrible pendulum swing. Sixty feet above the sea, with the rain lashing at his face, staring up at that menacing sky. Why? Would it make him a better leader of men? The mast reached the end of its trajectory and began its long swoop to leeward. He scuttled up and over into the blessed sanctuary of the maintop. Was he high enough? One glance assured him that he was not. He would have to climb to the next level, as Mr Lamb had done.

With a grim fatalism he began to scale the narrow shrouds of the foremast. This was pure madness, to be up here in this; to even consider a chase in this weather. But then as he looked out over the monstrous seas, he saw her. A scrap of sail through the driving rain. He hooked his arm through the shrouds and brought the glass to his eye. Yes, now he had her, and he forgot what was happening to the mast or even what any of the crew thought of him as he concentrated on keeping her in view. Lamb was right. She was ship-rigged but not quite as big as a frigate. Heeled right over like the *Unicorn*, so he could see her copper sheeting, even in this light. Her gunports, too. He counted ten of them, two more than *Sardine*. So that was it –

she was almost certainly French, and in the same class as
Unité.

He considered sliding down the backstay as Mr Lamb had
done but thought better of it and climbed, considerably more
sedately, down the ratlines.

'You were right, Mr Lamb,' he told him when he reached
the quarterdeck. 'And she is not one of ours, so we will have to
beat to quarters, Mr Duncan, and clear for action. And signal
Bonne Aventure to follow us.'

'And the guns, sir?'

Nathan peered down the heaving gundeck and decided to
leave them as they were for the time being, for it would be
some time before they were in a position to fire them. He made
an exception for the two long nines in the bows, however,
which might chance a shot if they drew any closer. If they could
shoot away a spar or even part a halyard in this weather they
could run down on her in a jiffy. But for some reason the
process of unshipping the two bow chasers appeared to be
causing more problems than it should have, even in this sea.
There were about a dozen hands engaged in the task under the
supervision of Mr Bailey, the officer who had been transferred
from the flagship. He was, as Nathan had surmised, an elderly
master's mate now made up to acting lieutenant, and he had a
considerably higher opinion of himself than was shared by his
fellows, or was tolerable in the confined quarters of a frigate.
With this went a tendency to express himself a good deal more
forcibly than was necessary in Nathan's view, and on this
occasion the object of his choler appeared to be George
Banjo.

The big African was inclined to offer his advice on a number
of matters that were not his proper concern, and despite the
friendliness of his manner this had been known to arouse
resentment at times, especially among his seniors. On this

occasion he had more justification to become involved than not, for even when Mr Clyde was alive he had considered the bow chasers to be his particular charge. Nathan was about to send for Mr Bailey to come aft and report what was amiss when he was distracted by a shout from Tully.

'You can see her from the deck now, sir.'

Nathan joined him at the lee rail, and as they rose on the next crest he caught sight of her through the rain. When they rose again, he had his glass ready. It confirmed his first impression.

'She has fallen off at least two points,' he said to Tully. 'And unless I am much mistook, crammed on more sail.'

If he did not follow her she would widen the gap between them, but it would bring them almost stern on to the wind and he knew his ship well enough to know she would not like that one bit. Nor would Mr Perry.

Nonetheless he gave the order to the quartermaster and waited in some concern for the ship's response. It was not long in coming. He felt the stern lift high under the following sea, and as it travelled under her keel the foresail drove the bows deep down into the trough. He almost heard the timbers groan under the weight of water but up she came like the thoroughbred she was, throwing the spray back from her mane. And at once the next wave began to lift her stern. They were in for a rough ride, but he could deal with that: his concern was for something else. He staggered over to the larboard rail, which still just about favoured the weather, and peered forward. As he had feared, on this new course the foresail was taking the wind from the foretop staysail and even the jib was beginning to flap wildly.

'I think we had better clew up on the weather side, Mr Perry,' he instructed the sailing master, who nodded urgently and lurched forward with his speaking trumpet. This eased things a little so far as the sails were concerned, but the next time Nathan saw the chase he felt the distance between them had increased. He looked to the sky with its scudding clouds. The light was fading fast and there had been little enough to start with. It would be dark in an hour or so.

He was aware of a presence at his shoulder.

'Yes, Mr Bailey?'

'Beg pardon, sir,' said the officer, touching his hat, 'but I think we can reach her with the bow chasers.'

Do you indeed, Nathan thought. And if we could, do you not think I would have had them firing by now? He curbed the inclination to utter this rebuke, however, and looked forward along the gun deck. He supposed that technically speaking it was true, certainly when they rose on the crests, but the likelihood of hitting anything at this range was minimal. And with the amount of sea coming over the bows he doubted they could keep the powder dry enough to get a shot off.

'What does Mr Banjo think?' he asked.

He was not sure why he said this. It was partly because he had thoughts of making the African up to ship's gunner in place of Mr Clyde, but it was possible that he wanted to put Bailey in his place. He instantly regretted the remark, but it was out now and he could only wait with a set expression for the officer's response.

'Banjo, sir? What does it . . .' But then he thought better of it. 'I am afraid I have not thought to consult him, sir.' The level of irony was just on the side of acceptable.

'Well, Mr Bailey, I appreciate your zeal, but I think we will wait until we close with her.'

But they never did close with her. With the wind directly astern of her the corvette was a better sailor, and certainly a faster one than the *Unicorn*, and within the hour, with darkness falling, Nathan conceded defeat.

'Bring her back on course, if you will,' he instructed the quartermaster with a reluctance that was almost entirely feigned, for he had had enough of this. He was very much intrigued, however, to know what a French ship-of-war, and a national ship in all probability, was doing so far down the coast of Italy. It might be that she was making for Naples or even heading round into the Adriatic. Or she might be bound for the southern shores of the Mediterranean to play havoc with the Levant trade. Either way, Nathan had a strange feeling he would see her again.

'And might I furl the fore course, sir?' Perry put in quickly, doing his best to hide his satisfaction, for the prospect of prize money was never enough to reconcile Mr Perry to the ruin of his precious sails.

'As you wish, Mr Perry.'

And so they ran to the south-east under storm staysails for most of the night until the Tramontana burned itself out in the early hours of the morning. Dawn found them in an empty sea: empty, that is, of anything more interesting than the *Bonne Aventure*, limping a mile or so behind with her foretopsail blown to pieces and her mainyard sprung. But the wind stayed fresh enough for them to continue at a goodly pace towards the Bay of Naples, and at six bells in the forenoon watch they sighted the twin peaks of the volcano to the south-east, with a long plume of cloud trailing away to windward.

'A fine landing, Mr Perry,' Nathan congratulated the sailing master; and to the officer of the watch, he said: 'Break out the ensign, Mr Holroyd, and let us have the Jack at the bow.'

And let us hope we are still welcome, he said to himself, as he stared out from the quarter rail at the smoking volcano off their larboard bow.

Part Two
The Sirocco

Chapter Nine

Venus and Vesuvius

———◦•◦———

Nathan watched from the quarterdeck as the city emerged from the haze to the south-east. Naples, the largest city in Italy. It sprawled almost voluptuously in the early afternoon sun, curving in a wide crescent along the shores of the bay that bore its name, flanked by the mountains of Vesuvius and Posillipo to north and south.

It was the first of these that naturally occupied Nathan's attention on their approach from the north, for though it was not the first volcano he had seen, it was by far the most active. The cloud they had observed from far out to sea was now revealed as a thick pyre of smoke, and he could see the smouldering ashes it had dumped along the rim and several small fires they had started in the sparse brush among the rocks and scree. The last eruption, only a few years before, had blown the top right off the mountain, leaving a distinctive crater between the two peaks, but there were few signs now of the devastation it must have wrought. The summit rose out of dense forest, and its lower slopes were clothed in the most abundant crops and vegetation: fields of golden wheat interspersed with olive and citrus groves and the more vibrant green of vineyards and other crops he could not name. And there were several very pretty villages close to the shore.

His concentration then shifted to Naples itself, and he thought it the most handsome city he had ever seen, at least from the sea. Every building appeared to have been painted a different colour, as if a demented artist had exhausted every variation of his palette in a bid to rival the extravagance of his surroundings. The classical shades of Antiquity were the most prevalent, but along with the Venetian reds and Egyptian blues, the saffrons and ochres and indigos, were more delicate hues: of pink and cream and lilac, like shells littered upon the shore. And presiding over this display, in all its majesty, the formidable ramparts and towers of Castel Sant'Elmo on the heights above, compensating for its grey solemnity with a great array of flags and banners bearing the arms and gules of the House of Bourbon.

But there was something disturbingly unreal about it all, something *wrong*. It took a moment or two for Nathan to realise what it was. It was the second largest city on mainland Europe, its population only a little less than that of Paris, but from the sea it appeared strangely deserted. Nothing moved, either on the shoreline or on the heights above. It seemed, indeed, as if the entire populace had been overwhelmed by an invisible gas released by the volcano on its northern shoulder.

He transferred his gaze to the harbour and its projecting mole where a fair amount of shipping could be seen. Studying it through his glass, Nathan made out the gunports of several ships-of-war – a two-decker and three – no, four – frigates, presumably of the Neapolitan Navy – but he could espy no movement either aloft or alow. If there were people aboard, they were afflicted by the same fatal torpor that had over-whelmed the city itself.

But even a city of the dead – if not actively engaged in hostilities with His Britannic Majesty – had to be accorded the customary respects, and in this case a 21-gun salute was in order for King Ferdinando of the Two Sicilies. Nathan considered sending one of his officers ashore to certify that the courtesy would be returned, for it would be a grave insult if it were not, but this would involve a long delay, so with some trepidation he decided to take a chance. To his relief, after the seventh cannon had been discharged in the general direction of Vesuvius, an answering salute issued from the quaintly named Castel d'Uovo, the Castle of the Egg, guarding the entrance to the harbour, and shortly after a launch could be seen leaving the two-decker and proceeding across the bay towards them.

'I suppose I had better make myself presentable,' Nathan sighed, for he was dressed in his shabbiest uniform and there were various formalities to be observed as the representative of King George.

Indeed, the approaching launch brought an officer of the Neapolitan Navy with the compliments of Admiral Caracciolo and an invitation for the *Unicorn* to moor in the lee of the flagship and for her Captain to come aboard. The occasion was more pleasurable than not, however, for the Admiral proved to be a hearty but courteous host who had fought for the British during the American Independence War and spoke enough English for them to converse amiably over a full-bodied wine from the Campania. He was eager for news of the war in the north – he had only lately heard of the French invasion of Tuscany – and Nathan did his best to present as agreeable a picture as was possible from the British point of view. He was not entirely sure if he had succeeded in this – it was not an easy task – but he was sent on his way with the Admiral's blessing

and an escort of Neapolitan Marines to conduct him to the
residence of the British Envoy, a former monastery known as
Palazzo Sussa, on the fashionable hillside of Pizzofalcone high
above the port. They also found him a sedan chair and four
stout chairmen to carry him there, for it would be hard going,
the Admiral warned him, in a full-dress uniform, and he would
be importuned by every beggar and *lazzaroni* in Naples, of
which there were not a few.

This opinion was confirmed by the view Nathan was
permitted from the windows of his new conveyance as it bore
him through the streets of the city. For here was a vastly
different perspective from that provided from the quarterdeck
of the *Unicorn*. It was as if he had turned over a stone to find
the cavity beneath teeming with secret life.

Pitiful figures, barefoot and in rags, sprawled in the shadows,
many of them blind or crippled, exhibiting the most alarming
sores and deformities, and exerting themselves only to extend
a scrawny hand towards the passing vehicle; and even those
who were not obviously beggars looked desperately in need of
alms. Nathan had never seen such poverty, not even in some of
the more degraded areas of London or Paris or even the ports
of the Caribbean. And the buildings, he saw, were in as parlous
a state as the people, with crumbling façades and grim shuttered
windows and the occasional line of washing hanging across
some dingy courtyard. The bright colours – and the large
frescos of Heaven, Hell and Purgatory which decorated many
of the walls – could not disguise a uniform squalor, the tenements rising up so high above the streets that no sunlight
penetrated the gloomy canyons between, and only the pigs that
rooted among the filth provided evidence of gainful employment.

Then, as Nathan proceeded up the hillside, he observed a
distinct improvement. There was still not much sign of life,

but the streets became broader and cleaner, the tenements gave way to elegant villas in luxuriant gardens – and the beggars vanished, as if they were swept up regularly and deposited with the rubbish on the meaner streets below. The higher they climbed, the more substantial were the buildings, until at length they reached the official residence of the British Envoy: the Palazzo Sussa, a substantial three-storey mansion set in a grove of myrtle trees just below the walls of Castel Sant'Elmo.

Nathan was deposited at the gate where he was greeted by the Envoy's secretary, Mr Smith. Sir William was expecting him, he said, having observed the arrival of the *Unicorn* from his study. He led Nathan through a surprisingly crowded antechamber – 'people trying to sell things,' he murmured mysteriously in Nathan's ear – and up a flight of stairs to a more elegant reception room on the first floor where the Minister was waiting to receive him.

Sir William Hamilton, His Britannic Majesty's Envoy Extraordinary and Minister Plenipotentiary, was a tall, thin, rather frail-looking gentleman in his mid-sixties whose air of studious repose put Nathan somewhat disturbingly in mind of a stick insect or a praying mantis – an impression enhanced by his long aquiline nose and a pair of deep-set eyes that subjected Nathan to a keen regard from beneath craggy brows. He even moved like a mantis, Nathan thought: stiffly and with creaking limbs, but with a peculiar grace, as if in time to a very slow drumbeat.

'Welcome to Naples, Captain,' he greeted Nathan, with an elegant bow and an ironic eye, as if mocking both the place and his own pretensions. But it became clear in the course of the conversation that whatever he thought of his position, he was entirely in love with the place, and the air of parody was something of a shield against those who might not share his enthusiasm.

They sat at a table in the enormous bow window with its astonishing view of the bay – 'though one cannot see Vesuvius very well,' Sir William complained, 'unless one ventures on to the balcony.'

Nathan made the appropriate remarks, but his attention was primarily directed to the room they were in, for it contained an astonishing number and variety of objects. Sir William, it transpired, was a devoted, even obsessive, collector. His particular interest was in Etruscan vases, he explained in answer to Nathan's query, but he also purchased paintings and artefacts, curios and antiquities – virtually anything, indeed, that caught his acquisitive eye. Even the volcano itself, whilst it could not be carted away wholesale, appeared to have been broken into small pieces for transfer into the rooms of the Palazzo. Glass cabinets displayed pieces of lava and pumice that Sir William had personally gathered from sixty-five visits to the volcano – he provided the number with a zeal for exactitude that was something between that of the scholar and the schoolboy – and bottled samples of salts and sulphurs he had harvested from the smoking crevices inside the crater itself.

'The last major eruption was, as you probably know, in ninety-four,' he told Nathan, 'and it has been bubbling and simmering like a witch's cauldron ever since – at times somewhat alarmingly, though I confess I am more charmed than distressed by the display.'

He was, alas, too old to continue these visits, he regretted, and could now only observe the volcano from a safe distance: 'But there is an excellent view from the observatory I have built on the second floor. I would show you myself, but I fear I must devote some time to the study of these documents you have brought me from His Excellency, for we may have need to discuss some of the intelligence he has sent me. However, my wife will be very pleased to entertain you while I am away.'

With this, he led Nathan through the house, pausing frequently to deliver a brief history of some object or painting he had acquired, until they came at length to the room in which he had installed the pride of his collection – and from Nathan's point of view the most extraordinary of all.

He had not supposed her ladyship to be an exact female replica of the Minister Plenipotentiary, but he was prepared for a woman of a certain age and station – something between a duchess and a clergyman's wife, perhaps – and had braced himself accordingly. But this wind was from an entirely different quarter and of a freshness and vigour that quite took his breath away. He was confronted by a vision of loveliness in white muslin and lace with a wide blue sash beneath her bosom and a velvet choker about her throat; heart-shaped features framed by a mass of chestnut to auburn curls, blue eyes that flashed with lively interest, and a perfect mouth formed in a brilliant smile of welcome as she rose from the couch on which she had been residing. She was no more than half Sir William's age.

'This is Captain Peake, m'dear,' announced her indulgent spouse. 'Commander of the frigate *Unicorn*.'

'Never!' declared the vision forcibly.

Sir William regarded his visitor with concern as if a recent acquisition had suddenly been exposed as a fake, but before Nathan could think of a convincing proof of his identity, her ladyship issued a gurgling noise which he took for laughter and exclaimed: 'Pray do not take offence, Captain! I only mean that you looks so young, don't 'e, Sir William?'

'General Wolfe was but twenty-four when he fell at Quebec, my dear,' the Ambassador pointed out tolerantly.

'Oh Captain, what must you think of me?' enquired Lady Emma with another giggle. She sat down again and patted the cushion beside her. 'Come and sit yourself down. You must 'ave 'ad a weary time of it, climbing up that 'ill in all that gear.'

Nathan confessed with a faint blush that he had been carried.

'Well there now,' Sir William declared with a smile, as if the question had been resolved to everyone's satisfaction. 'I will leave you to become better acquainted.'

This was a prospect which Nathan found by no means repugnant, for his hostess had the face of an angel and the body of a Venus, but her speech and manner was as startling as her appearance. She spoke in a mysterious brew of accents in which he detected both the North Country and the Cockney, and a variation of the genteel that appeared to be entirely of her own invention; all of which was expressed with a theatricality that exceeded anything he had witnessed upon the stage, and with frequent references to the Neapolitan Royal Family and other notables with whom she claimed to be intimate.

'Oh Cap'n, you must hexcuse me for I am all of a dither,' she assured him at the commencement of their discourse, 'only I'm just this minute back from attendin' upon 'er Royal 'ighness at Caserta, an' when I 'ears the guns I rushes in to Sir William screamin' that the French 'as landed.' She gave howl of mirth at her own folly. 'An' 'e's at the winder with 'is telescope and says as 'ow I'm not to be afeared for 'tis our gallant boys in blue what 'as come to bring us cheer and I'd best get meself ready to receive 'em, for they'll be up 'ere in two shakes of a dog's tail.' She gave out another alarming shriek. 'But what am I thinkin' on! You must be dyin' o' thirst – 'ow about a cup o' tea?'

She was so desperate to impress, her affectation so preposterous, Nathan found it difficult to feel at ease. Gradually, however, he began to unwind, for behind the gushing pretence was a genuine warmth and friendliness – and a desire to be liked – that could not but move him to sympathy. And as he relaxed, so did she. She insisted he call her Emma, as did all her intimates, and as their conversation progressed from the trivial to the more substantial, she revealed herself to be a shrewd judge of character and of politics, so that after an hour in her company, he felt he had learned more of Naples and the ruling House of Bourbon than if he had been briefed by the most eloquent of diplomats. She also talked, when prompted, about herself.

She had been born and raised in the North Country, in a small village in the Wirral, just a few miles from the port of Liverpool, but had moved to London in her teens, she informed him, working in a variety of households – she did not say in what capacity – but also as an artist's model. Nathan expressed genuine interest in this, for Sara, too, had posed as a model in Paris, and he found the prospect both titillating and alarming. It was mostly boring, Lady Hamilton confided, and imposed such a strain upon the body, 'keeping still so long and twisted about like the Scavenger's Daughter, not even the 'ores would do it.' But she had become the model for George Romney, whose fame as a painter was then growing and whose portraits of her had been so widely admired they had brought her to the attention of some of the most discerning collectors and connoisseurs in London – Sir William, Nathan assumed, being among them. And now here she was, she declared, with another giggle as if it was the greatest joke in Creation.

She was still prevailed upon to pose at times, she told him, and there were several of her portraits about the house, if he would care to see them. Nathan was nothing averse and though – rather to his disappointment – they were all clothed, they were so enchanting and revealed her in so many different moods and situations, he was persuaded that she would be remembered as one of the great beauties of the age.

At the completion of this tour they found Sir William awaiting them with one of the despatches Nathan had brought from Corsica.

'The Viceroy informs me that you are to proceed to Venice to communicate with Admiral Dandolo,' he began, somewhat to Nathan's consternation, for this was not information, he would have thought, to be shared with the Minister's wife. Possibly something in his expression indicated this for Sir William assured him, with his thin smile, that he might speak quite freely in front of her ladyship. 'Indeed, it was she who brought me the sad news, did you not, my dear, for she had it direct from Her Majesty who had it from her agents in Venice. I regret to have to inform you that Admiral Dandolo is dead.'

'Murdered!' exclaimed her ladyship in dramatic tones. 'Stabbed to death on the steps of the cathedral.'

'A convent, I believe you said it was, my dear,' Sir William corrected her mildly. And then to Nathan, who had been absorbing this exchange with difficulty: 'I was about to send to the Viceroy informing him of the event. I fear your mission is severely compromised, sir. More than that, it is very likely at an end.'

Chapter Ten

The Beggar King

F our bells into the first watch and Nathan leaned on the quarterdeck rail of the *Unicorn* watching the fireworks. They had commenced with several gouts of flame that leaped skywards from between the twin peaks. Red-hot chunks of rock were projected into the heavens and an enormous black cloud spread out across the sea. Tongues of fire licked the dark underbelly of cloud and a river of molten lava spilled over the rim of the volcano and proceeded with ponderous majesty down the upper slopes.

Even in his current mood, Nathan was impressed.

For two days *Unicorn* had lain becalmed off the mole, sweltering in the midsummer heat, while he puzzled over the various courses of action that were open to him. Or not, as the case may be.

Dandolo was dead. Or was he?

She had it direct from Her Majesty who had it from her agents in Venice . . .

This sounded very like moonshine to Nathan. If the Queen of Naples did maintain a string of agents in the *Serenissima*, which he very much doubted, he considered it unlikely that she would share their intelligence quite so freely with the wife of the British Ambassador.

But it was alarming enough that Dandolo had been spoken of at all.

'Whatever is said between Her Majesty and Lady Hamilton, you can be sure it will be in the strictest confidence,' Sir William had assured him.

Nathan wondered. He was by no means happy about this three-way converse between Sir William, Lady Hamilton and the Queen of Naples, no matter how confidential Sir William considered it.

'Her Majesty holds Lady Hamilton in the highest esteem,' the Minister insisted. 'She consults with her on a great many subjects and attaches considerable value to her opinion.'

Nathan wondered at this, too, but as he had no means of confirming it – or the information about Admiral Dandolo – he continued to stock up with provisions for his foray into the Adriatic.

He had interpreted the phrase *virgo intacta* – in the context in which it was uttered – to mean that he was not to become embroiled in Venetian politics, combined as they were, in some as yet undiscovered way, with sexual intrigue. This was difficult enough, given that he was being asked to bribe a senior government official, but if Dandolo was dead, it became considerably more so. Which was presumably why Sir William was advising him to abandon the mission.

Nathan did not for a moment consider this as an option. Even if the report was true, and he had reasons to doubt it, he still had to deal with the privateers operating out of Ancona.

He had been invited to stay at Palazzo Sussa while he was in port but he excused himself on the grounds that it was necessary for him to remain aboard the ship. The real reason was that he had no wish to be drawn into the intrigues that seemed to be the stuff of life at the Palazzo. But he had dined there on two occasions and had spent a pleasurable few hours being shown the sights of the city by Lady Hamilton in her carriage.

He turned away from the rail and caught the eye of Mr Tully, who was officer of the watch. 'I am going below,' he said, but with a certain reluctance, for the long, lonely night stretched before him.

Gabriel was already below, lighting the candles, for he knew it would be some hours before Nathan retired for the night. There was a packet ready to leave for Corsica as soon as the wind picked up and he had despatches and letters to write. He had already begun a letter to Sara but it was not going well. He had stopped in the middle of a description of Lady Hamilton and crossed it out as being both too critical and too enamoured. It sounded as if he was falling in love with the woman, if only he did not have a haughty distaste for her manner of speaking.

He tried a description of the city instead.

When I first arrived I thought it a City of the Dead. It transpired that this was because it was Siesta, which is observed as zealously in this part of Italy as it is in Spain, but at certain times of the morning and early evening it is as lively a place as any I have seen. The streets are full of lazzaroni, *a term which is used to describe the great mass of common people and which I took at first to mean the Lazy Ones, but though many are beggars, most work as messengers or porters or do all manner of odd jobs about the city, and the term approximates more to the Sans Culottes of Paris, except that they are said to be fanatically loyal to the Monarchy. If this report were to prove ill-founded I would not give two figs for the survival of the House of Bourbon, as they are a powerful presence and number above 50,000, I am told. King Ferdinando, however, is a very different creature from his cousin, the late King of France. Unlike that unfortunate he does not remain aloof from his subjects but appears to enjoy their company, especially the lowest amongst them, mingling with them on the streets and sporting with them, so much so that he is known as the Beggar King, or King Big Nose.*

Nathan paused for a moment's thought, for most of this information had come from Emma, Lady Hamilton, and he was not sure how much of it was true. She was a fanatical monarchist and may have exaggerated the King's popularity. But certainly she had painted a colourful picture. He smiled fondly at the recollection.

'Whenever 'e's bin out fishin' 'e goes down the fish market wiv 'is catch an' flogs it, same as the ordinary fisher-folk. As God's my witness, I swear it's true . . .' She had observed his look of disbelief. 'You see 'im there most mornings. Or 'e'll be down in the 'arbour sportin' with the *lazzaroni*. 'E pushed one of 'em in once, clownin' around like, and when 'e finds 'e can't swim, 'e strips off 'is coat an' dives in after 'im. Speaks their lingo, too, same as I do.'

And as if to demonstrate this, she had leaned from the carriage to exchange insults with a group of *lazzaroni* lounging on the street corner, informing Nathan that they were the King's regular hangers-on and were ready to die for him if the French tried to turn him off his throne.

But if there was any truth at all in her account, it seemed astonishing to Nathan that their loyalty could be bought so cheaply, for some of the images he had seen were disturbingly similar to reports of Paris before the Revolution. Gilded carriages racing about the streets preceded by large dogs scattering anyone and anything in their path, priests and monks in long processions bearing icons of the Virgin Mary or the saints, queues of women outside the bread shops, immense wealth and luxury contrasting with the dirt and the poverty – and a tendency for a mob to gather at the drop of a hat.

And then, of course, there was the coincidence of the two Queens – for Maria Carolina, Queen of Naples, was the sister of Queen Marie Antoinette.

'An' they was that close,' Emma informed him, 'that when they was becomin' young ladies, their mother, the Empress Maria Theresa, forbade 'em to ever see each other again, 'cos she said as 'ow they was a bad influence on each other. An' they never did,' she added tragically, he eyes filling with tears, 'for one is sent off to marry the King of Naples and the other is sent to France – and the 'orrible fate that awaits 'er there.'

It transpired that Emma had visited Marie Antoinette in Paris as a special emissary for her sister, when she had travelled back to England with Sir William before the war.

'"Give 'er this missive," says she, 'anding me a letter, "an' tell 'er as 'ow I still loves 'er and as 'ow she is never from my thoughts." The times I've sat with 'er,' she went on, 'when she's 'eard the news from France. Of 'ow 'er beloved sister was spat upon by the mob an' thrown into prison. And the dreadful accusations that was made concerning 'er. I was with 'er the day she 'eard the news of 'er death on the guillotine. I will not say the words she uttered to me, for it was in the privacy and the passion of 'er grief, but I will tell you this – that woman will not rest until she 'as avenged the death of 'er sister. Vengeance! That is all she lives for – that and 'er beloved children. An' now the King 'is Majesty wants peace with

France. Wants 'er to turn against 'er own family in Vienna. 'Ow do you think she feels about that?'

Nathan took up his quill again.

The King has very little interest in the practical business of government, devoting much of his time to the hunt and other earthly pursuits, whereas Queen Maria Carolina plays a very active role in his Council, particularly in matters of foreign policy, and this has aroused as much resentment in certain sections of society as did her sister Marie Antoinette in France.

He paused again, wondering if this was quite what he should be writing to the woman he loved and, more to the point, whether it was what she wanted to hear. It was more in the nature of a despatch than a love letter. But he felt inhibited in what he wrote to her, unsure of her feelings towards him, and – for that matter – of his towards her.

All of which reminds me very much of my time in Paris, he wrote, *when first we met, though, of course, the circumstances were very different.*

It had been Christmas when they met. Cold and wet. And the mob had been trying to string him up from a lamppost because he was not wearing the Revolutionary colours. And then later, when he had gone to her house, it had been snowing. But he felt the same sense of threat now as he did then, of being in a city and a nation that was on the brink of some great cataclysm; and the same sense of being caught up in the treadmill of history, and being unable to leap off or change its direction.

Emma had read his palm at Palazzo Sussa. A piece of nonsense, he had thought it. She had required the time and place of his birth and then embarked on some flummery about

his astrological sign and the winds that blew him hither and
thither, of rising waters and a bridge, and of how his fate was
bound up with the life of one who was King or Emperor, or
shortly to become one.

Of course it was. All their fates were bound up with the
lives of kings and emperors. That was the tragedy of it: that
they could not live their own lives free of such concerns. That
he could not spend the day with Sara at Cuckmere Haven with
a picnic, and no cloud on the horizon, no shadows of war or
conspiracy, no thoughts but of each other and the play of
sunlight upon the sea.

She must be in England now, he thought. But there was little
likelihood of hearing from her until he rejoined the squadron.
And by the time she received this letter – if he ever sent it – he
might be anywhere. Or dead.

A knock on the door, followed by the chubby features of
Mr Anson.

'Beg pardon, sir, but Mr Tully sends his compliments
and there is a launch come out from the shore with a message
for you.'

Nathan frowned. It was late to be receiving messages from
the shore. He took the letter and broke the seal. It was
from the British Minister. The King and Queen of Naples had
sent an invitation to Sir William and Lady Hamilton to join
them at their hunting lodge at Portici – and to bring Captain
Peake with them.

They picked him up at first light at the shore end of the mole
– so as to arrive before the sun became too hot, he was informed.
They were in three carriages – Sir William in the first with
Nathan and Mr Smith; Lady Hamilton in the second with her
maid, and her companion Mrs Cadogan, who was said to be
Emma's mother; and more servants in the third, for though

this was meant to be an informal visit, Sir William always travelled in style, Emma had explained to Nathan, adding in a conspiratorial whisper, 'On account of 'im bein' of royal blood.'

Nathan had expressed proper surprise at this announcement. He was aware that Sir William had been a kind of foster-brother to King George when they were both children, but not that they were linked by a more substantial bond. Oh yes, her ladyship had assured him, Sir William being the natural son of King George's father and his royal mistress the Duchess of—. Personally, Nathan could not see the faintest resemblance between the Praying Mantis and Farmer George, but stranger things had happened at court. It might even be the reason Hamilton had been sent to Naples: out of sight and out of mind.

He sat opposite Nathan in the carriage, shading his eyes with one elegant hand. He might have been asleep. Certainly, he was very still. He wore a blue silk suit with cream silk stockings and handsome shoes with large silver buckles. Possibly this was the proper rig for a diplomat attending the court of a prince, but he looked like a man from an earlier age – which in many ways, he was. Somewhat incongruously, he wore a rather louche wide-brimmed hat, such as the Revolutionists wore in Paris, presumably against the sun. Emma, in the carriage behind, was dressed in her hallmark muslin with a broad crimson sash at her waist and a kind of shepherdess hat tied with red ribbon. She looked slightly odd but ravishing. Nathan sweltered in his full-dress uniform, even this early in the morning.

Portici was on the slopes of the volcano – slumbering now after its exertions of the night; a gentle plume of smoke feathering out to sea – and to reach it they climbed through the fields and vineyards Nathan had viewed on his arrival from the deck of the *Unicorn*. At closer quarters, they appeared even more luxuriant than they had from out in the bay: oranges, lemons and figs hanging thick on the bough and the vines strung along trellises with tall cypress trees and magnificent elms planted at regular intervals either to provide shade or simply because someone thought they added to the visual effect. Certainly the whole landscape was so ordered and graceful it could have been sculpted by a master hand: oddly so, given the wild, unpredictable nature of the giant who presided over it. The dead city of Pompeii was not far from here, preserved as in aspic by a sea of lava and a cloud of deadly dust.

Nathan watched a file of workers toiling in the rising sun under the watchful eye of one of the many Madonnas that had been erected in the fields.

'Yea, though I walk through the valley of the shadow of death,' murmured Sir William who was not asleep after all, but observing Nathan from beneath the shade of his hat.

'Do you suppose they think of it at all?' enquired Nathan, who felt oddly uncomfortable under the Envoy's searching regard, the prey of the mantis.

'I doubt it,' Sir William replied. 'It is as God wills, like so much in their lives.'

He was silent a moment, then he added: 'The Queen once had a plan to make it safe. She brought in an expert who advised her to lop a thousand feet from the peak and to channel the lava in one great river to the sea. She seriously considered it – the labour would not have been a problem in Naples, it would have given the *lazzaroni* something useful to do – but happily it did not come to fruition, like so many other plans.'

'Happily?' Nathan could not help but respond.

A thin smile and Sir William inclined his head in acknowledgment of the jibe. 'For those of us who do not live in its shadow,' he acknowledged, 'but admire its wonders from afar.'

'So even the volcano comes under the Queen's authority,' Nathan prompted him, for he was slightly apprehensive about this meeting – his first ever with royalty – and eager for whatever information the Envoy might care to give him.

'The Queen likes to think so. I am not sure it has been discussed with the volcano.'

A note of censure there? Nathan wondered.

Sir William was still watching him keenly. 'You will find their Royal Highnesses to be the most amiable of sovereigns,' he said, as if divining Nathan's discomfort, 'if not the most gracious. They do not stand on ceremony, especially at Portici. It is the only one of the King's hunting lodges where the Queen is entirely at ease, largely because there is little for His Majesty to kill there.'

'The Queen is opposed to killing?'

'To the killing of animals. I am not sure she raises any objection to the killing of Frenchmen, so you need not fear her rebuke.'

Nathan smiled dutifully. 'I doubt we will do more than exchange the briefest of pleasantries,' he said.

'Oh, I would not count on that. Indeed, I expect the Queen will interrogate you mercilessly. She will wish to know every detail of the support you have been giving to the Austrians in the north. But do not worry; at least she is on our side, which is more than can be said for the King at present.'

Nathan frowned. 'He is opposed to the British interest?'

'I would not go so far as to say that, but his natural disposition is vacillating – inasmuch as he cares about politics at all. He will probably ask your opinion on fox-hunting. No, you will have no problems with either the King or the Queen. The man you must be wary of is the Chief Minister, Sir John Acton.'

Nathan looked surprised. 'He is English?'

'No, strangely, with a name like that. He is French. That is to say, he was born in France, though of English ancestry. He served in the French Navy for a time so you will have something in common. He is addressed as Admiral, by the way, though I do not believe he has ever attained a greater rank than that of lieutenant. He came to Naples to take over the duties of Minister of Marine, which is equivalent to the First Lord of the Admiralty. He is now also the Minister for War and the Minister of Finance, which is why I call him the King's Chief Minister, though there is no official title as such. He is also the Queen's lover.' He smiled at Nathan's look. 'But that is not an official title, either.'

'And does the King know of this?'

Sir William frowned thoughtfully. 'I must suppose he does, though he has never spoken to me of it. I am not sure that he would care very much. There is one thing you should know about the King,' he added after a moment's consideration. 'There has always been a taint of madness hanging over the Spanish House of Bourbon – a curse, one might call it, of hereditary madness and melancholia. For this reason his father, the King of Spain, directed that Ferdinand should not be over-taxed mentally. Indeed, he should be given no schooling whatsoever but be brought up entirely in ignorance. I am not sure if this was a wise decision – I will leave that to your own observation – but it may explain certain aspects of his behaviour which some have found childish at times, even oafish.'

Dear God, Nathan thought, another madman.

'But I am sure he will be quite charming to you personally,' Sir William assured him, smiling. 'And you will be quite – charmed.'

It was barely seven in the morning and the sun barely risen when they arrived at their destination. It was, of course, more palace than hunting lodge. Vast, sprawling and sumptuous, it was built in an eclectic style of Italian Baroque and neo-Classical – and put Nathan uncomfortably in mind of the Luxembourg Palace in Paris, where he had been imprisoned for a while during the Terror.

The King, they were told, was at breakfast, but he had left instructions for Sir William to join him as soon as he arrived. The Minister took off his broad-brimmed hat and replaced it with one more appropriate to his station and led the way into the royal presence.

The King of the Two Sicilies was standing at the far end of the breakfast room throwing food at the servants. They were covered in bits of fried egg and tomato and what looked like porridge or oatmeal, but they continued about their duties, some smiling, some stony-faced, while the King picked his targets and hurled his missiles. It was clearly his idea of a game, for he did not seem to be the least bit angry or ill-disposed towards them. On the contrary, he appeared in the best of spirits. He was using a spoon as a catapult and every time he scored a hit he roared with laughter, while his guests, of whom there were above a dozen, either clapped politely or cheered their approval or carried on eating as if nothing extraordinary was happening.

Nathan stood in the doorway, just behind the British Envoy, and stared in amazement. The King looked up and saw them there and aimed his spoon at them, but Lady Hamilton appeared from behind her husband and shouted something at him in the local dialect and he grinned bashfully and put the spoon down. The entourage, led by Sir William, then advanced and made their bows. Sir William introduced Nathan, in French, and the King made some kind of reply that might have been French but could have been any language on God's earth. He was probably in his mid-forties, Nathan thought, but he looked like a large, fat schoolboy. Apart from his size he was probably the most unprepossessing individual Nathan had ever encountered – the only outstanding feature of his appearance being his long bulbous nose. He seemed to be wearing a nightgown, or a kind of smock, tucked into a pair of pantaloons, and hessian boots. He was without his wig and the little hair he had was short and grey and stubbly. Some of the food he had been throwing had spattered over his own clothing, unless the servants were allowed to throw it back, which seemed unlikely. He did not look at Nathan properly when they were introduced but only in a kind of furtive, shifty way, as if he was shy, or a drooling idiot, but he was attentive enough to Sir William. In fact, he seemed slightly in awe of him.

They sat down to breakfast, not that Nathan felt like any after seeing most of it dripping from the servants or congealing in soggy dollops on the floor, but coffee was served and fresh rolls brought to the table. There was no sign of the Queen. Probably she had more sense than to put in an appearance at a food-throwing event, or perhaps it would not have happened had she been here. The King talked happily enough to Sir William and Lady Hamilton in his version of Italian – at least Nathan assumed it was Italian – but made no further attempt to talk to Nathan; for which Nathan was, on the whole, extremely grateful.

After a few minutes another guest arrived and was introduced as Sir John Acton. He, at least, greeted Nathan with apparent enthusiasm and in perfect English. It was delightful, he said, to have another naval officer at the table. Then, to Nathan's surprise, after addressing a few words to the King, who appeared to have fallen into a sulk, he proposed that he and Nathan take a turn around the garden. Nathan threw a questioning glance at Sir William but he appeared not to have noticed, or if he had, not to care.

'I felt you needed some air,' Sir John explained when they had emerged on to the long terrace at the rear of the palace. 'I certainly did.'

He was a man of about the same age as the Minister Plenipotentiary and somewhat resembling him in appearance, though more of the wasp than the mantis. Like Sir William, he was immaculately attired and bewigged, with silver buckles on his shoes and a silver-tipped cane: a courtier of the old school. But there was also something of the Admiral in him, if only in his brisk, bluff air and a face of broken veins, rosy with wind or wine or both. Indeed, Nathan had a suspicion that he had been drinking, even this early in the morning, and his conversation certainly lacked discretion.

'Well, I trust you have been sufficiently entertained since your arrival in Naples?' he began with the hint of a sneer. Nathan uttered some platitudes about the city and its surroundings which he interrupted impatiently: 'But what think you of the real wonder of Naples?'

'You mean Vesuvius?'

'Vesuvius be damned; I mean Venus, my boy. Lady Hamilton. Is she not the Eighth Wonder of the World? Has she shown you her Attitudes yet?'

Nathan confessed politely, but with some mild embarrassment, that he did not know what Sir John was talking about.

'Why then, I will not spoil it for you. I am sure she will not leave here without a show – the King will insist upon it. But you have not said what you think of her. Surely she has made some impression upon you?'

'I – why, she has been very kind . . .'

'Oh, I do not doubt it. She has the good nature and easy manners of a barmaid.' Nathan was at a loss for a reply but the Minister did not appear to expect one. 'Her real name is Amy. Amy Lyon, that was her maiden name, a blacksmith's daughter from, I forget precisely where, but like many a comely wench from the provinces she was soon attracted to London where she found employment in a number of establishments frequented by gentlemen of quality. She was the mistress of Sir William's nephew when he first met her . . .' He smiled at the expression on Nathan's face and took it for surprise. 'You did not know that?'

Nathan's expression, in fact, was one of disdain. He wondered if the man was deliberately trying to provoke him and he was preparing a dismissive remark when the Minister continued: 'Oh, do not mistake me. I have nothing but admiration for the woman, or at least, her skill in self-advancement. She is by no means stupid, but she acts upon instinct, not intellect – an instinct for survival.' There was barely a pause before he launched into the next topic, or perhaps it was the same one. 'She has become a great intimate of the Queen, as I expect you know.'

'I did not,' Nathan lied easily. So this is what vexes you, he thought. You have a rival – and a mere blacksmith's daughter at that.

'Oh, but it may very well become your concern, sir. The Queen is very much enamoured of her ladyship. A quite harmless passion, I would say, if their minds and energies did not turn so much to politics.'

So they were here at last, Nathan thought. Barmaids were very well in their sphere, even when they married into the quality, but when they became involved in politics . . .

'Lady Hamilton is of a . . . theatrical bent, as I expect you have noticed. Everything about her is artifice – a performance – and she loves to think that she occupies centre stage, or has some significant influence upon the people that do, like one of Molière's clever little maids. And the Queen, of course, has a murdered sister to avenge. So there you have it. Your plot.

Two women and not a brain between them.' He gave an awkward laugh. 'One recalls the phrase of John Knox and his monstrous regiment.'

Knox had, in fact, referred to the monstrous *regimen* of Elizabeth, Mary and Marie de Medici, the three Queens of England, Scotland and France, and for all his invective against them, Knox had never doubted their intelligence. But Nathan did not trouble to contradict him. He listened with increasing interest as Acton arrived at the heart of the matter: 'The conceived ambition of these two ladies is to secure an alliance of the Italian states, led by Naples and Venice, against the French.'

'And is that not in your own interest?' Nathan ventured after a moment.

'In what way would it be in *my* interest?'

'Only that I understood you had been influential in inclining Naples to the British interest.'

Acton arched his brow. 'My interest is the interest of my employers, the Royal House of Bourbon.' Then, after a moment: 'However, it is true that for some time I have considered those interests to be linked to those of Britain and Austria, if only to contain the spread of Revolution. Now . . .' He made a face. 'I think we must play a waiting game. See which way the wind blows. And at present, though you would not know it here, there is a very cold wind blowing from the north. Bonaparte's victories have given many people in Italy a great deal of unease. And if Spain enters the war on the side of the French, which I believe is only a matter of time . . .' He was watching Nathan's face for a reaction. 'Did the Viceroy not tell you this? Oh yes, I assure you it is true. When it happens, the British Admiralty will pull their fleet out of the Mediterranean, for they cannot hope to defeat the combined fleets of France and Spain. And where will that leave Naples?

Where will it leave *you*, my friend, if you persist in your journey to Venice?' He laughed at the expression on Nathan's face. 'Oh, I know all about your mission to the *Serenissima* – there is little that passes me by. But now that you know what has happened to Dandolo, perhaps you have had second thoughts.'

Nathan had tried to keep his face from showing the effect of these several blows, though clearly without success. The information about Spain he could dismiss as pure mischief, or at least speculation, but how did Acton know of his mission to Venice? It could only have come from Sir William Hamilton, or Emma. Unless he had his spies in the British Envoy's house . . . But of course he did. And in all probability so did the French. Acton was watching him carefully, waiting for his response.

'I have my orders,' Nathan replied coolly. 'As you seem to be aware.'

Acton snorted and shook his head. 'Madness,' he said.

Nathan forced a smile and delivered the one quote from Shakespeare he could always remember. ' "I am but mad north-north-west: when the wind is southerly . . ." ' But he was damned if he knew where it went thereafter.

' "I know a hawk from a handsaw," ' Acton finished for him. 'Yes. Quite. And you know what happened to Hamlet.'

Nathan was about to comment that Hamlet was not in the service of King George, when it occurred to him, perhaps a little later than it should have, that it would not betray British interests if Acton thought he *was* having second thoughts and had determined to return to Corsica.

'You may be right,' he conceded mildly. 'We *will* have to see which way the wind blows. Perhaps Sir William will advise me.'

'Oh, I am sure he will, if he has not already.' Acton glanced over Nathan's shoulder. 'Sir William.' He raised his voice. 'What is the plan for the day?'

Nathan, turning, saw the Minister emerge on to the terrace. But he also saw the quick glance that was exchanged between the two men and the terse nod that Acton delivered as if in confirmation of something. But what?

'The King is to go hunting,' Sir William replied when he had joined them. 'And we are to accompany him – with our little bows and arrows.'

'Now there is a surprise. And what has he determined to hunt today?'

'Hedgehogs,' announced Sir William with a sigh.

'So 'ow d'you 'unt 'edge'ogs?' enquired Emma of Nathan at the end of a long and trying day.

'With difficulty,' Nathan replied, collapsing in the chair beside her. He had shed his uniform coat and stock but his shirt was soaked with sweat and his feet ached cruelly. The King's normal method of hunting, he had been informed, was to stand in a brick enclosure, to safeguard his royal person from harm, while a small army of dogs and beaters drove the game towards him until they were close enough for him to fire upon them with the battery of guns he had assembled. Hedgehogs apparently being regarded as a low to negligible threat, the King had ventured outside his hide and forsaken the guns for a bow and a quiver of arrows, but his sport on this occasion had been limited by a regrettable tendency on the part of the game to roll itself into a small ball and refuse to move. The bearers had been compelled to pick the creatures up and carry them into range, but after pinioning several of them with his arrows the King had declared it was poor sport, and after experimenting for a little while by hurling them into the air so the King could shoot at a moving target they had switched to deer, but had been unable to find any.

'But why did 'e want to 'unt 'edge'ogs in the first place?' Emma demanded, quite reasonably.

'Apparently it was suggested to him by some of his friends among the *lazzaroni*,' Nathan informed her. 'And as the hedgehog appears to be the only creature he has not previously hunted and killed, and it is not the season for his usual game, His Majesty thought to chance his luck.'

'Oh, 'e'll try anything, that one,' Emma conceded with her startling laugh, 'but I could've told 'im 'e was a-wastin' 'is time. The gipsies used to 'unt 'em in the Wirral when I was little. They 'unt 'em with dogs, and when the 'otchis roll up into a ball they bash their 'eads in with a rock. Not much sport in that, even for 'is Nibs. An' you wouldn't want to eat 'em, not unless you're starvin'. Not that I ever 'ave,' she added when she saw Nathan's look, 'but me dad did once an' 'e said as 'ow 'e'd never tasted nothin' more disgustin' in 'is life, savin' badger.'

Several questions arose in Nathan's mind but he put them aside for a future occasion when he had the leisure.

'Well, as he did not catch more than two or three, we need not worry about having them for dinner,' he assured her, though privately it would not have surprised him if they had been served up in one form or another.

In the event he had no complaint for they dined on fresh fish and turtle with roast fowl and sweetmeats, washed down with plentiful quantities of wine, and on this occasion none of the food was hurled at the servants, possibly due to the presence of the Queen who was, Emma informed Nathan, a restraining influence.

'When she first met 'im, she said as 'ow they might as well 'ave drowned 'er in the sea,' she had confided to Nathan, shortly before dinner. 'But she goes 'er way and 'e goes 'is, and they 'ardly hever meets except when there's guests to entertain, like now, or when 'e gives 'er a poke, which don't 'appen so much these days, 'im bein' more inclined to 'ave 'is way with the washerwomen at Caserta.'

This was not altogether surprising. The Queen was said to resemble her sister, Marie Antoinette, in looks, but Nathan could see little of the doomed French Queen in her, save for the formidable Hapsburg jaw which they had both inherited from their mother, the Empress Maria Theresa. She was in her mid to late forties but looked older, possibly from the burdens of childbirth – she had brought sixteen children into the world, Emma said, though most had not survived their infancy – and it was said she bore the weight of the state on her own thin shoulders. She was credited with having inspired a Renaissance of the Arts since her arrival in Naples, but following the imprisonment and death of her sister, all her energy and passion had been directed towards plotting the downfall of France and instituting a policy of ruthless repression to prevent the same thing from happening to her. The news of Bonaparte's victories in the north – and her husband's abject reaction to them – had plunged her into deep depression, Emma said.

Certainly she displayed little interest in either the food or the company until, at the end of the meal, it was announced by a functionary that at the gracious request of their Royal Highnesses, Lady Hamilton had consented to perform a selection of her Attitudes. A spontaneous – and enthusiastic – burst of applause followed this announcement, led by the King himself, who uttered several loud whoops. A trio of musicians entered and set up their instruments, the curtains were drawn against the sun and the chairs moved to face the far end of the room where a small tableau had been prepared with screens and candles and a number of props. From where he was sitting, Nathan identified a pair of vases, a goblet, a lyre, a tambourine and a dagger. The musicians began to play – and Emma made her appearance.

She was wearing her muslin robe, but even the muted light could not disguise the fact that there was little or nothing beneath it. Nor, Nathan suspected, was it intended to. She was barefoot and her hair, which fell halfway down her shoulders, swirled around her as she began to dance. Nathan looked quickly towards Sir William but he appeared to be not in the least embarrassed by this performance; on the contrary he watched with the pride of a besotted lover or a doting parent as she took up the tambourine and raised it above her head so that her naked breasts threatened to burst from their muslin confines. Nathan glanced at the King and saw that he was transfixed. Emma clapped the tambourine with her hand, stamping her feet and swaying her hips, moving ever more rapidly about the stage, pausing only to snatch at the goblet and raise it to her lips, staggering now, as if drunk – Nathan wondered if she *was* drunk – until she collapsed to the ground and lay there still as a corpse, or a statue. The music stopped.

'*Bacchante*!' came the cry from the audience and a scattering of applause. The music resumed, but slower now and more sinister as Emma rose from the floor and picked up the dagger. And so it continued. Each time the music stopped, Emma would assume the pose of a statue from Antiquity and the audience would cry out its name. Medea, Iphigenia, Ariadne, Dido, Lucrece . . . With the aid of a few scarves and the props scattered about the stage – and the astonishing contortions of her body and countenance – she took on the attitudes of a range of Classical figures: in one instant a Sibyl, then a Fury, a Niobe weeping for the loss of her children, Sophonisba drinking poison, Agrippina at the tomb of Germanicus, Cleopatra reclining seductively for Mark Antony and then clasping the asp to her bosom. Nathan could hardly have cared less who they were and nor, he imagined, could many of those present. It was not simply erotic – though that was certainly a factor – it was surprisingly graceful and artistic. Emma Hamilton was a natural performer, as gifted a dancer as she was an actor. It was wonderful to watch how swiftly she moved from one tableau to another, exhibiting almost every human emotion, until she brought the performance to a climactic ending with the portrayal of a Neapolitan peasant woman dancing the *tarantella* with castanets.

Nathan remained entranced for some minutes after the performance ended. He was aware that people were talking to him but not of what they were saying nor of his response to them. He caught Acton's sardonic eye upon him but refused to acknowledge it. Then a servant filled up his wine glass and he saw that a note had been left beside it. It contained just three words. *The terras now*. And the single letter *E*.

The terras now? What could it possibly mean? He concealed the note in his palm and looked cautiously about him but no one seemed to have noticed. His heart was beating wildly. Clearly it was an assignation, but what or where were the terras? The curtains had been drawn back a little and the sun was still shining brightly on the lawns outside. Then he realised. The terrace!

He made his way outside. There were others here. Smoking and chattering and admiring the view. But no Emma. He walked to the far end, almost to the corner of the building, and stood there wondering if he had come to the wrong place or mistaken the meaning entirely. Then his hand was seized and he was yanked down the steps to the lawn. He glanced sideways at his assailant. A shawl was thrown about her head and shoulders but there was no mistaking the amplitude of that figure. She led him down the sloping lawn at a run, barefoot and laughing, and through a shrubbery to a kind of summerhouse or folly. She was still laughing when he grabbed her and pulled her to him, covering her face with kisses and feeling the wonderful soft, lovely lusciousness of her through the thin muslin.

'What are you doing?' she said, pulling violently away and looking up at him in apparent alarm. 'What are you thinking of? Be'ave yourself.' And she gave him an enormous whack over the ear.

He staggered back, blushing bright red, though possibly not as red as his ear. His confusion was increased by the impression that for a few seconds she had responded with as great a passion as his own. 'I beg your pardon,' he stammered. 'I thought . . .'

'I know what you thought, you wicked boy.' She pushed him in the chest and made to hit him again. He cowered. 'Go and sit over there and make yourself respectable before the Queen gets 'ere.'

'The Queen?' He stared at her in astonishment.

'Yes. The Queen wants to see you. Thank God she ain't 'ere already.' She looked out of the door. 'Oh Lordy, 'ere she comes now.' She rearranged her curls about her forehead and adjusted her neckline. 'Stop looking like a naughty schoolboy and act like a officer of 'is Majesty what 'as been hentrusted with a vital mission. Oh my God, the bloody nerve of you men!'

Nathan did his best to conform to her expectations, but his ear was singing from the blow she had dealt him and he was still trying to pull himself together when Her Majesty ducked through the low doorway. He leaped to his feet and made his bow but she was already addressing him in a heavily accented French.

'Captain Peake, I apologise for the irregularity of this meeting, but it is necessary to speak with you in confidence on a matter of vital import, and I regret that there is little that does not come to the attention of the wretched French. Please be seated.' She waved him to the bench he had recently vacated and, with some concern for her skirts, took the one opposite. Emma sat at some little distance from her, with a glare towards Nathan presumably intended to remind him of his status as an emissary of King George.

'I apprehend that you have been told of the murder of Admiral Dandolo?' Nathan confined his response to another small bow. 'It is not to be assumed that the news is true,' the Queen went on. 'It may well be a fake report spread by the French – for who can you trust? – but in any case it makes little or no difference to your mission.'

'My mission? Your Majesty, I—'

'Fortunately there are others of the same mind. They will contact you on your arrival in Venice.'

'Your Majesty, I think there has been some misapprehension,' Nathan persisted. 'My mission is confidential, but between these four walls I can assure you that it concerns only the activities of the corsairs in the Strait of Otranto . . .'

'Of course, of course.' A dismissive wave of the hand. 'And I can assure *you*, sir, that the details of your mission were known to us before you left San Fiorenzo. Before they were known to yourself, indeed.' She fixed him with a stern regard as if to say, let us have no more nonsense. 'I must impress upon you, sir, that it is vital to secure Venice for the alliance.'

Nathan spread his hands helplessly and looked towards Lady Hamilton, but there was no support to be had from that quarter.

'And even if we do not,' the Queen continued, 'it is as vital to ensure the resources of the *Serenissima* do not fall into the hands of the French. The empire may be in decline but there are above two million subjects who still owe allegiance to the flag of Saint Mark. Two million, sir. Including some of the best soldiers in Europe. Albanians, Croats, Macedonians. These were the soldiers of Alexander. Think what we might achieve with them. Think what Bonaparte might achieve. And then there is the fleet and the Ionians. No, sir, it is not to be contemplated. But of course you know that. That is why you are here.'

Nathan was reduced to silently shaking his head. The Queen's expression hardened. 'You do not tell me you seriously contemplate returning to Corsica.'

'That is something I must discuss with the British Envoy,' Nathan prevaricated.

The Queen turned her face towards Lady Hamilton. She looked, Nathan thought, like one of Emma's Attitudes, if nothing like as pretty. One of the Furies perhaps.

'Sir William will do anything for a quiet life,' returned Emma mildly. 'He has a sign above his bed that reads "*Ubi bene, ibi patria*" – where I am at ease, there is my homeland. His priority is to ensure that he continues to live peacefully in Naples until he dies. And in the present circumstances he thinks neutrality is the safest option.'

Nathan stared at her in amazement, not so much at what she had said but how she had said it. Her French – unlike her English – was flawless; it should not have mattered, but it gave him a completely different view of her.

'And did neutrality save Tuscany?' the Queen demanded. She was close to tears. 'Did it save Genoa? Is it saving the Veneto? When will these people learn? Did it save France, or my sister, when the King her husband decided *he* would do anything for a quiet life? Pah! It makes me sick.' She turned back to Nathan. 'You will go to Venice,' she said. It was like an order. 'And if Dandolo is dead, then another will take his place. It will be arranged.'

*

It was almost dusk when Nathan returned to the *Unicorn*. He felt as weary as if he had done a full day's hauling upon the ropes, and his brain felt as ill-used as his body. But he knew as soon as he stepped aboard that it was not yet over. The hands appeared sullen and apprehensive and the officers tense.

'What is amiss?' he enquired of Duncan, taking him aside.

'I regret to have to inform you, sir, that one of the officers has been struck by one of the men.' Duncan kept his voice low though every man aboard must have known of the incident. And Nathan knew at once who the officer must be.

'Mr Bailey,' he said.

'Yes, sir.'

Damn him to hell. For striking an officer was a hanging offence.

'And who struck him?' He knew this, too, but he hoped against hope that it was not true.

'George Banjo, sir. I have placed him in irons in the orlop.'

Chapter Eleven

The Consul of the Seven Islands

———◆———

'All hands to weigh!'

At the shrill wailing of the boatswain's pipes the two English men-o'-war seemed to stir restlessly at their moorings. Then came the rush of feet upon the decks as the hands began the laborious process of weighing anchor. Laborious but welcome, at least to the *Unicorn*'s Captain, who watched with grim satisfaction as his ship came alive with running, swarming men.

'Topmen aloft!'

'Ship capstan bars!'

Despite the wide variety of entertainment available ashore – and the antics of the Neapolitan court could not fail to appeal to anyone with the slightest sense of the absurd – Nathan was not at all sorry to be leaving the place; he only wished he could have left his problems with it. He lifted his gaze to the shore. It was barely sunrise and the city, all heedless of this busy, if orderly, bustle, slept on. But perhaps not entirely heedless. Nathan looked up towards the heights of Pizzofalcone and wondered if Sir William Hamilton was watching their departure from his observatory in the Palazzo Sussa, his lovely lady at his side.

'Pin and swift!'

Nathan had taken his leave of them both the night before and he writhed inwardly at the memory, and the look in Emma's eye, when she had wished him bon voyage. *I hope you will take fond memories with you, Captain, of your brief stay in Naples.* Indeed he would, and she knew what would be the most vivid of them in the lonely hours of the night, the saucy witch.

'Heave and rally!'

The hands leaned their weight into the capstan-bars, the messenger slowly coiled round the drumhead, and the cable gave a long groan as they took up the slack. The merest hint of a breeze stirred the still waters and swept away the thin cobwebs of mist lingering in the shallows.

'Heave and weigh!'

A brief clouding of the water at the bow as the heavy anchor stirred from its sandy bed in the depths below, and slowly, painfully slowly to the music of its own complaints and the rhythmic clicking of the pawls, the heavy cable came aboard. It was the only music permitted, at least aboard the frigate, for Mr Duncan frowned upon singing in the King's Navy while the men were at work. But from across the water came the jaunty chant of the shantyman aboard the *Bonne Aventure* where Lieutenant Compton clearly favoured a more relaxed regime.

> *What will we do with a drunken sailor,*
> *What will we do with a drunken sailor,*
> *What will we do with a drunken sailor,*
> *Earl-eye in the morning!*

An obvious choice but no less popular for that, judging from
the lusty chorus as they heaved the capstan round:

> *Way hay and up she rises*
> *Way hay and up she rises*
> *Way hay and up she rises*
> *Earl-eye in the morning!*

Slowly under topgallants and staysails, and with the merest
hint of a breeze from the south-west, the two vessels slipped
from their moorings off the mole. But whether or not they were
watched from the shore, there was one at least who observed
their departure from the sea. As they glided through the silent
anchorage, Nathan glanced towards the Neapolitan flagship
and saw the lone figure on the weather side of the poop deck.
Admiral Caracciolo had risen early to see them off. Nathan
could not help but wonder why – and at the nature of the
missive that had alerted him to their departure. He wondered,
more pointedly, if the Admiral had given orders to have them
shadowed out to sea, but there was no sign of life aboard the
three Neapolitan frigates. Their sails were furled, their flags
flapping idly in the breeze; they might have been moored in
cement.

The two men solemnly raised their hats and exchanged
bows across the half-cable's length that separated them as the
impudent canto of the shantyman rang out across the still
waters:

> *Shave his belly with a rusty razor,*
> *Shave his belly with a rusty razor,*
> *Shave his belly with a rusty razor,*
> *Earl-eye in the morning!*

'Let go the foretops'l. Let go the maintops'l.'

The capstan still turning steadily and the sails filling as the frigate cleared the mole and met the first gentle swell out in the bay. More music now to Nathan's ears as the ship gathered way, and to the groaning voice of the cable and the clicking castanets of the pawls was added the full orchestra of creaking ropes and spars and blocks and the harmonious rush of water along her sides.

'Helm-a-lee!'

'Course nor'-nor'-west.'

Nathan hoped they would get the message, those hidden watchers on the shore, as the frigate's bows came round to the north. Back to Corsica and be damned to the lot of you.

> *Give 'im a poke at Emmy Lyon*
> *Give 'im a poke at Emmy Lyon*
> *Give 'im a poke at Emmy Lyon*
> *Earl-eye in the morning!*

Nathan's head jerked round and he stared back towards the *Bonne Aventure*. It was not unusual to substitute bawdy lyrics for the orthodox version but he was startled to find Emma the subject of a capstan shanty. Was she known throughout the fleet, then – or was this a singular tribute? And how the hell did they know her by her maiden name?

There was a stamp of feet from the forecastle as his own hands joined in the lustful chorus. Mr Duncan reddened and raised his chin to bellow down the length of the gundeck but Nathan caught his eye and gently shook his head. It would reinforce the view that he was soft on the crew; they'd see a harder side soon enough when he dealt with the problem awaiting him down in the orlop deck.

Perhaps this would not have been a priority with other

Captains, but Nathan hated the idea of hanging any man, and besides, there was a personal bond with this one. He had purchased Banjo's freedom with his own money from the Governor of New Orleans when the African had helped to save the ship off the coast of Louisiana, and ever since he had been a valued, if occasionally difficult, member of the crew. He even acted as one of Nathan's unofficial bodyguards when the Captain took it upon himself to lead a boarding party or an action ashore. And now he was in chains in the dark limbo beneath the waterline.

There were two versions of the incident that had led to his arrest.

The official one – related to Nathan by the first lieutenant – was that Banjo had offered his unsought advice to Lieutenant Bailey as to the correct way of frapping the gun-tackle to the barrel of an 18-pounder, and the officer, taking exception to this, had called him a black heathen bastard, whereupon the gun captain had struck the officer in the face with his fist.

The unofficial version – related to Nathan by Gilbert Gabriel in the privacy of his cabin – was that the lieutenant had given a wrong instruction to the gun crew and when George 'being the cod's head that he is' had politely questioned him, the officer had called him a 'fucking black heathen bastard' and a 'horse marine' to boot. Whereupon the gun captain had grabbed him by the collar and thrown him across the deck.

It was not known whether Banjo had objected to being called black, heathen, a bastard or a horse marine – the common shipboard term for an awkward lubberly fellow – or to all four terms of abuse. It did not matter in the least. Nor which of the two versions of the incident was correct. The undisputed fact was that Banjo had struck an officer and the penalty was death.

'Right up and down, sir,' came the cry from the bosun on

the forecastle, and upon the first lieutenant's response Nathan gave a last look towards the shore and informed Mr Duncan he was going below for his breakfast.

A wonderful smell of coffee awaited him in his day cabin and there was a dish of fresh eggs and bacon from the provisions they had taken aboard at Naples. Nathan loaded up his plate and cut himself a hunk of fresh-baked bread, for there were few problems in this world, he had found, that could entirely remove his appetite. He suspected he would have dined heartily of the condemned man's breakfast, though it probably helped if the condemned man was not oneself.

'What would my father do?' Nathan enquired of his servant when he had poured his second cup of coffee. It was a legitimate question, given that Gabriel had been his father's servant for the best part of twenty years before entering Nathan's employ.

'What about?' Gabriel was never at his best first thing in the morning and possibly the problem did not weigh so heavily on his mind as it did on his Captain's.

'George Banjo.'

'Hang him,' replied Gabriel shortly.

'Just like that?'

'Oh, he'd give him a trial first – and give the officer a piece of his mind in private, like as not – but then he'd hang him. He wouldn't have any choice, no more'n you have.'

'He didn't hang you when he had you up for highway robbery.'

'I weren't in the Navy,' Gabriel pointed out reasonably.

Nathan knew most of the *Articles of War* by heart, but he had refreshed his memory as soon as the offence was brought to his attention; Article 22 was, as he already knew, unequivocal:

If any officer, mariner, soldier or other person in the fleet, shall strike any of his superior officers, or draw, or offer to draw, or lift up any weapon against him, being in the execution of his office, on any pretence whatsoever, every such person being convicted of any such offence, by the sentence of a court martial, shall suffer death.

The only let-out, for Nathan personally, if not Banjo, was that phrase *by the sentence of a court martial.*

In theory, the maximum punishment a Captain could order on his own authority without a court martial was a dozen lashes, though this was so often exceeded it had ceased to have any real meaning. But a hanging was a different matter. Nathan could legitimately wait until he returned to the squadron when a proper court martial could be convened with three Post Captains present. But that would mean keeping Banjo in irons for as long as the commission lasted – which could be a matter of months.

The alternative was to convene a drumhead court martial with himself and two of his officers in judgement.

But whatever he did, sooner or later, George Banjo would hang.

'You've spoken to him?'

Gabriel was reluctant to admit it, but he gave a grudging nod. Nathan knew that Gabriel had been as close to him as any of the men.

'How's he taking it?'

Gabriel shrugged. 'How'd you expect?' But then, after a short pause: 'He knows you'll have to hang him.'

'Not before we rejoin the squadron.'

'If I was him, I'd rather hang now than be stuck in chains in the orlop for God knows how long. Worse'n bein' a slave. An' still be hanged at the end of it.'

Nathan gave him a withering look. 'I call it a poor thing when a man may get off scot free for robbery with violence upon the King's highway, and be hanged for striking a man.'

Gabriel remained astonishingly unwithered. 'Aye well, an' there's some would say there's not that much difference between being a highwayman and servin' as an officer in the King's Navy,' he observed coolly, 'but that one may be hanged for it an' the other make his fortune with the blessings of His Majesty the King. Savin' your presence.'

A knock on the door prevented any further discussion of this contentious and potentially treasonable subject, and Mr Lamb made his usual timely entrance. 'Mr Duncan's respects, sir, and we are beyond sight of land.'

'Thank you, Mr Lamb, I shall be on deck shortly.'

He emerged to find the frigate under full sail, but barely heeling with the lightness of the breeze from the south-west. He could still make out Vesuvius and its attendant cloud to the east, but they were well out of sight of any watchers on the shore, even with the advantage of one of Sir William's excellent lenses.

'Very well, Mr Duncan, let us wear ship, and Mr Perry, you may set us a course for the Strait of Messina.'

But as he studied the charts in the master's day cabin, he began to think again. The Strait of Messina ran for twenty miles between the toe of Italy and the island of Sicily, a perfect short-cut to the Ionian Sea. But at its narrowest point it was barely two miles wide. Any ship passing through could be viewed along almost the whole of its length from either shore. The only possibility of evading detection was to make the journey by night or in a thick mist, but the massive amounts of water channelled into the narrows created dangerous currents and whirlpools. So dangerous, in fact, that it had given rise to the legend of Scylla and Charybdis, the two monsters said to reside on either side of the Strait.

Scylla, as Nathan recalled, was a kind of octopus with six long necks and six heads containing rows of razor-sharp teeth, while Charybdis was a whirlpool resembling a huge bladder with a mouth that could swallow a ship whole. The Strait being so narrow, mariners attempting to avoid Charybdis would pass too close to Scylla and vice versa.

The only alternative was to sail round the southern coast of Sicily, staying well out to sea, and this would add hundreds of miles to their voyage. It might take them a week longer to reach Corfu. And their problems would not end there. For within days of mooring in Corfu Town – or Kerkyra as the locals called it – the presence of two British men-o'-war would be known throughout the region. It might effectively curtail the activities of the corsairs, but it would not help *Unicorn*'s quest for prizes of her own.

But perhaps there was a solution to both problems. And the more Nathan thought about it, the more it appealed to the deceiver in him.

He discussed it with his first lieutenant and the sailing master. There was a natural reluctance from Duncan, who hated anything of the irregular and disorderly, but Mr Perry welcomed any alternative to sailing right round the island of Sicily. In deference to Duncan, Nathan waited until the morning watch on the third day out of Naples when they were, by the master's calculations, only a few hours' sailing distance from Castello di Scilla at the northern end of the Strait, but then the hands set to with exemplary, indeed almost distressing zeal. The perfect white stripe along the gunports was painted black to match the rest of the hull, the topgallants struck down and the remaining sails patched with oddments of canvas. More shoddy canvas was hung over the telltale beak of war and the proud unicorn at her bow; the frigate's name was painted over and the name *Gullveig* inscribed in its place with the port of origin given as Tergeste which Dr McLeish assured Nathan was the Old German for Trieste. And finally Mr Duncan's spotless decks were soiled with buckets of slush and other food waste from the galley which the hands took the greatest delight in treading in, just to see the look on the first lieutenant's face, even though they knew there would be long hours of holystoning to restore the decks to their former glory when there was no further need for deception.

Nathan had himself rowed out in the ship's launch to view the result. It would not pass a close scrutiny, but from a mile or so distant he thought it might pass muster. To add to the confusion for the watchers ashore he had resolved to send the *Gullveig* through the Strait first, with *Bonne Aventure* about a mile astern flying French colours and in apparent pursuit. She might even fire a few rounds from the 6-pounders at her bow, he conceded, though woe betide her commander and the gun crew if any came aboard.

And so halfway through the forenoon those putative watchers ashore might have observed an Austrian merchant vessel sailing close-hauled through the Strait of Messina chased by a French privateer which fired successive rounds vainly at her stern. Once clear of the Strait, however, *Unicorn* backed her mizzen and the two men-o'-war proceeded less dramatically around the toe of Italy and began the long haul across the Ionian Sea.

Nathan had set their course for Corfu, the largest of the seven Ionian Islands which lay off the western coastlines of Epirus and Morea, and were the main base for the Venetian fleet. The islands had been settled by the Greeks a thousand years before Christ. One of them – Ithaca – was believed to be the home of Odysseus and the place to which he had been trying to return during the adventures chronicled by Homer in the *Odyssey*. But they had been part of the Venetian Empire for the last five hundred years and were a key element in the *Serenissima*'s vital trading links with the Orient. Apart from his desire to view the Venetian fleet at close quarters, Nathan was also hopeful of meeting with Spiridion Foresti, British Consul to the Seven Islands and a valuable source of intelligence, he had been informed, on the politics of the Most Serene Republic. If anyone knew what had happened to Admiral Dandolo – and the British Ambassador, for that matter – it was likely to be Foresti.

On the morning after leaving the Strait of Messina the wind shifted to west-nor'-west, and for the next few days it did not depart from that quarter, or stir itself to propel them at more than two or three knots, often falling away altogether. There was little to do aboard the frigate, for the normal tasks of swabbing the decks and making everything shipshape had gone by the board in the interests of deceit. But the crew practised frequently at the guns, which had been spared the general air of neglect, and spent their leisure hours fishing or watching the dolphins that sported in the seas around them. Mr Lamb had set himself up as a naturalist and instructed Nathan in the identity and character of the large number of birds that trailed in their wake. Caspian and Slender-billed Gulls were the most common, but they also saw a pair of Glossy Ibis and once, in the distance, a flock of pink flamingos from the Sicilian lakes. In return, Nathan instructed him and the other young gentlemen in their navigation and mathematics, though he was but a poor tutor and was relieved for the most part to leave their education to Mr Perry and the schoolmaster. By night he watched the stars and tried to divert himself from considerations of policy and command and the thought of the prisoner in his chains down in the orlop.

And so at length, on the sixth day after leaving Naples, they came to Corfu.

*

'I fear it is true. Admiral Dandolo is dead. He was murdered on the steps of the Convent of San Paolo di Mare on Ascension Day – the last day of *Carnevale*. Stabbed to death by hired assassins. Which, even by the standards we have come to expect from the Serene Republic, is topping it a bit rich, as they say in the Navy.'

Spiridion Foresti, British Consul in the Ionian Islands, was a man of impressive stature and considerable presence who looked very like John Kemble's Othello on a poster Nathan had seen in Drury Lane. A paler version of the Moor, perhaps, but with the same swarthy, hawk-nosed air of a pirate turned diplomat – who was ready to turn back to piracy the moment it appeared to his advantage. He spoke excellent English with a hint of Wapping – he had served on an English merchant ship for many years in his youth, he said – but he was a native of Zante, the third largest of the Seven Islands, where he had his official residence. Nathan was lucky to find him in Corfu, he disclosed, for he only came here in pursuit of his own business concerns. He had extensive shipping and trading interests throughout the region and, indeed, as far afield as the Levant. Nathan assessed him as an honest rogue. He had warmed to him within minutes of their acquaintance.

His confirmation of Dandolo's death was a blow, though not unexpected.

'Do we know who killed him?' Nathan enquired. 'And why?'

The Consul spread his arms in a generous embrace. 'In Venice, that is like asking why are the streets filled with water and who put it there. It could have been agents of the French, the Austrians, any one of a dozen Italian states – the Papacy or the Florentines are the usual suspects when a knife or poison is involved – or agents of the Republic itself, always assuming the motive was political. But it could as easily have been a crime of passion, or a family feud, or some deadly insult demanding instant revenge. And a deadly insult in Venice can be as trivial as treading on someone's toe. It takes very little to require the employment of a *bravo* in the *Serenissima*.'

Nathan confessed he was not acquainted with the term.

'Nor would you wish to be,' the Consul assured him. 'A *bravo* is a hired assassin – as common in Venice as are chimney-sweeps in London, and almost as cheap.' He topped up Nathan's glass with wine. 'But did you have a particular reason for wishing to meet with him – if it is not to betray a confidence?'

It probably was but Nathan told him anyway. There seemed little reason not to now. 'In the event of a French invasion, Dandolo was prepared to come over to the British,' he said, 'and bring the fleet with him.'

'Ah.' This was clearly news to the Consul. 'Well, in that case we need not trouble ourselves with crimes of passion. If that had become known to the French, or even the Venetian authorities, his life would not have been worth a single *denaro*. But I am intrigued. He offered to bring over the fleet, you say?'

'That surprises you?'

'No, it does not surprise me. Only that someone would take him up on the offer.'

Nathan queried this with a frown, and by way of a reply the Consul rose from his chair and opened the window to the balcony.

'Come,' he said, 'and I will show you.'

The Consul's house was on the waterfront and offered a panoramic view over the harbour and across the North Channel to the distant mountains of Epirus on the mainland. Immediately below them was the little Bay of Faliraki where some twenty or thirty sea-going vessels were moored, including the *Bonne Aventure* in her present guise of a packet bringing despatches for the British Consul – but not the *Unicorn*, which they had left in the sheltered bay of Kassiópi a few miles along the northern coast.

Nathan had glimpsed the masts of several ships-of-war on his way up the Channel from the south, but the Consul's balcony afforded him a far better view. Lying under the guns of the old fortress on the headland were eight ships of the line and as many frigates and sloops, all flying the winged lion of St Mark. The Consul invited him to study them at his leisure through the telescope mounted on the balcony.

When Nathan finally withdrew his eye, Spiridion Foresti smiled at the expression on his face.

'What do you think?' he enquired.

'I think they could never put to sea,' Nathan ventured. 'Not in that condition.'

'Never,' the Consul agreed complacently.

'They have no halyards, no braces, some of them have no yards or topmasts,' Nathan announced in a tone of wonder. 'It is as if they are laid up in ordinary. I think some are without guns.'

'Most of them are without crews.'

'But . . .' Nathan struggled to make sense of this. 'How long have they been like that?'

The Consul shrugged. 'Years, in some cases.'

'*Years?*'

The Consul invited him to re-enter the building. 'You must understand that nothing in the *Serenissima* is real,' he said, when they had resumed their seats and he had filled their glasses. 'All is artifice and illusion. Like *Carnevale*. A mask upon a mask. "*We depend entirely on the idea of Venice that others have of us.*" This was said by the last Doge, Paolo

Renier, who was more of a realist than most, much good it did him. So – we have ships-of-war that can never put to sea, forts that would crumble to pieces the first time they fired a gun, an army without weapons, or the powder to fire them, a Doge who is a mere figurehead, a Senate that goes through the motions of debate, and no one cares. Music, dancing, gambling, theatre and debauchery, they are the chief objects that excite interest. For the rest . . .' He spread his fingers in the manner of a conjuror making an object vanish into thin air. But Nathan's mind was still on the ships.

'Are they all like that?' he asked, jerking his head towards the window and its view across the bay. 'The entire fleet?'

'Oh, I would suppose there are three or four that could take their place in the line of battle, though not in the British Navy. You might find them in Venice or Porto Quieto. As to the rest . . .'

'But have you not reported this?'

'I have. I have reported it to Sir William Hamilton in Naples and to Sir Gilbert Elliot in Corsica.'

'So the Viceroy is aware of the situation?'

A mild inclination of the head. 'Sir Gilbert has been *informed* of it. But he hears what he wishes to hear. The Viceroy is an idealist. A dreamer. He dreams of a united Italy. A bulwark against French expansion. He does not wish to hear, or believe, anything that would shatter this illusion. In this, he is very like the Venetians. If the late Admiral Dandolo tells him the Venetian fleet is the most formidable in the eastern Mediterranean, then that is what he will believe.'

'But what of the English Ambassador in Venice? Surely he . . .'

'Sir Richard Worsley. Yes, well, he is more of a realist, but he has his own – what is the expression – fish in the fire?' The Consul's English was not without its quirks. 'Besides, I have not heard from the Ambassador for several months. Not since the murder of Dandolo, in fact. And he does not reply to my despatches.'

'Could he have been killed at the same time – and by the same people?'

'No.' A firm shake of the head. 'I would have heard.'

Nathan considered. 'You say there are three or four ships that could still take their place in the line of battle?'

'About that number.' The Consul ticked them off on his fingers. 'The *San Giorgio*, the *Vulcano*, the *Medea*, the *Vittoria*. Oh, and possibly the *Eolo*. All of seventy guns or more.'

'And the ships under construction in the Arsenale . . .' Nathan saw the look on the Consul's face. 'What?'

'The Arsenale. The Wonder of the Age. The greatest shipyard, the greatest workforce, the greatest ships. Once upon a time. But now . . . ? Another illusion. I doubt there are more than a thousand men employed at the Arsenale, and most of them have never picked up a tool in anger.' He saw the disbelief on Nathan's face. 'What you must understand is that in Venice places are given to men not according to their ability, but according to their means. Or their birthright. The son of a shipwright will follow him into the trade – after paying his dues – even though he serves no apprenticeship, has no skills at shipbuilding nor any inclination to learn them. He does not even go to work. He simply signs his name in a book and draws his pay.'

'But I was told there are thirteen ships of the line on the stocks.'

'True. So there are. And they have been on the stocks for several years. They were built with green oak from Istria. It was not allowed to weather. And what happens when you use green oak? It shrinks. The ships will remain on the stocks until they rot, or until someone strips them down to the keel and builds them again from scratch, with weathered timber. But I will not see that day, nor will you.'

Nathan was silent for a moment. He did not doubt what the Consul had told him – and he had seen the evidence with his own eyes – but he was reluctant to accept that his mission was entirely futile. Besides, five ships of the line was still a formidable fighting force – in the right hands. Certainly, they must be prevented from falling into the hands of the French.

'Who has been appointed in Dandolo's place? Do we know this?'

But before Signor Foresti could answer, there came a knock upon the door and a servant entered with a message for the Consul's private ear.

'Forgive me,' he said. 'There is something that requires my immediate attention. I will not be long.'

While he was gone Nathan returned to the balcony and resumed his study of the Venetian men-o'-war. He saw nothing to correct his first impression. Those ships would never put to sea, not in the state they were in. Judging from the amount of marine growth and rust on the anchor cables, they had not moved for many months.

The Consul was frowning on his return. 'I have just had report that there is a French ship-of-war moored in Alipa Bay,' he said, 'on the far side of the island.'

Nathan emerged from the realms of speculation to grapple with this new and alarming reality. If it *was* real.

'You are sure she is French?'

'My informant has just come from there. He has spoken to some fishermen who went out to her and *they* were sure of it. She is called the *Jean-Bart* and she is about the size of a frigate, he says.'

Chapter Twelve

The Jean-Bart

───•◆•───

Nathan had but one thought – to return to his ship, and by the fastest route possible. But that meant taking the *Bonne Aventure* up through the Corfu Channel. For which he would need a pilot. And a wind.

There had been a light offshore breeze when he had landed, but it had fallen away to almost nothing. Even if he could find a pilot at such short notice, they would have to tow the brig in the boats – a distance of about twenty miles in the full heat of the afternoon. And there would almost certainly be strong currents running in the narrows between Corfu and the mainland.

'I can find you a pilot,' the Consul assured him, 'that is not a problem – but it will take six or seven hours to tow the brig to Kassiópi. Whereas we could ride across the island in three hours or less, take a look at this Frenchman and rejoin your ship before dark.'

'Ride?' Nathan was so used to living and thinking on water it was often difficult to envisage an alternative form of transport, but he had been told that several possibilities existed and that other people found them quite convenient at times.

'In the meantime we can send a courier overland to Kassiópi to warn your ship to be prepared,' the Consul pressed him. 'If we set out now, we could reach Alipa by late afternoon.'

'We?'

'Yes, I will come with you,' Foresti said with a smile. 'To show you the way.'

While their mounts were being saddled up, Nathan wrote a short note for Lieutenant Duncan apprising him of the situation and requesting him to bring the *Unicorn* westward along the coast 'with all due speed'. This would depend upon the wind but they could meet her part-way, the Consul said, after they had seen what awaited them in Alipa Bay. He showed Nathan on the map. There was a road, of sorts, between Corfu Town and Paleokastritsa, which would give them a wide view of the bay and much of the surrounding coast. From there, a winding mule-track led to Sidari, on the north-west corner of the island, about six or seven miles west of where the *Unicorn* was presently moored.

It all looked very simple on a map. The reality, Nathan suspected, would be very different. He had spent much of his childhood in the saddle – or more often riding bareback across the South Downs – but he had been constantly at sea for over a year now and the prospect of trekking several hours on a pony was not an experience he anticipated with any degree of pleasure.

In the event it was much less of an ordeal than he had imagined. Their ponies were of a breed brought to the island by the Crusaders in the twelfth century, sure-footed and sturdy – and of a placid disposition. They needed to be, given the height and weight of the two men they were obliged to carry. Nathan had shed his uniform coat and wore a wide-brimmed straw hat against the sun, but the heat was intense and the flies a constant distraction – and from the moment they left the town they were overwhelmed by a deafening chorus of cicadas that kept up their din for the entire journey. The Consul's 'road' was little better than a mule-track winding through the undulating hillsides, and the ubiquitous olive groves soon gave way to a dense furze of golden thistle and other hardy shrubs, impregnated with the scent of wild mint and thyme. As they climbed they left the flies behind and encountered more attractive insects, at least on minor acquaintance, and a great variety of butterflies and flying beetles, and as they advanced deeper into the interior they saw remnants of the great oak forests that had once covered the islands, Spiridion informed him, before the Venetians cut them down for their fleets. They were on first-name terms now and the Consul proved an amiable travelling companion, pointing out various features of interest on the way. There were several picturesque villages down in the valleys with whitewashed houses nestling among pretty orchards of pomegranate, pear and fig, while on the craggy summits of the hills they espied ancient monasteries. Catholic for the most part, Spiridion explained, though most islanders were of Greek extraction and inclined to the Eastern Orthodox religion, if any. Most, he said, were happily pagan.

They had been travelling for almost two hours when they glimpsed the sea on the far side of the island, and an hour later they emerged on to a ridge looking down into the turquoise waters of Alipa Bay. And there, anchored off the far point, was their ship. Nathan knew at once that it was the corvette they had seen coming down to Naples.

He observed her for a while through Spiridion's glass. She was moored by the head and several of her boats were out in the bay, though they did not seem to be heading for the shore, or anywhere else that made any sense. After a few moments it dawned on him. He had spent his first years in the Navy on a hydrographical vessel in the South Seas and had done more than his fair share of removing samples of the seabed from a small boat.

'They are taking soundings,' he said.

'Why would they do that?' Spiridion frowned.

There could only be one good reason that Nathan acknowledged, but he said nothing for the present. He was even more anxious now to rejoin the *Unicorn*, for if the corvette remained here overnight they had every chance of coming up with her by first light and she would not escape them as easily as she had in the Tyrrhenian Sea.

It was a little over twenty kilometres to Sidari, Spiridion declared, but they must first rest their ponies. There was a monastery nearby where he was known to the monks and they could give Nathan any information he needed about the coastline hereabouts. Besides, he added with a broad grin, they served an excellent wine.

And so they sat on a shaded terrace overlooking the bay while their horses were fed and watered. The monks brought them bread and olives and a tangy goat's cheese washed down with the wine Spiridion had recommended – a mellow white from their own vineyards infused with a resin of pine. They were Benedictines and the Prior was a Venetian who chatted amiably with them in a mixture of Latin and French, and Nathan continued their conversation privately while Spiridion went to see if their ponies were ready for the next stage of the journey.

'You are planning a retreat?' the Consul quizzed him curiously when he returned.

'One could do worse,' Nathan observed, for it was as peaceful and as lovely a setting as he had found anywhere on his travels, with its view across the vineyards and orchards to the sea. Such a place as Odysseus must have dreamed of, as he fought his way home from Troy.

As the afternoon merged into evening they resumed their journey, pushing their mounts hard now for Sidari. It was about the same distance as they had already travelled, but cooler now as the sun slipped down towards the sea and a slight breeze came up from the north-west – the prevailing wind, Spiridion declared confidently, which would carry them to Alipa Bay before dawn. The cicadas had ceased their frantic chorus and there was a pleasant scent of jasmine and stock in the air which Nathan might have appreciated more, had he not been so impatient to reach his destination before dark. But the sun was low on the horizon and their shadows long on the path ahead when they finally came in sight of the sea. And there was the *Unicorn* creeping along the coastline towards them under as great a spread of sail as its shortened masts would allow.

'My plan is to cut her out,' Nathan informed his officers at a council of war in his cabin, 'under cover of darkness.'

He had given this careful consideration on the ride over from the bay. He was not comfortable with the idea of engaging an enemy in the territorial waters of a neutral state, not if there was any means of avoiding it. It was possible that the corvette had permission from the Serene Republic to carry out a marine survey – she might even be doing it partly on their behalf – and he had been warned by the Viceroy of Corsica to do nothing to offend the Venetians or give them cause to take sides with the French.

'We will hug the coast as far as the opposite headland,' he explained, 'and then send in the ship's boats.'

Once aboard they would cut her cable and send topmen aloft to loose the sails, he said, and then they would steer her out to sea where the frigate would be waiting. But everything depended on them launching their attack in the hours of darkness – and for that they needed the wind to keep up, at least until they reached Paleokastritsa on the opposite side of the bay.

'You may rely on it for a few hours yet,' Spiridion assured them, 'but it may drop a little before dawn.'

'If it does, we will tow her out to sea,' said Nathan, 'but we will need every man we can fit into the boats.'

The ship's boats consisted of the Captain's barge, the launch, two cutters and the jolly boat. Normally, in a calm sea, they would be towed behind the ship, but in the *Unicorn*'s guise as an Austrian merchant trader, all except the jolly boat had been stowed in the waist and covered with canvas. It would take some time to get them into the water and it were best done while there was still some light in the sky. Crammed to the gunwales, the boats could carry about 120 men between them. A large corvette of twenty guns or more would carry about the same number, but most of the French crew would still be asleep below decks – provided the *Unicorn* reached the bay before dawn.

The first lieutenant, of course, begged to be allowed to lead the attack, but Nathan was of a different mind.

'I am sorry,' he said, with entirely bogus regret, 'but I have had the advantage of seeing where she lies in daylight.' This was not the only reason. Duncan was a solid and reliable officer but he was not the man to be leading an attack in small boats off an unknown coast in the darkness. 'I will take Mr Tully as second-in-command,' he said, 'and Lieutenant Whiteley with his Marines.'

'And I beg you will allow me to accompany you, sir,' Spiridion said, 'for I know the coast well hereabouts – and I fought against Turks and Barbary pirates in my time.'

'It will be an honour,' Nathan assured him with a bow, though for all his Turks and pirates, he had no wish to see the

British Consul killed by Frenchmen while under his command.

But there was one other decision he had to make – and it was more difficult.

'I intend to take George Banjo,' he informed the first lieutenant privately.

Duncan frowned. 'I cannot advise it, sir,' he replied. 'In the interests of discipline . . .'

'Even so,' Nathan interrupted briskly. 'Banjo is worth five men in a boarding party. It is absurd to leave him chained in the orlop when we need every man we have got.'

'Very well, sir, but I believe we must inform Mr Bailey.'

'Then be so good as to send him to me.'

Bailey, of course, took it badly. 'With respect, sir, I must register an official protest,' he complained stiffly when his Captain's decision had been put to him.

'I appreciate your concern,' Nathan told him, 'and I will note it in my report, but I am persuaded it is in our best interest. He will be returned into custody as soon as the operation is over. And by way of compensation you may command the large cutter – I cannot say fairer than that.'

He was not sure if the officer regarded this as a reasonable exchange but it gave some small satisfaction to Nathan.

'Fetch Banjo here,' he told Gabriel, when Bailey was dismissed. 'I would have a few words with him in private.'

When he went on deck the men were already armed to the teeth with the usual array of boarding pikes, cutlasses and axes – but no guns. Nathan would take no chances of issuing firearms to the crew for fear of alerting the corvette to their approach with an accidental discharge. He took his own pistols, though, which had caps to prevent such a misfortune and to keep the powder dry, and of course the Marines had their muskets and bayonets. Banjo, he noted, had armed himself with his favourite weapon – a machete he had brought from the swamps of Louisiana with a blade that had been honed to a razor sharpness. He looked none the worse for his incarceration in the orlop deck, but Nathan caught him looking at Mr Bailey once with an expression he did not at all care for while testing the blade with his thumb.

The wind dropped a little after midnight and despite Spiridion's assurance it had fallen away altogether long before dawn. At a little after six bells in the middle watch, Nathan ordered the men into the boats and they left the *Unicorn* becalmed in the middle of St George's Bay. They rowed on in line ahead, led by the Captain's barge, towards the dark hump of Paleokastritsa, with its ancient monastery and the ruins of a Byzantine fortress high on the cliffs. It was a bright, starlit night and when they reached the headland they could see the corvette still in her position off the opposite point. But if the French kept any kind of a lookout they would be able to see them just as clearly as they crossed the mouth of the bay. It would be safer to stay close inshore against the dark backdrop of cliffs, even though it would add another couple of miles to their journey. So they muffled the oars and rowed on, across the narrow mouth of Spyridon Cove and round the long curve of the bay to Kassiópi, where Nathan let them rest while he viewed the enemy at close quarters and made his final plans for the attack.

The *Jean-Bart* was moored by the head, about two cables' lengths off the end of the point. She had lights at her stern and masthead and she had taken the precaution of rigging nets against boarders. Her gunports were closed, however, and Nathan could see no sign of life on the decks. His initial plan had been to seize the quarterdeck and the forecastle, cut the cable and send the men aloft to loose the topsails. Then, even if the French continued to fight on, they could steer the corvette out to sea under the guns of the *Unicorn*. But they had left the

frigate hove to in St George's Bay. They would have to over-
come the entire crew and then tow the corvette back along the
coast. Their best chance of success, he figured, was to secure
the quarterdeck and forecastle and turn the ship's own cannon
against the men in the waist. He had taken the precaution of
bringing cartridge and powder and several bags of grapeshot in
boxes in case none were kept near the guns.

He explained this plan to the officers as the boats nuzzled
together off the headland. Then they made their final approach.

They were within half a cable's length before they heard the
first shouts of alarm, and they covered the last few yards in a
frantic dash with no attempt now at hiding their intent. Nathan
led his barge and the two cutters straight for the quarterdeck
with most of the Marines, while Tully made for the forecastle
with forty men in the launch and the gig. They reached the side
without a single shot being fired, but there was an inevitable
delay while they hacked their way through the anti-boarding
nets. Then they poured aboard with wild yells.

There was little resistance on the quarterdeck. Two or three
of the crew had taken up belaying pins but they threw them
down when they saw the press of armed men swarming aboard.
An officer came rushing up sword in hand, but he was swiftly
cut down by half a dozen men with pikes and axes. Others
battened down the hatch and secured the companion leading
down to the Captain's cabin. But then a great flood of
Frenchmen came pouring up out of the hatches in the waist,
including a number of soldiers armed with muskets and
bayonets. Whiteley had his Marines lined up on the rail pouring
a disciplined volley down into them, but the fire was swiftly
returned, and there seemed to be a desperate struggle going on
up in the forecastle where Tully had boarded with his own
contingent.

Nathan had made straight for the foremost gun on the

quarterdeck with Banjo and Michael Connor, the two biggest men in the crew, and the Angel Gabriel at his back. It was a 6-pounder as he had expected, nothing like the big 18-pounders aboard the *Unicorn*, but it still weighed a good 3 hundredweight, and it took all four of them to cast it loose from the muzzle and lever it round with crowbars to face down into the waist. It was already loaded, as was normal in wartime, with a lead apron over the touch hole to prevent accidental ignition, and Nathan noted with relief that everything else was laid out in tubs next to it — handspikes, sponges and worms, wads and matches, even a powder horn and a lantern. But no cartridges or spare rounds.

Nathan looked about the deck — a certain number were usually kept in special holes drilled in the hatch coamings, but in the darkness he could see no sign of them. Possibly they only sent up for them from the magazine when they were clearing for action. He could not tell if the gun was presently loaded with round shot or grape, but the quickest way to find out was to fire it, and he was about to do so when the door of the companion flew open and a number of men came rushing up on to the quarterdeck led by an officer with a brace of pistols. He discharged them straight at the men at the 6-pounder and Connor fell back across it with a smoking wound in his chest. Nathan drew his own pistols but before he could fire the officer was upon him with his sword. He ducked under one wild slash but slipped on Connor's blood, and he was sprawling on the deck with the officer poised to run him through when Banjo stepped up and took the man's head off at the neck with one slash of his machete. Nathan scrambled to his feet, wiping the blood from his eyes, while Banjo and Gabriel laid about them like berserkers. There was a savage hand-to-hand struggle going on all over the quarterdeck now. Spiridion had his back to the helm fighting off two men with a sword in one hand and an axe in the other. Bailey was calling on the men to rally round him at the stern. Whiteley still had his Marines at the rail but back-to-back now, fighting to keep the French pinned down on the quarterdeck while other of the ship's complement engaged them from the rear. Nathan found the slow match burning on the deck and he stepped up to the gun again and put it to the touch hole.

The cannon turned out to be loaded with round shot and the effect was disappointing, but they reloaded with cartridge and grape brought up from the barge while the fighting continued all around them. The second discharge was far more effective. The grape cut a huge swathe through the crowded deck and it was followed a few seconds later by a second salvo from up forward where Tully had finally gained control of the forecastle. When the smoke cleared Nathan stared down at a waist that seemed to be full of dead and dying men.

Whiteley wheeled his Marines about and they advanced across the quarterdeck with their bayonets, driving the remaining Frenchmen before them to the stern. Several leaped overboard and struck for the shore. The rest threw down their arms. The officer Banjo had killed turned out to be the Captain, and the only officer they could find unwounded was a young ensign who gave Nathan his sword.

They herded the prisoners down into the orlop deck and Nathan headed straight down into the Captain's cabin and blew open the safe with one of his pistols. Their surprise had been so complete that the code book and the Captain's orders were still there, and he stuffed them into his coat pocket to read later. When he went back on deck there was a pale light in the sky and they could see a huddle of people watching them from the headland. There was still not a breath of wind.

'Get the men into the boats,' he instructed Tully. 'They will have to tow us out. The Marines may stay aboard,' he told

Whiteley, 'but they must take a turn at the capstan and haul in the cable.'

'And the wounded, sir?' Nathan looked about him. There appeared to be a dreadful number of corpses lying about the decks and the wounded among them, many crying out for help, French and British together.

'They must have had a doctor aboard,' Nathan said. 'Ask among the prisoners and send him up with four or five members of the crew. And we had better have as many of our own men with them.' He cursed himself now for not thinking of this before, and bringing the *Unicorn*'s doctor and his loblolly boys, but he had thought it would not be long before they were back aboard the frigate. 'Perhaps you would be good enough to take over here,' he instructed Tully, 'for I have business with the Consul below.'

He and Spiridion went through the Captain's orders together.

'It is as I thought,' Nathan said. 'They had orders to take soundings in all the major bays and harbours. Not only at Corfu but at Paxos and Zante.'

Spiridion scanned the document. 'Do they give a reason?'

'No, but I think we can guess.'

'The French mean to seize the islands.'

'A bigger question is why,' mused Nathan.

'It would mean war with Venice.'

'I do not think that would trouble them overmuch, but it would certainly interest the Venetians if they knew.' Nathan ran his fingers through his hair and encountered a sticky mess of blood. He frowned and looked about the cabin. The French had not had time to clear for action and he availed himself of the pitcher and bowl on the Captain's dresser. There was even a mirror, he noted with interest. Sometimes he thought he had joined the wrong Navy. While he was thus engaged, Spiridion had applied himself to the wine store and poured two full glasses from what proved to be a hearty claret.

'I have a mind to go to Venice,' Nathan announced when he had finished his ablutions.

Spiridion looked startled. 'What good would that do?'

'Well . . .' Nathan considered. 'I might find out what has happened to the British Ambassador. He might tell me what happened to Dandolo – and why. The Ambassador might have other friends in high places. We would appear to need them if the French have designs on the Seven Islands.'

'A lot of mights for such a risk,' Spiridion observed. Then, after a moment's reflection: 'It is possible they have made a deal.'

'Who?'

'The French and the Venetians. The Ionian Isles in return for peace.'

'Is that likely?'

'The French have a significant following in Venice, even among members of the government.'

'Well, there is only one way to find out,' Nathan proposed.

'There is never only one way to find out. For you to go to Venice would, in my view, be perfect folly.'

'Why is that?'

'Because Venice is crawling with French agents who would have you knifed the moment you stepped ashore. There are any number of *bravi* who would not think twice about killing an English officer – though they might ask for more than the going rate.'

'I was thinking of posing as an American,' Nathan confided. 'Their relations with the French have deteriorated somewhat of late but they are still counted as neutrals. Or do you not think that would make a difference?'

Spiridion regarded him warily. 'You think you can pass for an American?'

'I have done it before,' Nathan assured him. 'And it was generally regarded as convincing. My mother is an American. It is necessary only to speak more slowly and spit a lot.'

'Well, it may serve,' Spiridion conceded grudgingly. 'But how will you travel? You cannot go in the *Unicorn*, even in her present disguise. She may look like an old tramp from a distance, but she will not deceive the port authorities of the *Serenissima*.'

'I was thinking of the *Bonne Aventure* under an American flag.'

But the Consul shook his head. 'It is not permitted for a foreign ship-of-war to enter the lagoon of Venice,' he explained. 'Besides, what manner of American are we speaking of here?'

'Well, something in the merchant shipping line, I believe. I should have something to trade. Otherwise, I might be a wealthy gentleman embarking upon the Grand Tour.'

'Travelling by sea?'

'There is no reason why not. Though it still poses the question of a suitable conveyance,' Nathan added thoughtfully. He felt a sudden movement as the corvette began to take the tow, and experienced a small measure of guilt at not being on deck to at least give the appearance of command. An apologetic cough at the cabin door alerted him to the presence of Mr Holroyd who begged to report that they had found a doctor, but that he was insisting the wounded be carried below.

'Well, can we not do that?'

'I did not know if you wished to take the risk, sir.'

'I do not think there is a great risk, Mr Holroyd. How many are there?'

It was a shocking number. Twenty-three from the *Jean-Bart*, eleven from the *Unicorn*.

'And the dead?'

'Fourteen Frenchies, sir. Five of our own. And one missing.'

More than in many a battle with broadsides. Almost a third of the corvette's crew dead or wounded.

'One missing?' Nathan repeated.

'George Banjo, sir,' Holroyd replied without expression. 'Two of the hands saw him leap overboard after the French surrender and swim for the shore.'

'Very well. There is no point in going after him now. Log him as a deserter and we will bury the dead when we are well out to sea; I do not want them washed up on shore.' Then, considering that this might sound more callous than not, he added: 'But let us try to ensure there are no more of them.'

'If you insist upon going to Venice,' Spiridion continued when the officer had gone, 'I have a schooner in Corfu Town that might be of some use to you. The Captain is a man called Kyrgyakos. Perhaps not the most amiable of men, but reliable. He will see you safely ashore and perform any translating that may be necessary. The common language of the Venetians is a sort of bastard Latin, though the better-off speak French. I would come with you myself but I have urgent business to attend to in Paxos. However, I still think it is folly. Dangerous folly.'

'Even so.' Nathan shrugged. 'I think it is expected of me.'

'Even though Dandolo is dead.'

'I would not feel I had completed my commission to the best of my ability,' Nathan confessed, 'if I had not explored every possibility of success.'

'Well, I suppose that is very British of you.'

Nathan regarded him curiously. 'Do you consider yourself to be British, Spiridion?'

'No, my friend, I think of myself as a Venetian, and sometimes a Greek, and sometimes, when I have been exceptionally clever, or devious, a Levanter.'

'I thought that was a wind. Or a ship.'

'It is both of these things. It also describes a man with trading interests in the Levant, or one who absconds with large debts. Between which two, regrettably, there is often no distinction.'

'And how did you come to be British Consul of the Seven Islands?'

'I really have no idea,' Spiridion admitted frankly. 'Perhaps they could find no one else to do it.' But then after a moment he added thoughtfully: 'I have always admired the British.'

'Why?'

'Why do you think?'

'I have no idea. That is why I ask.'

'Well, there are many things. But – a sense of justice? Fair play. And perhaps your sense of humour.'

Nathan sniffed. 'Well, we have a sense of humour, I suppose. I am not so sure about our sense of justice – certainly it is not apparent in our courts of law. But on that score, I have a favour to ask of you.'

'It will be my pleasure.'

'You may not think so when you hear what it is. It concerns the man who swam for the shore. George Banjo. He is in the monastery above the headland, where we had that wine you recommended.'

Spiridion regarded him with a bemused smile. 'How do you know that?'

'Because I gave him the directions to it. And before I left I made sure he would be given sanctuary there. He was on a charge, for striking an officer. I believe it to be unjust, but – he would have hanged.' The Consul was still staring at him, though he may have blinked a little. 'I have given him some money and told him to make for Corfu Town where he may find a ship. He is a good seaman – and a good man. He has saved my life on at least two occasions. But he is an African and he speaks no Italian or Greek. He may need an introduction. Of course, I will understand if this is an embarrassment . . .'

Spiridion shook his head. He was smiling. 'It will remind me of why I am the British Consul,' he said. 'I will send for him when I return to Corfu. I take it you met with no objection from the Prior when you spoke with him?'

'None whatsoever. I gave him a small donation to Saint George.'

'That was probably wise. It is always good to have Saint George on one's side. You will certainly have need of him in Venice if the Devil sniffs you out.'

'The Devil? Is he a particular problem in Venice?'

'He is. He goes under the name of Cristoforo Cristolfi and he is the chief agent of the Inquisition. Which in Venice is an instrument of the State, not the Church, and dispenses what passes for justice in the Republic. But the three Inquisitors are changed every month. Cristolfi is not, so you could say he is the most powerful man in Venice. Pray God and Saint George you do not encounter him.'

'Anything else – before I set off on this little venture?'

'Yes. The wind.' Nathan smiled, if a little uncertainly, but Spiridion's expression was serious. 'There is a wind which the Venetians call the Sirocco. You may have heard of it?' Nathan was nodding. 'Good. But you will not wish to experience it, my friend. At sea it comes upon you of a sudden and with a tremendous violence, driving you before it until you run upon the rocks. On land it has a more subtle but no less extreme effect. It drives men mad and women wanton. There are some who call it the Wind of Eris – the Goddess of Strife who haunts the battlefield and delights in human bloodshed. It was she who caused the discord that led to the Trojan War. And all wars since. She is adroit in the manipulation of human folly.

When she wishes to stir it up, she sends the Sirocco. The Wind of Eris. The Wind of Folly.'

'So.' Nathan regarded him curiously, for this was a side of Spiridion he had not hitherto observed. 'French agents and assassins. Eris and the Devil. You paint a grim picture. And I had heard it was one long Carnival.'

'Oh, it has its diversions, as I hope you will discover. However, in Venice one must always watch one's back. The Republic has been ruled by the same clique of noble families for a thousand years. They allow of no dissent, not even among themselves. And they do not trouble with trial by jury, as you do in England. If you offend against their authority and their own narrow sense of order, they will look to the Devil for redress. And the Devil will dispose of you, my friend, in the most convenient manner that is available to him.'

Another presence at the door, this time Mr Bailey. 'Mr Tully's compliments, sir, and he thought you would wish to know that the *Unicorn* is in sight.' The merest pause. 'And the dead are ready for burial, sir.'

Chapter Thirteen

The Bride of the Sea

—◆—

'*Seigneur Dieu, par la puissance de Ta Parole . . .*'

'*Lord God, by the power of Thy Word that stilled the chaos of the primeval seas, made the raging waters of the Flood subside, and calmed the storm on the Sea of Galilee . . .*'

Nathan listened solemnly while Ensign Leveque, as the only surviving French officer present, intoned the words of the Catholic Prayer for the Dead.

'*As we commit the bodies of our brothers to the deep, grant them peace and tranquillity until that day when all who believe in Thee will be raised to the glory of new life promised in the waters of Baptism.*'

They were, Nathan reflected, rather more comforting than the words he had himself spoken from *The Book of Common Prayer*, with its emphasis on the corruption of the body and the eventual, but by no means certain, absorption into the body of Christ. But then as they were spoken in French they were unlikely to win any converts among the Protestant and, in some cases, downright disbelieving crewmen of the *Unicorn* who had come aboard. And as for the Frenchmen . . . Nathan wondered if the Resurrection of the Dead complied with the hopes and aspirations of the French Revolution. But the young ensign did not appear to be unduly troubled on this score and there were no vocal objections from the prisoners as they stood in the waist of the corvette under the watchful eyes of the Marines.

He realised with a start that the ensign was looking towards him, waiting for the signal. He nodded. Then, six at a time, the shrouded figures of the French dead slid from the sloping mess tables into the sea. Eighteen of them now, four more having died since the battle, and three more from the *Unicorn*. All sharing the same watery grave off Cape Drastis: 'until the sea shall give up her dead.'

The service over, Nathan retired to the stern rail of the *Jean-Bart* as the hands returned to their duties and the French prisoners were despatched to their gloomy confinement in the orlop deck.

'Martin, I want you to take command here,' Nathan told Tully when he came aft. 'I am afraid I cannot spare you much in the way of a crew, but some of the prisoners may agree to serve – I note there are a number of Italians among them – and we will put the rest ashore on the mainland.'

And so they proceeded northward: the *Unicorn*, restored to her former pristine lines, the *Bonne Aventure*, the *Jean-Bart*, and the schooner *Angelika*, named for one of Spiridion's daughters, which joined them from Corfu. They were desperately short-crewed and the corvette scarcely had enough people aboard to fire half her broadside, but they made an impressive picture as they cruised in line ahead off the Italian coast. It was Nathan's own little squadron and he was about to abandon it.

'Well, good luck,' he said to Mr Duncan, 'and remember, if

I have not rejoined you or sent word within ten days, you must sail for Naples without me.'

Duncan's expression was stern. He did not approve of his Captain's jaunts ashore, as he doubtless referred to them privately. But equally he would relish a few days of command, even with a third of his crew aboard the *Jean-Bart*.

Nathan was greeted with little ceremony on the *Angelika*. Captain Kyrgyakos was not, as Spiridion had put it, of an amiable disposition, and though his crew appeared cheerful enough there was not a one of them that spoke a word of English or French. Nathan felt a pang of loneliness as he stood at the rail and watched the squadron fade into the distant haze. When he went below he found his cabin was the size of a cupboard, and the Angel Gabriel, who was the only man he had permitted to accompany him, complaining that they had missed dinner and there was no prospect of lighting the galley fire until morning.

'I expect we will eat well in Venice,' Nathan assured him gloomily, 'when we get there.'

This, as it transpired, was by no means assured. For within a few hours of leaving the squadron, the Sirocco found them – and it was every bit as bad as Spiridion had advised.

It was almost sunset, the sea the colour of molten lead and the sky so like a burnished shield that Nathan was about to comment upon it to the Captain when, with a blast as of the Devil's breath, a sudden gust laid them over almost on their beam ends. The next few minutes were a desperate fight for survival as they struggled to take in canvas in a lather of flying ropes and warm stinging spray. Then the wind drove them before it under bare poles or at best a scrap of staysail, always northerly and at such a pace Nathan feared they might run out of sea room in the murky shallows of the Gulf of Venice and drive upon the Doge's Palace in the dark.

He need not have worried. The wind dropped as the sun rose and then blew fitfully in brief scorching bursts that felt like the opening and closing of an oven door until halfway through the afternoon watch it died away altogether and left them to their other demons. Standing, high in the prow, beneath the limp staysails, Nathan felt a subtle stiffening through the keel, as if the sea were resisting them, pushing them back or dragging them down. The gurgling water under the hull seemed oddly ominous, like a muttered curse, and he had the oddest feeling that the sea was draining away beneath them down a giant plughole, leaking away from under their hull. And then a shout from the lookout alerted him to the presence of land.

Nathan took his glass and, with the Captain's permission, went aloft. They were approaching what appeared to be a long, low shoreline which the charts informed him were the barrier islands blocking access to the Lagoon of Venice. There were several gaps between them but a foreign vessel could only enter by way of the Porto di Lido, the skipper had informed him, and then only with a qualified pilot. Kyrgyakos himself, though he knew these waters as well as any Venetian – and better than most, he sneered – was not allowed to guide them there, on pain of blinding and four years in the Doge's prison. Nathan thought he was joking but could not be entirely sure. The Venetians had lost an empire, but they had a jealous regard for what remained.

Further north, he could see other ships, large and small, standing in for the port, or waiting stoically for permission to do so.

But where *was* the port?

Nathan scanned the nearby shore. Not here, for sure. His questing gaze dwelled upon nothing more substantial than a long, low island of mud and shale with a few reed beds and some soggy grasses, limp as the schooner's sails in the breathless air. To the south lay the sparse huts and nets of a fishing village, its boats drawn up on the strand with cabalistic signs on their jaunty prows: of horses, angels and ancient gods, and a single evil-warding eye. The sluggish sea was studded with black flags – Dan buoys they called them in his native Sussex, employed to mark fishing nets or lobster pots – with a scum of herring gulls bobbing on the oily swell. He could have been off the shingle banks of Dungeness or the Romney Marshes, or the bleak, black mudflats on the approaches to Rye Harbour: the desolate world of fishermen and salt-gatherers and smugglers. This was the Venice of old, surely, when the refugees from the mainland had fled here from Attila's hordes and scratched a barren living from the mud, before they began to build their churches and palaces – and ships.

He moved his glass to the north, following a line of stout wooden piles rising from the water in clusters of three, like tripods of stacked muskets guarding some vital channel: some with lanterns or little shrines on top, and on one a cormorant, spreading its wings to dry in the warm air. Through the gap into the lagoon, across the wastes of murky water, there were a few small sails: of fishing smacks and coastal traders. And then, in the middle of this desolate inland sea, he espied a man walking. He had to focus the lens to be sure of it, for at first he thought it was another marker flag, or a large bird, but no, it was a man: a solitary Neptune prodding with trident or net, at least a mile from the nearest land. Or was he? For even more ludicrously there was a woman, too, not far from him, hanging washing on a line. A line that appeared to be strung out across the sea. Then he looked again and saw it was an island, or mud bank, scarcely breaking the surface of the water, but with little low shacks, and fishing nets hung up to dry. And there were others like it: flat, featureless lumps of mud, lying about like stranded whales driven into the shallows by the tide and left to rot. For there was a tide in this corner of the Adriatic, Nathan had learned: a startling, treacherous rip tide that rushed in across the mudflats, covering the lower islands and pouring into the canals of Venice itself, sometimes flooding the streets and piazzas, sloshing into the ground floors of houses – wherever they were. Perhaps they were under water now.

Then the Sirocco breathed on them again, and the sails filled and flapped, then filled and stayed filled, bearing them northwards, skirting the muddy shores of Pellestrina and bringing them closer to the sails they had seen earlier, clustered about the Porto di Lido. And then, rounding a promontory, they saw her. With a shocking suddenness as if she had risen like Aphrodite from the waters. A wondrous city of towers and domes, steeples, columns and campaniles topped with statues of saints and angels and Christian crosses: a mirage in a watery desert. Venice, the Bride of the Sea.

They joined the flow of shipping waiting for permission to approach the gilded throne. Ships of England and of France, of Spain and Portugal, the Low Countries and Scandinavia, of Genoa, Naples, the Papacy, and the *Serenissima* herself. And there they lay, netted in the shallows of the Adriatic, for across the channel between the two islands there was a barrier: an immense chain stretched between the two fortresses of Castelvecchio on the Lido and the Fortezza di Sant'Andrea on its own island opposite. And though it was lowered during the day, its massive iron links resting upon the seabed, everyone could see the great winches that raised and lowered it, and the floating batteries that were moored at intervals along its length. Venice, even in decline, was no ripe plum to be plucked by the first adventurer bold enough to mount an assault. The fleets of Pepin the Frank, of Genoese and Turk, the pirate Slavs and Uskoks, the Moors from North Africa, the mercenary armies of Popes, Medicis and Hapsburgs, all had tried and failed to breach those massive sea defences. The *Serenissima* remained inviolate in her marshy backwater on the edge of land and sea.

They spent the night here, in this unfriendly anchorage, and most of the day that followed, awaiting inspection by customs and harbour officials, sweltering in the heat and swatting at pestiferous insects, but finally, towards late afternoon, cleared of illness and ill-intent, they took their pilot aboard and proceeded slowly up the channel, wafted by the fitful Sirocco past the guns of Sant'Andrea, round the tip of the Arsenale and into the Basin of St Mark with the Isola San Giorgio Maggiore to larboard and the great, magical city close on their lee, brilliant now in the early evening sun, the domes and rooftops gleaming with a deep golden light.

And three dead bodies hanging from a rope between two stone columns on the waterfront.

'Welcome to Venice,' remarked Kyrgyakos as he noted the direction of Nathan's gaze.

'Is that normal?'

'As normal as anything in this city. More normal than most. This is how they dispose of the common criminals. Others have a less public execution.'

But Nathan's attention had been attracted by something of more professional interest. There were four ships-of-war moored in the Basin of St Mark. He studied them closely through his glass as the schooner glided slowly by. Two 70-gun two-deckers, the *San Giorgio* and the *Vittoria* – both of which Spiridion had said could take their place in the line of battle – and two frigates, the 42-gun *Bellona* and the 36-gun *Artemise*. They were certainly in far better shape than those he had seen in Corfu: the sails were neatly furled, the ropes all in place with no loose ends showing, no rust or refuse running down from the gun ports – the hulls seemed newly painted, in fact – and the guns, what he could see of them, appeared to be well maintained. But there didn't seem to be many people aboard. He could see no more than a dozen or so figures, alow and aloft. It was possible they were all ashore, but still . . .

Their pilot led them to a mooring at the edge of the Canale Orfano – the Canal of the Orphans – where, in the not so distant past, Kyrgyakos informed Nathan, condemned prisoners were given a less public execution by drowning. They were taken at dead of night from the Doge's dungeons, bound and burdened with heavy weights, and tossed without ceremony into the murky waters of the lagoon.

'It is said that they still dispose of certain prisoners in this fashion,' he confided. 'Political prisoners. Those who might cause them some embarrassment if they were hanged in public, on which account it is forbidden to fish here. Not out of consideration for the dead, you understand,' he added, lest Nathan attribute so feminine a sentiment to these pitiless rulers of the *Serenissima*, 'but for the living.'

For all its beauty and all its splendour, Nathan did not think he had ever moored in so hostile a haven, nor beheld a city where he had felt such a strong sense of foreboding, or of watchful hostility; not even when he had come to Paris at the height of the Terror, with the grim Goddess of the Guillotine under her black shroud on the Place de la Révolution.

'Well, are you ready to go ashore?' enquired the Captain with a smirk.

They landed on the Riva degli Schiavoni, not far from where the three bodies were hanging, and Kyrgyakos sought directions to the American Consul's house and a gondola to take them there. While he was thus engaged, Nathan took a short stroll across the Piazza San Marco, marvelling at the splendour of the buildings that rose up on either side. If this was an empire in decline, it hid its failings well. Here was the Venice of old, the wonder of the medieval world. The Great Basilica of St Mark, the towering campanile or bell-tower, the magnificent Logetta erected at its foot, the Library and the Mint, the awe-inspiring Palazzo Ducale . . . Such ornamentation, such statuary, such columns and towers and domes and spires . . . it was like something out of a fairytale, or rather a great many fairytales, with bits and pieces from each and every one, all jumbled together in some glorious fantasia, with the gingerbread cottage grafted on to the ogre's castle and a clocktower stuck on top.

The Doge's Palace was a masterpiece of Gothic architecture, while the Basilica looked as if it had been lifted bodily from the heart of Baghdad, blessed with Holy Water, girt about with saints and angels, studded with crosses and dropped into a convenient corner of the Piazza. And given the Venetians' appetite for plunder, this was by no means unlikely. Throughout the Middle Ages there was hardly a vessel that did not return from the Orient without bringing a column or a capital, a statue or a frieze taken from some ancient building to glorify the fabric of the Basilica. Gradually the exterior brickwork had become covered with various marbles and carvings, many of them much older than the building itself. Even the supposed body of St Mark the Evangelist – the Patron Saint of Venice – had been stolen from Alexandria. And the four bronze horses that fronted the Doge's Palace had been scavenged from a palace in Constantinople. But whatever their inspiration or origin, the buildings formed a complex that was essentially Venetian. Nathan could only stare in wonder and amazement. On one side of the piazza stood Ancient Rome, on the other Byzantium. And between them the three grim puppets of dancing Death, twisting on their ropes in the stagnant air as a warning to those who thought to flout the continuing authority of those who ruled here.

The Doge might be as empty a title as Spiridion implied, the relic of St Mark a fraudulent collection of old bones, but their pretence was clothed in such magnificence one might be forgiven for thinking the camel trains still staggered into the caravanserai of Aleppo under their weight of treasure, and that the Venetian factories of the Levant still bulged with merchandise waiting to be despatched across the seas to this jewel of an island that had made itself, by its own initiative and industry, its prudence and guile, into the crossroads of the world.

But then Nathan boarded the gondola Kyrgyakos had hired for them and as they headed northward into the labyrinth of narrow canals behind the Piazza he saw the reality behind the glittering façade: the derelict warehouses, the disused cranes and pulleys, the abandoned, boarded-up townhouses of the merchant princes and the squalid tenements of the poor; the lines of washing strung from the windows, the effluvia that poured into the canals from a thousand waste-pipes and sewers, the collapsed pavements and the rotting piles – everywhere the evidence of decomposition and decay.

Then they came out on to the Grand Canal and were caught up in a frenetic bustle of boats and barges and sandolos and gondolas and countless other craft that Nathan could not have named, all loaded to the gunwales with people and produce, darting about like so many water boatmen. And here, on a bend of the canal just to the north of the Rialto Bridge they found the house where they had been told the American Consul lived – the Ca' da Mosto – not so much a house as a palace with a massive Stars and Stripes trailing from the flagpole on the third floor and almost dragging its hem in the water below.

He had Kyrgyakos drop him off at the water steps and advanced alone to the immense, brass-studded door fronting the canal. His summons was answered by an impressively liveried black footman in a powdered wig who spoke to him in the deep, musical English of the Southern States, took his letter of introduction from Signor Foresti and invited him to wait in an elegantly-furnished reception room while he enquired if the Consul was at home.

The Consul was, and he did not keep Nathan waiting for more than a few minutes or so. A tall, lean, elderly gentleman with the elegant periwig of an older generation and the genteel manners of a Virginian, which indeed he was: Mr James Hamilton Devereux of Albemarle County, Virginia, not far from Mr Jefferson's house at Monticello, did Mr Turner know it? Mr Turner regretted he did not. Nor, even more regrettably, did he know Mr Jefferson.

Nathan had laid out the bare bones of his deceit in the letter he had dictated for Spiridion and which the Consul now held in his hand. 'So you have met Signor Foresti? An excellent fellow, even though he represents the British.' The Consul had met him several times in Venice, he said, and had once had the pleasure of visiting him in Corfu in his yacht.

His yacht. This was clearly one of the better class of Consul, but then Nathan had known it from the moment the footman had opened the door and he had followed him across the magnificent tiled courtyard with its brass-covered cistern.

'And he says here,' peering at the letter through his spectacles without troubling to set them on his nose, 'that you are from New York.' Raising his bushy brows in polite enquiry.

'Indeed.'

But the enquiry, though courteously expressed, demanded a more fulsome response than this, so Nathan regaled this honest Virginian gentleman with a brief and entirely mendacious account of his activities as a merchant sea captain who had made his fortune trading between New York and London, but now wished to see a little more of the world than the grey wastes of the North Atlantic. He had come to Venice primarily as a tourist, he said, but he also had an eye for any business opportunities that might arise in the region.

'But of course,' Mr Devereux murmured with a polite bow and perhaps the merest hint of irony in his blue-grey eyes. He regretted, however, that such opportunities might be difficult to find in modern Venice. They stood in the window and looked down on the traffic in the Grand Canal.

'Oh, there is still plenty of local trade,' the Consul assured him, 'but it is mostly for the table and the salon. Foodstuffs, wine and the requirements of a woman's toilette – and a man's, too, of course, this being Venice – this is what sustains the *Serenissima*. You would not believe how long these people can spend before a mirror or how much money on a banquet or a suit of clothes.'

While his expression fell well short of a sneer, there was a sufficient note of censure in his tone to sharpen Nathan's perception of him.

'I have always been a great admirer of the Venetians,' the Consul confided. 'That is why my friend Mr Jefferson was kind enough to despatch me here. Like yours, Mr Turner, my family's wealth came from shipping and trade. As did that of the Venetians of old.

'What a history this place has had! They came here as refugees, fleeing from the hordes of Attila the Hun, scavenging what poor living they could from the marshes and the mudflats. And through ships and trade they built an empire. "One quarter and one half of what was Rome's." This was their proud boast. They conquered large parts of mainland Italy, they planted their colonies and their forts all down the coast of Dalmatia. In Albania, in the Morea, the Greek islands, Cyprus, Crete . . . Their fleets carried the Crusaders to the Holy Land and brought most of its wealth back with them. They sacked Constantinople and stripped it of all they could carry. They brought back the wealth of the Orient by camel train along the Silk Route through Samarkand and Isfahan to Aleppo. And their ships carried it to all the ports of the western world. They were the richest and most powerful nation in Europe – before Europe knew what nations were. But then a Portuguese explorer Vasco da Gama discovered a new route to the Orient, around Cape Horn, and they had lost their monopoly on the wealth of the East. And about the same time, the Turks took Constantinople and closed their doors to them, shutting off the Silk Route. And that was the end of it.

'Venice has been in decline for more than three hundred years, Mr Turner. I knew that when I came here. It was not a surprise to me. I expected to see decline. I did not expect to see . . . decadence.

'You ask what opportunities there are for trade in Venice. I am sorry to say, Mr Turner, that there is but one. And I will tell you what it is, in the privacy of my own home and because there are no ladies present, and because Mr Foresti has vouched for you as an honourable man. It is the trade in sexual favours.'

Nathan exchanged his expression of polite interest for one of shock and dismay. So embroiled was he in the character of Nathaniel Turner, as he understood it, he could not be sure if this was genuine or not. The Consul appeared to find it gratifying.

'Venice, as you must know, Mr Turner, has become the premier destination on the Grand Tour,' he continued in the same confidential vein. 'People come here to see the fine architecture and the works of art, the churches, the canals . . . They come to marvel at the miracle that is Venice, this city on the sea. But they also come for the grossest forms of pleasure – and they find them, I am sorry to say, in the most unlikely of places.' He paused a moment and Nathan observed that he was blushing. 'But this is not proper of me,' he said, in a different tone. 'I am afraid I have become carried away by my own abhorrence of these practices, my disappointment in these people, the modern Venetians.' He shook his head. 'Suffice to say that in its heyday there were sixteen thousand people employed in shipbuilding at the Arsenale. Now there are but a quarter of that number. Only a few years ago, there were twelve thousand employed in the silk industry. Now there are a thousand. There are as many people employed in dressing hair. I could go on. It is part of my job to advise my fellow countrymen, Mr Turner, on opportunities for trade. But I will not be their pimp, sir. I will not be their pander.'

Not another Udny then, Nathan reflected.

'I had no idea,' he said wonderingly. 'And I had thought they came to see the works of Titian and of Tintoretto, of Tiepolo and Bellini – as I do.'

The Consul laid a hand on his arm. 'My dear sir, please do not think for a moment that I intended to imply . . . My goodness, not for a moment.' Now he was truly embarrassed. 'Not when you have been recommended to me by Mr Spiridion Foresti, upon my word. No, and I shall be very glad to tell you where you may find these wonders, and others beside. In fact, it would give me the greatest of pleasure if you would accompany me – and my wife and daughter – to a concert tomorrow evening. A selection of the arias of Mr Handel is being performed to a select gathering at the house of Carlos Goldoni.'

Nathan murmured that he would be delighted, of course, if Signor Goldoni did not mind an extra guest. A small shadow crossed the Consul's face. 'Signor Goldoni has been dead for many years,' he revealed. 'But he is still revered as the most accomplished playwright that Venice has ever produced. The Venetian Molière, I have heard him called. His house is now something of a shrine – and you will be most welcome to worship at it.'

And so it was agreed that Nathan should call upon the Consul again the following evening at seven and they should travel there together in the Consul's private gondola. 'For we use gondolas as others use a carriage,' Mr Devereux assured him jocularly as they rose to their feet, 'and glide upon water with more ease and comfort, I do assure you, than you will ever have experienced on the streets of New York.'

This was certainly true.

The Consul conducted him down the stairs and across the stone courtyard to the steps where Nathan's own gondola was awaiting him. The house had been built for a wealthy Venetian nobleman of the Querini family, Mr Devereux informed him, which had in the past contributed several members to the office of Doge.

'Which is, in a manner of speaking, the equivalent of our President,' he said, 'though not, alas, elected by the people as is the case in our own country. For the electors must be of noble birth and their names enshrined in what they call the Golden Book. There are but twelve hundred of them, though I doubt but one-tenth are now men of substance.'

'And the rest?'

'Impoverished. Noble, but near-destitute. That is the truth of it, Mr Turner. That is the glory that was Venice.'

Throughout this discourse, Nathan had a strange feeling that they were being observed from above, and under pretence of admiring their surroundings his gaze swept the upper floors to observe a blonde head and a pale face hastily drawn back from the surrounding balustrade, leaving him with an impression of a grave and secluded beauty.

'Until tomorrow,' said the Consul, as he saw him to the door.

*

'Where now?' enquired Kyrgyakos with a scowl. Clearly the role of guide was not one to which he aspired.

'The British Ambassador's house,' Nathan told him as he sank into the cushioned seats of the cabin with a sigh of remorse and self-disgust. Was this the facility that made Imlay so pleased with himself, like some smug conjuror or illusionist who alone knows that things are not what they appear to be; that it is all smoke and mirrors – the effortless trick of deception? But it could never be that for Nathan. He was ruined by his upbringing as the son of a Tory squire and a New York feminist: it bred a certain peculiar integrity. And yet . . . Sometimes he wondered at himself, sometimes he wondered if he was just a bit too good at it, that it might come naturally, after all. He did not mind tricking the French. They were there to be tricked. But there was no credit in deceiving an elderly gentleman of Virginia, not unless you were one of his slaves when, admittedly, it might compensate a little for the inconveniences he caused you from time to time.

He wondered who the blonde beauty was that he had seen upon the stair. Devereux's daughter? Surely not his wife? If it was his wife, well, perhaps *he* was not quite what he appeared to be, for she was much less than half his age. But it *must* be his daughter. Nathan would find out, presumably, when he joined them for an evening of Handel arias at the house of Carlo Goldoni.

He was already beginning to look forward to this. It would not be the most arduous of the tasks he had performed as a spy in the service of His Britannic Majesty, nor the most foolish.

They were entering another labyrinth of waterways, so cut off from the light of the sun – and so stinking and putrid – he might almost have imagined himself in the sewers under Paris on another misadventure imposed upon him by one of the

King's Ministers. But then they glided out of darkness into light, light so dazzlingly reflected off the surface of the water and the bleached buildings that surrounded it, he was obliged to raise his arm to his eyes as if to ward off a blow.

'The house of the British Ambassador, your honour,' Kyrgyakos informed him with an ironic bow.

But the British Ambassador was not at home.

Nathan gazed doubtfully up at the imposing façade of the palazzo in the Campo dei Miracoli where Sir Richard Worsley was said to reside. Not quite as imposing as the American Consulate, though possibly of an earlier vintage. There was an air of dilapidation about the place and most of the windows were shuttered. And there was no flag.

'Ask him where he is,' Nathan instructed Kyrgyakos, for the footman who had answered the door improbably claimed to speak no English.

'He says he is not at liberty to reveal, your honour.'

'Tell him I have vital despatches for His Excellency.' Nathan tapped the canvas bag he carried over his shoulder. 'And he will not be pleased if they are not delivered.'

A brief exchange.

'He says to give him the despatches and he will ensure that His Excellency receives them.'

'Then be so good as to tell him that *I* am not at liberty to part with them. Not to any but the British Ambassador.'

A lengthier dialogue ensued, apparently of some import, judging from the reactions it elicited. Nathan controlled his impatience with difficulty.

'He says the Ambassador has been poisoned,' Kyrgyakos declared with grim satisfaction.

'Poisoned?'

A shrug. 'We are in Venice. It is not so very strange.'

'You mean he is dead?'

'Not dead, but dying.' He considered this interpretation for a moment and modified it to 'very ill'.

'Then where is he?' Nathan demanded when he had digested this information as well as he was able. There was a further interchange with a great deal of shrugging on both sides.

'In Murano,' Kyrgyakos said. 'Where they make the glass.'

'And where is that?'

Murano, it appeared, was one of the other islands – of which there were above a hundred – in the lagoon. Nathan considered. He had been hopeful that if he were being watched by agents of the Ten – as Spiridion had said he would be – they might think he had come here as the result of some casual remark by the American Consul, perhaps to see Sir Richard's collection of paintings and antiquities. A journey out to some remote island in pursuit of a dying, or at least very ill Ambassador could not be explained quite so readily. But it was a journey he persuaded himself he was obliged to make.

'Can we go there?' he enquired of his guide.

'But of course. You can see it from the Fondamenta Nuove.'

Not so remote then, but somewhat perplexing, for at first sight, as they crossed the intervening half-mile or so of water, it appeared to be composed entirely of tall chimneys belching forth an immense cloud of thick black smoke. Kyrgyakos supplied the information that the glass industry had been moved here by government decree many years before, after the furnaces had caused a number of fires in Venice. It now employed some 30,000 people and Murano glass had become the *Serenissima*'s chief export.

Nathan wondered why the American Consul had not mentioned this in his summary of the Venetian economy. He also wondered, rather more pertinently, why the British

Ambassador should consider it a suitable place to recover from being poisoned. However, as their vessel glided up the eastern shore of the island, they left the tall chimneys and the fiery furnaces behind them and entered a pastoral idyll of vineyards and citrus groves, interlaced by pleasant rambling waterways and rural lanes. This, it appeared, was where Sir Richard Worsley had chosen to hide himself.

He was not dying. He did not even look very ill. But he *had* been poisoned.

'By the Devil. Or one of his accursed agents,' he told Nathan when the latter was admitted to his company.

Nathan gathered that he meant the man Spiridion had warned him about, not the Prince of Darkness, though the Ambassador gave him to understand that there was little to distinguish between the two.

'First he butchers Dandolo before my very eyes – on the steps of a convent, forsooth – and then he bribes one of my own servants to feed me some foul toxin. I have been sick as a dog these past few weeks or more. I have shed several stone in weight, my intestines are near destroyed.' He clutched his lower abdomen to ensure they were still there. 'God knows what substance I have been subjected to, but I assure you I am a shadow of the man I once was.'

He was by no means insubstantial now, Nathan thought, though the flesh sagged about his jowls and there was an unhealthy pallor to his complexion that might have been the result of the toxin or too little exposure to the light of day.

Nathan knew of his reputation, of course. His divorce from Lady Worsley had been one of the great scandals of the age, Sir Richard having brought a case of 'criminal conversation' against her lover, thus exposing the details of their private life to public appraisal. Though he had won the case, the jury had been so unimpressed by Sir Richard's own lack of integrity that they had awarded him a mere shilling in damages. But despite this embarrassment and his more recent misadventures at the hands of the Devil, the 7th Baronet clearly maintained an extremely high opinion of himself and a corresponding concern for his own safety.

He had come to Murano, he said, because it was one of the few places in the *Serenissima* not infested with the Devil's agents, the Ten having made an agreement with the 'glass men' to spare them the inconvenience of police surveillance, provided they retained their skills for the exclusive use of the *Serenissima*.

'I will not say I feel secure here,' he informed Nathan, 'but I am as secure as I ever will be in this damned hellhole.'

Unfortunately, it had caused him to be rather more cut off from human contact than was desirable in a foreign envoy. He had brought with him only a handful of English-speaking servants and a woman who had introduced herself as Mrs Smith, a lady of about his own age who was more in the nature of a companion, Nathan was led to believe. Nathan was left in her company while the Ambassador retired to read the despatches he had brought, and they did their best to entertain each other as the sun slipped below the distant peaks of the Dolomites on the mainland and the shadows spread out over the lagoon. A servant came with a taper to light the lamps and Nathan wondered if he was here for the night. He was about to ask if he might speak with Kyrgyakos, who had been left with the boatman and would be becoming more surly and disgruntled by the minute, when Sir Richard returned. Mrs Smith murmured her excuses and left them to their private consultation.

'You say Dandolo was murdered by Cristolfi,' Nathan prompted him. 'Or at least on his orders. But what could be the reason?'

'How would I know? Possibly because Dandolo had a degree of ambition. That is quite enough to get you killed in Venice. Perhaps the other members of the Ten thought he would endanger their precious neutrality. It will not save them, of course. The French could move on them any time they wished. I have already packed up my collection and pretty well shut up shop. Damned place is finished one way or another.'

He appraised Nathan slyly. 'So you have a squadron at your disposal?'

'I would not say a squadron, sir,' Nathan corrected him, but not without a degree of pride. 'I have a frigate and a pair of sloops.'

'Even so, it is reassuring to know that we have the means of deliverance, should it become necessary. I do not fear for my own safety, you understand, but it would be a tragedy to lose my collections. A tragedy.' He dwelled upon the momentousness of this for a moment. 'I have some Old Masters that I was able to obtain at an excellent price due to the uncertainties of war and revolution, and I do not mind telling you I had rather see them in the hold of a British man-o'-war than in Bonaparte's baggage train on their way to the Louvre.'

Nathan declined to inform him that this was not the main purpose of his mission to the Adriatic. 'But why would Bonaparte take the trouble of coming to Venice?' he chose to enquire. 'Surely it would be a mere diversion for him, when his prime concern is to knock Austria out of the war.'

'Then why does he have troops in the Veneto?' Sir Richard demanded forcefully. 'The French have had garrisons in Verona and Vicenza for the past month or more. Their cavalry press to the very edge of the lagoon. Besides, he may not *have* to come to Venice. Venice is by way of coming to him.'

Nathan queried this phenomenon with a frown and the Ambassador went on to confirm Spiridion's assertion that

the city was infested with French agents and sympathisers –
'Freemasons and the like' – and that every success of Bonaparte
added strength to their importuning.

'So where would that leave the Venetian fleet?'

The Ambassador sighed. 'Well, I did entertain hopes of
securing it for the alliance, of course, as you will know, and
the Ionians with it, until the murder of Dandolo. Now we have
old Nani to contend with.'

It had been on Nathan's mind to tell the Ambassador of his
capture of the *Jean-Bart* and what he had learned of the French
interest in the islands, but now something held him back. Sir
Richard was not a man to inspire confidence, or the disclosure
of confidences. The information would keep, Nathan decided,
until he returned to Corsica.

'Old nanny?' he said instead.

'Nani. Giacomo Nani, the old Admiral. Dandolo's successor.'

'And he is not inclined in our support?'

'He is inclined to a quiet life. He is seventy-six years of age
and he will do whatever the Ten tell him to do. He knows
what will happen if he does not.'

'And there is no one else?'

'In the Navy?' The Ambassador thought about it. 'Well,
there is Tommaso Condulmer – his deputy. He is efficient
enough. And I am told he is ambitious. As to his loyalties . . .'
He shrugged. 'I expect they might be bought for the right sum,
as any commodity in Venice.'

'Might he be approached?'

'Not directly. If it were to be reported that the Venetian
Vice-Admiral had been enticed by an officer of the British
Navy, there would be hell to pay.'

Nathan confided that he had not presented himself as an
officer of the British Navy, but as a wealthy American merchant
embarked upon the Grand Tour.

'I see.' Sir Richard observed him shrewdly. Then, after a moment's pause: 'And this is something our masters have set their minds upon?'

'I believe they consider it vital to keep the Venetian fleet out of French hands,' Nathan informed him. But he must know that already if he had read the despatches from the Viceroy. Nathan could tell from his face that he had and that he did – and was working out how to keep his own neck out of the noose.

'Well, I am not personally acquainted with Condulmer, but there is someone I know who is. Certainly, she is better placed to advise you than I am. She was a close friend of Dandolo's. In fact . . .' But whatever he was going to say he thought better of it.

'She?'

'Yes. Her names is Sister Caterina.'

'She is a nun?'

'She is the Deputy Prioress of the Convent of San Paolo di Mare. That, at least, is her official function. In truth she is a great deal more than that. A very powerful and dangerous woman: there are some who call her the uncrowned Queen of Venice. Others say she is involved in the Black Arts, but of course, this is said of many women. Fortunately for us, she is very much opposed to the French interest. She is almost certainly in the pay of the Austrians. I know they are our Allies but our interests do not always coincide, and besides, she has other motives. I suppose one might say she was a patriot, if she were not a woman. She is as addicted to political intrigue as other women are to cards or the exigencies of fashion. But she is closely watched. The death of Dandolo on the steps of her own convent was a warning to her – not to meddle in the affairs of the Ten. I doubt she has heeded it, but she must be approached with care. Are you a gambling man, sir? Do you frequent houses of ill-repute?'

Nathan was somewhat startled by this sudden change of subject. But apparently it was not.

'The Convent of San Paolo possesses a certain notoriety as a bawdy house,' the Ambassador informed him. 'Also, it has a very fine gaming room. You look surprised, sir. Be assured it does not raise an eyebrow in Venice. There are several convents that provide, shall we say, *specialist* forms of entertainment. Indeed, they pride themselves on catering for every taste. Very *catholic*, do you see, ha ha.'

Nathan shook his head. 'I am sorry to be so naive. I had been told to expect a certain level of depravity, but I had not thought to find the convents so affected.'

'Shocking, is it not? It could never happen in England, at least not with real nuns. But it does give you an approach that might succeed in misleading the Devil's acolytes. In your role as an American abroad, eager to sample all the *Serenissima* has to offer, you might conceivably be attracted to such an amenity, do you not think?'

So much for *virgo intacta*, Nathan reflected privately.

'But beware, my friend: these people are not to be trifled with. These are not "Honourable Gentlemen" who call each other names across the floor of the House of Commons, or fight with pistols at dawn. And do not think for one moment that I can save you. This is a country of intrigue, poison and the *stiletto*. One false move and you will feel it twisting in your guts. Or, if they take an especial dislike to you, they will cut off the parts you prize the most and toss you into the Canale Orfano with a rock where once they resided.'

Chapter Fourteen

Sister Caterina

———◆◆◆———

Though not without his failings, Nathan had never before visited a brothel; nor, for that matter, a convent. It was convenient to find them unexpectedly combined.

And despite his reservations, he did admit to a certain curiosity as to how the business was managed, so to speak.

It was unfortunate that it clashed with the prior invitation from Mr Devereux to accompany him to an evening of Handel arias with his wife and daughter, but Nathan sent a note round to the American Consulate with his regrets, explaining that he was indisposed – something he had eaten, perhaps – and braced himself for a very different evening with the nuns of San Paolo di Mare.

He left Kyrgyakos behind for once – the Ambassador had said that the nuns, being educated women, all spoke sufficient French for him to make himself understood – and walked the short distance from St Mark's.

The convent was as brightly lit as Vauxhall Pleasure Gardens on a Saturday night and exerted as strong a pull, it appeared, on the less principled members of society. Nathan stood in the shadows opposite and watched them flutter into the lamplight, like brightly patterned moths only too eager to be burned. Some came on foot, others in a series of uniformly black gondolas, while two burly male attendants subjected them to critical examination at the door. Nathan chose a moment when two gentlemen had been turned away by these guardians of virtue and then crossed the footbridge and presented himself for inspection. He had timed it well – or possessed the qualities of the affluent debauchee – for they admitted him without question. He crossed the stone-flagged *corte* and was directed by another gentleman up a broad flight of stairs to the *piano nobile* where, after being relieved of his cloak and hat by yet another attendant, he entered the reception room.

This was distinguished by a large iron grille which divided it down the middle, rather as the nave is divided from the choir in a church. Behind it sat a number of young women – presumably the nuns, or their pupils, though none of them wore the traditional habit and veil. On the contrary, all were attired in the finest silks and satins and with scant concern for modesty. Their visitors conversed with them through the grille or with each other, while servants circulated with refreshments and a dwarf performed handstands for their entertainment. Nathan joined the fringes of this happy throng and attempted to make himself inconspicuous by studying the paintings on the walls and on the ceiling, though he was too nervous to be as engrossed as he might have been, and he kept a weather eye upon the dwarf, who had begun to make a nuisance of himself. At the same time, he made a careful study of the features that were most relevant to his mission.

In Venice, the Ambassador had assured him, appearance was everything. And as far as appearances went, this was an entirely proper occasion, providing an opportunity for the nuns of a semi-closed Order to enjoy a visit from friends and family under the careful supervision of their superiors. Indeed, some of the visitors, perhaps the majority, *were* friends and family. But others were not. Others were here for entirely less honourable reasons and everyone knew it, but – for appearance's sake – they were obliged to follow certain procedures, which had been outlined to Nathan in some detail by the Ambassador.

In the wall to the right of the grille was a half-open door, behind which stood a nun: a mature woman dressed in the traditional robes of her calling. And behind her, somewhat in the shadows, stood two lay sisters, or servants. Their function, it appeared, was to receive the gifts – of food and other small comforts – brought by family and friends for their loved ones. And also those of a more substantial nature brought by the gentlemen who were not family and friends. Or if they were, had no intention of letting the relationship inhibit them.

The gifts these gentlemen deposited normally took the form of a purse containing a sum of money, sometimes accompanied by an envelope upon which was inscribed the name of the nun or novice for whom it was intended. This permitted entrance to the gaming room and the rooms above and beyond it, where other more private transactions were conducted.

The fact that everyone in the room, on both sides of the grille, was perfectly aware of these arrangements, that they were known to the agents of the Inquisitors, to the Council of Ten, to most of the Senate and to a large section of the populace – that they were most likely known in Rome, even – was entirely inconsequential. Appearance was everything.

And so, after observing these proceedings for a while, Nathan advanced to the door and presented his gift and the accompanying missive to the doorkeeper. She glanced down at the name written upon the envelope and exposed Nathan to a searching regard. He smiled confidently. Her own features

remained impassive. She took the offering but indicated with a
nod that he was to wait in the salon. Nathan retreated to his
previous position on the fringes of the crowd, which was now
considerably diminished, and continued his study of the ceiling
and the artwork on the walls. Unhappily, he had finally
attracted the attentions of the dwarf who subjected him to
some considerable insult. He also became aware that some of
the remaining visitors, and many of the young women on
the far side of the screen, were regarding him with a speculative
interest. He tried not to notice. But at last he saw the eye of the
doorkeeper was upon him. She beckoned him to her. Drawing
a deep breath, Nathan disentangled himself from the dwarf,
who had gripped his legs in a passionate but mocking embrace,
and made his way towards her. Still without a word she stood
aside and he was admitted to whatever greater or lesser
embarrassments awaited him within.

At the end of the corridor there was a room of about the
same proportion as the first but with several notable differences.
A dozen or so green-baized gaming tables occupied the floor,
there was no iron grille, and most of the women he had seen
behind it now mingled freely with the guests. At least, he
assumed they were the same women, for everyone in the room,
apart from himself, wore a mask. This, Nathan had been
informed, was expressly forbidden in a place of worship, but
possibly this description did not apply to the gaming room of a
convent. Certainly, the paintings on the wall appeared to have
no religious significance, being mostly of naked or scantily clad
women.

Nathan paused in the doorway, conscious of his singularity,
and wondered what he was supposed to do next. He was
instantly approached by a young woman wearing the mask of
a cat and a low-cut gown of shimmering gold who took him by
the hand and guided him to a flight of stairs. These led to a

long gallery overlooking the room below and with a number of doors leading, he supposed, to bedrooms. The woman stopped before one of them and dusted her knuckles upon the gilded panelling. A voice from within invited her to enter.

'Sister Caterina,' murmured his guide as she opened the door.

Nathan stepped into a large elegant room, hung about with paintings, but with little furniture beside a few chairs and a desk at the far end. For a second Nathan was himself, his body parts arranged more or less in the right order. Then his heart and his throat came into violent conflict and he stood transfixed, gaping like an idiot.

He had never met the Deputy Prioress of a convent but he had anticipated some grizzled ancient, or at least a woman of mature years, with the parchment complexion of one who was rarely exposed to anything more enlivening than a religious icon or a book of prayer. But Sister Caterina was no older than he was, and possibly the most beautiful woman he had ever seen.

Each individual feature was exactly right – the generous lips, the straight Roman nose, the high cheekbones and the delicate brows – but the sum was far greater than the parts. This was the work of a sculptor of genius whose commission had been to design perfection and who had achieved it admirably. Her dark hair was coiled in bands and covered in a mesh of pearls which added to the somewhat ethereal effect, and her eyes . . . No sculptor, even of genius, could have created eyes like that. Nathan was spellbound. He stood there in the doorway while she regarded him with a half-smile on her lips until he was recalled to his manners, if not his senses, and completed his bow. She returned it with a gentle inclination of her head.

'Welcome, *monsieur*,' she addressed him in French. 'I have been expecting you.'

Somehow Nathan found it in him to speak. Certainly someone did, though he was not convinced it was himself. 'Then you have the gift of prescience,' he said, 'for it is only a few hours since I made up my mind to come here.'

'Even so,' she replied, 'I have known you were on your way these past two weeks or more.'

And yet a fortnight ago he had barely arrived in Corfu.

'Then you are surely an enchantress,' he assured her. 'And I have been summoned here by your charms.' He had never before flirted with a nun. He had a suspicion he was not very good at it.

'Please, be seated.' She gestured graciously to one of the easy chairs in the window and came round from behind the desk to join him. She was tall, as tall as Emma Hamilton if nothing like as Junoesque. Her figure was slender and she moved with the easy poise of a dancer. If he had looked for a goddess to compare her with, he might have thought of Diana, the Huntress. Or Titania, perhaps, in *A Midsummer Night's Dream* – not a goddess as such but sufficiently superior to humankind – and indeed she might have been the model for this creature, for she had the same queenly presence. She wore a gown of shot silk in midnight blue, such as Titania might have worn, that rippled as she walked, like a second skin. All she lacked was wings, and if she had suddenly spread them and flown to the ceiling, Nathan would not have been entirely surprised, though he might have looked for the wires.

Instead she sat in a chair opposite and regarded him with quiet amusement.

'Do not look so worried,' she said. 'You are as safe here as in the British Admiralty. Safer, in fact, for I am not about to send you off to fight the French fleet. Not immediately, at least.'

This did nothing to allay his concern. On the contrary. In

his note, which he had signed in the name of Turner, he had said only that he had a message from the British Ambassador. Had Worsley sent a different message, or was she gifted with more than mere looks?

'Who do you think I am?' he asked her with a frown.

'I know exactly who you are,' she said. 'You are Captain Nathaniel Peake of His Britannic Majesty's frigate *Unicorn*, which is presently in the Adriatic. Although you are an Englishman, you were born in America – in New York. And tomorrow is your birthday.'

This was beyond belief. She might conceivably know his name, even the name of the *Unicorn*. Even that it was in the Adriatic. But only one man in all of Italy knew the time and place of his birth and that was Gilbert Gabriel who had not yet set foot in Venice and whose discretion, in some things at least, could be relied upon.

Only one man . . . *but one woman.*

Of course. When she had read his Tarot. The time and the place of his birth . . . Emma Hamilton.

Could she have sent a message to say he was on his way? How long would a message take to reach Venice from Naples? He supposed it might be done, travelling overland, by post. But why? And besides, he had said nothing to Emma Hamilton about coming to Venice. Admittedly she might have learned it from Sir William – but he could recall no reference to Sister Caterina. Nathan had not even known of her existence until the Ambassador had told him just a few hours ago. He remembered what Worsley had said of her:

'*Others say she is involved in the Black Arts, but of course this is said of many women.*'

This was absurd. He did not believe in witchcraft. Nor was he a misogynist.

The nun was watching him with that whimsical smile,

almost as if she could read his thoughts. 'Please.' She moved her hands in a gesture of reassurance. 'Your secret is safe with me.' Her voice was low and husky, pleasant, but . . . was there something slightly contrived about it, as there was about that movement of the hands, as if . . . *she was acting a part in a play?* She had been an actress, the Ambassador had said, before she entered Holy Orders.

'Very well,' Nathan acknowledged with a shrug. 'You were warned that I might come here. You know who I am. We need not play games with each other. I am here because of what happened to Admiral Dandolo.'

There was a subtle change in her expression. The smile now was more chilling than whimsical, her voice as even as his. 'I know why you are here. You are my Avenging Angel who comes from the sea.'

Nathan frowned. He wondered suddenly if she was entirely sane.

'Well, certainly I come from the sea. And I sincerely hope the Admiral's death might be avenged, if only by continuing with what he set out to do.'

'And what was that?'

How much was it safe to say? Probably not very much.

'My understanding is that he intended to keep the Venetian fleet safe from the French.'

'Only that? Not a great ambition for which to lose one's life.' The thought appeared to depress her. Her tone was listless. 'So how do you plan to continue the life's work of Admiral Dandolo?'

'I had thought that perhaps one of his successors . . .'

'Ah yes. I understand.'

He had hoped she would, but her next words confounded him.

'And how do you think I can help you?'

'I was told that you might know one of them. The Vice-Admiral. Tommaso Condulmer.' Her expression did not alter. She repeated the name, but flatly, with no apparent knowledge of its owner. 'You do not know him?'

'Oh, I know him.' Carelessly. 'Or at least I know one who does.' Nathan had the sense of being on a carousel. Round and round we go, up and down. 'He is *cicisbeo* to one of my acquaintance.'

'*Cicisbeo?*'

'It means whisperer in English.'

'I am sorry, but . . .'

'The *cicisbeo* is the companion of a woman of fashion. The man she walks out with. Her great admirer, her adviser on matters of taste and etiquette: the clothes she wears, the rouge, the eye make-up. He is the man to whom she can confide her secrets and the secrets of her friends. Who they are sleeping with, who they would like to be sleeping with. Other matters of importance. Far more important than affairs of state. He is her escort, her confidant, her whisperer. You do not have them in England?'

'Not as such,' he replied carefully. 'And this is a common occupation in Venice?'

'Well, it is not an occupation as such – they are not paid a stipend – but it is very common. Every woman must have one. Every woman of fashion, that is. Where would she be without him? She cannot confide in her husband. She cannot go out with her husband. Good heavens, you will be wanting her to sleep with him next! No, a woman's *cicisbeo* is her essential. He is written into the marriage contract.' And when Nathan smiled dutifully: 'Oh, I assure you it is true. Just as it is specified what personal servants she is to have, or her hairdresser or her hatmaker, or the conditions upon which she agrees to surrender her virginity.'

'I see.' He doubted that he did. 'And Tommaso Condulmer is such a man?'

'He is. To the Contessa Juliana Contarini. It is important, you understand, that the *cicisbeo* is a man of influence, who can be of use to the family. He is not simply decorative. And for the *cicisbeo*, it confers a degree of influence with the family. The Contarini are one of the most important families in Venice.'

'And the Contessa is your particular friend.'

'Not my *particular* friend. But we are acquainted.'

'And would it be possible, do you think, for her to affect an introduction?'

'Between you and her *cicisbeo*?' Sister Caterina considered it. 'I expect it would. But what am I to tell her? That an English naval officer wishes to bribe the Venetian Vice-Admiral to sell the fleet to England?'

'It would perhaps be necessary only to tell her that a gentleman of your acquaintance desires the honour of an interview.'

'I suppose that is possible. But then, if it could be arranged, this interview, what would you tell *him*?'

Nathan had been giving some thought to this, but he was not sure how much he wished to reveal to Sister Caterina.

'I would introduce myself as an American man of commerce who has been sent on a particular mission by his government to secure the assistance of the Venetian fleet.'

'Ah, you want him to sell it to the Americans!'

'Well, they do not have a fleet of their own. But I did not say that precisely. I said to secure its assistance. American commerce in the Mediterranean is, as you probably know, much troubled by pirates off the Barbary coast.'

'I did know that. Very plausible. Unfortunately, you could still be hanged for it. And so could he. Except that the Ten would probably not put themselves to the trouble of hanging you. They would just send someone to slit your throat one night when you were walking back from a house of ill-repute – or a convent – and throw you to the fishes.'

'So I have been told. Well, I would have to take my chance on that. Unless you have an alternative suggestion.'

'Oh, but I do. That is why you are here.'

'I am sorry?'

'Where is your ship-of-war, the *Unicorn* – an excellent name, by the way?'

'Well . . .'

'Oh, you do not have to tell me its exact position on the chart. It would mean nothing to me, anyway. But could it be brought to Venice at short notice? And the other ship that is with it – the *Bonne Aventure* – another excellent name, by the way – for our endeavour?'

He winced inwardly at the extent of her knowledge, but at least she did not know about the *Jean-Bart*. That was something, he supposed. And it probably meant her intelligence came from Naples. Either from the Queen or Lady Hamilton or Sir John Acton. Or all three. 'It is possible,' he agreed. 'But for what purpose?'

'How many men do you have?'

'Well, a ship of that size has a crew of about two hundred and fifty or so. Officers and men.'

'And soldiers? You have soldiers?'

'Yes. Marines. We call them Marines.'

'How many?'

He hesitated a moment but it was not a military secret. 'The normal contingent in a ship of that size is about forty.'

'So few?' She frowned. 'Still, a show of force . . . The red coats – they wear red coats?' She shot him another fierce glance. He nodded in affirmation, despite himself. 'Good. And we would have plenty of assistance.'

'What exactly did you have in mind?' he enquired politely.

'Listen to me. You think I am mad – yes, you do,' as he began to shake his head. 'You think all women are mad. All men do, in their hearts. Mad, bad and dangerous. Especially women who meddle in things that should not concern them, like politics. But I am not mad. Nor am I stupid. Do you know the size of the Venetian Army?'

'I am told it numbers about five thousand or so.'

'They are mostly Slavs and Albanians from the Dalmatian Coast, and a few Greeks,' she explained. 'Mercenaries, of course. The Venetians, they no longer serve in their own Army. Over two thousand are scattered in small garrisons in the Veneto – the most, they are in Verona, eighty miles away. In Venice, there are fewer than five hundred men who are fit for active service. Have you ever seen them?' Nathan shook his head. 'No, I did not think so. You do not often see them. Mostly they are in their barracks, drunk, scratching the fleas, picking from each other the lice. Some of them have muskets but they are not permitted to carry them, or even to practise with powder or shot. Too expensive. Also too dangerous. The Ten, they have always feared their own army, more than they fear the army of a foreign power. Then there are the *sbirri* – the police. You will have seen them, they are everywhere. They number around a thousand on paper, their actual strength probably a little less. But they are not soldiers. Nor are they armed with guns, only swords and staves – and the officers, they carry pistols. The *sbirri* is good to break up a mob, but a company of trained soldiers with muskets – Marines, you call them, yes? And your sailors, too, they can fight, I have heard?'

'They have been known to on occasion, but—'

'And we would have the *Arsenalotti* on our side.' She saw that the term was unfamiliar to him. 'The trained bands of the Arsenale. A militia. The only militia in the city. Fanatically loyal to the *Serenissima*. They guard the Doge's Palace on all state occasions.'

'But if they are fanatically loyal . . . ?'

'Why would they support a coup? Ah, that is what is so clever about it. Because we will convince them the government is about to surrender to the French. And then your ships they sail into the lagoon, the sailors and the Marines they come ashore . . .'

'And the Two Castles – the Fortezza di Sant'Andrea and the Castelvecchio? We just sail past them?'

She was unmoved. 'We will have bribed the Commandants not to fire upon you.'

'I see. But can we not bribe the Vice-Admiral of the Venetian fleet?'

But she was already shaking her head. 'He is already bribed. By the French.'

He stared at her. 'You are certain?'

'I am.'

'So it would be useless for me to contact him?'

'Not only useless, but extremely dangerous. He is also, in his heart, a supporter of the Revolution and a great admirer of General Bonaparte who is winning all these victories against the Austrians. He will keep the fleet safe for the French when they come here – and they will come, if we let them. So, you see, you have no alternative but to support my plan.'

'And the French? You think they will stand idly by?'

'Now listen to me. The Austrians are marching down the Adige Valley to the relief of Mantua. General von Wurmser has fifty thousand men under his command. Bonaparte will have enough to occupy him. He could not spare a single troop of horse to come to the help of his friends in Venice, even if they had the means of crossing the lagoon. We can do this. All it needs is a little courage.'

'I am afraid this is well beyond the terms of my commission. I have no authority to risk my ships or my men in such an enterprise.'

'It is a risk others would take in your position. Your Commodore Nelson would not hesitate, I think.'

'Commodore Nelson is also an acquaintance of yours?' He was prepared to believe it.

'I have never met him, but I know of his reputation from others. And I know he would not spurn such an opportunity to win for his country the fleet of the Venetians, and the islands of Corfu and Cephalonia, and for himself the Glory.' She was probably right. 'A bold plan, he would call it,' she concluded.

Nathan considered. It was impossible, of course. Even for Nelson. With a single frigate and two sloops – and one crew between them. Even to take Leghorn, Nelson had asked for 2,000 regular British infantry.

But Leghorn had been occupied by the French, whereas Venice . . .

Could he trust her, and her assessment of the Venetian Army – and the *sbirri*, and the *Arsenalotti* – and, most of all, the Two Castles? It was a hell of a lot to take on trust from one nun.

'So, you are talking of a coup against the present government of the *Serenissima*.' She gave him a look as if to say, What else do you think I have been talking about this past half-hour or more? 'And who or what would take its place?'

'You cannot expect me to tell you that before you have agreed to take part in it.' He supposed this was a fair point. 'But you may rest assured,' she continued, 'that I have no personal ambition to replace the present Doge, or to take my place in the Council of Ten.'

'Then what *is* your motive?'

'Revenge. And also, of course, to serve the best interests of my country.'

'Of course.' But he looked at her curiously. 'For Dandolo's murder?'

'There are other reasons, but that will do.'

'And who do you think murdered him?'

'I *know* who murdered him. The Devil.'

'Cristolfi.'

'Ah, so you know who the Devil is.'

'And the reason?'

'Because Dandolo had a mind of his own. It is enough – in Venice.' She stood up. 'You will wish to think about this,' she concluded briskly. 'But please do not take too long over it. Or the French may move first.'

He looked at her sharply. 'But you said . . .'

'I said they would not be able to land troops. But they will not have to, if they have enough support in Venice – and no one is prepared to fight against them.'

Nathan also rose, but he was not as anxious to leave as he had been just a few minutes before. If the French were to seize power in Venice, did he not have a duty to resist – to the best of his ability? Certainly to aid the forces of resistance. And if he had the chance to pre-empt such a move . . .

'I will think on it,' he promised.

'Good. Please do. Now, it is necessary, if you are to sustain your credibility as the young American, Mr Nathaniel Turner, intent only upon pleasure, that you should be seen to pleasure yourself a little, is it not?' She smiled at his expression. 'But you will need to wear this.'

He caught the object which she threw in his direction. It was a mask. He turned it over in his hands.

'Put it on,' she commanded him firmly. 'It is a half-mask that we call the Colombine. Because you have a pretty mouth and a pretty chin and it would be a pity to hide them.'

Nathan put it on.

'Good. And I too. For appearance's sake.'

She, too, wore a Colombine, possibly because she, too, had a pretty mouth and a pretty chin.

'Where are we going?' he asked her.

'Below.'

'But I have been seen without the mask. People will know me for who I am. And you . . .'

'Oh, the mask is not to hide your identity from others. Or at least that is not the most important of its functions. It is to mask your inhibitions, to free you from guilt. It is not *you*, it is the mask. Now,' she gave him her arm. 'We are ready.'

Dawn presumed upon Venice like a botched breakfast, a raw egg leaking down the streaky back of the sky. It found Nathan making his careful progress to the Piazza San Marco where he had hopes of finding a boat to take him back to the *Angelika* and his neglected cot. He was still rather unsteady on his feet on a platform that did not move with the steady rhythms of the sea. He concentrated on walking in a straight line, one foot in front of the other, as if he was walking on a tightrope.

He was crossing a footbridge over one of the canals when the men came up behind him. He was first aware of their presence when they took him by the arms, shouting at him in dialect. He thrust them away from him and reached for his sword but inexplicably it was not there. He struck out with his fists and knocked one of them into the canal before a blow from a stave laid him out cold and mercifully he did not feel their boots going in.

Chapter Fifteen

Canal of the Orphans

———◆———

He was in his day cabin on *Unicorn* with sunlight pouring through the stern windows, but strangely he seemed to be lying on the deck. Why was that? Still, it was good to be back. He had been away, he remembered. Or half-remembered. It would come back to him in a moment, if only it did not hurt so much to think, or move. Too much wine the night before. Red wine and champagne. It was not wise to mix the two. But where had he been drinking champagne? And why was he lying on the deck? Had he not been able to make it to his cot? Had he fallen? It was not good for discipline if someone found him here. He tried to stand up but he was aching all over.

A quantity of water hit him in the face and he half-rose, gasping and cursing, and then holding his head as he was racked with a violent, shocking pain. He felt sick. He *was* sick, rolling over as he felt it rise into his throat. It hurt to be sick. It hurt his head but it hurt his chest most. He crouched there for a moment, trying to breathe, trying to vanquish the pain, or at least come to terms with it. It did begin to ease a little, at least in his head, but there was now a worse pain in his ribs. He wiped his mouth. Where had the water come from?

He squirmed round, opening his eyes and then shutting them again as another violent spasm shot through his head. But he had seen enough to assure him that this was not his cabin. If there had been any remaining doubt it would have been dispelled by the names people were calling him. Pig was one of them. *Porco*. Which meant pig, or swine, in Italian. *Porco inglese*. English pig. He knew that much, but not the other words they were shouting at him. He had no idea where he was or how he had got here, but he remembered the convent, and some at least of what had happened there, and walking back along the canal towards the Piazza San Marco. There had been some kind of argument, he thought. He had insisted on walking back alone. And some men had set upon him. Presumably the men who were abusing him now.

He tried to climb to his feet, to continue the fight, for the one thing you must not do in a street brawl or a fight on the deck of a ship was stay down; you had to get up, no matter how badly hurt you were, and keep moving, or they would kick your head in. But he could not get up. He was in irons. But at least they were not kicking him. He sat up and put his head in his hands. He could do that, though his wrists were shackled. His wrists and his ankles. The pain in his head had now retreated to a point just beyond the crown. He put a hand to it and felt crusted blood and a lump the size of a pigeon's egg. He sat there for a moment, trying to get his strength back.

Someone was pulling at him, taking his hands away from his face. He tried to resist but others joined in, forcing his arms down. Someone was peering into his face, tugging at his eyelids, and he thought of butting him, but then he heard the word *dottore.* Another word he knew. Doctor. They had brought a doctor to him. Surely this had to be a good sign, though in truth the man looked like a villain. He reminded Nathan of Dr Roach, their family doctor back in Sussex when he was a child. The youngsters called him Dr Cockroach.

Nathan submitted to having his head examined. The doctor applied some salve to the wound and dressed it. Then he pulled up Nathan's shirt. There was a great livid bruise all down his right side, possibly several run into one, but after feeling for breaks the doctor merely shrugged and applied more salve. While he was doing this Nathan looked about him. A plain, unfurnished room. Stone walls. Arched ceiling. Wooden floor. A window with an iron grille. Some kind of prison, then. Two guards. There had been more, he thought, when they had attacked him.

He asked the doctor if he spoke French. The doctor said nothing. Latin? But of course he spoke Latin: he was a doctor.

'*Civis* . . .' Nathan began. '*Civis* . . .' But there was no word for American in Latin. He made it up. '*Civis Americanus sum.*' That should be clear enough, and he said it in French, too. '*Je suis un citoyen Américain. Je suis un citoyen des États-Unis. Je demande à voir le Consul Américain.*'

The doctor said nothing, not to Nathan. He stood up and spoke to the two men in dialect and then closed up his bag and left. The men unlocked the chain that attached Nathan to the floor and led him off like a bear, a dancing bear, out of the room and down the corridor, but shambling rather than dancing because his ankles were still chained together.

The room they brought him to was much larger than the other and clearly not a prison cell, though there were grilles on the window. It was more like a courtroom. It had panelled walls and tiered bench seats arranged in a semi-circle and a large desk, like a judge's bench, on a raised platform at the far end.

In front of this platform there was a man, sitting in a chair, reading some papers. He looked up when Nathan entered and put the papers on the floor beside him. His presence was not reassuring. He was dressed in black and he had a face like a skull. He looked, Nathan thought, like the figure of Death.

They stood Nathan before him at a distance of about five or six yards, his manacled hands held in front of him. He kept his head lowered and his shoulders hunched in defeat, but he felt some of his strength returning to him. A sudden leap and he could pull the guards off their feet. The chain would then become his weapon, his flail. He needed only a few seconds and he could wrap it round the man's throat.

'Mr Turner?' The man spoke. It was almost a sigh. Nathan said nothing but it was encouraging to be addressed as Turner. His next words, however, were not so encouraging. 'My name is Cristolfi. Does that mean anything to you?'

It did. And not only because he had spoken in English. Spiridion had warned him about Cristolfi. The man they called *Il Diavolo*. The Devil.

Nathan looked up and met the man's eyes. They were as cold as a serpent's. 'Where am I?' he asked.

'You are in the *Palazzo Ducale*. To be precise, in the *Magistrato alle Leggi*, where criminals are brought to answer for their crimes.'

'I am not a criminal. I have committed no crime.'

'Oh.' The Devil reflected a moment, scratching the side of his head. He had very short, grizzled hair. In fact, he was almost bald; it was strange that he did not wear a wig. Perhaps he thought the absence of a wig added to the fear he evoked, and he was probably right. He was a man of about forty or fifty, Nathan reckoned, and in good condition physically. Lean, quite strong-looking. He had a long face, a long jaw, clean-shaven. *Il Diavolo*. What else had Spiridion said about him?

He was not Venetian-born – he came from somewhere in Dalmatia – but he was fanatically loyal to the Republic.

'What crime am I charged with?' Nathan persisted.

'I hardly know where to begin. But let me try. Conspiracy to overthrow the Republic. That would do to start with. It carries the death sentence, in case you were wondering. Traffic with the agent of a foreign power. That, too. Lewd and offensive behaviour of a nature inclined to the perversion of public morals. You might get away with thirty years for that. Wearing a mask in a place of worship. Five years.' He frowned. 'That seems rather excessive. Quite illiberal, do you not think? No matter. I doubt it will figure in the charge sheet, given the choices available. Resisting arrest. Assault upon agents of the *sbirri*. Shall I go on? There is more.'

'I did not know they were agents of the *sbirri*. They fell on me without warning.'

'They told you exactly who they were and you assaulted them. I myself was a witness to it.'

'I do not speak Italian. I thought they were *bravi*, come to slit my throat.'

Cristolfi looked shocked. 'You thought our good *sbirri* were *bravi*? That will not speak well in your defence.'

'I am an American citizen. I have the right to speak with the American Consul.'

This was in the nature of a test, for his interrogator had said nothing thus far to indicate he was aware of Nathan's true identity – or nationality. The fact that the guards had called him an English pig meant nothing. They would not distinguish between an American and an Englishman in such a context.

'But I do not think the good Mr Devereux will wish to speak with *you*. Not when he hears of the charges against you. He is a man of strict moral principle and he has a beautiful daughter to protect from the likes of you. Lewd and offensive behaviour,' he repeated thoughtfully. 'Behaviour of a nature inclined to the perversion of public morals . . .'

'Oh, for pity's sake, you would have to arrest half Venice.' A better argument occurred to him. 'Certainly you would have to arrest half the foreigners who come here.'

'You mean they do not come for the beauty of the place? For the architecture, for the paintings? "*To see the works of Titian and of Tintoretto, of Tiepolo and Bellini – as I do.*"'

His exact words to Devereux. So who had repeated them? A servant in the pay of Cristolfi, or the Consul himself?

'I do not think he would be pleased to know you were arrested coming home from the Convent of San Paolo di Mare at dawn,' the Devil pointed out. 'I do not think he would believe you had been there to pray.'

Nathan's head was beginning to hurt again. 'So what do you want of me?' he enquired. 'Am I permitted to see a lawyer?'

The Devil laughed. He appeared to be genuinely amused. Nathan remembered what Spiridion had told him about Venetian justice. And corruption.

'Then, is there something I can offer in mitigation of my alleged offences?'

'Attempt to bribe a senior official of the Republic? That, too, carries the death penalty.'

'I do not believe I spoke of money. I spoke in a spirit of co-operation.'

'Oh. Co-operation. Now, that is a very good word. Co-operation. Yes, I like the sound of that. And how are you prepared to co-operate, may I enquire?'

'I expect you are going to tell me that.'

'Indeed, I am. Very well.' He spoke in his own language to the guards and one of them brought a chair for Nathan to sit upon. 'You can begin by telling me why you have come to

Venice. And do not tell me it is to see the works of Tiepolo and the rest.'

Nathan considered. Clearly, given Cristolfi's position and the power he held over him, it was futile to tell the story he had told the American Consul. But there was another that might serve almost as well.

So he embarked on the fiction he had prepared for Admiral Condulmer and rehearsed upon Sister Caterina, with some elaborations that had occurred to him since.

It was well-known that the government of the United States was much concerned by the atrocities committed upon their shipping by the Barbary pirates, he began. These rogues, many of whom were under the protection of the Bey of Algiers, were indiscriminating in their attentions, requiring only that their victims should be non-believers; since there was little in the way of Jewish, Hindoo or Buddhist shipping in the Mediterranean, these victims tended to be Christian, of one denomination or another.

The Devil leaned back, folding his arms across his chest, frowning a little, but Nathan could see he had his complete attention.

While regarding any Christian vessel as legitimate prey, Nathan continued, these jihadists of the sea were inclined to be more tolerant of vessels of those nations possessing a navy capable of inflicting retribution, either upon themselves or upon the ports and commerce of the Bey of Algiers, and by and large they extended a like dispensation to those whose governments paid an annual fee by way of exemption. The government of the United States, however, possessed not a single ship-of-war, and were disinclined to pay a large tribute annually to men they regarded, not to put too fine a point on it and without disrespect to their professed religion, as a bunch of thieves and cut-throats. Unhappily for their merchant ships and the men

who sailed in them, this policy left them vulnerable to attack
– and attacked they were. Their ships were boarded upon the
high seas, their cargoes pillaged, the crews – and passengers if
there were any – subjected to gross abuse and sold into slavery.
The slave markets of Tunis, Algiers, Cairo and even as far
distant as Constantinople and Baghdad paying a premium
for healthy, fair-skinned males and an even greater amount for
the female of the species, should they be so fortunate as to
come by such a prize.

The Devil nodded comprehendingly and settled his long
chin upon his fist.

Not surprisingly, Nathan continued, the government of the
United States was much disturbed by this practice, but had
failed to come up with a solution – until some enlightened
diplomat in the service of President Adams had thought of
seeking the protection of the Venetian Navy.

The Devil's eyes widened a little in surprise and enlightenment.

Encouraged, Nathan went on to explain that the Venetians,
unlike the English, French and Spaniards, had no previous
history with the American people that might, for reasons of
national pride and honour, preclude such an arrangement, or
make it a subject of critical debate in the American press.
Besides which, the Venetian Navy in times past, under the
leadership of Admiral Emo, had delivered such a blow to
the pirates of Algiers that they had desisted in their attacks for
many years.

And so it was decided to send an emissary to make discreet
enquiries.

'You?'

Nathan nodded. 'It was thought advisable to keep my
mission confidential,' he said, 'for fear that it might come to
the attention of the English.'

The Devil clapped his hands. A slow clap, with the rhythm of a dead march. 'An excellent tale,' he declared. 'I do not think there is a better in the *Thousand and One Tales of the Arabian Nights*. I congratulate you, sir. Were it my decision, I would almost certainly commute the death sentence to one of fifty years in the Doge's Prison, at the *Serenissima*'s expense. But alas, I am a mere public servant, and my masters are less impressed by the fabrications of a plausible rogue.' He silenced Nathan's protest with a gesture. 'Now you must listen to me, sir, for I must inform you that only the truth will save you, even if it is considerably less entertaining than what we have just heard.'

He signalled to his associates, who at once threw a loop of chain around Nathan's throat, making it impossible for him to execute the manoeuvre he had previously contemplated. He then spoke some words to them in their own tongue and Nathan was yanked to his feet and led from the room.

They took him up a short flight of steps and along a passage with two grilled windows on one side through which Nathan caught a glimpse of the lagoon and the island known as San Giorgio. This, then, must be the Ponte dei Sospiri, of which Spiridion had advised him – the Bridge of Sighs, which was used to take prisoners from the courtrooms of the Doge's Palace across the adjoining canal to the building known as the New Prison – though it had been built more than a century ago. These windows afforded the convicted felon his last sight of the outside world before his incarceration, hence the sighs.

For Nathan, however, the sight of the lagoon gave him more cause for hope than despair. Somewhere out there, just off the tip of the island, was the *Angelika* where his absence would now have been noted. It would not be long before Gilbert Gabriel, at least, began to question his whereabouts and to make strenuous efforts to find him. But would it lead him to the Doge's Prison?

They had reached a staircase with steps leading both up and down. With a small shove the guards indicated he should take the steps going down. They were steep and narrow and increasingly wet. The walls, too, were dripping. Nathan concentrated on not stumbling. When they reached the bottom, they proceeded along another corridor and through a door into a large, windowless room very like a cellar or storeroom. As Nathan's eyes adjusted to the gloom, he made out the shapes of several large pieces of equipment whose purpose was shockingly plain. He could even put names to some of them. The rack, the garrotte, the grid-iron – and a brazier for heating some of the other instruments that hung from hooks on the walls. The bile rose to his throat as he took them in. But on this occasion, at least, he was here only to look, and reflect. This was what awaited him should he fail to satisfy his grim interrogator.

A jerk on his chain and he stumbled back into the corridor, through another door and into – sunlight. A muted sunlight, admittedly, for it was a small courtyard enclosed on all sides by the walls of the prison. Even so, he gazed greedily up at the sky, squinting against the harshness of the light. He counted four floors, each marked by a row of square grilled windows – but not a sight nor sound of a single occupant.

They led him across the courtyard, past the cistern in the middle and through the opposite door into what was apparently the prison reception area. Here he was handed over to his new guardian, a man who bore as much resemblance to a toad as was possible, Nathan thought, whilst still remaining a member of the human race. He subjected Nathan to another search, though everything of use to him had been removed while he was still unconscious. Then, relieved of his chain and manacles, he was introduced to his new quarters – a dank cell of about three yards by four, whose only source of light was a small window with an iron grille set high in one of the walls, its only furniture a wooden pallet resting on two stone plinths and a leather bucket. Despite the intense heat, the ceiling, floor and walls were running with damp and there was a tide-mark of mottled green-and-black slime up to a height of about two to three feet on the walls.

He was in the *Pozzi*. The Wells. Known as such, Spiridion had informed him, because their proximity to the canal meant that they were flooded to a depth of between two and three feet at high tide. So twice in every twenty-four hours, for several hours at a time, the prisoner was obliged to wade up to his thights in water, or stand on the wooden pallet. And unless he took the bucket with him, the waters would be fouled with his own filth, though as the canal was more or less an open sewer this was a minor consideration. Far worse was the prospect of being overrun by the large rats that infested the place, for they could swim as well as they could climb, Spiridion had assured him, and only waited for you to lie down before subjecting you to their foul attentions.

The door was slammed shut. The bolts slotted into place.

Nathan remembered that it was his birthday. He was twenty-eight years old.

He sat down on the wooden pallet and subjected the room to closer study. Apart from the grating the only objects of interest were two small holes at floor-level, presumably to let the water out – and the rats in – and the *graffiato* scratched by previous occupants on the walls and ceiling. A few names, some individual words in Italian, some drawings, mostly lewd – and a few lines of what appeared to be verse.

Nathan took off his coat and folded it into a pillow. Then he lay down on the pallet, clasping his hands behind his head, and contemplated the verse above his head. Though he spoke little or no Italian, some of the words seemed familiar to him from his knowledge of the Latin. Perhaps they contained some useful message from a previous inmate, an aid to survival. Lacking anything better to do, he set himself to translating them. *O voi che entrate* must mean *O you who enter here* . . . He could guess the next line. *Abandon all hope.* It was from Dante's *Inferno.* Hardly the most inspiring of messages, or the most original. He did not bother with the rest.

Instead he applied himself to an exercise that had served him during previous incarcerations in Paris. He tried to make a mental picture of the night sky as he had last viewed it from the *Unicorn* and to project it on to the ceiling of his meagre quarters. The concentration required for this, however, combined with exhaustion and the beating he had received, caused his eyelids to feel heavy and within a few moments he had fallen fast asleep.

Unhappily it was neither as sound nor as relaxed a slumber as he could have wished. He was tormented by a succession of nightmares in which an army of beautiful nuns armed with flails and other instruments embarked on an endless battle with another army that appeared to be composed entirely of lizards. Nathan, who had been recruited as a General in the army of the nuns, was engaged in conflict with a lizard that looked remarkably like Cristolfi when he awoke to find the water seeping steadily into his cell from the gap under the door.

For the next hour or so he watched it rise with gloomy interest. He was not unduly alarmed, for the tidemark on the walls assured him that it would stop more or less at the level of his refuge. As the water continued to advance, however, he grew rather more anxious. When it began to slop over the pallet he was obliged to put his coat back on and stand upright.

The water gradually advanced over his boots. The only positive note was that thus far there were no rats. None that he could see, at any rate. His main complaints were the stench, which was foul in the extreme, the sweltering heat, and – ironically in view of the amount of water in his cell – an immense thirst.

The prospect of drowning, of course, was another factor in his discomfort. Although he told himself that the water would only rise to the level on the wall, his imagination persisted in informing him of the likely situation if it did not. It had advanced almost to the top of his boots before it began to retreat. The atmosphere remained extremely humid, however; the pallet was too damp to sit or lie upon and his thirst had not abated.

At last, when the waters had entirely receded and only a few puddles remained, a small hatch was opened in the door and a mug of water was thrust through with a hunk of stale bread on a wooden plate. This apparently constituted his rations for the day. He drank half the water straight away and kept the rest to aid him through the hours of darkness. The bread he put in his pocket for later as he was not at all hungry.

The hours slid slowly by. The jailers had taken away his watch and everything else in his pockets but he marked the passage of time by the bells of the clock in St Mark's Square, and to divert himself he returned to his study of the Cosmos. Once he had fixed all the major constellations in position he set himself to exploring them in a conveyance of his own imagining which he called a starship.

This craft, which was conical in shape, was propelled according to the principles discovered by the late Sir Isaac Newton, after whom it was named. It was projected into the heavens by a number of rockets, each of which ignited its neighbour before reaching the limit of its trajectory and falling away. Once the craft had risen by these means above the gravitational pull of the earth it would continue to move, consistent with Newton's theories, at the same speed and in the same direction until some other force diverted it. Accordingly, Nathan had designed an ingenious system of magnets which could be raised and lowered and otherwise manipulated by means of several wheels or windlasses, whose purpose was to lock on to the diverse magnetic fields emanating from the planets: not unlike the practice of mariners in following the trade winds. When the time came to return to Earth – and the gravitational pull of that planet caused the craft to drop more rapidly than was desirable – the crew would remove themselves to the detachable chamber at the rear of the craft, inflate the balloon by means of a small furnace, and float safely back to Mother Earth.

Thus Nathan traversed his imaginary universe, stopping off from time to time at planets that appeared of interest to him and exploring them further as the mood took him and whenever he had nothing better to do. His present situation fitting into this category, he settled himself as comfortably as he was able upon his meagre platform and embarked upon a journey to the constellation Monoceros, otherwise known as the Unicorn.

Little was known of this constellation beyond the recent studies of Sir William Herschel, which had revealed it as having four stars. It was bound to have a great many more planets, however, and though nothing was known of them, Nathan gave his imagination full play by applying to them a character and an identity which conformed to his particular fancies, rather in the manner of a Gulliver or a Voltaire. In common with these literary figures, Nathan took the opportunity to satirise those social and political systems on Earth which seemed most absurd, or unsatisfactory, or venomous to him. Such as the one he was in at present.

And so he created the Planet Serenissima.

The Planet Serenissima was in theory governed by a

Legislature composed of several hundred members chosen by the electorate. This institution met regularly to represent the grievances of the people and to enact laws that would address them. In reality, however, the members treated the assembly as an exclusive club which endowed them with great privileges and generous expenses, provided they approved the laws passed down to them by a select few known as the Ten. The Ten were the real rulers of the planet, but to avoid giving this impression they appointed an individual they called the Doge, who had all the appearance and apparatus of power but none of the reality. That is to say, he lived in a great palace, rode about in a golden carriage, or barge, appeared before the public on grand occasions and gave his approval to all the laws that were enacted in his name.

To deflect them from criticism, or rebellion, the people were permitted every indulgence in terms of bread and circuses. They had a Carnival which lasted above half the year and numerous sporting occasions and festivals. Cheap drink was supplied to keep them at a level of drunkenness, or in an abject state of recovery from it, that made them incapable of any sustained level of political protest. The cooking and eating of food became a national preoccupation; dance, music, the fashion industry and the cult of celebrity were all promoted as additional diversions. And the people were allowed every facility to express themselves in writing or in some form of public performance. Almost everyone was writing a novel or a play – usually a reflection upon his or her own life – or singing or dancing or playing upon a musical instrument. On the surface, at least, it seemed that they were all thoroughly enjoying themselves.

Unhappily, very few people were doing any work. The planet was becoming poorer and poorer. The poorer it became, the more pleasure was provided, almost always now at government expense. Paper money was printed to pay for it. This, of course, brought its own problems. As the government's critics began to multiply, the government resorted to oppression. They began to rely more and more upon the police, led by a man people called *Il Diavolo*.

This worked for a while, but eventually they confronted a new critic who could not be kept down. She was a woman – a nun, in fact. Soon she became the leader of a large protest movement. Civil war appeared imminent.

At which point Nathan landed upon the planet in his starship. His natural instinct was to support the rebels, even though he did not entirely trust the woman who led them. He was further inhibited by the fact that the planet which had sent him here – the Mother Planet – was desirous of making a treaty with the Planet Serenissima and recruiting its help in a war they were engaged in with their neighbour and arch-enemy, the Planet of the Frogs. But while he dithered, the Devil pounced. The starship was impounded and its Captain arrested and thrown into their deepest, darkest dungeon.

And now he had to find a way out of it.

Reality impinged upon these fantasies. It was, in fact, becoming darker. By the time the clock on St Mark's Tower had struck nine, it was black as pitch and the nightmares of Nathan's earlier imagining were replaced by the real thing.

First came the mosquitoes. He could not see them but he heard them buzzing around his head. He sat on the pallet flapping blindly at them with his hands. Then he felt the water at his feet. High tide, he estimated, would be at about eleven o'clock. It would be at least an hour after that before it had receded sufficiently to uncover the pallet, another hour before it was dry enough for him to lie down on it again. It was like camping for the night in a bog. He took off his stock and wound it round his face, leaving a small gap for his eyes, even though he could see nothing, but the insects were so bold they even settled on his eyelids. He thought he would go mad. But there was worse to come.

He heard the squeaking first, that distinctive high-pitched squeak that announced the presence of rats. Normally rats were of no concern to him: he had grown used to them aboard ship. But ship's rats were sustained largely upon a diet of ship's biscuit, or whatever stores they could find; they were denied a diet of refuse and human waste because it went straight into the sea. And they usually kept out of your way. You did not encounter them in pitch darkness on their own territory. Sewer rats were an entirely different matter.

Where were they? He stared into the dark, the mosquitoes now a minor irritant. He was sitting on the pallet with his legs folded under him, and the first intimation of their proximity was when he moved his hand and touched one.

He scrambled to his feet and stamped around the pallet, kicking out to mark his territory. This was greeted with a great many squeals and some splashes. He remembered the bread he had stuffed in his pocket and broke it into small pieces, though it was almost as hard as ship's biscuit, and threw them into the furthest corners of his cell. He heard the rats fighting over them. How many of them were there, for God's sake? If only he had a light. He felt the water once more at his feet and one of the creatures crawled on to his boot. He lashed out and he heard the thud and squeal as it hit the far wall and then the splash as it landed in the water. This gave him some small satisfaction. But he was so tired. He had slept for barely two hours in the last thirty-six. Sooner or later he would have to lie down and then they would be all over him. He turned up his coat collar and fastened the buttons up to his chin, though it was already unbearably hot. St Mark's clock struck midnight. Five or six hours before dawn. He would have welcomed another interview with the Devil. He wondered if it would do any harm to tell him who he really was and the reason for his visit.

Shortly after the clock struck two he heard footsteps in the passage outside. Then the bolts of his door were drawn back and it was forced open. The water still lay a few inches deep on the floor but they splashed through it and dragged him out of the cell. There were four of them, with a fifth outside holding a torch. The roughness with which they handled him convinced him that they were taking him to the torture chamber. He had been wrong in thinking they would be inhibited by his presumed nationality. They did not care. The only question was what instruments they would use.

But they did not take him to the torture chamber. They took him back across the Bridge of Sighs to the room where he had met the Devil. And the Devil was still there, reading his papers by the light of several candles. He looked up when Nathan was brought in and put the papers down, just as before. But this time they did not bring Nathan a chair.

'So, have you had sufficient time to think who you are and what you are doing here in Venice?' he enquired in his excellent English.

Nathan considered. There was really no reason not to tell him the truth, or at least an approximation of it. It could do no damage to his country and it could harm no one in Venice, for he had not yet had time to contact anyone apart from Sister Caterina, and they must know about her. It might conceivably embarrass the Ambassador, of course, but Nathan was not sure he cared overmuch about that.

He sighed, for he knew himself too well. 'My name is Nathaniel Turner,' he said. 'I am an American citizen and I have told you why I am here. I demand to speak with the American Consul.'

He was not sure why he said this. It was part foolishness, of course, and pride. A stubborn resolve not to be intimidated. But perhaps there was a more reflective view that he should hold the truth back for when he really needed it, for when the torture became unbearable and the need to convince them became pressing.

The Devil, too, sighed. Then he spoke to Nathan's guards. He spoke in the Venetian dialect but either because it so closely resembled Latin or because something in his tone and gesture spoke for itself, Nathan understood him to say: 'Take this thing and dispose of it.'

Nathan tried to resist but he was stiff from his ordeal in the cell and weakened by the blows he had already received. And there were four of them. They threw him to the ground and tied his hands behind him. Then they dragged him away. Along another passage, through a door and down a flight of stairs. He saw lights reflected in water. He looked up and saw the night sky. Stars. His universe. Not the courtyard, either. They were beside a canal. He could see the Bridge of Sighs to his right. And at his feet there was a boat of the type the Venetians called a *mascareta*, very like a British dory. A shove in the back told him he was to climb into it.

'Where are you taking me?' he asked them, in French and Latin, even in English. No reply. Instead, they thrust a gag into his mouth. It was only when they forced him to the deck and tied an anchor to his feet that he had his answer. They were taking him to the Canale Orfano – the Canal of the Orphans.

He remembered what Kyrgyakos had said when they had first moored here.

'It is said that they still dispose of certain prisoners in this fashion. Political prisoners. Those who might cause them some embarrassment if they were hanged in public.'

He kicked out and strained at his bonds, but it was useless.

Now, if anyone had asked him, he would have told them everything. But no one did, and nor could he have replied with the filthy rag in his mouth. He raged at his own stupidity for not telling Cristolfi the truth, for coming to Venice in the first place, for not heeding Spiridion's words of warning.

'If you offend against their authority and their own narrow sense of order, they will look to the Devil for redress. And the Devil will dispose of you, my friend, in the most convenient manner that is available to him.'

They glided out from the little canal into the Basin of St Mark. Even lying in the scuppers Nathan could see the lights of the Piazza and of the shipping moored in the Basin. Somewhere out here was the schooner *Angelika*. If only he could shout they might hear him. But it was useless to even think about that.

They left the lights behind them. Now all he could see were the stars. He concentrated on them, trying to pick out the constellations. He identified Lyra, Aquila and Cygnus. The moon had set, but August was the month of the meteor showers known as the Perseids and he looked for them greedily, not having seen them before. It seemed only fair that he should see them before he died, or perhaps just one, as if it was his starship cruising through the heavens, waiting for him to join it.

These whimsical reflections were disturbed by a more practical consideration, for it suddenly occurred to him that the steel hook on the anchor might provide a means of freeing him from his bonds. He squirmed around in the bottom of the boat but his contortions only succeeded in lodging the anchor rather painfully in his buttocks. He was trying to manoeuvre it into a more suitable position so that he might chafe the rope on it, when there was a sudden shout from one of the oarsmen and another boat loomed up out of the darkness on their starboard side. There was a confused moment – and then with a crunch of oars and a splintering of timbers the two boats collided.

Nathan was sent rolling around the scuppers but he took the opportunity to rub his bonds even more vigorously against the steel hook which was now more or less embedded in his rear. It was only when a large body landed on top of him and there was the flash and report of a pistol that he realised this was no accidental collision. Then the boat was full of struggling figures, fighting with cutlasses and cudgels. Nathan struggled to sit up. Was it the launch from *Angelika*? Had Gabriel discovered what had happened to him and prevailed upon Kyrgyakos to attempt a rescue? Another pistol report and one of his guards fell across him with half his head blown off. Another went overboard. And then it was over. Laughter now. Hands reached down for him, the gag was pulled from his mouth.

'Capitaine Turner?' It was not a voice or a face he recognised.

'Yes. I am Captain Turner. Would you mind getting this anchor out of my arse?'

'*Venez avec nous, s'il vous plaît.*'

Well, he had no objection to going with them, given the alternative, but who were they and why had they come for him? And, rather more to the point, where were they taking him?

'Be at ease, Citizen,' one of them assured him when Nathan put these questions to them. 'You are in the hands of the French Army – the glorious Army of Italy. And we are taking you to General Bonaparte.'

Part Three
The Levanter

———◆———

Chapter Sixteen

Il Liberatore

Nathan was not naturally inclined to the optimistic. Some of his intimates had, unkindly, accused him of being overly inclined to the reverse. He was the kind of man, they said, who would have subjected the Good Samaritan to searching enquiry before accepting his offer of a soothing massage and assistance to the nearest inn. So although there was an immediate improvement in his circumstances – he was relieved of the anchor that was to have been his tombstone; they cut the ropes that bound his wrists; they handled him into their own boat with care, as if he was a frail old gentleman and not the Captain of an English frigate; they settled him comfortably in the sternsheets and gave him water to drink and even a flask of wine – he could not help but wonder why the glorious Army of Italy should put themselves to such inconvenience for one insignificant prisoner of the *Serenissima*.

He did not, of course, believe he was being taken to General Bonaparte. But clearly someone in French headquarters had taken an interest in him, and doubtless at some time in the

near future the reason would be explained to him and he would
be exposed to new forms of torment.

But in the meantime, being unable to do anything about it
– and being, by his own estimation, a cheerful pessimist – he
settled himself in the sternsheets with his flask of wine and
watched with satisfaction as his rescuers stove in the timbers of
the *mascareta* and let it sink to the bottom of the lagoon taking
the bodies of his former tormentors with it. Having accomplished this with an efficiency that persuaded him it was not
the first time they had performed such a task, they hoisted sail
and headed off into the darkness of the lagoon.

Nathan took stock of his new accommodation, which
appeared to be a broad-beamed sailing barge with a simple
lateen rig and a leeboard, not unlike the Dutch *skutsje*. The
eight or nine men who crewed it did not look like French soldiers,
they looked like smugglers, and after a few moments Nathan
concluded that most of them were. They clearly knew what they
were about, even at night and at low tide, expertly manoeuvring
their way through the shoal waters and mud banks of the lagoon
and making steady progress towards the mainland.

It was not a part of the coast that Nathan knew at all well,
even from his study of the charts, and it appeared to be devoid
of human habitation. But as they approached the shore, one of
the crew exposed a lantern in the bow, and after a few moments
an answering light appeared in the darkness ahead of them, a
little to starboard. They altered course towards it and then
lowered the sail and proceeded inshore with the help of a pair
of sweeps until, with a gentle jolt – and still some fifty yards or
so out – they grounded.

'From here, I am afraid you must walk,' Nathan was
instructed.

The water was warm and no more than a couple of feet
deep, and he was glad of the opportunity to wash away some

of the slime and stench of the *Pozzi*. But it was only when he reached the shore that he realised no one else had accompanied him. His rescuers had already shoved off from the mud bank and were heading back towards the distant lights of Venice.

And waiting for him on the secluded shore was the real French Army.

He heard them before he saw them. The jingle of harness. The snort and stamp of horses. And dimly in the darkness, a little back from the waterline, he discerned a troop of horse and a coach and four. A figure detached itself from the group and came forward to greet him. He wore a riding cloak and a military shako but all Nathan could make out of his features was a moustache and the white of his eyes. His voice sounded young.

'Citizen, I have the honour to command your escort, if you will be so good as to follow me.'

He led the way to the coach and a trooper leaped forward to open the door. Nathan glanced into the dim interior. 'I am very wet,' he pointed out doubtfully, in consideration of the upholstery.

'That cannot be helped, *monsieur*,' replied the officer firmly. 'We will find you some dry clothing at the first stop.'

'Are we going far?' Nathan enquired.

But his new guardians appeared even less inclined to enlighten him than those who had preceded them. The officer inclined his head towards the interior of the coach. 'Please, *monsieur*, we must not delay.'

Nathan climbed into the coach. The officer closed the door and slapped his hand sharply on the side. As the vehicle lurched off into the darkness, Nathan was left to contemplate an uncertain future. He consoled himself with the thought that at least he had one.

*

They jolted for about a mile along a dirt track but soon reached a more substantial road which enabled them to set a reasonable pace, even in the darkness. Nathan stuck his head out of the window and looked back to see his escort riding some little way behind, but not so far as to permit any serious thought of escape. Besides, even if he could have leaped from the coach without injury and made a dash for the trees, what was he to do next? He had no money, no knowledge of the language and no idea where he was. Better, he thought, to wait for daybreak and see what fortune it brought.

They seemed to be travelling through a pine forest but at times he caught glimpses of a river and some fine villas through the trees to the left which suggested they were following the course of the River Brenta eastward towards Padua. But the British Ambassador had said the French were further east than that, at Vicenza and Verona.

Nathan thought again about the reference to Bonaparte. It was possible, he supposed, that his presence in Venice had been reported by one of the French agents in the city, but it seemed unlikely that it had been brought to the attention of the General himself, and even more unlikely that after nine months and almost as many battles, Bonaparte would remember who he was. But if it *had* been brought to his attention, and he *did* remember, then it could only be because it had crossed his mind that the mysterious Captain Turner, the erstwhile associate of his time in Paris, was not who he said he was, and that instead of being an American merchant mariner in good standing with the Revolutionary authorities, he was in fact a spy for the British. Nathan's sudden disappearance from the French capital could only have reinforced this view, and so he had instructed his minions to extract the truth from him before placing him in front of a firing squad.

But this, admittedly, was a pessimistic view.

They were coming to a halt. Nathan looked out of the window. A coaching inn. Apparently the 'first stop' the officer had mentioned. But when Nathan tried to alight he was politely requested to remain in the coach. It was too dangerous, the officer informed him. 'These Italians, you cannot trust them. They rob you and slit your throat.' They brought food and drink out to him, however, and the promised change of clothing – nothing like as elegant as he had chosen for his visit to the Convent of San Paolo di Mare and about two sizes too small, but it was clean and dry and he changed into it without complaint. Then he sat gazing out of the window, drinking his wine and eating his bread and cheese, while they changed the horses.

He noted that two of the troopers were stationed on either side of the coach, either to protect him from having his throat cut or to stop him from escaping. He suspected the latter. The rest of them were standing about outside the inn, smoking and drinking while their own mounts were watered at the troughs. He noted that both men and mounts appeared to be in remarkably good condition for an army that was said to be starving and in rags only a few months earlier, when they had crossed the border into Italy. The men wore green uniforms with hussar-style braided coats and helmets, and though Nathan was no military expert he took them for *chasseurs à cheval* – light cavalry. He could no longer see the officer but presumably he was inside the inn, eating something rather more substantial than bread and cheese.

It seemed to be a regular staging-post – another coach came in from the opposite direction shortly after their arrival – and there were plenty of people about, even in the early hours of the morning. But no one appeared to question the presence of a troop of French cavalry on Venetian territory. He found himself wondering what would happen if a troop of French horse had ridden boldly through the English shires, and concluded they would probably get away with it there, too. Certainly he could see them trotting through Lewes without much more than a nod and a wink from the local Constable, much the same as if they were smugglers. There was a strong tradition of looking the other way in Sussex. *Turn your face to the wall, my dear, while the gentlemen go by.*

The officer emerged from the tavern, the sergeant began to shout orders, and they were off again, on their madcap dash across the Veneto. And within a few minutes, replete with food and drink and in his new suit of dry clothing, Nathan was asleep.

He woke with sunlight pouring through the windows; they had come to a halt again and there was a figure standing at the open door. Nathan shaded his eyes against the glare. The face appeared familiar to him but it was a moment before he knew why.

'Good God,' he said. 'Sergeant Junot!'

'*Colonel* Junot,' the apparition informed him. 'I've been promoted. Move over.'

Junot. The first time Nathan had met him was in Paris, outside White's Philadelphia Hotel in the Street of the Little Fathers. He had thought he was a tramp or a police spy. But he turned out to be aide de camp to General Buonaparte, who then still used the Italian version of his name, and he had come on his Commander's behalf to challenge Nathan to a duel. Nathan had insulted the Citizen General, he said, by making disparaging remarks about him to a woman whom he held in the highest esteem.

The woman was Rose Beauharnais and Nathan *had* made disparaging remarks, though not deliberately, being under the impression at the time, thanks largely to Rose, that Citizen General Buonaparte was a street entertainer and circus performer who made his living by being shot out of a cannon. Nathan had wriggled out of the situation by humbly apologising and buying the General dinner at the Procope in the Cour de Commerce, where Danton and Desmoulins used to eat. Buonaparte was in need of a good dinner at the time, being penniless and unemployed – he had been promoted Brigadier General, or *Chef de Brigade*, for his services as an artillery officer at the Siege of Toulon, but he had never been given a brigade to command and he was generally regarded in Paris as a bit of a joke: Captain Cannon. Hence Nathan's unfortunate error.

The meal had been a success and Junot had turned up at the end of the meal to carry the General home. The next time Nathan met them both was during the Royalist uprising of Vendémiaire when, purely out of desperation, Bonaparte had been given the job of commanding the troops who remained loyal to the government. Even after his success he was still widely sneered at in the Army as the General who had fired on the mob. General Vendémiaire. Not any more. And Junot had obviously shared in his good fortune. He wore the uniform of a Colonel of the horse artillery with half a ton of gold lace and a large plume in his hat. He took it off when he climbed in the coach and put it on his lap, smoothing the feathers. A trooper shut the door after him and they were off again. Nathan looked out of the window. They were following the walls of a city with the French tricolour flying from the battlements.

'Where are we?' he asked.

'Vicenza,' replied Junot shortly. Now he was banging the dust off his thighs. There was a lot of it. Nathan flapped his hand in front of his face.

'And where are we going?'

'Verona. Then Roverbella.'

'What's at Roverbella?'

'You ask a lot of questions for a fucking prisoner.'

'Am I a prisoner? No one told me.'

'Well, let's say for the sake of argument you're in protective custody. It amounts to the same fucking thing.'

Nathan observed him mordantly. He still spoke with the trace of a rural accent – he came from a village in Burgundy, Nathan recalled – but there was something of the schoolmaster or the lawyer's clerk about him, even in his smart new uniform. Certainly he was an educated man: he had been Bonaparte's secretary in Paris as well as his boot-cleaner. Nathan had an idea he had once trained for the priesthood. He tried to remember if he had sworn as much in Paris and thought not; there was something rather showy about it, as if it came with rank. He had filled out a bit and grown florid since his days on the scrounge with his unemployed General, but he had the same sharp, ferrety eyes and thin nose, the red mark of the glasses he usually wore across the bridge. He was about twenty-four or twenty-five years old. Colonel Jean-Ardèche Junot. It had a ring. Better than sergeant, anyway. 'I'm glad success hasn't changed you,' Nathan said.

'What's that supposed to mean?'

'That you haven't lost your natural affability.'

'I've just saved your fucking life, isn't that affable enough for you? From what I hear the Venetians were about to feed you to the fish.'

'Really? I thought they were just trying to put the wind up my sails. But thank you, if it was you who saved me. How did you know?'

'How did I know what?'

'That I was trussed up in a boat with an anchor up my arse.'

'Well, I didn't, to be honest. If I had I might have left you there – far be it from me to interfere with the way a man pleasures himself. But I knew you were in the *Pozzi* – we get regular reports from our agents in Venice – and I asked myself, "Hello, what is our American friend who left us so suddenly in

Paris without so much as a goodbye, good riddance, now doing in the Serene Knocking Shop?" And knowing what a fine upstanding citizen you are, I knew it couldn't be for the sex. So what *were* you doing there? If you don't mind answering a few questions yourself for a change.'

'Not at all. I was on holiday, as a matter of fact.'

'The hell you were. Was that why Cristolfi threw you in prison? Were you having too good a time?'

'You know Cristolfi, do you?'

'Look, you just don't get this, do you? I am here to interrogate you, not the other way around. That is why I rode up from Lake Garda where I was having quite a pleasant time, since you ask. I thought it would be quite civilised to question you in the coach, but if you'd rather we did it the usual way in a cellar with whips and nut grinders, it can be arranged.'

Nathan grinned at him. 'Thank you,' Nathan smiled agreeably, 'but I'm quite comfortable where we are. I don't know why the bastard threw me in prison. I'd like to ask him, with my hands round his throat. Perhaps he thought I was a spy – for the French.'

'Or the British. That's wiped the smile off your face, hasn't it? I read the reports. You've been asking questions about the Venetian Navy.'

'It's an interest of mine,' Nathan told him. 'I'm a Navy man, remember? All right.' He saw he had pushed him far enough. 'I was doing a favour for the government.'

'What government?'

'My government, of course. The government of the United States.'

Junot frowned and wrinkled his nose, greatly increasing his resemblance to a ferret that's had a bit too much rabbit for its dinner. 'What kind of favour?'

Nathan told him the same story he had told Cristolfi, with

minor embellishments – and rather more success, apparently. Certainly Junot did not react with the same level of sarcasm, or shout for the guards to throw him back in the *Pozzi*.

'Interesting. So the Americans want the Venetian fleet.'

'Well, a couple of frigates would do.'

'Even so. I think you will have to talk to Bonaparte about that.'

Nathan regarded him curiously. 'Am I going to talk to Bonaparte?'

Junot thought about it. 'He wants to see you,' he admitted.

'Really? I would have thought he had more on his mind at the moment, with the Austrians at his throat.'

'Stuff the Austrians. They're nowhere near his throat, nor ever likely to be. His wife gives him more problems than the Austrians. You saved his life in Paris. He will never forget that. Even if you did try to fuck his wife.'

Nathan thought of pointing out that this was a gross exaggeration, and that in any case she was not married to him then, but he could not summon the energy.

They were both silent for a moment. Nathan looked out of the window. They had left the river and were climbing between steep hillsides covered with vines. Workers tending them in straw hats, women mostly, stopped to watch as they passed by. They did not wave. One of them shook her fist. Nathan remembered the streets of Paris in October, the smell of gunpowder and the smoke hanging in the air. The National Guard cut to pieces with grapeshot on the Pont de la Révolution. He was in a little street off the Rue Saint-Honoré, a cul-de-sac with a church at the far end. The Church of Saint-Roch: all the saints' names had come back in France since the end of the Terror. There were a couple of hundred Royalist rebels on the church steps, some in the uniform of the National Guard, others in their shirtsleeves, hurling defiance at the so-called

Patriot Brigade of People's Deputies who had come out of the Convention to fight them and changed their minds when they saw that it might involve dying.

Then Bonaparte came riding up on a white horse someone had found for him. All night long he'd been on his feet, dashing about from gun to gun in the pouring rain with Nathan and Junot running after him, taking turns to bend over so he could use them as a table for his street map. 'Now he has to go poncing around on a horse,' Junot had just said, worrying about him being shot at. Next minute, the horse was rolling on the cobbles and Bonaparte with it. The mount was up before anyone could get to it, its eyeballs rolling, bolting down the street dragging the little man with it, his boot caught up in the stirrup, straight towards the rebels on the steps of the church. Nathan ran after it and caught hold of the bridle before he could think what he was doing. A musket round took off his hat and another took the horse in the head and put it down for good, and then Junot was there with a squad of infantry and Bonaparte was on his feet calling for them to bring up cannon.

'All I did was hold his horse,' he told Junot.

'Yes, well, you know that and I know that, but His Holiness thinks you're his lucky star.'

This was true, though he had thought little of it at the time. Bonaparte took a particular interest in stars, not quite as scientific as Nathan liked to think his own interest was, but no less passionate. 'Every man has a star, you know,' he had assured Nathan when they had dined together at the Procope. His had been depressed at the time; he thought it had abandoned him for good. He had given up all hope of a career and was writing a novel.

'I thought his star was in the heavens,' Nathan said to Junot.

'It is complicated,' Junot agreed. 'Maybe he thinks you are its personification on earth, Christ knows why. Or it might have something to do with magnetism.'

'Excuse me?'

'He thinks every single body in the universe has an effect on everything else. Like magnetism. You'll have to ask him about it, I'm damned if I know what it's about. Anyway, he's nervous at the moment. He thinks the stars are pissing him about. Pulling the wrong way or something. So when I told him that a certain American ponce was in Venice he said, "Get him out, bring him over here." He wants his lucky star. Either that or he wants to know why you left Paris in such a hurry. He was asking for you, you know, as soon as the dust settled. He wanted to invite you to the wedding.'

'The wedding?'

'To Rose. Joséphine as he calls her now. Madame Bonaparte.'

'Oh.' It was all he could say, really. Rose. An enchanting image sprang to mind of her standing stark naked at her own dinner-table and trying to cover herself with a napkin while her lover, Paul Barras, stood in the doorway in a blue uniform and a plumed hat and told her to put her clothes on. And now she was married to Bonaparte. Nathan had an immense fondness for Rose. She looked gorgeous naked. He wondered what her wedding had been like. Glamorous, no doubt.

'So where *did* you scurry off to, then, you rogue, if it's not an awkward question?'

It *was* an awkward question. Nathan tried to think of a good answer besides the true one, which was that he had gone to London to report back to the Admiralty, but for once his imagination failed him. Fortunately Junot was distracted. They were coming to a halt again. 'What's the matter now?' he grumbled. He thrust his head out of the window and shouted something at the escort; then swore an oath and jumped down from the coach. Nathan peered after him. There appeared to be a convoy on the road, coming in the opposite direction. Junot was talking to the officer in charge of the escort. Nathan could see him properly now: a young man with a drooping moustache and a long braid of hair hanging over his shoulder, like the Paris dandies. And doubtless it would have looked fine in Paris, but on a dusty road in the Veneto it looked like he had a rat on his head and its tail was hanging down from under his hat. His uniform was caked in dust and so was his face except where the sweat had caused tiny rivulets to run through it, like cracks in a clay sculpture. A sergeant came running up with a map and Junot put a thin pair of spectacles on his nose and peered at it, jabbing down from time to time with his finger. Then he came back to the coach.

'The Austrians are in Verona,' he said.

'Is that bad?'

Junot gave him a look. 'It's bad for you,' he said. 'You'll have to get up off your arse and ride.'

'A horse?'

'No, a fucking camel. Of course a horse! You can ride, can't you?'

'I'm in the merchant marine, not the cavalry.'

'Oh God.' Junot put his hands on his hips and stared at the sky.

Nathan took pity on him. 'I suppose I could manage at a pinch,' he said, 'but why do we have to?'

'Because the Austrians are between us and Bonaparte. We'll have to take the back roads.'

But it was not so easy to find him a mount. They had to take one of the coach horses. Nathan eyed it doubtfully as they saddled it up. 'How far do we have to go?' he asked.

Junot showed him on the map. The Austrians had followed the Adige Valley down from Trento, and the French Army was on the far side, to the south of Lake Garda, about twenty kilometres to the west. But there were only two bridges across the Adige, apparently: one at Verona and one at Bussolengo, twenty kilometres further to the north. They were hoping the Austrians had not left a garrison there.

'And you want to ride there now?' Nathan was dubious.

'Well, I'm not hanging around here picking grapes.'

So they rode to Bussolengo. Despite what he had said to Junot, Nathan was perfectly at home in the saddle, but the horse they had found him didn't like being saddled and it didn't like being ridden. Nor was it at ease with the route they were forced to take, twisting and climbing through the vineyards until they came to a ridge overlooking the Valley of the Adige. Below them, sparkling in the evening sun, was the river. And spanning it, a small town with an ancient keep and a bridge. Bussolengo. It was clear, even from a mile away, that the Austrians were there.

'Can we not try further upstream,' Nathan enquired, 'and swim across?'

But the Adige, it appeared, was too deep and too fast – and Junot could not swim.

'We will wait for dark,' said he, 'and make a dash for the bridge.'

Nathan did not like the sound of that. Nor did the cavalry officer. The mounts were blown, he said, and the men exhausted. They had ridden over fifty miles since they had picked Nathan up from the lagoon. The horses would never descend the slope in the dark, he said, much less raise a gallop to cross the bridge.

'Very well,' Junot conceded reluctantly. 'We will rest up until dawn.'

So they rode back two or three miles to a small village set among the vineyards and billeted themselves on the unfortunate inhabitants for the night. Junot took the best house for himself but was gracious enough to share it with Nathan. A woman cooked them a stew of beans and onions with some straggly bits of meat that could have been anything, but they mopped it up with hunks of bread and washed it down with the golden-white wine of the region.

'This is the life,' said Junot, who was a peasant at heart.

But Nathan had one pressing concern.

'What happens at dawn?' he wanted to know.

At dawn they crossed the Adige. They came down from the hills in the half-light with their bridles greased and muffled, the horses' hooves clad in leather. A low mist hung over the river and extended across the fields on either side. They could no longer see the bridge, or very much of the town except the top of the keep rising out of the mist – like the tower of an ogre's castle, Nathan thought, in a fairytale. He was not, otherwise, inclined to the whimsical. Junot had offered him a pistol but he had turned it down, not wanting to shoot upon Britain's allies, but telling Junot that as an American he was a non-combatant in this war, and that to kill anyone, Frenchman or Austrian, would be murder. Junot looked at him as if he was trying to be funny.

'Well, I doubt you'll need it,' he said, when he realised this was not the case. 'The last thing they will expect is an attack from east of the river.'

He might have been right, for their approach elicited no challenge until they reached the town, though Nathan was more inclined to thank the mist for that. But then, as they saw the outlines of the first houses, there was a shout, followed a moment later by the blast of a trumpet, and a line of white-clad troops seemed to rise up out of the ground almost at their feet.

'Ride!' yelled Junot, drawing his sword and urging his mount forward.

Nathan seriously thought of letting them go, but his own horse, which could only be induced to walk by kicks and curses the day before, was perversely caught up in the excitement of the moment and broke into a wild gallop. The mist saved them. The mist and the sun, which splintered into a thousand spears in the vapid air, lancing directly into the defenders' eyes. They burst through the thin white line without losing a single man and charged on through the town. But when they reached the bridge there was a wagon drawn across the middle of the road and a double line of infantry drawn up in front of it.

The line erupted in smoke and flame. Men went down. Men and horses in a confused mêlée of lashing hooves and screams and blood. Nathan saw the lieutenant's face shattered, his body leaning sideways but his hands still clinging to the reins until he and his mount went over together. He saw a gap between the wagon and the side of the bridge and urged his mount towards it. There were figures rushing at him with bayonets but the charge swept them away. Four of them were carried through the gap together, jammed tight and jostling each other in their frenzy. One went right over the wall into the river. Nathan saw the horse's rolling eyes, the white foam on its muzzle. Junot was lashing about him with his sword, his face a demonic mask in the witch's brew of smoke and mist and fiery light. Then they were through and charging for the far end of the bridge. But there were men here, too, with their muskets levelled. Nathan lay low over his horse's neck, a roaring in his ears that he was surprised to find came from him. The thunderous report of the volley. More screams of beasts and men. Junot's horse went down and Nathan leaned forward and snatched him up, threw him over the pommel and rode on. It was instinctive, a part of the roaring in his ears, the fury of the moment. If he had thought about it, he would not have done it. But by the time he did they were through. They did not stop until they reached the vineyards on the far side of the river and he put Junot down. There were four of them, five with Junot. They had been thirty when they started out.

Junot fell upon him, covering his face with kisses. 'You save another life for France,' he declared. Nathan thought this was very French.

They rode on towards Lake Garda, the troopers taking turns to double up so Junot could have his own mount. There was no pursuit. They rode in a dazed silence. Nathan felt they were shocked by their losses, bewildered to be still alive. He knew he was. He felt he was to blame. He had brought Death with him, out of the lagoon of Venice.

They rode along the eastern shore of Lake Garda until they came to a small fishing village where they found a ferry: a broad-beamed sailing barge which took all five of them with their horses to Desenzano on the southern shore. There were more Frenchmen here – infantry, maybe a thousand or so. Nathan thought they looked beaten: an army in retreat. They had been part of the force besieging Mantua, Junot said. An officer told him Bonaparte had moved his headquarters to Lonato, a few kilometres to the south-west.

So they rode on to Lonato.

The bulk of the French Army of Italy was camped in and around an ancient fortress known as the Rocca which sprawled over the hillside above the town with a distant view of the lake. It was impossible to make an accurate estimate of how many troops were gathered here but Nathan tried – he thought it might be important. At least 10,000, he reckoned, but there could easily have been twice that. Mostly infantry but at least one regiment of *chasseurs à cheval* in their green uniforms and a long train of artillery with gun limbers and wagons trailing back towards the lake. Nathan had a chance to look them over at his leisure for they rode right up to the castle and back down again in their search for Bonaparte. No one seemed to know where he was, or if they did they were not willing to disclose it, even when Junot lost his temper and threw his hat on the ground. But finally he met another Colonel who told him he had just been to see Bonaparte and that he was down in the town, in a villa called the House of the Podestà – the residence of the Venetian Governor.

'What do I call him, if I speak to him?' Nathan asked as they rode into the town.

'What do you mean, what do you call him?' Junot had recovered some of his old charm since the incident on the Adige. 'What – do you think you call him *Nabolione*, like his mother, or his brothers and sisters? Even they don't dare call him that now. You call him "my General", like the rest of us, with respect. He is not the man you knew in Paris. He's *Il Liberatore*. The Liberator of Italy.'

'I treated him with respect in Paris,' Nathan objected.

'I'm fucked if I noticed,' Junot grunted. 'And he certainly didn't.'

'Well, I do not suppose for a minute that he will have time to speak with me,' Nathan said. 'Now he is so important.'

'Oh, he will speak with you, don't you worry – *if* we ever find him,' said Junot.

But they did find him – where the Colonel said they would, at the House of the Podestà in Lonato. He was sitting in a chair in one of the upper rooms, surrounded by lesser mortals, with his eyes closed and his head lolling. *Il Liberatore*, the saviour of the Revolution, the new God of War. He had not changed much since Nathan knew him in Paris, except he had a better uniform. But he had the same lank, straggling hair cut off in a ragged line at the collar, the same sallow complexion and sharp, almost haggard features, so sharp you felt they could strike sparks off iron. If anything he looked younger than he had in Paris – he was possibly the youngest man in the room, Nathan reckoned, apart from Junot, though there was hardly anyone who looked much above thirty. There was a map spread out on the table and the officers were arguing over it. Nathan gathered they had lost the cavalry; some said it was at Peschiera and others that it was still at Vicenza. He heard the name Kilmaine and some disparaging remarks about the Irish.

'They're not at Vicenza,' said Junot. 'I've just come from there. The last time I saw Kilmaine he was at Roverbella.'

'Are the Irish fighting for you now?' Nathan asked Junot.

'Only Kilmaine,' said Junot. 'And he's one too many.'

One of the other officers shushed them. 'Keep your voices down,' he told them with a glance at Bonaparte. 'He's been in the saddle for three days.'

'So have I,' said Junot. 'No one's worried if I've had enough sleep.' But he dropped his voice. 'Come here,' he said to Nathan, 'and I'll show you what we're up against.'

Nathan stood next to him at the map. It showed the whole of the Veneto from Venice to west of Lake Garda, and from Mantua in the south to Trento in the north.

'We are here with about eighteen thousand men.' Junot stabbed a finger on Lonato, south of the lake. He swept his hand to the south. 'Wurmser is here, marching up from Mantua, with thirty thousand Austrians. Somewhere behind him . . .' he frowned '. . . or in front of him is Sérurier with ten thousand of our men from Mantua. Behind us is Kilmaine, with the cavalry. Except that we do not know where they are. But when we find them, and when we get our men back from Mantua . . .'

There was a slow hand-clap behind him. Bonaparte had

woken up, or perhaps he had never been asleep.

'Brilliant,' he said. 'Junot is back. We can all go home.'

Junot grinned a little uncomfortably. 'Good day, my General. How goes it?'

'Not bad until you showed up.' Bonaparte peered at him through his sleepy eyes. 'Where the devil have you been?'

'I went to Venice as you ordered, my General. To fetch the American.' He presented Nathan with an awkward flourish, like a conjuror upon the stage after a trick that has gone badly. Several of the officers looked at Nathan curiously. Bonaparte frowned.

'Captain Turner. Welcome back. We missed you in Paris. I wanted to invite you to my wedding.' He still had that thick Corsican accent. One of the reasons they used to laugh at him in Paris. *Nabolione*, they'd say, like an Italian mama beseechingly. *Buonaparte*.

'I am desolate to have missed it, my General,' he said. 'Please permit me to offer my belated congratulations. And how is Ro— Madame Bonaparte?'

'Very well, I trust. I was obliged to leave her in Milan and now she has gone back to Paris. What were you doing in Venice?'

Nathan opened his mouth to reply – though not entirely sure what he was going to say – but Junot stepped forward and spoke quietly in the General's ear. Bonaparte closed his eyes again but nodded once or twice, then opened them and looked at Nathan sharply. Nathan wondered what Junot was telling him. He braced himself for the interrogation but Bonaparte raised a hand. 'Well, it appears we have a great deal to talk about – when we have the leisure. But now, I am afraid, we have greater priorities.'

He levered himself out of the chair and crossed stiffly to the table. The other officers drew respectfully back.

'So, now Junot has explained the position to you, with his usual exactitude, what are we to do about it?'

'I have no idea, my General,' replied Nathan truthfully, with a smile that was not entirely convincing.

'Well,' Bonaparte surveyed the map as if he were seeing it for the first time, 'imagine we are in Paris. No, it is not easy, I agree, with all these mountains and the lake. But essentially it is the same. We are outnumbered and surrounded with our backs to the wall . . .' He frowned. 'Can you be surrounded with your back to the wall? Perhaps not.' Nathan wondered if he was feeling the pressure. At Paris he had commanded a few hundred men and fifty or sixty guns. He had forty thousand in the Army of Italy, the Viceroy had said, though if Junot could be believed he had no more than half that number at Castiglioni.

'Outnumbered and surrounded,' Bonaparte repeated thoughtfully, still gazing down at the map, 'but we have one advantage that they do not.'

He did not say what it was. Perhaps he thought they all knew.

He looked at Nathan. 'Remember, *monsieur le Capitaine*, how you held the map for me, at the Tuileries, you and Junot?'

'I do,' said Nathan. 'It was raining.'

Bonaparte stared at him as if he was being flippant, but Nathan was a Navy man: you always had to think of the weather. 'Was it? I do not remember. Perhaps it was. Now listen to me, and I will teach you how to be a General.' He peered at the map. He looked, Nathan thought, like a wasp buzzing over a pot of jam. 'A month ago the Austrians were in retreat. Here at Trento. Twenty thousand of them at most. Defeated, demoralised – under a General they did not trust. They were no longer a threat to me, no longer an army. So

I went to Milan to see my wife. I drew a new map of Italy. I took tribute from the Pope in return for Rome. I even had time to kick the English out of Livorno.'

Nathan remembered that, too, but did not say. He wondered if Bonaparte had been there, up on the hillside with his beloved artillery, looking out towards the *Unicorn*, that irritating English frigate, guarding her chickens, plucking the English to safety. But Bonaparte had moved on from Livorno.

'But then the Emperor took twenty-five thousand men out of his Army of the Rhine and sent them south, under Wurmser, to Trento. Generalfeldmarschall Graf von Wurmser, one of the old school. You know that he is seventy-two? I am twenty-six. War is not a game for old men. But . . .' he shrugged. 'The Emperor trusts his old men. *Die alte Herren*. So now I have this old man with his twenty-five thousand veterans at Trento and twenty thousand of the men I have already defeated – how many times is it, Junot?'

'Three times, my General.'

'Only three? It feels like more. And last week they marched down the Adige. I was not too worried, to tell the truth. I thought Masséna would stop them at La Corona but . . .' He shrugged again. 'He did not. He let me down. His troops let *him* down. Some of our battalions did not behave very well, not like one expects Frenchmen to behave, did they, Junot?'

'No, my General.'

'How would you know? You were in Venice. Hiding behind your mask. Playing at Carnival.'

Nathan had taken Junot's remark about being in Venice as a lie, or an exaggeration, but now he wondered. Had he been in Venice while Nathan was there? Had he been in the Convent of San Paolo, in his mask? But he forced his attention back on the map. He had the feeling that for some reason Bonaparte wanted his approval, but why? Unless Junot was right.

'But then Wurmser makes a mistake. The first mistake. He divides his army. He sends eighteen thousand men down the west of Lake Garda under Quasdanovich.' He drew the line with his finger, the narrow trail between the lake and the mountains. 'The rest he brings down the Adige.' He drew another line, down the east of the lake, towards Verona and Mantua. 'Now why does he do that? Why does General-feldmarschall Graf von Wurmser, with all his experience, send half his men down one side of the lake and half down the other?'

He looked sharply at Nathan. Nathan shook his head.

'I have no idea,' he said.

'Nor have I,' said Bonaparte with a sigh. 'But let us think about it. Look at the map.'

Nathan took a guess. 'To catch you between two pincers? Squeeze you like a lemon.'

Bonaparte looked at him. 'You are sure you have not been a General?'

Nathan smiled thinly – he took it to be sarcastic but no, Bonaparte thought that might very well have been what Wurmser had intended – and that it might have had every chance of success, if he had seen it through.

'See, he has cut my lines of communication with Milan, and if he unites the two wings of his army here, south of Lake Garda . . .' Bonaparte shrugged. 'Well, I will not say we are finished but we have a fight on our hands. But then he makes his second mistake. He takes Verona but then he carries on marching . . . marching south to Mantua.' He frowned at Nathan. 'Why do you think he does that?'

It seemed reasonable enough to Nathan, given that Mantua was his objective. He said as much.

'But consider, what is his priority? What should *be* his priority?'

Nathan thought what Nelson would do. 'To defeat the enemy,' he said. 'To smash them. To go right at them.' That was what Nelson would have said.

'Excellent.' Bonaparte clapped his hands together twice. 'We will make a General of you yet. His priority is to defeat me. To smash me. The French Army of Italy. He smashes the field army of the French and not only does he raise the Siege of Mantua, he takes back the whole of northern Italy. For we have no other army in the field. So why does he march on Mantua?' This did not seem to be a rhetorical question: he seemed to be genuinely puzzled. 'Is it because he wishes for the glory? To become the General who breaks the Siege of Mantua? Maybe he thinks the Emperor will make him the Duke of Mantua, along with his other titles. Or maybe it is just that he is an old man and fights the old wars. In the old wars you do not fight battles, not unless you have to. Armies are too precious to lose. You move them around the map, you take a city here, a city there. It is a war of sieges and fortresses. But we have changed all that. For see, I have raised the siege, I have abandoned my siege guns, all those trenches we have been digging all summer, I have pulled back Sérurier's division from Mantua and I have concentrated my forces here, south of the lake. I am between his two armies. The lemon, you say? Very good. Imagine this is the Tuileries in Paris. It is Vendémiaire. The enemy have me surrounded and outnumbered. But at any one point if I strike out from the circle, it is I who have the advantage – me. And this is what I have done. Yesterday we took Quasdanovich here at Lonato – Masséna did. He makes up for his defeat at La Corona and he has sent him scuttling back to the Tyrol, with the loss of how many men, Junot?'

'I do not know, my General, I was not here.' Sulkily.

'Tell him, somebody.'

'Seven thousand,' said several voices at once.

'Seven thousand men. And he is out of the fight. And now Wurmser is marching up the Mincio from Mantua with his twenty-five thousand men to save him, not knowing he is already defeated, and tomorrow we will do the same to him. Except he has nowhere to run, and *if we can find the cavalry . . .*' raising his voice for the benefit of the others in the room '. . . *we will wipe him out!*' He looked at Nathan again. 'Someone will tell us sooner or later where the cavalry are. Kilmaine is an Irishman, you know. His family name is Jennings. I cannot even pronounce it.' He had difficulty with some of the French names, too. 'So what have I left out, my General?'

Nathan looked at the map again. He scratched his chin. 'The weather?' he guessed.

'The weather?' A frown. Bonaparte looked at Junot; he looked at the other officers. They aped his frown. 'What is the weather to do with it? Do we think it might snow, in August?' He looked to his officers again. Nathan could see they were thinking about it. 'Why do you say this? I ask if you remember Vendémiaire and you say, "Yes, my General, it was raining." You are like my mother. "Take your coat, *Nabolione*, it is going to rain. Remember, my son, it is cold in the Alps in winter."'

The officers laughed. Apparently it was all right for Bonaparte to make jokes about his mother, and his name.

'No, not the weather, not the wind or the rain or the snow. What I have left out is *the luck*. A General must have the luck. If Wurmser has the luck and I do not . . .' Suddenly he looked depressed and very tired. 'Well, a General must make his own luck. Give our friend here an armband, Junot,' he said, 'and find him a horse. He can hold the map. It may bring us the luck.'

He walked back to his chair and fell into it, closing his eyes again.

*

Next day they marched to Castiglione.

Nathan spent the night wrapped in a horse blanket on the floor. He thought of escape but dismissed it as impractical. Even if he could have made his way to the Austrian lines without being shot by the French *videttes*, there was every likelihood of being shot by the Austrians. He did not underestimate the difficulty of convincing a nervous and excitable Austrian picket that he was a Captain in His Britannic Majesty's Navy who found himself stranded 100 miles from the sea in the uniform of a French cavalry officer. Especially as the only German he spoke was *Guten Tag* and *Danke*. Good-day and Thank you would not, he thought, prove overly persuasive.

His chief hope was of an Austrian victory. In the chaos of a French retreat, he thought it might not be impossible to make his way back to the coast, especially if he was now supplied with a reliable mount. Finding a boat that would convey him to the *Angelika* – if she was still at her mooring – was a problem he would consider at the appropriate time and place.

And so a little after dawn on the fifth day of August, or eighteenth Thermidor as the French still insisted upon calling it, Nathan rode out with General-in-Chief Bonaparte and his staff to fight a battle that would, the General informed them, determine the fate of Italy, possibly the whole of Europe. Nathan rode a big bay gelding with a more amiable disposition and considerably better gait than the last horse they had given him, and he wore the green-braided coat of a Major in the 21st Regiment of *chasseurs à cheval*. Junot had also found him a red-and-white silk scarf which he had tied about his right arm to signify that he was one of the Commander-in-Chief's elite *aides de camp*. The map was folded in his pocket. The weather, albeit irrelevant, was fine. Clear blue skies, the sun already warming the parched earth. He had been given a sword and a pair of pistols. Junot rode at his side, Bonaparte a little ahead of them both.

The Austrians were drawn up on a ridge of high ground running east from Castiglione to the small town of Solferino, marked by the distant tower of La Rocca which guarded their right flank. Their left was guarded by the redoubt of Monte Medolano. There had been an exchange of artillery fire and the morning mist was thickened with smoke, shrouding the ridge where the Austrians were. Nathan saw the white-uniformed figures moving through it like ghosts. Not that they appeared to be moving much. They seemed content to hold their position and let the French do all the work.

His first impression was hopeful. The French troops looked exhausted. They had been marching and fighting for three days now and many of them were dead on their feet. The Austrians commanded the high ground and they had a large advantage in numbers. From remarks he had overheard, Nathan gathered that Wurmser had about 28,000 men with his veterans from the Army of the Rhine, and more he had picked up from the garrison at Mantua. Bonaparte had about 22,000 but with 10,000 more marching up the Oglio after raising the Siege of Mantua. He had Masséna on his left and Augereau on his right and Kilmaine with his cavalry – which had either been found or had not been missing in the first place – massed in his rear.

If Bonaparte had asked his opinion, and Nathan had been inclined to the French cause, he would have advised him to stay where he was until his reinforcements arrived and then hope to turn one or other of the Austrian flanks. But Bonaparte did not ask his opinion. He launched an immediate attack on the Austrian centre.

For most of the morning Nathan watched the French columns advancing towards the opposite ridge and then falling back. But they always fell back in good order and it occurred to Nathan, after some private deliberation, that the attacks were feints, designed to persuade Wurmser to strengthen his centre at the expense of his flanks. He had no idea if this was working or not. Although the mist had dispersed, the smoke lay thick over the entire battlefield. He could no longer see either Solferino or Monte Medolano. There was a continuous roar of artillery all along the line, though it seemed rather a tame roar to Nathan after the confined discharge of a ship's broadside.

He had leisure to observe Bonaparte directing a battle, but in truth he learned little from it. The General seemed lost in his thoughts and he did not choose to share them. He looked, Nathan thought, like a mathematician working out a very complicated sum in his head. Gallopers came and went bringing news from his divisional commanders, but mostly they brought notes, scribbled in the heat of battle, and Bonaparte sent written notes in return. The first indication of a tactical manoeuvre was when Nathan heard Bonaparte emphasising that both Masséna and Augereau were to make the retreat look real. What retreat? Nathan wondered. He could see no signs of a retreat from either side. Then he saw the Austrians pouring down from the ridge over towards Solferino. He understood now what was meant by 'the fog of war'. A little later, a galloper came in with news that the French troops from Mantua were attacking the Austrians' left flank. Then, for the first time, Bonaparte consulted the map. He nodded to himself a few times and then called out to one of his aides.

'Ride to Marmont. Tell him now.'

The staff shifted their position to the right to watch the attack on Monte Medolano. The *masse de rupture*, Bonaparte called it. Even through the smoke, Nathan could see the French horse artillery gallop up to point-blank range and open fire on the Austrian flank. And behind the horse artillery came the grenadiers. Even Nathan, who hoped for a French defeat, felt a thrill of excitement as he watched those blue-uniformed troops in their bearskin helmets marching into battle to the sound of the drums. The little drummer boys almost running to keep up with the marching troops, beating out the rhythm of the march, rat-a-tat-tat, rat-a-tat-tat. He heard the roar of the Austrian artillery and the distant spiteful whine of the falling shot. He saw the swathes it opened in the ranks of the marching men, but they did not stop marching and the drums did not stop beating.

News now came thick and fast. The grenadiers had taken Monte Medolano. Leclerc had captured Solferino. Wurmser was falling back on the Mincio. Bonaparte ordered a general advance.

It was evening, the sun low in the sky but still hot. Smoke everywhere now, and the dead and the wounded, and the heat rising in waves from the scorched earth. They had ridden down to Borghetto, Bonaparte and the whole of his staff. The Austrians, it was said, were now crossing the bridge over the Mincio. Wurmser himself was there in person. Bonaparte was still shouting for his cavalry, where were the cavalry? Now was the time to smash the enemy, before they escaped over the river, but he needed his cavalry. Then someone came in with news that the Austrians were bringing up reinforcements from the south. 'Where is Kilmaine?' Bonaparte was bawling. Kilmaine appeared to be what every army needed – a scapegoat.

Nathan turned his horse round and rode back through the smoke. He would never have a better chance, he thought. He had a fresh horse and his map. He pulled it out of his pocket. Even riding by easy stages he could reach the coast in two days. But first he would have to cross the river. Clearly it was impossible to join the Austrian retreat and cross the bridge at Borghetto – but if he rode north to Peschiera by the lake, even if there was no bridge there he might find a boat. If anyone tried to stop him – anyone French, that is – he would say he had been sent to find Kilmaine and his cavalry. It seemed to serve for most.

But it was not the French he had to worry about. It was the Austrians. Suddenly he was among a confusion of gun limbers and shouting men. He asked an officer what was going on. The Austrians had broken out of Borghetto, the officer said. A desperate, last-ditch attempt, probably, to cover the retreat. Nathan was putting his map away when he saw them coming through the smoke: Austrian cavalry, Uhlans, cutting down everyone in their path. He wheeled his horse about and urged it into a gallop, back towards where he thought the French would be, but in the smoke and the confusion, he galloped the wrong way. He realised his mistake when he saw the glint of sunlight on the river and the Austrian bayonets; saw the long white column crossing the bridge and the others on the far side of the river winding back into the distance, a whole army in retreat. There were flames in the smoke and he heard the crash of musketry: they were firing back from across the river – and they seemed to be firing at him. Several rounds whined about his ears or struck dust from the ground.

Bending low over the horse's neck, he kicked his heels in its flanks, thinking to ride through them as he had at Bussolengo on the Adige. But this time his luck was out. He felt a tearing pain in his thigh and then a terrible blow to his chest. The force of it lifted him up out of the saddle but he was still clutching the reins and he was thinking he had to stay on the horse, he had to stay conscious. But then he saw the ground coming up to meet him and he stopped thinking anything.

Chapter Seventeen

A Hero of France

———◦•◦———

They told him he was an American called Turner. Nathaniel Turner – a New York Yankee fighting for the French – and that he had been wounded at the Battle of Castiglioni. He was a hero, they said. A hero of France.

'Turner?' he repeated. 'Nat-aniel Turner?' This meant nothing to him.

'That is because you have lost your memory,' they said. 'You fell off your horse and banged your head, and now you do not even know your name.'

This was not his only problem.

He had fallen off his horse because he had been shot. He had been shot in the chest and in the leg. He was lucky to be alive, they told him. Both shots had been fired at extreme range from the far side of the river and the musket balls had not penetrated very far. The surgeon had been able to dig the ball out of his leg without much trouble while he was still unconscious, but the ball in his chest had penetrated the ribcage, cracking one of his ribs, and had lodged close to his right lung. Too close for the surgeon to remove it. They were hoping it would work its way to the surface, as often happened in such cases.

'What if it does not?' he asked them.

They did not say, but he suspected that he would die.

He was quite lucid in his mind and in his speech. He could converse with them in French, but not Italian. His French was excellent, they said. He spoke it like a native. They would have taken him for a Frenchman if they had not been told he was American.

'But are you sure?' he asked them.

'Quite sure,' they said, smiling. An American sea captain, an adventurer, fighting for the French.

They were nuns. Or to be more accurate, they told him, sisters. Nursing sisters. The Hospitaller Sisters of St John of Jerusalem. Their hospital was on the shores of Lake Garda on the edge of the Veneto, the mainland territory of the Most Serene Republic of St Mark. For some reason this troubled him, but he was not to worry, they said, because he was under the protection of the French. More than that, he was a friend of General Bonaparte.

'He has asked us to take especially good care of you,' they said. 'He has said that if you die it will be on our heads so, you see, you must not die.'

'Who is General Bonaparte?' he said.

His memory puzzled him. He knew who the French were but he had no memory of having been to France. He vaguely knew who the Americans were, and even the Austrians, but again, he had no memory of being to either of these countries or of having ever met an American or an Austrian. He had no memory of the battle they said he had been in, but he asked after his horse.

'Your horse was shot at the same time as you were,' they told him. 'It died.'

There was another hero of France in the hospital, they said. His name was Colonel Junot and he had been wounded in the head. He had not lost his memory and his wits were intact, as far as they could tell, but there were still some splinters in his skull and he suffered from headaches. He spoke very warmly of le Capitaine Turner. The Captain had saved his life, he said. He was in the next room. Soon, when he was feeling a little better, the Colonel would come and visit him.

There was one young nun who was from Ireland and she spoke to him in English which he found he understood as well as he did French. Her name was Sister Francesca and she had the face of an angel. She had been born in Dublin where her father was a doctor, but when she was eleven the whole family had gone to live in Rome. One day she brought a book for him.

'It's about a sea captain,' she said, 'the same as you.'

His only complaint about Sister Francesca and her sisters was that they spoke to him as if he were a child.

The book was *Gulliver' Travels* by Jonathan Swift and she read it to him aloud in the hope that it would help to bring his memory back. So far it had not, but he liked her reading to him.

He had been here almost a month and his memory was no better than when he had first arrived. What's more, the wound in his chest was growing worse. They put hot poultices on it to draw out the poison but he grew weak and feverish. He drifted in and out of consciousness. He could not eat. He was wasting away.

'They are bringing a famous physician from Milan,' Sister Francesca told him. 'General Bonaparte has ordered it.'

The famous physician was called Dr Calvaresi. He was a small man of middling years and lugubrious expression. He looked more like an undertaker than a doctor to his patient

but there was often little distinction, and besides, Nathan was
past caring: an undertaker seemed fairly appropriate to him.
He began to care more when the doctor removed the dressing
and started to poke around in his wound. He expressed himself
fairly forcibly on the subject but the doctor, not a whit dis-
comfited, declared that the ball had carried particles of clothing
into the wound which had caused an infection; it would have
to be extracted. There was no time to be lost, he said. The
operation must be performed immediately.

The patient was stripped to the waist and laid on a wooden
table with a cushion beneath his head. They also provided him
with a leather gag to bite upon. The same surgeon who had
removed the ball from Nathan's leg was in attendance, but his
main function seemed to be to assist in holding him down. It
was Dr Calvaresi himself who performed the operation. He
explained the procedure. He would use a long metal probe,
like a hollow tube, which would grip the musket ball and
prevent it from penetrating to the lung. Then he would insert a
device very like a corkscrew down the centre of the probe,
which could be gently screwed into the soft lead of the ball and
permit it to be drawn out through the tube. Then he would use
a pair of tweezers to remove the cloth and any other foreign
tissue. Once the wound had been thoroughly cleaned it would
be irrigated with a mixture of turpentine and lime water and
then packed with honey. This, though it seemed unduly
eccentric, was not Nathan's prime concern. His prime concern
was the probe.

In this he was entirely justified. The agony was beyond
anything he had anticipated, and he had anticipated the worst.
Despite the attentions of the surgeon and two stalwart nuns,
his movement was such that they were obliged to strap him
down. He exhausted his repertoire of abuse. Shortly after they
resumed the operation, he passed out.

When he came to, he found himself back in his bed between clean white sheets with a bandage round his chest. There was a great deal of pain but it was not unbearable. Sister Francesca was there. She looked pale and frightened. The operation had been successful, she said. The doctor had removed the bullet and a piece of cloth from Nathan's shirt. The wound had been drained of pus and packed with honey. Now they could only wait and see.

The next day the fever came upon him. For almost a week he hovered between life and death. Sometimes it seemed as if he was already dead. He revisited places he felt he had been before in a previous life, though he had no real memory of them, only a vague feeling of familiarity. The sea figured largely in these places but also a city in which there were many churches but also a great deal of pain and squalor and suffering. He was conscious sometimes of the presence of Sister Francesca and other of the nurses. They bathed his face and even his whole body with cool, damp cloths. They changed his dressing. They gave him water to drink.

And then one night he woke up and knew who he was.

It was the middle of the night. Four bells in the middle watch. There was a narrow gap between the curtains, and the starlight penetrated the dark sanctuary of his room. He wanted to draw the curtains further back so he could look out at the stars, but he did not have the strength to rise from his bed. Otherwise he felt quite well, better than he had for a long time. Very much at peace but thirsty. He thought about who he was and was not entirely surprised. He had never been convinced about the man called Turner who was an American. But he knew why it had been necessary. He lay there for a long time taking pleasure in the return of his memory. Running through the names in his head. His mother, his father, the *Unicorn*. Tully and the Angel Gabriel. Sara. It was very satisfying for him to remember these people whom he had loved and who were his friends. It felt like they were returning to him. He wondered vaguely if this was because he was about to die.

But he did not die. And when he woke up in the morning he announced to the nuns that he thought he could manage a slice of game pie with a little preserve on the side.

To his disgust they gave him bread and milk instead but greeted his completion of the feast with the applause due to a man who had consumed an entire bullock, horns and all.

He did not tell them who he was. He felt bad about this but he considered that it would only be an embarrassment to them. However, it was never as easy as that. He was obliged of necessity to elaborate upon his disguise: to invent an entire background for himself – as he had for the American Consul in Venice – and he felt even worse than he had on that occasion. He felt particularly bad about lying to Sister Francesca. He longed to tell her who he really was, but he knew that she would be obliged then either to confess it to her superiors or to commit a sin in hiding it from them.

Unfortunately, Sister Francesca possessed an insatiable appetite for stories, particularly stories about Mr Turner, and in search of the material for this fiction, Nathan found himself delving ever more wildly into the territory of a man who was possibly the most untrustworthy individual he had ever met.

And so in this new spectral form, Gilbert Imlay walked back into his life.

Nathan had first met Imlay in Paris at the time of the Terror. Imlay was an American who occupied a role which he described as 'something between a diplomat and a shipping agent'. In reality, as Nathan subsequently discovered, he was a spy. He had at one time or another been a spy for the Americans, the British, the French and the Spanish, often when one or another of these governments harboured the illusion that he was working exclusively for them. And his private life was no less complicated. Whilst in Paris, Imlay had encountered the English writer and feminist, Miss Mary Wollstonecraft, and subsequently married her – in a ceremony of doubtful legality – to save her, he said, from being imprisoned as an enemy alien. This act of selfless chivalry had not prevented him from getting her with child – and then breaking her heart by embarking upon an affair with an actress from a strolling theatre company.

Nathan could have had no greater master in the dark arts of subterfuge and deception. Even as he spoke, he heard Imlay's voice in his own and was filled with a dread that he was becoming uncomfortably like him.

To divert Sister Francesca – and himself – from this topic, he began to express an interest in religion. It was not entirely feigned. Death was no stranger to him but in the past few months it had been his constant companion. He was haunted by the words of the burial service he had read off Cape Drastis.

We therefore commit his body to the deep, to be turned into corruption, looking for the resurrection of the body and the life of the world to come, through our Lord Jesus Christ; Who at His coming shall change our vile body, that it may be like His glorious body, according to the mighty working whereby He is able to subdue all things unto Himself.

How many times had he read those words? Yet only now did he begin to wonder what they meant. But if he hoped that Sister Francesca might enlighten him, he was disappointed. 'Christ is perfection,' she told him, 'and we must work our way towards Him.'

'But what does that *mean*?' he said.

'It means we must strive to be as like to Christ as it is possible for any human to be. Would you like me to fetch you a priest?' she asked him doubtfully.

'No. I don't want a priest. I want to know what *you* believe.'

'I believe in the Apostles' Creed,' she said with a smile. 'Shall we say it together? I believe in God the Father, Almighty Creator of Heaven and Earth . . .'

'No,' he said. 'No, no, no. I know all that. But what do you *believe* in?'

But she would not discuss it any further with him. She was not qualified, she said. She was not a theologian. If he was troubled in his mind he must speak to a priest. But clearly it worried her, for one night she came back to him and renewed the discussion. She told him that she believed that all Christian souls, men and women, were in the process of a journey that would bring them to perfection, perfection in Christ.

'A journey?' he said. He could understand that.

'Yes. But . . .' She hesitated and then it came out in a rush. 'Perhaps more than one.'

'You mean more than one life?'

She did not answer but he could tell that this was what she meant. 'Is that not a heresy?' he asked.

'I rely upon you not to tell on me,' she said with a smile.

'Oh, I will not tell on you.'

He liked the idea of life as a journey. More than one journey was even better. What he did not like was the idea of arriving at the end of it. In life or in death. He did not look for a resolution; only a continuance of the unresolved.

But he was curious that she could hold such an opinion and still feel she could remain within the Church.

'One finds one's own way to Christ,' she said. 'But the Church provides one with a shield – and a set of moral standards.'

He thought of the standards set by the convent in Venice.

'I was brought up to believe that the Church of Rome had

no moral standards,' he said truthfully. 'And that the Pope was the anti-Christ.'

'And now you believe in Revolution,' she said, mocking him with her eyes. 'And that has become your God.'

'I did not say that.'

'But you fight for the French.'

'Yes, but that is not necessarily the same as fighting for Revolution. Most of us, most men, fight for their friends and family. Their comrades-in-arms. Their shipmates.'

'Are the French your friends? Your family? Your shipmates?'

'No.' He was not entirely comfortable with where this was leading him. 'Well, I have friends amongst them, but . . .'

'But you do not believe in Revolution?'

'No, not as such. But if it appears to be the only means of opposing tyranny . . . I mean, we had a Revolution in England – we cut off the head of a King.'

'We?'

'I mean, they. The English.' He felt the colour flood to his face. 'At the time of King Charles we were all English. Even in America.'

But he could tell from the look she gave him that he had done little to remedy matters. For the next day or so he saw nothing of her. He worried that she was avoiding him; that she might report her suspicions to a superior. But she would never do that. She had no reason to love the French, and nor did the Church. If she was avoiding him it was because she knew he had lied to her.

Nathan was surprised by how much time had passed since he was wounded. It was now mid-October. The leaves were falling and there was snow on the high mountains. He wondered what had happened to the *Unicorn*. And the *Angelika*. Had Kyrgyakos discovered what had happened to him? It seemed unlikely. They must think he was dead.

One day Junot came to see him. His head was wrapped in a bandage and he was almost as thin as Nathan. He suffered from terrible headaches and the doctors said his wits were scrambled but he seemed the same old Junot to Nathan. He said that the Austrians had recovered from their defeat at Castiglioni and that Mantua continued to hold out. It was only a matter of time before it fell, however, and then Bonaparte would march on Vienna. Meanwhile, Spain had come into the war on the side of the French. The English, he said, would soon be driven from the Mediterranean. Then the war would be over.

Nathan began to think of leaving. They had stopped packing his chest with honey and the wound was healing. Irritatingly, it was his leg that caused him the most inconvenience. He could only hobble around with the aid of a stick. But he was eating well and putting on weight. He felt fitter by the day. He wondered if he could contrive to steal a horse and ride back to Venice. But he was more worried about Cristolfi than he was about the French. It might be safer, if a lot further, to try to reach the opposite coast and find a boat to take him to Corsica.

Then, while he was thinking about this, he had another visitor.

His name was Landrieux. Jean Landrieux. He introduced himself as Adjutant-Général to the Army of Italy. He had taken a break from shuffling paper to call at the hospital, he said, and see how Captain Turner was progressing.

'General Bonaparte sends his best regards,' he said, 'and his hopes for your continued recovery.'

'It is due to the General's regard that you find me almost fully recovered,' Nathan told him. 'If it had not been for the physician he sent from Milan, I would have been feeding the worms long since.'

Landrieux smiled, but from the look in his eyes his sympathies were entirely with the worms. He wore the uniform of a Colonel in the cavalry but he had the look of a thorough ruffian. Dark, saturnine and hairy. He was a large man, but he sat hunched up into himself, as if he was afraid of bursting out at the seams. His hair, however, was beyond control and was in the process of bursting out from wherever it found an opening to do so – his scalp, his nostrils, his brows and ears, even out of his collar where it pressed into his neck. He rather put Nathan in mind of a troll.

'The General will be pleased to hear it,' he said. He glanced towards the stick resting beside Nathan's chair. 'But you are still convalescing, I see?'

It was more a question than an observation. 'Oh, I need the stick less and less,' Nathan assured him. Indeed, he had begun to think of it as more of an affectation than a necessity. 'I believe I am playing the old soldier.'

The officer laughed good-naturedly, inasmuch as he could achieve that happy state. 'Then you will soon be off on your travels,' he said.

Nathan's hopes rose. Perhaps he was to be sent on his way, with the thanks of a grateful nation. Someone had seen the doctor's bill and sent this bully boy to put a boot under his arse.

'Well, I think I will not go back to Venice,' he said. The officer obliged him with a tight little smile. Nathan wondered if he had been informed of the circumstances in which he had left the city. 'But I thought perhaps I might find an American vessel in Genoa or Livorno heading back across the Atlantic,' he added artlessly.

'Then you intend to return to America?'

'Indeed, I cannot let my interests in New York languish much longer, or I am a ruined man.'

'Livorno is probably your best hope of finding a suitable ship,' reflected Landrieux thoughtfully. And then, after only the slightest of pauses, but as if it had just occurred to him: 'And it is possible that you might be able to do the General a small service while you are there.'

'I would be glad of the opportunity,' Nathan replied with a bow, hoping it would not involve as much injury and inconvenience as the last 'small service' he had done the General.

'I do not suppose you have heard much about the course of the war while you have been here,' Landrieux ventured.

'Not a great deal.'

'Then you do not know that Spain has now joined the conflict on the side of France.'

'Well, I had heard a rumour to that effect,' Nathan replied.

'It throws the balance of power in the Mediterranean decisively in our favour. Especially at sea. The combined fleets of France and Spain far outnumber the British – certainly in the Mediterranean.'

Nathan was aware of this. It had been preying on his mind ever since Junot told him of the event. But why was Landrieux telling him now?

'In consequence of this, the British Admiralty has withdrawn its fleet from the region and abandoned all its outposts apart from the Rock of Gibraltar. However . . .' he drew his chair forward and lowered his voice. 'What I am about to tell you is in the strictest confidence, you understand?'

Nathan nodded and tried to keep his expression one of polite interest, no more.

'Before the withdrawal could be effected, one of our vessels encountered an English frigate off Corfu in the Ionian Sea.' His dark eyes bored into Nathan's. 'You did not hear anything of this while you were in Corfu?'

Nathan slowly shook his head. 'Not a thing.' Was this a

mistake? There was no way of knowing from the officer's expression.

'Well, it was not widely known but the Englishman got the better of the exchange. The French ship was taken and the survivors were landed at Ancona. They reported that the name of the frigate was the *Unicorn*, Captain Nathan Peake.'

Nathan felt like a rabbit fixed by the glare of a snake. It was hard not to swallow. He said nothing. Nor did he trust his voice. After a moment the Frenchman went on: 'The *Unicorn* has since been reported in Naples, presumably on her way to rejoin the British fleet.' Now Nathan struggled not to show his relief. 'Our fear is that she may have taken with her certain . . . documents. Evidence, of a sort, of our intentions in the region.'

It was necessary for Nathan to speak, if only to permit him to swallow. 'I see.' His voice sounded normal. Then: 'Forgive me, but what has this to do with me?'

Landrieux leaned back a little. His regard was more speculative now than intense. 'We would like you to drop a word in someone's ear,' he said.

Nathan frowned enquiringly.

'There is a woman in Livorno called Adelaide Correglia.'

This was becoming more bizarre by the minute. Nathan wondered if Landrieux knew of his acquaintance with Signora Correglia; knew exactly who he was, in fact, and was playing a game with him for his own amusement, like a cat with a mouse. When he had finished playing with him, he would hang him.

'Signora Correglia is a whore. She is also a spy for the British. We have known this for some time. And so we feed her the occasional scrap of misinformation to pass on to her English friends.'

Nathan continued to stare mutely at him but there was a

strange ringing sensation in his ears. Did Landrieux know that one of those friends was Commodore Nelson? Certainly he did. So how long had Signora Correglia been feeding Nelson these 'scraps of misinformation' – for as long as he had known her, or only since the French had been in Livorno? It occurred to Nathan that if he agreed to go along with this proposal, it was possible he would find the answer to this. It also occurred to him that the duties of an Adjutant-Général in the Army of Italy clearly involved a lot more than shuffling paper.

'How can I be of assistance?' he enquired.

'We would very much appreciate it if you were to call upon Signora Correglia on your way through Livorno. You may bring her the regards of a certain Colonel Murat who is acquainted with her . . .'

This did not surprise Nathan in the least. He had known Murat in Paris.

'You may tell her that whilst in Venice you were approached by Colonel Murat with a view to making a hydrographical survey of the Ionian Islands. The reason for which was to use them as a French naval base for an attack upon the port of Trieste.' He regarded Nathan thoughtfully. 'Is that clear to you, Citizen?'

'Of course, but—'

'And it is agreeable to you?'

'Why, yes, but why do you want me to . . .' He affected enlightenment. 'Ah. This is another piece of misinformation you want me to feed her.'

Landrieux regarded him evenly but said nothing.

'Well.' Nathan spread his arms. 'I am ready to go whenever it pleases you.'

'Excellent. You would be ready to leave tomorrow?'

'Tomorrow? Why – yes. There is no reason why I should not.'

Landrieux stood. 'Then I will make the arrangements.' He bowed. 'The General will once more be in your debt.'

'What did that bastard want?' Junot enquired later that evening, when he came round to play chess.

'Is he a bastard?' enquired Nathan mildly as he moved a rook.

'In the early days of the Revolution he raised a corps of irregular cavalry known as the Hussards Braconniers,' Junot offered by way of a reply.

Nathan was puzzled for a moment. *Hussards* meant hussars but he had to think about *braconniers*. The best he could come up with was 'poachers'. The Poacher Hussars?

'He placed them at the disposal of the Jacobin committees to hunt down traitors – mostly nobles, but virtually anyone might qualify if Landrieux and his thugs took against them, or there was money in it. They were bandits, brigands. Don't get me wrong, I'm as much in favour of the Revolution as any man, but it brought a few scorpions out from under the stones – and Landrieux was one of them.'

'So what does he do now?' Adjutant-Général was an office rather than a rank; it could cover a multitude of sins.

'He runs Army intelligence in the whole of Italy. Among other things. So what did he want?'

The whole of Italy. Dear God. Junot was waiting for an answer. 'It is probably confidential,' Nathan said.

Junot shrugged. 'Suit yourself.' He moved one of his knights to threaten Nathan's king. There seemed to be no reason why Nathan should not take it. But Junot only sulked if he lost. He moved a pawn instead.

'He wants me to undertake a hydrographical survey of the Ionian Islands,' he said.

Junot looked at him. 'The hell he does.' Now Nathan

shrugged. Junot was still looking at him. 'Now why would he want you to do that?'

Nathan said nothing. He was thinking about it himself. Junot took his pawn. 'He's always been interested in the Ionian Islands,' he said.

'Landrieux?'

'No. Bugger Landrieux. This is nothing to do with him. Buonaparte.' He used the Italian pronunciation. 'Landrieux is just the messenger boy. Did you say you would do it?'

'I said I would think about it. Why is Bonaparte interested in the Ionian Islands?'

'He says they are more important than the rest of Italy put together.'

'Good God, why?'

'As a stepping stone to the East.'

Nathan frowned. 'What do you mean, *the East*?'

'The Orient. He is fascinated by the East. Always has been. As long as I have known him, anyway. Remember when he was in Paris – and the Turks wanted him to come and command their artillery? He was all for it.'

'I thought that was just because he didn't have a job.'

'Well, that was part of it – but he liked the idea. And now he's just one step and a jump from Constantinople.'

'I would have thought Vienna was far enough,' Nathan said.

'Oh, he's not interested in Austria – apart from knocking them out of the war. Then he'll march on India.'

He made a move but Nathan ignored it. 'What are you taking about?' he said. 'Why would he want to march on India?'

Junot shrugged. 'Why not? You know our boy.' He was staring intently at the board. 'Your move,' he said.

Nathan moved a bishop. 'The Directory would never let him.'

'Don't you believe it. It would be the end for the British if they lost India. Barras knows that.'

'Barras?'

'*The* Barras.' He tutted. 'Director Barras. Our new King, in all but name. I thought you'd got your memory back, not lost your wits.'

'I'm sorry. I'm confused. So Barras is involved in this?'

'It wouldn't surprise me. He fought against the British in India – in the old King's army. He was at the fall of Pondicherry. He's always going on about how important India is to the British, that without India they're nothing. But this will be Buonaparte's idea. To march in the footsteps of Alexander the Great.'

'And that's why he wants me . . .' Nathan stopped himself from saying more. 'Good God.' He tried to picture it on the map. 'But he would need a fleet.'

'He's got a fleet. The Venetian fleet. And the British are not going to stop him. Not now.' He moved his Queen. 'Checkmate!' he declared triumphantly.

Absently, Nathan took his Queen. 'It would never work,' he said.

But it *could* work. Junot was right. Now the British fleet had withdrawn from the Mediterranean, there was nothing to stop Bonaparte moving his pieces across the board, taking whatever he liked. Venice. The Ionian Islands. And then? What was he planning next?

Chapter Eighteen

Escape to Elba

———◆———

He left at dawn with an escort of dragoons. The nuns turned out to see him go, but Sister Francesca was not among them. He thanked them for all they had done for him. They said they would pray for him. Then, just before he stepped into the coach he looked back and saw her standing there, in the shadows by the door. He thought of going over to her, but in the end he just lifted his hand in half-wave, half-salute. He did not know if she waved back. He knew that she did not care that he was an Englishman, but she would care that he had lied to her. He felt like Gilbert Imlay.

They travelled due south to Florence, skirting Mantua – its Austrian garrison still holding out after six long months – but the French seemed to be everywhere else. All the way from the Veneto down through Modena and into Tuscany, Nathan saw the signs of French occupation. Garrisons in all the towns, checkpoints on all the roads. A constant demand for '*vos papiers*'. It was like France at the time of the Terror. The dragoon escort and the safe conduct from Landrieux saw Nathan through them all without undue hindrance, but there were constant delays from convoys moving supplies and munitions up to the front at Mantua and Lake Garda.

Nathan was tired and depressed. Tired from his wounds, depressed by what he saw from the coach window. Evidence, if it were needed, of how badly the war was going for Britain and her few remaining allies. It was only a matter of time, he thought, before Austria threw in the towel. The German princes would follow suit. Then Britain would be fighting with Portugal as her sole ally against the combined might of France, Spain and Holland. The three most powerful navies in the world after her own.

A year ago it had seemed to Nathan that England was fighting for a few sugar islands in the Caribbean. Now she was fighting for her very survival.

But if he had ever puzzled over what he was fighting for, he knew now, he thought, as he watched the French troops swaggering around Modena.

There was heavy snow coming over the Tuscan Hills and they were held up for two days at an inn before a mild thaw set in. Then it was mud for the rest of the way. They had been four days on the road before they passed through Florence, and it was another day before they arrived at Leghorn. Back to the place where it had all started – and with an escort of French dragoons. It seemed only yesterday that he had stood off the mole in the *Unicorn* and watched the French cavalry advancing down from the surrounding hills.

He had never set foot in the place when it was the main British naval base in Italy. Never called at the house of Mr Udny to view his collection of harpsichords and loose women; or paid a visit to the opera, where you picked them up. But now he was a hero of France and it was nothing but the best. The best hotel, the best food – and the best whore in town.

He had been furnished with the address by Citizen Landrieux

but he waited until the following day – and the civilised hour of noon – before presenting himself at her door. He owned to some trepidation. Their relations had improved somewhat since the incident of the rats on board the *Unicorn*, but he wondered how she would greet his sudden appearance in French-occupied Livorno, in a French uniform. But at least he did not have to take his escort with him.

A maid answered the door and Nathan gave his name as Captain Turner, a friend of Colonel Murat. He was passing through Livorno, he said, and the Colonel had asked him to call upon the Signora to pay his respects. The maid regarded him shrewdly, assessing his potential. The Signora was presently engaged, she said, but if he were to call back in an hour or so she might be free to see him.

Nathan kicked his heels down by the harbour. There were several ships-of-war moored off the mole – privateers, by the look of them. But not many merchant vessels. In fact, it was bizarrely quiet for a major port, which suggested the British still maintained their blockade. This was one good sign, at least.

He returned to the Signora's house and this time he was admitted. And there was Signora Correglia sitting in the window of her little salon, little changed from when he had last seen her. Her welcoming smile faded when she saw who he was, but she recovered herself well under the watchful eye of the maid.

'Why, Captain Turner,' she said in excellent French, 'and have you brought any rats with you this time?'

He was tempted to tell her only one, and she was looking at it. He had no intention of giving her false information to pass on to her English friends, as Landrieux called them, but he did mean to use her.

There was nothing for it but to throw himself on her good

graces. He told her he had undertaken a confidential mission for Commodore Nelson under false colours but that he was now desirous of making his escape from Italy.

'And so you come to me,' she said, 'bringing the respects of a French Colonel.'

'I met Colonel Murat in the north,' he told her, 'and when he heard I was coming to Livorno he gave me your address.'

'As one French officer to another.'

'Precisely.'

But he could not leave it there. If Landrieux suspected the Signora of being a spy for the British, he had a duty to warn her.

'A little later I was summoned to the office of the Adjutant-Général,' he said. 'And he told me you were in the practice of passing on pieces of information to your English friends.'

She stared at him for a moment and he sensed the fear beneath that bold front.

'He thinks I am a spy?'

'He did not use the word spy as such.'

'That is a gross slander!' she exploded, following up with some choice slanders of her own in French and Italian directed upon the Adjutant-Général's character and family antecedents. She had come back to Livorno because the facilities in Corsica were less than adequate, she said, and the company fell a great deal short of her expectations. But there was no question of her being a spy for the British. '*Non. Absolument pas!*'

'Then you no longer have any communication with Commodore Nelson?' Nathan enquired mildly.

'How could that be possible,' she demanded hotly, 'when I am here in Livorno and Commodore Nelson is in Portugal – or back in England, for all that I know of it?'

The maid came back with tea and some tiny biscuits dusted with icing sugar. Signora Correglia calmed herself a little.

Nathan regarded her speculatively. She had lost some weight since he had last seen her aboard the *Unicorn* but she looked no less fetching for that. Several unhelpful thoughts crossed his mind. She caught his eye upon her.

'So what will you do now?' she enquired when the maid had left.

'I shall leave word for Citizen Landrieux that I have done what he required of me,' he said, 'and then take the first ship I can that is heading for the Atlantic.'

'And what am *I* to do, if the French think I am a spy?'

'You can come with me, if you like,' he offered engagingly. 'But I do not suppose you are in danger, so long as they think you are of use to them.'

She mulled over this for a moment in silence. Nathan offered to pour the tea.

'No, I will pour the tea,' she said. She said something else in Italian that he suspected was not very polite. But she poured the tea. He took the cup and saucer from her and a biscuit and thanked her politely.

'So you will not go to Elba?' she said.

He frowned. 'Why would I wish to go to Elba?'

'To join your friends there.'

This was equally puzzling. 'What friends do I have in Elba?' he enquired, as one might humour a lunatic.

She was looking at him with much the same expression. 'You do not know that the British are there?'

'What?'

'Fremantle and Sir Gilbert Elliot and five thousand soldiers.'

'Good God, no.' He stared at her in bewilderment. 'What are they doing in Elba?' Elba was the largest of the several islands of the Tuscan Archipelago, halfway between Corsica and the mainland. When he was last in the vicinity it had been in the possession of the Grand Duke of Tuscany. But now, according to Signora Correglia, it had been taken by the British. Most of the troops evacuated from Corsica were stationed there – with a small naval detachment under Captain Fremantle to maintain a blockade of Leghorn and Genoa.

This made no sense to Nathan. 'Why would we do that,' he demanded, 'if the main battle fleet has been withdrawn into the Atlantic?'

The Signora shrugged as if the decisions of the British High Command had very little to do with her: which, to be fair, they probably did not.

'Is it possible for me to get there?' he asked her. He read the obvious challenge in her expression. 'I can pay,' he said, for the Adjutant-Général had supplied him with sufficient funds to impress with his largesse.

'Well,' she replied cautiously, 'there are some fishermen that have been known to visit the island from time to time.'

He supposed them to be more smugglers than fishermen, but he had no objection to that. 'Do you know any personally?' he enquired.

'And what am *I* to do?' she insisted.

He repeated his invitation to her to come with him.

'To Elba?' She looked at him as if he was mad.

'Genoa?' he offered.

'My mother is in Genoa,' she said. He gathered this was not in its favour. She considered a moment in silence. Then she said: 'No, Elba is not for me. I will stay in Livorno.'

He waited expectantly, but when nothing was forthcoming he coughed politely and prompted her: 'And the fishermen? Do you think something can be arranged?'

She sighed. 'I suppose it is possible,' she conceded. 'You had better wait here while I see what I can do.'

*

They sailed just before dark, heading southward about a mile out from the coast. It was very cold, with a bitter north-west wind and a hint of sleet in the air. No night to be out at sea in a small fishing boat. Nathan sat in the sternsheets, huddled up in the French Army greatcoat they had given him at the hospital; its last owner, he suspected, having died on them. He could not help wondering if it would not be a great deal easier for the crew if he were to die now. They could dump him overboard as soon as they were out of sight of land and head back to Livorno and their warm beds and wives. None of them spoke any French but the skipper had a smattering of English, and Nathan attempted to ingratiate himself with him at every opportunity. There was no obvious sign that it was working. Why did the Signor not go below, the man enquired. He would wake him before dawn when, if the wind held, they should be off the coast of Elba.

Nathan demurred at first. If they planned to cut his throat he thought he had a better chance of survival if he stayed awake, but by midnight he was nodding off anyway so he thought he might as well.

The only space below deck was for a small saloon and a galley, but at least it was out of the wind and there was a wooden shelf for the crew to sleep on if they were so minded. Nathan stretched himself out on it, pulling his greatcoat around him. Surprisingly he slept quite well and the skipper had to shake him awake. Nathan gathered they were approaching land.

He made his way up on deck to find the crew peering out over the leeward rail. They seemed nervous. It was still dark and it was raining – a dense drizzle that cut visibility down to a few yards. Nathan could see no sign of Elba, or anything else.

'Where will you land me?' Nathan asked, but the skipper

shook his head with a frown. He seemed to be listening. Nathan listened too. Nothing at first. Nothing beside the normal sounds of the sea. The waves slapping against the side of the boat, the wind in the rigging, the creaking of the ropes. Then . . . He could not quite place it. Breakers? It sounded more like a gust of wind, yet the sails had fallen slack. He looked questioningly at the skipper – and then all at once he realised and turned to face the threat rushing down upon them, his mouth open in a shout of warning that never came.

The ghostly figure of a woman loomed out of the darkness. Mad, staring eyes in a white face, a gaping mouth and wild flowing hair. A great lance of a bowsprit pierced the air above Nathan's head, carrying away the sail and most of the mast as the great beak of a bow smashed down on them.

At the last moment he jumped. Not out, but up. It was pure instinct, the instant he saw that white face bearing down on him. He leaped on to the gunwale and then straight up at that ghoulish countenance, his outstretched hands clawing. He was falling back into the sea when his clutching hands encountered a rope and he held on to it, soaked in spray while the bows rose and fell, a dangling puppet carried before the onrushing ship. He tried to haul himself up towards that glaring figurehead, but he lacked the strength. He had been too long ill. There was a terrible pain in his chest: he thought it would split open, the blood gushing from the open wound. He glared back at the face of his oppressor. He thought it was the last face he would ever see. Then there were others beside it, even uglier, and a moment later hands were reaching down to him, hauling him up. Passing him back along the bowsprit and up over the heads where the hands, in normal times, were wont to relieve themselves. It was not a part of the ship with which he was at all familiar.

'Thank you,' he gasped. 'Thank you kindly. Thank you.'

'Speakee English, do ye?' said one.

'Frenchie, is 'ee?' said another.

'I am English,' said Nathan. He sensed them staring at him, the white eyes in the dark faces. Harsh, grim features in the light from the belfry but he loved them all.

'What's that, mate?'

'Says as 'e's English.'

'I *am* English,' he stated, more firmly now as the habit of command came back to him a little. 'What ship is this?'

Inconstant, they said. 'And what's it to you, mate?'

Inconstant. He laughed out loud, coughing.

'All right, mate, it's not that funny.'

'Is Captain Fremantle aboard?' Astonished silence. 'Perhaps you would be good enough to take me to Captain Fremantle.'

They took him to the officer of the watch.

'Captain Nathaniel Peake. *Unicorn*,' he introduced himself formally.

'The devil you are!'

'You have just run down a fishing boat,' Nathan informed him coldly. 'There will be men in the water.'

They fetched Fremantle up from below. 'Good God, Peake,' he said after a moment to get used to the idea. 'I thought you were dead.'

'I very nearly was,' said Nathan. 'And there are others soon will be if you do not come about and search for them.'

Fremantle gave the necessary order but he insisted Nathan come below. 'Else we might as well have left you in the sea,' he said.

'What in God's name happened to you?' he demanded when they were settled in his cabin. 'And what are you doing in French Army uniform?'

Fremantle was not the most discreet of confidants. Nathan told him only that he had been taken prisoner in Venice, escaped, and made his way overland to Leghorn disguised as a French officer. 'I paid the fishermen to bring me here,' he said, 'and I fear I have brought them to their deaths.'

He looked about the cabin. It was divided by hangings and there were certain telltale signs. 'Have you got a woman here?' he said.

'For God's sake, keep your voice down,' Fremantle rebuked him. Nathan had noticed he was speaking in scarce more than a whisper. 'I'll have you know she is my wife.'

'Your *wife*? Good God, Fremantle, when were you married?' Belatedly Nathan dropped his voice. 'Who to?'

'Betsey Wynne – you remember. That we took out of Leghorn. We were married a week ago in Naples.'

'What were you doing in Naples?'

'Nelson sent us.'

'Nelson sent you?' Nathan tried to make sense of this. 'I thought Nelson was in Lisbon. I thought the fleet was ordered out of the Med.'

'So it was – all except us – but he came back. The Admiral sent him to evacuate Elba. But the General ain't leaving, he says, not till he gets a proper order from the Duke of York, so Nelson sent us to Naples to fetch the Viceroy.'

Nathan stared at him in utter confusion. *The General, the Duke of York, the Viceroy . . . ?*

'Look, I have been away for a long time,' he said. 'I got a nasty crack on the head. Do you think you could take me through that again, a little more slowly.'

It took a while but he got there in the end.

General De Burgh was the officer commanding at Elba. He had 5,000 troops that had been evacuated from Corsica and a small squadron of frigates and sloops under Fremantle to protect them and maintain a loose blockade of Leghorn. They were the last British forces in the Med. But then the Admiralty had sent orders to evacuate them. So Admiral Jervis had sent Nelson with two frigates, the *La Minerve* and the *Blanche*. They had arrived the day after Christmas, but General De Burgh refused to leave without a written order from his Commander-in-Chief, the Duke of York. Failing which, he would only take an order from the Viceroy of Corsica, Sir Gilbert Elliot. But the Viceroy was in Naples on diplomatic business. So Nelson had sent Fremantle to fetch him to Elba.

'And while I was there, Betsey and I got married,' he finished with a smirk.

This made as much sense as anything else he had told him.

'Congratulations,' said Nathan. 'I am sorry I was not there.'

'Well, we will drink a glass to it later,' declared Fremantle complacently.

'So where is the Viceroy now?'

Fremantle jerked his head towards the bulkhead partition. 'In my night cabin,' he said. 'He is not the best of sailors, I am afraid. But we will be in Porto Ferraio within the hour.'

Nathan leaned back in his chair and closed his eyes with a sigh. It seemed that he had made it. After all this time. Then he opened them again.

'And where is the *Unicorn*?' he asked.

'The *Unicorn*?' Fremantle stared at him. 'You mean you do not know?'

A knife twisted in Nathan's guts. 'What do I not know?'

'Oh, my dear fellow, I am so sorry,' said Fremantle. He looked stricken. 'The *Unicorn* ran upon the Rock of Montecristo. In a gale in November. She went down with all hands.'

Chapter Nineteen

Break Out

———◆———

He pieced it together as best he could from the reports. The *Unicorn* had been on her way north from Naples, in company with the *Jean-Bart* and *Bonne Aventure*, when they ran into a powerful Spanish squadron: two ships of the line and three frigates under Vice-Admiral Moreno. It must have been their first action since coming into the war. There was a strong south-westerly wind and a heavy sea. A murky, ugly sky.

They ran to the north under all the sail they could carry, but the *Bonne Aventure* was soon in trouble. *Unicorn* hung back for her and exchanged shots with the leading Spaniards. It saved the brig but the *Unicorn* took some damage aloft. Tully, on the *Jean-Bart*, reported that he thought her spanker boom had gone. Then they lost her in the murk. The last they saw of her, she was running to the north-west with the Spaniards in hot pursuit, but they thought she would be safe enough. It was a Spanish newspaper that reported her as having run upon the Rock.

Nathan found it on the chart. Montecristo. The mountain

of Christ. The tip of a volcano, barely two-and-a-half miles across. Nothing there except a monastery. He could imagine it in a storm.

'It would not have helped if her spanker had gone,' said Fremantle, thinking he might hold Duncan to blame.

But he did not blame Duncan.

'It would not have helped that I stripped her of one-third of her crew,' he said, 'for a prize.'

They left him alone with his grief. All those men who had been with him in the Caribbean. Duncan and Holroyd, McLeish, Whiteley, the midshipmen, Anson and Quinn, McIvor the purser and Mr Lloyd the carpenter, William Brown the master at arms, and Jacob Young, his coxswain, Mr Sweeney the sailmaker who had made him his tent; on and on it went, the grim toll. Tully, at least, had been spared aboard the *Jean-Bart*. Who else had been with him? Lamb, of course, thank God. Who else? Desperately he tried to remember, who had gone and who had stayed. The living and the dead.

And what of Gilbert Gabriel?

Something like panic gripped his chest. He felt short of breath. Not Gabriel. Had he rejoined the ship after their trip to Venice? Pray God he had not. He could not lose Gabriel. He felt a sob rise in his throat and it unleashed the tears.

Nelson came on board shortly after their arrival in Porto Ferraio.

'I am sorry about the *Unicorn*,' he told Nathan, 'but thank God you were spared.' He regarded him shrewdly. 'You have been in the wars, I think.'

Nathan nodded, his face expressionless.

'I am anxious to hear your report,' said Nelson briskly, 'but I must first make myself known to the Viceroy.'

The Viceroy was still below; still suffering from the effects of seasickness, according to Fremantle. But it was to be presumed that his stomach would settle a little in the sheltered waters of Porto Ferraio.

Despite his grief, Nathan agreed to join Fremantle and the other officers in the gunroom for breakfast.

'What with my wife and her family, not to speak of Viceroys and their staff, my own quarters are somewhat crowded at present,' Fremantle confessed a little bleakly. Nathan wondered how he was finding marriage after so many happy years of bachelorhood – but now was not the time to ask. He told him that Signora Correglia sent her regards and had arranged his trip to Elba.

'She is a good friend to us,' Fremantle said, but they left it at that.

They dined off salt pork and eggs washed down with pints of hot coffee, and Nathan was on his second cup when word came that he was required in the Captain's cabin.

He found the Viceroy somewhat the worse for wear, wrapped in a blanket with his smelling salts to hand, but he said he was bearing up and was as anxious as the Commodore to hear Nathan's report from Venice.

It was what Nathan told them about the French intentions towards the Ionian Islands that interested them the most.

'You had not heard?' he said, looking from one to the other.

'How could we have heard?' demanded Nelson. 'Who else did you tell?'

'Only Mr Duncan – but I thought he had been in Naples . . .' But if he had, clearly he had not thought to convey Nathan's report to Sir William Hamilton. 'He must have been bringing the news to you when he died,' he told Nelson.

'So these documents you found in the *Jean-Bart*,' Elliot prompted him, 'they were with the *Unicorn* when she foundered?'

'I thought they were safer with the *Unicorn* than with me,' Nathan told him.

'And did they give any reason for the survey?' demanded Nelson.

Nathan shook his head. But then he revealed what Junot had told him.

'He was Bonaparte's sergeant at Toulon,' he explained. 'When Bonaparte was imprisoned as a terrorist Junot stood by him, took him food, even planned his escape. Then he came with him to Paris. He was his only companion there all those months when Bonaparte was unemployed. Bonaparte called him his aide-de-camp.'

They looked at each other. Nathan asked himself again how much they knew of his own time in Paris.

'So he is in Bonaparte's confidence?' Elliot said.

'Absolutely,' said Nathan. He wondered privately if this was entirely true, but he let it go for the time being.

'But the Ionian Islands are a long way from India,' Nelson pointed out unnecessarily. 'He would have to march across Turkey. Would the Directory want war with the Sultan?'

Nathan mentioned what Junot had said about Barras.

'This is true,' Elliot agreed eagerly. 'Barras was in the French Army of India.'

The Viceroy was surprisingly ready to believe the report. Soon it became clear why. He wanted the Army to stay in Elba. It would give Britain a toehold in the Mediterranean. 'For when the fleet returns,' he said.

Nelson looked doubtful. 'I am not sure when that will be,' he said.

'But the Admiralty must think again,' Elliot insisted, 'especially when they hear about this. They cannot afford to let the French take the Ionian Islands. And a threat to march overland to India . . .'

'Is a pipe-dream,' Nelson declared coldly. 'Even if we can believe the report. I do not doubt you personally,' he assured Nathan, 'and you do right to alert us to the possibility. But who is this Junot? Besides, there is a much greater threat to England at present.'

'I think it is imperative that Captain Peake returns to London,' the Viceroy argued, 'and reports directly to their lordships. For without the document itself . . .'

He left it unsaid but Nelson finished it for him. 'Their lordships will take some persuading,' he said.

But the Viceroy was firm about Elba. He had no authority, he said, to order General De Burgh to evacuate his troops. If the Navy wanted to pull out, that was their concern, but the Army must remain until they had direct orders from their own Commander-in-Chief, the Duke of York. Nelson had no choice but to concur. A small naval force would remain under Fremantle.

'Ridiculous!' Fremantle complained to Nathan when he heard the news. 'I will be like a fish in a net.'

Privately Nathan agreed. It was a nonsense. Elliot, it was clear, still had hopes of uniting Italy against the French. But if he thought 5,000 British troops in Elba would persuade the Italian princes to take up arms against Bonaparte he was an even greater dreamer than Spiridion had implied.

Nathan was by no means reluctant to return to England, however. He had had quite enough of Italy for the time being. And for the first time since the war began he was without a ship.

They sailed for Gibraltar at the end of January and arrived ten days later without incident. Nelson waited only a day at the Rock. He was impatient to rejoin the fleet off Lisbon. His sixth sense told him there was a battle in the offing, he said, and he could not bear the thought of missing it.

Nathan thought there was little chance of that, but it might not be the battle Nelson desired. There was a Spanish squadron in the bay, waiting for them to come out. *La Minerve* was a fine ship – a captured French frigate of 38 guns – but she was no match for an entire squadron including two ships of the line, and Nathan reckoned she would need all her much-vaunted sailing qualities to outrun them. To make matters worse, she had to fight the currents coming out of Gibraltar, and the Spanish ships had the benefit of a steady Levanter wind blowing from the east.

Looking back at the Rock, Nathan saw it was crowded with spectators come to watch the fight. He doubted they would enjoy it much more than the men aboard.

The ship was cleared for action and Nathan asked Captain Cockburn was there anything he wanted him to do.

'Aye, you can make yourself useful by talking to the wee man there, and keeping him from talking to me,' the Captain instructed him grimly, without taking his eyes from the sails. This was the longest conversation Nathan had enjoyed with him since coming aboard. He gathered the wee man was Nelson.

It was the Levanter that saved them. It was blowing up too much of a storm for the Spaniards to aim their guns with any degree of accuracy, and as soon as the frigate reached the middle of the Strait, Cockburn ordered the studding sails set and they began to put some clear water between them. Nelson was confident enough to propose the other officers join him for dinner and they were sitting down to it in the day cabin a little after three when they were perturbed to hear the cry of 'Man overboard!'

'It's Barnes,' the midshipman of the watch informed Cockburn when the officers emerged on deck. 'Lieutenant Hardy has gone to look for him, sir.'

Nathan could see the jolly boat about a cable's length astern, apparently searching for the missing man. He glanced back towards the Spaniards. They were still at a reasonable distance but in his own humble opinion it would not do to hang about too long, and judging from the look on Cockburn's face he shared it.

The jolly boat was heading back, having apparently abandoned their quest. They watched it anxiously from the quarterdeck. It did not appear to be making much headway.

'The current is against them,' Nelson observed. He looked worried.

Cockburn muttered something under his breath.

'I'll not lose Hardy,' said the Commodore firmly. 'Back the mizzen topsail.'

Cockburn looked grimmer even than usual, but he had no choice but to obey the order and it slowed them down sufficiently for the boat to catch up. Inexplicably, their pursuers held back.

'They think we have sighted the British fleet,' Nelson speculated. But whatever the reason, the Spanish ships remained at a distance while the last light faded from the sky.

'Well, gentlemen, shall we see if they have kept dinner for us?' suggested the Commodore.

They had given Nathan a tiny cabin off the gunroom but he found he could not sleep. The loss of his ship lay heavy on him and he counted the dead as he might have counted sheep. He saw the end as clearly as if he had been there. His beloved ship broken on the rocks of Montecristo. And the cold bodies strewn upon the shingle in the grey light of dawn.

After tossing and turning for most of the night and listening to the snores of his neighbours through the thin partitions, he decided to abandon the quest for sleep and go up on deck. It was just after six bells in the middle watch. The Levanter was still blowing and a thick fog swirled around them in the darkness. He was reminded of his journey to Corsica and his fight with the privateers. But then he had been in the *Unicorn* and all his friends still alive. He looked about him and to his surprise he saw that Nelson and Cockburn were also up on deck. He opened his mouth to address them but Cockburn froze him with a fierce frown, raising his finger to his lips.

They seemed to be listening for something. Nathan squinted out into the night. Cliffs, breakers? But they were in open sea. There was nothing between here and America. Then there was a sudden flash in the gloom and a muffled report. A signal gun. Something lurched out of the murk to starboard. But not a cliff. It was a ship. The fog closed around it again. They heard voices. And with a shock Nathan realised they were Spanish.

He looked questioningly at Cockburn but the fierce frown enjoined him to silence. Another flash and boom. More sails to larboard. More voices, on both sides now. They were in the middle of a fleet. A fleet or a convoy. Dim, spectral shapes in the murk, and their own ship ghosting through. Not a sound from anyone on deck or aloft. Even the groaning of the ropes seemed strangely muted, the ship's bell struck dumb by Cockburn's frown. Then, at last, they were in open waters again. The signal guns a distant melancholy bark in the fog.

Nathan let out his breath. 'What in God's name was that?' he said.

'That, laddie, was the Spanish battle fleet,' said Cockburn. 'You'll know it, no doubt, next time you see it.'

'Next time we see it,' said Nelson, staring into the fog, 'we will have company.'

They found them at dawn, sheltering under the lee of Cape St Vincent: fifteen ships of the line under Admiral Sir John Jervis – the British Mediterranean fleet that was.

Nelson went aboard the flagship to report, taking Nathan with him.

'You should tell the Admiral what you told the Viceroy,' he said. 'He'll not thank you if he learns it from the Admiralty.'

But when Nelson came out of his meeting with the Admiral, he simply said, 'Now is not the time.' Jervis had too much on his mind with the present threat to be concerned with French ambitions in India or even the Adriatic. There could be only one reason, in his view, for the Spanish Mediterranean fleet to leave its base in Cartagena and come out into the Atlantic, and that was to combine with the French fleet at Brest. Together they could overwhelm Britain's last line of defence and land an army on the south coast of England.

'I must return to my ship,' Nelson said. 'You can stay aboard the flagship or come with me.'

When Nelson said his ship, he meant the *Captain*, the 74 that had been his flagship when they were off Leghorn. *La Minerve* had served only as his transport to Elba. Now he was anxious to return to his place in the line of battle.

'I will come with you, sir,' Nathan said, 'if I may.'

As night fell the fleet stood to the south-east with the fog once more closing around them. They could hear the muffled thump of signal guns from the Spanish fleet somewhere in the darkness ahead. The wind had shifted to the south-west and they were sailing close-hauled on the starboard tack in two columns. Nathan snatched a couple of hours' sleep in the wardroom but he was on deck again long before daylight to join the silent throng of officers on the quarterdeck, peering southward into the gloom, waiting for the battle they all knew was coming.

Dawn scarcely broke but seeped in through the ragged holes in the murky sky. And with it came a British sloop, hurrying from the south-east under a full press of sail and firing her bow chasers to warn that the enemy was in sight. With a shock of recognition Nathan saw that she was the *Jean-Bart*. He leaned over the weather rail, peering through the murk for a glimpse of Tully or some other of his old crew, but the mist closed around her and she was gone.

At eight-thirty they had breakfast as usual. There was some discussion about the strength of the Spanish fleet. Noble, the signal officer, had seen it assembled at Cartagena before the war and claimed it numbered twenty-six ships of the line including six three-deckers of 112 guns apiece. The flagship, the *Santissima Trinidad*, was even bigger: she carried 130 guns and she was the only four-decker in the world. The biggest ship in the British fleet was their own flagship, the *Victory*, with 100 guns.

'We all know they're big,' growled Berry, 'but can they fight?'

They all knew the answer to that, too. The press always said the Dons could not fight and nor could the French – and they were wrong on both counts. The only hope was that the Dons were out of practice.

A little after four bells in the forenoon watch they caught their first glimpse of them from the deck, strung out over several miles of ocean. The masthead lookout reported thirty sail, including twenty-five ships of the line. But they seemed to be in two separate divisions with a widening gap between.

'Flagship is signalling, sir,' called out the officer of the watch.

It was flag number 31 – *form line of battle ahead and astern of the flagship.*

And they headed straight for the gap.

Chapter Twenty

Line of Battle

———◆———

Nathan asked the Flag Captain if there was anything he could do.

'You can stand next to the Commodore,' growled Miller, 'and give them something bigger to aim at.'

Nathan felt like a passenger, which was more or less what he was. A Captain without a ship. But he was wearing a borrowed coat of Miller's, which would mark him out as a target. He wished he had kept his Army greatcoat now, but it had seemed disloyal on the quarterdeck of a British ship of the line. He was glad of the *sauve-tête* netting that had been strung up above the quarterdeck, to protect them from falling timbers. It would hide them from sharpshooters too, to some extent, and the smoke would help more.

He put it out of his mind.

The wind was light and there was hardly any sea running. At the last reading of the log they had been making a little under five knots. The fleet had cleared for action and the sea was strewn with empty casks and other debris, even live animals, for many were penned on deck and there was nowhere else to put them. Steers, pigs and sheep could be seen swimming among the debris. There was even a cockerel on top of one of the casks and two miserable hens. This seemed unnecessary to Nathan, but then he had been attacked by a cockerel at the Battle of the Glorious First. It was his only wound – in that battle.

Culloden was leading the line with the flagship somewhere in the centre. *Captain* was positioned towards the rear with just two ships behind her, the *Diadem* and the *Excellent*. The signals officer, Noble, pointed out that they were number thirteen in line.

Nathan stood at the weather rail gazing out towards the Spanish fleet – or at least that part of it that was to windward of them. He could see them clearly now, though he wished he had his glass. They were all bunched together, a forest of masts. Several of them were abreast of each other, masking each other's broadsides.

Then, as he watched, they began to wear on to the larboard tack.

'They are coming up on our weather side,' Nelson said.

Nathan watched as slowly, ponderously, the Spanish ships came about. They would pass right along the British line, in the opposite direction, at a range of about 1,000 yards.

'Why do we not close with the brutes?' Miller complained at Nathan's shoulder.

But the British were already sailing as close to the wind as they could, and the Spaniards clearly had no intention of coming any closer themselves. *Culloden* was already in action and one by one the ships in her wake followed suit as the Spaniards drew level with them. Nathan saw some hits, but not many. The sea between the two fleets was peppered with shot. As usual, the Spaniards seemed to be aiming high in a bid to bring down the British rigging. At eleven-thirty, *Captain* was in action, blazing away with her starboard broadside as the leading Spanish ships came within range.

For forty-five minutes the guns roared, pouring broadside after broadside into the Spanish ships as they sailed past in the opposite direction, like ducks in a row, Nathan thought. And like ducks, they kept bobbing along. He observed very few hits at this distance. Nelson was frowning fiercely. Nathan saw him shouting into Miller's ear but he could not hear what he was saying. His own ears were deafened by the thunder of the cannon. Men moved through the smoke in apparent silence, working the guns. They took some hits, mainly aloft, but he could not hear them, only see the effect. Blocks and tackle tumbling down from above in an eerie silence. Nelson had moved *Captain* slightly to leeward so he could keep the rest of the fleet in sight, but the whole of the centre of the line was wreathed in black smoke and they could barely see the mastheads. But at the head of the line *Culloden* was coming round on the tail of the Spanish fleet – snapping at their heels as they cruised steadily northward. And now the lookouts were shouting down to the quarterdeck. The flagship was signalling. Nathan moved closer to Noble so he could catch what orders were relayed.

'Signal number eighty,' he shouted towards Nelson. '*Ships will tack in succession.*'

'Tack in succession?' Nathan repeated. He caught Noble's eye and could see they were both thinking the same thing. Jervis clearly meant to keep his fleet in line. Each ship would sail to the point where *Culloden* had turned and then follow her round. But then they would be trailing the Spanish fleet, much as the British ships had trailed the Armada up the Channel at the time of Drake. And unless the Spaniards turned again, they would lose them. Already a gap of about half a mile had opened between *Culloden* and the next ship in the

British line. By the time *Captain* turned she would be two or three miles behind, effectively out of the battle. And she would not be the only one.

But Jervis must have realised this. The flagship was flying another signal. They all waited impatiently for Noble to tell them what it meant.

'Signal number forty-one,' he sang out after consulting the book. '*Take suitable stations for mutual support and engage the enemy as coming up in succession.*'

'What in God's name does that mean?' demanded Berry, bringing a glare from Miller. But no answer. Nor from Nelson who was gazing out at the Spaniards with his hands clenched behind his back. On this tack the last of them was just out of reach of his guns, but every minute widened the distance between them.

He said something. No one seemed to hear. Nelson turned and looked towards Captain Miller with his eyebrows raised slightly. He wore his green eye-patch under his hat, to shield his bad eye from the light, and it was difficult to read his expression. He raised his voice and this time Nathan heard him.

'Do you hear me, Captain? Wear to starboard.'

The order was swiftly relayed down the deck to the hands at the braces, and as the yards came round the ship fell off the wind and dropped out of the line of battle. There was a different kind of silence now on the quarterdeck. The tension was almost palpable. It was unheard-of to drop out of the line of battle, even in fleet manoeuvres. But at the height of a battle, in the face of the enemy, it was unthinkable. It would mean a court martial, disgrace. They had shot Byng for less.

But Nelson was not running from the enemy. He was running towards it.

Round came the *Captain*'s bows. Further. Round came her

yards. She was taking the wind on her larboard quarter now, her bows facing the enemy. Heading straight for the gap between *Diadem* and *Excellent*, the last two ships in line.

On her present course she would run straight for the centre of the Spanish division: the forest Nathan had remarked upon earlier where the biggest trees were gathered. The *Santissima Trinidad*, the largest ship afloat, four gun decks, 130 guns, the *San Josef*, the *Salvador del Mundo*, the *Mexicano*, all of 112 guns . . . several others he could not name.

He glanced astern. Not a single ship had broken line to follow them. They were all sailing on to the point at which *Culloden* had turned. Already *Captain* was closer to the Spanish fleet than to the British. And they were firing at her. The air was full of hurtling metal. Nathan could hear it now, smashing through their rigging. A forest in a gale. Bits of splintered timber were falling down on to the netting. Men were swarming aloft, making temporary repairs. The sails were full of holes but they still did their job, carrying them into the heart of the Spanish fleet. The gun crews standing silently by their loaded guns, waiting for the order to fire back. And then Nathan heard Nelson's voice again: 'Take us straight for the flagship,' he said.

Dear God, as if they were not in enough trouble already! He was taking them straight at the *Santissima Trinidad*. She was blanketed in smoke and flame, but as the wind took it away Nathan could see her sides, bright yellow streaked in black like some massive hornet.

They were in amongst them now, firing both broadsides. The *Salvador del Mundo* on one side, the *Mexicano* on the other, the great walls of their gundecks rising like tall cliffs on either side. But that was the last he saw of them before they vanished in an eruption of fire and smoke. The noise was incredible. Smashing, splintering timbers. So much rigging had fallen from above, the net was sagging under its weight. Part of it came down as he looked, bringing an avalanche of timber on to the deck. The *Captain*'s gun crews worked in a silent intense fury. Loading, firing, sponging, worming. No need to take aim; they were too close to miss. But the ship was being shot to pieces around them. The fore topmast had gone and her jib, every yard seemed to be cock-a-bill, as if the ship was in mourning, the stays, halyards and sails torn to ribbons. Nathan looked around the shattered quarterdeck. There were bodies everywhere. The wheel was shot away, the helmsmen lying dead around it. The deck was slippery with blood, several guns disabled. He saw Nelson go down, bowled over by a huge chunk of timber, part of a splintered block. Miller caught him and set him on his feet. He dusted himself down but Nathan saw the pain on his face.

Still their guns were firing. Faster, much faster than the Spaniards'. But how long could they keep this up? They were hardly moving in the water now, and half a dozen Spanish ships were around them. They had hauled their wind, Nathan realised in some dim recess of his brain, hauled their wind to larboard. *Captain* had turned them, like a sheepdog turning a flock of sheep. Much good it would do her. For these were not sheep.

Then another ship came through the smoke, blazing away with both broadsides.

Culloden.

Troubridge had come up at the head of the British line.

He brought the 74 up between *Captain* and the flagship, mercifully diverting their fire. And there were others behind her. The *Blenheim*, the *Prince George* driving their blunt bows into the heart of the battle.

Nathan had lost his bearings. He did not know where they were in relation to the Spanish line. But here was a ship looming up out of the smoke to larboard. 'The *San Nicolas*,' someone shouted. It hardly seemed to matter. She had fouled another Spaniard on her windward side and the two were locked together by the yards, like two crippled stags. The *Captain* smashed into her starboard quarter. Her bowsprit was thrust over the Spanish poop like a long lance, the spritsail yard locked into her mizzen shrouds. God, what a mess, Nathan thought. What a bloody shambles.

Nelson was calling for boarders. Thank Christ Nathan had something to do at last. He drew his borrowed cutlass.

Men were pouring up from below armed with pistols and cutlasses, boarding pikes and tomahawks. Soldiers with them – men of the 11th and 69th Foot serving as Marines – with their muskets and bayonets. Some Austrians, too, in their white uniforms. That gave him a shock. God only knew where *they* had come from. For a moment Nathan had problems working out whose side they were on. The last time he had seen them had been at Castiglioni, shooting at him.

He followed Nelson to the bows. The Commodore drew his sword and climbed on to the anchor cathead. He had lost his hat, and with his shock of hair, even greying as it was, he looked like some little boy dressed up in a costume. His followers gathered below. Nathan knew some of them. Berry, Noble, Pearson, Tom Allen, the coxswain William Fearney . . . Nelson looked down at them, an expression of pure joy on his face.

'Glory,' he said. 'Glory – or a tomb at Westminster.'

They went in through the stern windows. One of the soldiers smashed them in with the butt of his musket. The cabin door was locked and men were on the other side firing through it, but they smashed it open and swept them aside, rushing up to the quarterdeck. Christ, if the *Captain* had been bad, this was far, far worse. There were more dead than living. Bits of

smashed body, limbs, heads . . . Nathan slipped on the blood.
A soldier came rushing at him with a musket and bayonet but
somebody shot him before he could use it. Nathan walked
through it all, shocked, bemused. There was no one to fight.
There was no fight in them. A Spanish officer gave Nelson his
sword.

But they were still firing from somewhere. Nathan looked
about him and saw that it was coming from the other ship, the
one locked against the larboard side. A much bigger ship, rising
above them. Nelson was rallying people to him, calling on
them to board her.

Board another ship? It was impossible. Shaking his head,
Nathan followed. Berry was helping the Commodore into the
main chains and there were Spanish officers staring at them
from the quarter rail, shouting that they had surrendered.

Nathan let his sword arm fall. He felt so tired. He had never
felt this tired after a battle. It must be his wounds, he
thought.

Nelson was taking another sword. He had two of them now.
He gave them to his bargeman, Fearney, who put them under
his arm.

'Victory!' somebody shouted. Men were clapping each other
on the shoulders, shaking hands. They were even shaking hands
with the Spaniards.

Nathan climbed up the shrouds a little to look around. The
gunfire seemed to have slackened somewhat. There were two
more Spanish ships with British colours hanging above their
own. It's over, he thought. Another battle won. And he was on
the right side this time. He felt the wind on his cheek, a wind
from the south-west, and wondered if it had a name.

Epilogue

The Death of Venice

———◄•►———

Venice, May 1797

The Devil splashed through the flooded paving of the *Fondamenta San Severo*, holding the skirts of his coat out of the wet. Unfortunately he could do little for his shoes or his stockings other than take them off, and despite recent events he considered this to be one indignity too far.

The two men were waiting for him on the bridge, well above the level of the tide.

'Greetings,' said the Greek. 'You've got your feet wet.'

Cristolfi ignored this but reflected privately that even a man as heedless as Spiridion Foresti would have considered such a remark unwise when *Il Diavolo* was still at the height of his powers.

He glanced at Foresti's companion. A large African, presumably a bodyguard.

'My associate,' the Greek murmured. 'Mr Banjo.'

Cristolfi nodded curtly. He looked about him. The light was fast fading and they appeared to be unobserved. Not that you could count on it. French spies were everywhere, even with 3,000 of their soldiers garrisoned in the city and a French General installed in the Doge's Palace.

Cristolfi's fall had been as rapid as that of the Republic. Faced with Bonaparte's ultimatum, the Senate had capitulated without a fight. 'I will have no Inquisition,' Bonaparte had informed them, 'no antique barbarities.' Rather ruining the munificence of this remark by adding that he would be 'an Attila to the Venetian state'.

But no one wanted to fight him and there was nowhere to run to. Instead the Venetians extinguished their glorious past and embraced the Revolution. The winged lion was toppled from his perch and a Liberty Tree erected on the Piazza San Marco. The 120th Doge abdicated with the curious remark that to an honest man every place is his country, and he may as easily occupy himself in Switzerland.

But he had stayed on to dance around the Liberty Tree with the rest of the Great Council. The Devil had watched from the shadows. The end of a thousand years of history.

No one had come for him yet, but he expected they would soon enough. There were too many scores to settle, too many families of those he had been obliged to consign to the *Pozzi*, or the Canale Orfano. Too many tortures and judicial murders. It would be useless to argue that he was only a loyal servant of the *Serenissima*.

So he must look to himself for once.

'Well, I have brought what you wanted,' he said, patting the leather satchel on his shoulder. It was a risk, but if they made a move towards him it would be in the canal and they probably knew it. The Greek stretched out a hand.

'So what have you brought *me*?' the Devil enquired.

'You have not made enough, over the years?'

'I took nothing more than my salary as an official of the

state. There was a saying: there are only two things you cannot buy in Venice – the Devil and the Sirocco.'

'So I had heard,' Foresti acknowledged. 'I did not know if it was true.'

'It was true of me,' the Devil told him. 'I do not know about the Sirocco.'

'Very well, but before we go any further, you must give me some indication of what you are selling.'

The Devil shrugged. 'Nothing you could not guess, but I expect your masters will need proofs and I have them here. We have ceded the Seven Islands to the French, the colonies in Dalmatia – and the entire Venetian fleet. Nine ships of the line, three frigates and eleven galleys.'

'What of the vessels on the stocks at the Arsenale?'

'They are to be burned. Every one.'

The Greek inclined his head towards his companion who took a purse from under his cloak and the exchange was made.

The Devil untied the string of the purse and glanced at the contents. He nodded in grim approval. 'There is one thing more,' he said. 'A French squadron has arrived in Corfu – four ships of the line and three frigates. And I have heard they are looking for the British Consul.' He regarded Foresti with satisfaction. It was a small revenge for the remark about his shoes. 'You would not happen to know where he is, I suppose?'

Foresti appeared unmoved. 'I do not suppose they have despatched a French squadron from Toulon solely on my account,' he remarked. 'Have you heard what else they may be doing there?'

'I have heard they are preparing an expedition,' Cristolfi replied. 'To the Orient.'

'The Orient is a large place. You cannot be more precise?'

'What is it worth?'

'Nothing at present. But your co-operation would be appreciated. And remembered.'

'Very well. You may tell the British they have the Devil on their side. They may have need of him.'

'The place?'

'I have heard Egypt mentioned,' said the Devil, watching him slyly.

'I see.' Foresti did not appear overly surprised. 'And these ships, do you have any idea of their names?'

The Devil pulled a list from his pocket. 'They are the *Guillaume Tell* and the *Tonnant*, both of eighty guns, the *Aquillon* and the *Généraux*, of seventy-four guns, and three frigates – the *Junon*, the *Justice*, and a captured British ship – the *Unicorn*.'

Acknowledgements

With special thanks to: Cate Olsen and Nash Robbins of Much Ado Books in Alfriston, East Sussex, for digging up so many outstanding and often obscure works of reference; to my daughter Elesa for researching the Naples chapters and finding such good material on Emma Hamilton and King Ferdinand of the Two Sicilies; to Elizabeth Molinari for helping me with Italian translations and Marcello Molinari for showing me some of the less familiar sights of Venice; to Sharon Goulds for the pleasure of her company while exploring the Veneto and other parts of Italy; to Tobias Ercolino for his advice and hospitality in Venice; to Judy Lever and Roger Taylor for enlivening my stay there; to Dr Tom Sutherland for his advice on the treatment of gunshot wounds; and to my publisher Martin Fletcher and his assistant Emily Griffin at Headline for all their help, ideas and encouragement.

History

When a writer mixes fiction with fact – and real-life characters with ones that are purely imaginary – there is always a risk of distortion.

As a child reading about the English Civil War, I was on the side of the Cavaliers, so when I saw the movie *Cromwell* I was incensed by the portrayal of Prince Rupert as an effeminate fop with a miniature poodle which he carried around with him on his horse. In fact, he did have a dog – it was called Boy – but poodle or not, it was a large hunting dog. In contemporary engravings it looks a bit like a lion. Puritan pamphleteers at the time portrayed it as the Devil. A minor detail, perhaps, but one that has always made me suspicious of the way historical facts can be twisted to suit the purpose of the writer or director.

So I'd better come clean about what I've done in this novel.

Nathan Peake and the crew of the *Unicorn* are entirely fictitious. The *Unicorn*, however, did exist. She was a 32-gun frigate launched in 1794 at Chatham and she had an illustrious career in both the French Revolutionary and the Napoleonic Wars. But she was *not* part of Nelson's squadron in the Mediterranean in 1796 and she did *not* take part in the evacuation of Leghorn. Generally speaking, I've used real ships throughout the story, and on the whole I've put them in the right place at the right time. Interestingly, at least to me, the French corvette *Unité*, which is mentioned in Chapter Seven, was in reality captured off Algiers in 1796, bought into the service and renamed the *Surprise*, the name of Jack Aubrey's frigate in the Patrick O'Brian series.

The man who captured her – Captain Thomas Fremantle – is real, of course, and so is his improbably named frigate *Inconstant*. Fremantle's part in the evacuation of Leghorn is based on the true history – and he *did* marry Betsey Wynne; a full description of the evacuation and subsequent events can be found in the relevant volumes of *The Wynne Diaries*. I've probably taken a few liberties with Fremantle's character, but the fact that he was a notorious womaniser is evidenced by what survives of his own diaries. It is from these that we learn of the services provided by Mr Udny, of Fremantle's dealings with several 'dollies' as he called them, and of Adelaide Correglia's long relationship with Nelson. Whether she was a spy is more contentious, but there are several references in Nelson's despatches that indicate he may have used her in this capacity in both Genoa and Livorno. On the other hand, he might simply have been justifying his expenses.

As for Nelson himself, I hope I've kept him in character – or at least what we know about his character in the summer of 1796 when he was thirty-seven and the years of fame were yet to come. For well over a hundred years after Trafalgar, almost all the books written about him tended to be hagiographies, portraying him as an almost saintly figure. One of the few exceptions to this, *Memoirs of the Life of Vice-Admiral Lord Viscount Nelson* by Thomas Pettigrew, published in 1849, which included an insight into Nelson's private life with Emma Hamilton, was hounded out of print. But Nelson, Fremantle and many of his 'band of brothers' were youngish men in their twenties and thirties, away from their wives and families for long periods, and living at the height of what T.H. White called

The Age of Scandal. They didn't always behave themselves. Certainly, they weren't the pure, virtuous *Boy's Own* heroes idolised by the Victorians — they were actually a lot more interesting than that, though no less heroic. I had the privilege of working with the late Colin White on the dramatised documentary *Nelson's Trafalgar* for Channel Four (2005) and of interviewing Terence Coleman and Brian Lavery, all three of whom have given us a far more honest account of Nelson's life and times, warts and all, without in any way detracting from his genius. And one of the most recent biographies — John Sugden's *Nelson: A Dream of Glory* (2004) — has given us a comprehensive portrait of our hero as a young man which has the ring of truth about it, unclouded by either sentiment or iconoclasm.

As for Emma Hamilton, her own early life is still clouded in mystery. We don't even know her real name but it was probably Amy Lyon and she was the daughter of a blacksmith from Neston in the Wirral — the peninsula between Liverpool and Chester. We know she moved to London when she was about thirteen, and there are unproven accounts that she worked as a prostitute in an exclusive brothel called Madame Kelly's. Perhaps more reliable is her own testimony that she was one of the 'goddesses' employed by the sex therapist and showman James Graham in his so-called 'Temple of Health' off the London Strand. This bizarre establishment combined straightforward voyeurism with pseudo-medical science, and claimed to provide a cure for impotence or sterility. Its main feature was a large bedroom containing the 'Celestial Bed' — a king-sized edifice of brass and purple silk with panels carved with erotic scenes and a canopy fitted with mirrors, available for hire at £50 a night, around which the 'goddesses' danced semi-nude while the client couples attempted to beget an heir — aided by such visual stimulation as was available and a series of electric shocks. Contemporary newspapers claimed that Sir William Hamilton fell in love with Emma after witnessing such a performance. It seems unlikely. In fact, she had become the mistress of Hamilton's nephew, but when the latter decided it was time to marry a wealthy heiress he passed her on to his widowed uncle. Hamilton tried to do a Pygmalion on her, with limited success, though she had a natural talent for singing, dancing, acting and generally showing off. Her Attitudes were a must for rich voyeurs on the Grand Tour: the performance she gives to the Royal Family and their guests is based on eye-witness accounts from such tourists including Goethe and the Marquis de Sade. The speech patterns I've given her are copied from the letters she wrote and may not be entirely fair, since the speech of the upper classes was also a bit odd at the time (see *The Wynne Diaries*), but I thought they helped to bring her alive, and pointed up the contrast when she speaks French or Italian. Emma was nobody's fool. It's just a pity she got involved in politics.

I've based the characters of King Ferdinand and Queen Maria Carolina on various accounts given by travellers, including *The Grand Tours of Katherine Wilmot* and J.B.S. Morritt's *A Grand Tour: Letters and Journeys 1794–96*. Their Chief Minister, Sir John Acton, is another real-life character and was widely believed, even by the King himself, to have been the Queen's lover, though of course there is no real evidence of this. Nor is there any evidence that the Queen and Emma conspired to form an alliance with the anti-French party in Venice, though they were active in many other conspiracies against the French and their supporters.

Both Sir William Hamilton and the Viceroy of Corsica worked at uniting the Italian states against the French. They were unsuccessful. Bonaparte overran most of northern Italy and bullied the rest of the country into submission. Venice tried to stay neutral but was plunged into chaos as the patriots fought against the pro-French factions. After the massacre of a French garrison in Verona, Bonaparte delivered his ultimatum and Venice capitulated. A few months later, *La Serenissima* was handed over to the Austrians as part of the peace process, ending 1,000 years of history as an independent republic. Some of the political intrigues in the novel are based on contemporary accounts of the events leading to this, but the characters of Sister Caterina and Admiral Dandolo are fictitious. Sir Richard Worsley *was* the British Minister in Venice and the character I've given him is based on what I've read. His role in one of the most notorious sex scandals of the eighteenth century is brilliantly documented in *Lady Worsley's Whim* by Hallie Rubenhold (2008). As for the sexual scandals in Venice at the time, particularly in the convents, these are based on a host of literature on the subject. Cristolfi is a real-life character – and he was the chief agent of the Ten – but the character and role I've given him in the novel are entirely invented.

Similarly with Spiridion Foresti. A real person, and a fascinating character – but I've no idea if his personality was anything like the one I've created for him in the novel. He was a native of Zante and was British Consul and then Resident Minister in the Ionian Islands for the entire length of the Revolutionary and Napoleonic Wars. He ran an extensive network of agents and informants throughout the region and across the Levant, and he reported regularly to the British Foreign Secretary, to Sir Gilbert Elliot in Corsica and Sir William Hamilton in Naples, and to the various British naval commanders in the Mediterranean including Nelson and Sir Sydney Smith. Nathan's mission in the novel is based on Spiridion's reports to the Admiralty on the state of the Venetian fleet in Corfu and the dangers of its falling into French hands. Nelson thought very highly of Spiridion Foresti and came to rely greatly on the intelligence he provided of French activities and ambitions in the region. The records of their correspondence and Foresti's despatches to the British Foreign Secretary provide a fascinating insight into intelligence-gathering during this period.

For details of Bonaparte's Italian campaign I have relied on the memoirs of another spymaster – Adjutant-Général Jean Landrieux who was in charge of the Bureau des Affaires Secrètes – the central office for controlling spies and French agitators throughout northern Italy. My description of Landrieux is entirely fictitious, however, and is based on the notoriety he earned as a leader of irregular cavalry during the early days of the French Revolution. The character of Junot, too, though he was also a real person, is largely imagined.

As for Bonaparte's character, I've taken that from various sources, including some excellent descriptions of him by the Venetian envoys sent to treat with him in the autumn of 1796. The problem with Napoleon, of course, as with Nelson, is that so much is written from the perspective of history, when we know what they *became* rather than what they were at the time. I've tried to imagine what they were like as relatively young men before they were gilded in glory, but I'm well aware that I might have done a Prince Rupert on them and reduced them to caricatures, with or without poodles.

A Note on the Winds

———•··•·•··•———

The **Tramontana**, from the Latin, trans montanus, meaning 'from across the mountains' – in this case the Alps of Northern Italy. A cold, northerly wind, the continuous howling noise of the Tramontana is said to have a disturbing effect upon the psyche. In his poem 'Gastibelza', Victor Hugo wrote:

Le vent qui vient à travers la montagne
Me rendra fou

(The wind that comes from across the mountains
Will drive me mad)

Tramontana has other meanings not related to the wind. It can refer to anything seen as foreign, strange or barbarous.

The **Sirocco**, or **Scirocco** is the Italian word for the Ghibli, a desert wind that rises in the Sahara and sweeps across North Africa and the Mediterranean, often reaching hurricane speeds. Hot and dry in Africa, hot and moist in Europe, it causes sand storms in the desert and wet weather in Italy and the Adriatic. 'C'e Scirocco', they say in Venice, usually with a resigned shrug, when everyone is irritable and petulant and more prone than usual to madness. In southern Spain it is known as the

Leveche – or Xaloc in Catalan – where it brings rains laced with red dust from the Sahara, sometimes mistaken for blood.

The **Levanter,** an easterly wind with fog and rain, rises in the central Mediterranean and reaches its greatest intensity through the Strait of Gibraltar where it is funnelled between the heights on either side before burning itself out in the Atlantic.